Books by Farley Mowat

People of the Deer (1952, revised edition 1975)
The Regiment (1955, new edition 1973)
Lost in the Barrens (1956)
The Dog Who Wouldn't Be (1957)
Grey Seas Under (1959)
The Desperate People (1959, revised edition 1975)
Owls in the Family (1961)
The Serpent's Coil (1961)
The Black Joke (1962)
Never Cry Wolf (1963, new edition 1973)
Westviking (1965)
The Curse of the Viking Grave (1966)
Canada North (illustrated edition 1967)
Canada North Now (revised paperback edition 1976)
This Rock Within the Sea (with John de Visser)
(1968, reissued 1976)
The Boat Who Wouldn't Float
(1969, illustrated edition 1974)
Sibir (1970, new edition 1973)
A Whale for the Killing (1972)
Wake of the Great Sealers
(with David Blackwood) (1973)
The Snow Walker (1975)
And No Birds Sang (1979)
The World of Farley Mowat, a selection
from his works (edited by Peter Davison) (1980)
Sea of Slaughter (1984)
My Discovery of America (1985)
Virunga: The Passion of Dian Fossey (1987)
New Founde Land (1989)

Edited by Farley Mowat

Coppermine Journey (1958)

The Top of the World Trilogy

Ordeal by Ice (1960, revised edition 1973)
The Polar Passion (1967, revised edition 1973)
Tundra (1973)

FARLEY MOWAT

THE REGIMENT

An M&S Paperback from
McClelland & Stewart Inc.
The Canadian Publishers

An M&S Paperback from McClelland & Stewart Inc.

First printing October 1989

First edition copyright © 1955 by McClelland and Stewart
Limited
Second edition copyright © 1973 by Farley Mowat

Canadian Cataloguing in Publication Data

Mowat, Farley, 1921 –
The regiment

(M&S paperback)
Includes index.
ISBN 0-7710-6694-5

1. Canada. Canadian Armed Forces. Hastings and Prince
Edward Regiment. 2. World War, 1939 – 1945 - Regimental
histories – Canada. 3. World War, 1939 – 1945 – Campaigns –
Italy.   I. Title.

D768.15.M68 1989   940.54′12′71   C89-094259-5

Cover design by Pronk & Associates

Detail from "The Hitler Line" by Charles Comfort, Accession
#12296, Collection of Canadian War Museum, Canadian
Museum of Civilization, National Museums of Canada

Typesetting by Trigraph Inc.
Printed and bound in Canada

McClelland & Stewart Inc.
The Canadian Publishers
481 University Avenue
Toronto, Ontario
M5G 2E9

*For those who have joined the ranks of
the White Battalion of the Hastings
and Prince Edward Regiment – and
for their comrades who remain.*

Maps

Contents

Foreword

THE STORY of an infantry regiment has a hundred facets; some obvious, and others most obscure. The majority of those that have been turned to the public eye have particularly disclosed what is heroic, what is glittering in deed and memory; or, in sharp contrast, they have reflected what is grotesque and bestial in war and in the men who fight in war.

Yet neither the dark mirror of an obsessed realism nor the shallow one of a determined romanticism properly reflects the true shape of that amorphous but vital creation of men's emotions – which is called the regiment.

With full understanding of the fact that a regiment is the sum of the attributes of its myriad human elements, I have nevertheless chosen to write of it as a substantive entity – a thing possessed of special animation. I have attempted to tell the story of one regiment in birth, in growth, in dissolution; and throughout this book the regiment itself remains entire in all its moodss. I have tried to show these moods without partiality, and without exaggerated emphasis on any one of them.

The result is not a history in the accepted sense of the word, since I have made no great attempt to evaluate the past through the cold and retrospective eye of the historian. I have chosen instead to concern myself primarily with the living understanding that fighting men had of events that were yet in being; and with the emotions which belonged to those men in the days when war was here – was now.

I could not have accomplished my task without the wholehearted assistance of the Hastings and Prince Edward Regiment. Nothing was kept from me. The full details of the sombre hours when the Regiment faltered, have been given to me as freely as were the details of its greatest moments. At no time was any effort made to persuade me to soften or to evade the truth.

These men – these comrades – to whom I owe so much will understand that I cannot acknowledge my immeasurable debt to them individually and can personally identify so few of them in this story which touches upon the lives of more than four thousand men. I think they will forgive me when I choose one of their number to be the particular recipient of my gratitude. He is Freddy Goforth – Major F. Goforth, M.C. Without him, there would have been no book.

FARLEY MOWAT

Palgrave, Ontario
September, 1955

The Years Before

THE DAY was hot with the glare of sun on water and heavy with the stench of a million silvered fish, dull-eyed, decaying on the sandy beach. Replete beyond repletion, gulls squatted fatly amongst the schools of dying shad and gazed with bloated incuriosity towards the rolling dunes inland. Sounds came to them, unruly sounds, the faint refrain of singing men.

One gull, less bloated than his fellows, lifted idle wings and rose above the dunes to hang suspended on the air.

Below him in the shimmering heat two platoons of soldiers marched in fours along an old cart track, their puttees flapping at their ankles, their forage caps sliding wetly over sweating brows. Slung at their shoulders, Lee-Enfield rifles winked sharply as the sun struck metal that had long since been polished from metallic blue to gleaming silver. The platoons marched on and the sound of their voices faded and the beach grew quiet and nothing remained upon its yellow face except the gulls and the decaying shad.

The year was 1933; the place, a sandy strip of wasteland on the southwestern shores of Prince Edward County in the Province of Ontario. The Outlet, it was called, and here in the sweltering days of July the Hastings and Prince Edward Regiment was holding summer camp. One hundred and thirteen private soldiers, N.C.O.s, and officers were there – they were the Regiment. Two weeks earlier they had taken off their civilian clothes, put on motley remnants of uniforms from the war of 1914 and, aboard a collection of hired trucks, they had gone off to play at war.

That, at least, was what the country of Canada at large thought at the time. And the civilians spoke of the soldier games in scornful tones as if to imply that the whole matter of the Militia was a disgrace to a God-fearing and hard-working democracy. The people in the little towns of the two counties said it – some of them, but they were only echoing the words of the politicians at Ottawa who had long since taken their stubborn stand. They *knew* there would be no more wars. There would be no further need for soldiers; no further need to perpetuate the mechanism for a nation's self-defence. It was the time when Canada stood slack-bellied and would not look across an ocean at the apocalyptic birth.

The mechanism rusted. The army dwindled away until it became hardly more than a pile of dusty papers – dusty names. In the whole of a country that bordered on three oceans, there were three infantry battalions under arms. For a nation five thousand miles across, there were a few dozen antiquated aircraft that the few serving pilots hardly dared to taxi on the ground. And for those three oceans, there was a pitiful handful of little ships – a navy that the Swiss could very nearly have outmatched.

This was the sum total of the visible arsenal of defence. Yet there was one hidden weapon; one ignored by most of those who calculated military strength, ignored by the very government itself – and yet a weapon infinitely more powerful, and more ready than any in the official armoury.

It was called the Militia.

Now there are not many men who love war. Few welcome it unless they have their early youth to shield them from a knowledge of its nature. Peace is the good thing; and yet it is a bitter truth that peace does not live long in our times. During the decades after the Armistice of 1918 there were a few men in Canada who recognized this truth. Hating war with a depth of understanding born of a bloody experience, these men alone were not deluded into the soft complacency that filled the country in the years between. Knowing war for what it was, these men – the few – foresaw the day when they, and their sons and grandsons too perhaps, must needs go out again to battle that the unborn generations might survive.

These were the men of the Militia; to which the 'playtime soldiers' of the Hastings and Prince Edward Regiment belonged.

The twin counties of Hastings and of Prince Edward lie on the south central boundaries of Ontario. Prince Edward has a coastline along the wide waters of Lake Ontario itself, while Hastings stands at Prince Edward's back, stretching northward into a world of rock and stunted trees. The counties are new enough, for they were first settled in the last years of the 18th century. English and Scots regiments, that had fought in the war with the Thirteen Colonies, gave freely of their men and officers to the new lands of Upper Canada and it was from these expatriates that the early settlers in the two counties were drawn.

Those were unsettled times, as threatening as the times we know, and the soldier-settlers, reinforced by families of United Empire Loyalists (voluntary exiles from the rebellious southern colonies), were quick to see the need for strength. Thus it was that in 1800 Col. Archibald Macdonnel organized one of the earliest native units to be formed in the new country; and he called it the First Regiment of Prince Edward Militia. To the north, Col. John Ferguson was not far behind, and in 1804 he fathered the First Regiment of Hastings Militia.

These two units were an army of the people, and were therefore true militia. Their organization was quite independent of the uncertain government of Upper Canada. Their outward shape and nature was what could be made by the banding together of men who had a clear eye for the future, and who trusted in no protectors save themselves. In those two early units there was no thirsting for military glory and the armoured way of life – no yearning for distant fields of battle where medals and promotions could be won. The two regiments existed for one purpose, and one only – to defend themselves and what was theirs.

There was no desire, and no chance either, for them to build a military reputation and renown during the century which followed birth. There were no wars to blood them, except the brief interlude when the Americans invaded Canada in 1812 and were sent scuttling home again. Both regiments sent volunteer companies post-haste to drive the intruders out, but the campaign offered little glory to any of the participants.

During the Mackenzie Rebellion, and the Riel Rebellion in the West, both regiments again contributed detachments of volunteers, but again there was little action, and even less glory – except in long retrospect.

That there were no great battles upon which regimental spirit and tradition could nurture themselves, mattered less than nothing to the militia men. Their spirit was a prosaic one, devoid of the need of trumpet blasts and martial splendour. Yet it was the manifestation of a strength incalculable.

The strength of that spirit in the two counties must have been almost unique. It was so strong that at times it verged on the ridiculous as when, in 1851, the Prince Edward Militia burgeoned into four battalions while the Hastings Militia swelled to seven. Each of these eleven battalions had a full complement of officers and senior N.C.O.s, but it would have required nearly 7,000 other ranks to bring them up to strength – and there were not that many men, women and children in the whole of the two counties! It was an army, but one that would have been hard put to it to find enough riflemen for one platoon.

The absurdity was purely superficial. What mattered was the power of the belief that the Militia was a thing to be preserved in readiness.

It was not until 1863 that the authorities took formal notice of the phenomena in the two counties. On February 6 of that year the distended Prince Edward Regiment was forcibly condensed to form the 16th Battalion Volunteer Militia Unit of Canada; and in 1866 the Hastings unit suffered a like fate and became the 49th Regiment (Hastings Rifles).

It was more than a century after the founding of the militia units before the first real war came into being. The Government made no effort to maintain unit identifications in the Canadian contingents which volunteered for the Boer War. Nevertheless, numbers of the men of the two counties joined the colours and for the first time learned what battle was.

They were not favourably impressed. If anything, their dislike of war for its own sake, or as a means of empire-building, was strengthened. And yet, instead of sinking into the oblivion which overwhelmed many militia units after the Boer War, the two county units remained active, setting a pace that their successors were to maintain throughout the next half-century.

By 1905 the character of the two units had become firmly established. They were rural regiments and of necessity decentralized and spread across the thinly populated face of two large counties. Separate companies had been established at Picton, Consecon, Northport, Milford, Madoc, Sidney, Tyendinaga and Trenton. Because of their virile and unbroken existence over an entire century, the two militia units had now become an integral part of the ordinary pattern of men's lives throughout the counties. They belonged, as certainly as did the fields, the forests and rocks themselves.

That era closed in 1914.

Overnight, with the announcement of war, the two units swelled into full-blown infantry regiments clamouring for a part in the "crusade to end all wars." Here, so the civilian soldiers were persuaded, was the vindication of all that for which the militia units had existed. Unlike the Boer War, with its taint of Imperialism and self-interest, the Great War now beginning appeared to them to be a struggle for survival against a colossus that, if left unchecked, would overwhelm the world. The threat seemed real and clear to the descendants of the soldier-settlers of a century past. Flushed with belief, and filled with an unquestioning conviction of the truth, the men of the militia swamped the recruiting stations.

They were to know a deep disappointment.

With a lack of understanding that can hardly be credited, the authorities decided to discard the strongest weapon that the potential army had, its strength of name and pride of age, and to ignore the regiments that had been in being for a century. Instead, the volunteers were mustered into a hodge-podge of shapeless new units which bore only numerals to distinguish them one from the other.

Despite the ignominy, the men of the counties volunteered for service anyway – and how they volunteered!

During the years of the Great War the two counties were responsible for the formation of the 39th, 80th, 155th, 235th, and 254th Infantry Battalions. In addition they made major contributions to the 2nd, 21st, and 59th Infantry Battalions; to the First Forestry Battalion, and to the Artillery, the Engineers and to most of the other branches of the Army.

It was a remarkable record. There could hardly have been a man of military age, fit for service, in the two counties who did not volunteer. The spirits of Archibald Macdonnel and John Ferguson, and of the soldier-settlers, was still abroad – perhaps stronger than it had even been.

Dispersed amongst so many units and intermingled with men from every other part of Canada, the county men saw the war through. There were too many who did not return but their names remained alive in the outlying farms, in the bush holdings, and along the shores of the Bay of Quinte and Lake Ontario. As for the ones who lived, they brought back a deep and abiding horror of war in all its shapes. They brought with them, too, the bitterness of disillusionment, for during the four years of the cataclysm they had come to understand that wars will end no wars, and that much of what they had been told, and had believed, about this war was false. Yet they knew that despite the fact that some of those who had cried them on had done so for the most selfish of reasons, there had remained one truth to make their journey into hell a worthy thing. They understood that Man cannot refrain from plunging nations into holocausts; and while this is the way of things, then those who comprehend the full futility of war must nevertheless be prepared to take up arms in defence of the values which alone redeem the human animal.

When, after the Armistice, a general public reaction against maintaining the weapons of defence sprang into vociferous activity, those who so violently decried the very existence of all armed forces were not the ones who had miraculously survived the Somme and Ypres and Belleau Wood.

During the years between 1919 and 1939 the people of Canada were deluged with a spate of propaganda from those who would have disarmed the country. Much of the propaganda was sincere – some of it was not. Political expediency entered into the pronouncements of some statesmen when they condemned all military activity. There were even those, and not a few of them, who held strong sympathies with the new fascist forces of destruction, and who spoke out in high places against the folly of defence.

Most of the country listened; and believed what it was told.

Only a handful did not believe. These were the men who had known war and who hated it with all their beings.

In the two counties they were the men who bore the names of the settlers of Macdonnel's day. They were the sons and nephews of those who had died in France short years before. The continuity was there in blood; the continuity was there in spirit.

When, in 1920, the two old militia battalions of the counties were amalgamated into one, the new unit, bearing the name The Hastings and Prince Edward Regiment, was not still-born as many other units which amalgamated in the post-war period were. Instead it came into life a lusty entity, essentially unchanged from what it had always been. The continuity remained unbroken.

Nevertheless, the space between the wars was a sufficiently disheartening period. For the Regiment, as for all its sisters throughout the land, there was starvation. There were no boots, no weapons, no interest, and often no pay. Instead there was the thinly veiled dislike of the politicians, echoed by the contempt of almost the entire civilian populace, and even finding fertile ground within the two counties themselves.

This is the way the Regiment survived.

Once a week a handful of men in civilian clothes, or in bits of last-war uniforms, gathered in an old garage, a packing shed, or, if they were lucky, in an armoury that echoed emptily to the sound of their few feet. And as they came to the evening drill they were sometimes sneered at by the loungers on the streets.

A few of the luckier of these skeletal companies had ancient rifles, and one or two had managed to acquire a war-time Lewis gun. This was the full extent of their fighting equipment. And if there was no ammunition for practice purposes, these men who were the sons of stead-fast men, nevertheless, at least learned how to handle the weapons of defence. They came from the farms and from the shops. Their officers laboured unceasingly, giving not only of their time, but out of their own pockets to buy boots for the men. Against a growing feeling of apathy, or of outright antipathy, the Regiment survived – stood ready against the day of need.

Once a year the companies gathered for a two-week period in camp, and to make that journey the men gave up their annual holidays. Their vehicles were usually their own cars and trucks. Their clothing was often their own. Often, there was not even the recompense of the miserly militia pay.

There were never many of them. A company that could muster forty men at camp-time was exceptional. But these forty were worth five hundred, for they were the strong fibres deep in the tree trunk, and they could support the strain that would be laid upon them in the time to come.

Play soldiers all, the men of the militia received nothing

but the opprobrium of their fellow citizens; yet they endured. They endured the years between, and because of that, Canada was not utterly impotent when the day of danger came.

In the autumn of 1939 that day dawned.

The Regiment received its mobilization orders on September 2, 1939. Six years later, on October 4, 1945, it laid down its arms. The story of those six years is the story of four thousand volunteers. It is the story of men who came from the relief rolls of the depression, from the aimless wandering of the unemployed; from the law courts; from business offices; from wealthy homes; and from tar-paper shacks.

These were the men. They were a living tide channelled into that amorphous thing they called the Regiment. They came out of nowhere and from everywhere, and for a while they were a part of that entity which was no more that a projection of themselves. They were a tide that flowed without cessation for six years, sometimes slackly, and sometimes with a thunderous current. And for each man in that stream there was the moment when he belonged – when he was a sentient atom in the structure of the Regiment itself. And for each man there was the moment when the flood, implacable and irresistible, broke loose his slender hold and cast him out – to die, to drift amongst the broken flotsam of the wounded, or to sink into the oblivion of peace.

They were not all born with the blood of the counties in their veins. Some drifted westward from the fishing hamlets of the Maritimes; some drifted southward from the hard-rock mines under the Laurentian Shield; some wandered eastward from the golden plains. It did not matter where they took their origins. It mattered only that they came, and that for an hour of their lives they too belonged as truly as if their flesh had grown in the county soil.

There were four thousand of them. They were the Regiment.

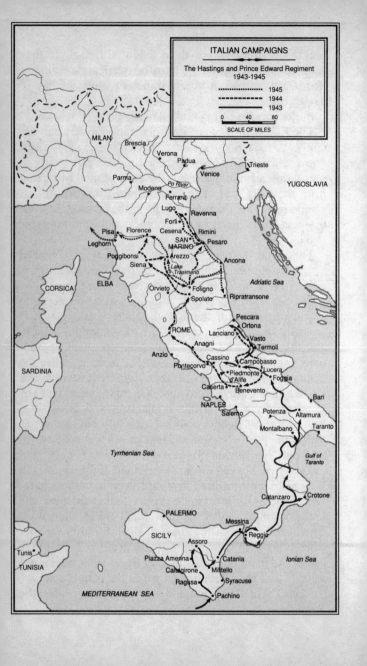

ITALIAN CAMPAIGNS

The Hastings and Prince Edward Regiment
1943-1945

.... 1945
---------- 1944
————— 1943

0   40   80
SCALE OF MILES

MILAN
Brescia
Verona
Padua
Trieste
Parma
Modena   Venice
Po River   YUGOSLAVIA
Ferrara
Lugo
Forli   Ravenna
Cesena   Rimini
Pisa   Florence   SAN MARINO
Leghorn   Pesaro
Poggibonsi   Arezzo   Ancona
Siena   Lake Trasimeno
CORSICA   Adriatic Sea
ELBA   Orvieto   Foligno
Spolato
Ripratransone
ROME   Pescara
Lanciano   Ortona
Anagni   Vasto
Anzio   Termoli
Pontecorvo   Cassino   Campobasso
Piedmonte   Lucera
d'Alife   Foggia
SARDINIA   Caserta   Benevento
NAPLES   Bari
Salerno   Potenza   Altamura
Montalbano   Taranto

Tyrrhenian Sea   Gulf of Taranto

Catanzaro   Crotone

PALERMO   Messina
SICILY   Reggio
Assoro
Tunis   Piazza Amenna   Catania
TUNISIA   Calfagirone   Militello   Ionian Sea
Ragusa   Syracuse
MEDITERRANEAN SEA   Pachino

ONE

Phoenix in Uniform

IN THE last days of August the two counties were at peace within themselves. In the northern country, men drove lumber trucks along stony roads leading into a wilderness of rock and scanty forest. In the back settlements men stood in the yards of frame shanties and looked over the lean desolation of stone ridges, of muskegs, of dark lakes, and of stunted copses of birch and spruce that clung hungrily to the meagre soil. Men who were almost a law unto themselves shaped the pattern of the approaching winter and saw in it the days when hounds would run white-tailed deer through snow-filled draws. They looked to their crosscut saws and speculated on the remote valleys amongst rounded rock where they would begin the work of cutting cordwood. Some looked through the doorways of their cabins with hard eyes, for it was still a time of hunger, and it was a hard land at best. In 1939 the evil of the depression was still vivid and those who lived in the outer settlements of North Hastings were often men of adversity.

Nevertheless, they looked out over their land in the last days of August, and they were at peace with it.

In the towns and villages of the northern county it was much the same. In Bancroft, Stirling, Madoc and Marmora the frame houses held the same sort of men though they might be shopkeepers, or garage men, or workers in the little mines that pocked the surface of the ancient rock. They, too, considered the future during the last days of August and they, too, looked ahead to a time of hunger for some, of adversity for many. In the smoky and crowded beer rooms of the hotels men still spoke of relief cheques, of work in the lumber camps far to the north, of mines that were closing down, or of stores that could not collect their debts and could not pay their debts. For these were vital things and the dark whispers of disruption on a distant continent were not yet loud enough to sound above these things.

In the southern part of Hastings, and in Prince Edward County, the land was softer, but the people were the same and their thoughts were much the same. Along the smooth and lovely shores of the Bay of Quinte, on the great isthmus which lies between the Bay and the green waters of the open lake, there was the sound and smell of the harvest. In the towns of Trenton on the mainland, and Picton and Wellington on the isthmus, the canning factories steamed into blue skies while wagons and old trucks, carrying the fruits of a rich soil, came to them. Orchards held high promise in their laden boughs; yellowing fields marked a good catch of grain; tomato fields gave up their tons of bloody pulp. It was not like the land to the north, yet it was the same nonetheless.

For even here the bitter years had not yet come to an end. And on the farms men looked with constrained hopes at the abundancy of their fields, for there was little sale for the fruit. The canning factories laboured but dully, for they could not sell all that they packed. There were no prices for the farmers. The winter ahead was as shadowed for the men of the south as for the northern men.

It did not matter.

A hundred and seventy years earlier the forefathers had broken these fields, and some had gone farther north to live by gun and trap. And in that stretch of time men had grown old on the land of the two counties, and it was their land, and though it might disappoint them, it would not permit them to pass from it. And in the time of adversity it would put food in their bellies, if it could do no more than that.

In the last days of the month, the peoples of the two counties were at peace within their land.

On the second day of September a boy on a bicycle carried a telegram down the main street of Picton and delivered it to a sleepy clerk in the Armouries.

"LT.-COL. S. YOUNG – KM2 – MOBILIZE."

PICTON is a farming town, remote from the world beyond it even as Prince Edward County is remote. Almost an island but for a narrow neck of land at its western end, the county lies with its south face to the great lake, and its northern shore upon the placid waters of the bay. It is an unhurried county where things move leisurely, and Picton, the largest town, partakes of the quietude that, in the summer days, is close to somnolence.

The main street winds casually down from the high ground to an abrupt fiord that is the little harbour. Stores with cluttered old-fashioned fronts line the pavement, but half-way between high land and water a building of a different sort rises in grotesque grandeur.

This is the Picton Armouries, a rococo monstrosity whose red brick face with its foolish little battle towers had looked out on the main street for more than four decades. But in all that time it had seen little of the things for which it was designed. Nominally the headquarters of the Hastings and Prince Edward Regiment it had, before 1939, a good deal more social than military significance.

Within the iron-studded doors a drill hall stretched into dimness. At the farther end, overhanging the empty space like the deck of an ancient ship-of-war, was a broad gallery. From it, in the years between, the shades of other times looked down once a week and watched as twenty or thirty local men came straggling through the massive door to gather in little groups, lost in that immensity of space. In the years between, the men of Charlie company gathered here one night a week to listen to lectures on how to dig a trench, bayonet an enemy, read a map, or keep a rifle clean. For the rest of the time the mausoleum stood empty and silent except on those occasions when the townsfolk needed a space to hold a dance, a chicken social or some other great event in the course of country life.

In the first days of September 1939, the Armouries was an empty and dusty vault. In the orderly-room office a fly buzzed with a shocking resonance in a silence that had become almost tangible.

It was nearly noon when the telegraph boy rode his bicycle down the main street of the town.

The cryptic telegram he carried was to set off a detonation that was to shatter utterly the peace of the two counties. Its delivery was the firing of the cap. The musty air of the orderly-room in the Armouries was rent asunder as three men in civilian clothes pushed in through the half-open door and set off a flurry of telephone calls that tied up the local exchange and threw the woman operator into utter confusion. So the primer fired. In Marmora, Trenton, Madoc and a half-dozen other towns, the recipients of the calls threw down their shop aprons or stripped off their mechanic's overalls and rushed to their local company armouries. And the shell exploded. From the five company offices in five different towns the telephone calls multiplied across the counties. Men listened briefly, then drove furiously to back-county farms to pass the news by word-of-mouth. In pool rooms and beer parlours men were silent for one long instant, and then they crowded to the doors. Within a few hours of its receipt, the word had penetrated to every corner of the counties and to every man.

With all explosions there is an aftermath of chaos, and Picton Armouries, the focal point of this sudden detonation, was no exception. The officers of battalion headquarters assembled quickly enough and the clerical staff appeared soon afterwards. But now that the die was cast, each man found himself stunned by the magnitude of the task ahead. In less than twenty days the unit was ordered to turn itself from a peace-time group of a hundred civilians, into an organized regiment of more than nine hundred soldiers. Each of the nine hundred had to be properly documented, each had to be medically examined; provided with a place to sleep and with three meals a day; given uniforms and boots; paid, and set about the tasks that would make him into a fighting soldier. But this was only a part of it. An even more formidable aspect lay in the gigantic amount of paper-work that was involved; the indents for stores; the returns in quintuplicate; the records and the endless frantic correspondence with the slumbering branches of the Service in high places. The story was the same with two dozen other militia units across the country, as, caught in a shameful and pitiful state of unpreparedness, the nation turned towards that despised band of peacetime civilian soldiers to implement the bold order to mobilize for war.

It was well for the country that the militia units had so well endured the decades of neglect and national ill-will. And it was doubly well that the spirit of the old Militia had so deeply permeated the affairs of men.

Within two hours of the telegram's arrival at Picton, mobilization had begun and within two days enlistments were mounting rapidly towards the unit goal.

On a picnic beach near Lake Ontario, a twenty-two-year-old company sergeant-major was dallying with a pretty girl. It was a day and hour for unhurried romance. A stranger approached suddenly and muttered half a dozen words. The young man leapt to his feet, abandoned love, and drove off with the stranger leaving his maiden marooned and far from home. An hour later, in full uniform, he was reporting on parade – and for six years he did not doff that uniform again.

In a Trenton rooming-house two young men had come into an unexpected windfall and they were drinking it with full enjoyment. They heard the news about the time that they were down to their last half-dozen pints. For a long moment they eyed each other speculatively, and then, without a word, picked up the sum total of their worldly goods, four yet-unopened bottles, and marched off to enlist. They were both county men with names from Macdonnel's time. One of them won the M.C. in Italy. Neither came back.

On a distant farm a man of late middle-age heard the word over the party line. His son drove him to the nearest company headquarters, for he could not drive himself, having lost most of his sight and most of his lungs to mustard gas in 1918. He wept when they gently turned him away. But the Regiment did not forget him, for the son enlisted before the two returned to their farm that night.

The word was slower in passing out of the counties, but within twenty-four hours men who had been born in Trenton, in Picton, in Bancroft, had heard the news in places as far distant as Wyoming and British Columbia. Before the next dawn, telegrams were pouring into the Armouries. "*Returning first train east stop hold a place.*" In Toronto, one man, but recently escaped from the grip of the depression and having found his first job in three years, took the two dollars advance pay he had just received and bought gasoline for his motorcycle. All through the night he drove, and in the morning was waiting at the Armouries door.

For some it was an easy thing to do, for others it was desperately hard. There were the men who had laboriously built up small businesses which were to have been their sons' heritage – but they left their shops and their life work, knowing full well how great the loss must be. There were the young men, some recently married, who had struggled against black odds through the years of their youth in the effort to survive and to build, in a world of darkness and despair. They left their wives and threw away their hopes.

On no man was there a compulsion, save that which came from his own heart. Indeed there were grave reasons why most of them should have held back. But they were not that kind of men. Even as the volunteers had rallied from the counties to die at Ypres – so did they rally now.

Why did they come? Not out of the empty patriotism of a bygone age – that much is certain. Perhaps some of them came simply to escape the insecurity of hard times. Perhaps some of them came to escape the consequences of failure. Perhaps some came only to escape from boredom, from ugliness, from misery at home. Yet these were the minority. Most of them came because they could not help the spirit that was in them; because the Regiment itself had meaning for them that few could have expressed in words. They came because it was the hour of their pride, the hour of need.

There was much heartbreak in those first days. The authorities had set exceedingly high medical standards, as if in a deliberate attempt to discourage enlistment, and these standards struck down many of the officers and other ranks who had given so largely of themselves during the years between. Nearly half of them failed their first medical examinations. But they persevered. They waged a furious battle to have their categories raised. They bullied or tried to bribe the Medical Officers, they pleaded with them, threatened them – and those who failed to change their fate, ignored it. In uniform, or out of it, with or without official sanction, they continued to serve the Regiment with a steadfastness that was blind to the most cruel rebuff.

These were the men, the ones who made their Medical Boards, and the ones who failed, who performed the miracles of the twenty days of mobilization. It is well that they who were so soon forgotten be remembered now.

There was inevitable confusion in those first days; confusion multiplied into chaos from which slowly emerged the entity that was being born in such travail.

In Trenton a man who had been a railroad hand four days previously now stood on the open land behind the Cold Storage Building, wearing the puttees, breeches and stiff jacket of 1918, shouting drill orders to his platoon.

The men wore what they had worn when they had left their homes. There were bright sweaters, worn jackets, flannel trousers, and grease-stained mechanic's overalls. On their shoulders they carried lengths of wood, broomsticks or pieces of planking shaped roughly to resemble the Lee-Enfield, for there were not even enough antiquated rifles to go round.

It was a time of enthusiasm such as men seldom know. It was a time of patch-work improvisation, of getting down to the job with what there was at hand.

Then, on September 10, Canada declared war on Germany. On that day seventy-five men enlisted.

There was nothing grim about the atmosphere of those days. The excitement of the moment, and the satisfying feeling of creating something out of nothing contributed to a general atmosphere of carnival. The end result to which all the preliminaries must inevitably lead was so far distant that it was beyond comprehension. What was war? Dimly, it was the recollections of the men of 1914-18, a hazed nightmare of anguish deeply obscured under the good memories which alone remained vivid in men's minds. The fellowship of volunteer soldiers, the stimulating – because of its novelty – effect of an easy military regimentation, the release of peace-time tensions and restraints, all these contributed to the new mood; the mood of youth reaching out towards adventure that had suddenly been born in a drab and shoddy world. In those early months of its existence the Regiment felt little antagonism towards the enemy. Men were concerned with more immediate things. They possessed a simple and unreasoned certainty that this war must be fought and won, a certainty that demanded no buttress of inflammatory words to make it stand. Dimly they understood the issues, but they did not dwell upon them. There was no time, and less inclination, for *now* was the moment, and it was a moment fraught with fascination.

It was also a fleeting moment. Less than four months were to elapse from the day the mobilization order was received until the Regiment was on the Atlantic, bound for Britain. Those months rushed into the past with such furious speed, that only momentary glimpses could be caught and held in memory.

The things which loomed large and left their mark were often trivial. There was the chronic boot shortage for instance. One sergeant-major solved his personal problem by appearing regularly on parade wearing a pair of crimson romeos. Most of the men wore their civilian shoes until these disintegrated, then, out of their own pockets, they bought farm boots from the Picton stores.

Uniforms were another sore point. No man can properly identify himself with military habit when he is dressed in dungarees, a sweat-shirt and an old felt hat. What uniforms were available came out of damp storage bins where they had lain since 1919. They were moth-eaten and shabby – and they never fitted. Some men were issued khaki breeches while their comrades received the tunics. They took these relics to the local tailors and at their own expense had miracles worked over them. But on parade they still looked like a motley collection of comic-opera soldiers from a third-rate vaudeville production.

There was a desperate individual desire to attain military perfection in the shortest possible time. Eagerly, farmers, store clerks and lumbermen studied the drill books and the training pamphlets which had survived the First World War. No one considered the obvious inadequacy of methods already two decades old. No one knew anything whatever about modern warfare, so there was no alternative except to model oneself on the pattern of 1918.

There were no weapons except a few score outmoded rifles. A few ancient Lewis guns represented the sole 'heavy' armament. The platoons clamoured angrily to be allowed to have these guns for drill, despite the fact that the Lewis gun had long since been replaced on active service by the Bren light machine gun.

And on that memorable day when a real Bren was first produced, in the care of a squad of staff officers, who guarded it like a royal personage, the men of the Regiment could only stare in awe, and feel that they were in the presence of a shining vision. The Bren was to remain a vision for many months to come.

Towards the end of September arrangements were made to concentrate the entire Regiment in Picton, and to this end squads of carpenters and masons set to preparing the dungeon-like cellars of the Armouries to accommodate nearly a thousand soldiers. Not far from the Armouries was the Tecumseh Canning Factory, and this was requisitioned, converted into a barracks, and promptly named the 'Chicken Coop'. In early October the outlying companies arrived, by truck convoy or by train and bus. They flooded into Picton and the little town turned khaki-coloured over night. Now the Regiment was whole, its fragments gathered in to make the unit in its entirety. There was a full dress parade, and for the first time the C.O. stood at the head of the Regiment. It was also the first time most of the men had ever participated in anything like it, and they were deeply stirred. Nine hundred men, as one, who wore, or would soon wear, the same badge above the same uniform. Dimly they perceived the existence of that living entity which had no shape, no physical existence, but which had an infinite capacity to stir men's emotions and to claim their loyalty. They knew for the first time the spirit of a regiment.

It was heady stuff. Shortly after that first parade these volunteers were asked to sign a supplementary declaration expressing their willingness to proceed overseas to battle. The reaction was violent when they were offered time to think it over before signing. A heavy voice was raised. "Time, hell! We'll sign the damn thing now!"

Autumn drew on and there was a visible change from day to day. The first issues of modern battledress arrived and the lucky few who received them were envied mightily. Rifles were issued and their new owners stripped and re-assembled these ancient weapons until they were ready to fall apart.

First pay-days came and with them a new aspect of civilian-soldier relationships. Never before in Picton's history had such a flood of money appeared in so brief a time. There were abuses on both sides. New young soldiers, inwardly abashed, and outwardly truculent, drank too much beer and made too much noise. It was enough to make some of the citizens of the town, and of nearby towns, swell with outrage. The soldiers had less difficulty adjusting to the new tenor of their lives than did the town in assimilating the gargantuan military growth which had sprung, full-blown, out of its flesh in a matter of weeks. Nevertheless, there was a waxing feeling of respect for the Regiment, and of pride in it, on the part of the civilians. There was also a feeling of uneasiness, for this was no play-acting militia unit – it was a battalion of soldiers imbued with an incalculable potential power.

Leaves were granted and most of the men were lucky, for in their antique cars, and on motorcycles, they could reach their homes in a matter of hours. From home to war, the transition was an easy one while the physical link remained so strong. And yet even in early November there were signs that the link was weakening. Rumours, which are the breath of an army, were filling the barracks. Cold rumours they were, yet ones that made men's hearts pound with suppressed excitement. The Regiment would not be in Picton long.

No man who did not live in those days can grasp the full feeling of them; the strange sensation of existing in a world divorced from all previous experience, and not quite real, despite the impact of a thousand solid details, each laden with its warning of a grim reality. They were days of magnificent weather, the finest autumn that the counties had ever seen. They were days made vivid by the overwhelming sensation of being freed from a routine existence and at the same moment irrevocably committed to what might be an adventure into death. No one had time to consider what the future might hold – no one, that is, except the insurance salesmen who gathered vulture-like about the barracks, even finding their way into the men's quarters to peddle their wares and to plant fear. The soil was arid. It was too soon for fear to grow.

The days passed, the rumours spread, and military routine became a man's second nature. Discipline, which had been something in the books before, became the real, if somewhat casual and self-imposed discipline of willing men anxious to get on with a job.

As for training, it was largely a case of the blind leading the blind. A regimental sergeant-major had been imported from the miniscule Permanent Force to run a course for N.C.O.S; a course whose students consisted of the handful of militia corporals and sergeants, and a balance composed of those new soldiers who seemed to be a little brighter than their fellows. These were the instructors, and they would of necessity stay up half the night instructing themselves on the next day's training lesson before passing on the information to the rank and file. Enthusiasm had need to substitute for knowledge. Sometimes these tyros suffered for their insufficient preparation. Drill was carried out in the open spaces of the Picton Fair Grounds and one October morning a drill instructor, after much trouble, manoeuvred an entire company into a marching column. Now a company being drilled is in some ways like a large elephant on a lead; an amenable elephant with no will of its own, that must be directed clearly and accurately, or trouble follows. That day the instructor saw his column coming perilously close to a building, and in panic he ordered a right turn without pausing to consider his own relative position. As one, the hundred and fifty marching men turned on him. He tried to scramble out of the way, but tripped and fell, and the company stolidly marched over him without, let it be said, so much as breaking step.

Instructors and men were learning together, and so was the regimental staff. The quartermaster's department in particular showed a fine and typical spirit in the manner in which it became proficient in the ancient technique of 'scrounging' – the obtaining of the unobtainable by unmentionable methods.

In the battalion and company orderly-rooms, staff-sergeants and corporal clerks wrestled hopelessly with the flood of paper that became known later in the war as 'bumph'. The term was apt. It is beyond question that more time, energy and money was spent on returns, proformas, forms, statements and tabulations during those early months, than was spent on soldiering in all of its real aspects. The administrative personnel had much to learn, and their primary task was to discover how nine-tenths of the 'bumph' could be avoided or diverted elsewhere. They were learning, slowly and painfully, to deal with the 'Staff' on higher levels. A vital lesson, this, for to most infantry soldiers the staff remains an enemy, and sometimes a formidable one.

Through October and November the Regiment was 'shaking down' and the fact that it was actually learning next to nothing about how to fight was not of great importance. It was learning to be itself, it was developing its own particular individuality and characteristics. It was passing out of its swaddling clothes.

The succeeding days began to take on familiar tones and to blend into each other in that form of calculated monotony which is the essential protection of the soldier in time of peace, and his vital armour in times of stress. There was no variety in the training now, for the men had exhausted the limited novelty of the textbooks. There was only a faintly hypnotic repetition of words and phrases, and the less pleasant repetition of drill movements, and of long and tedious route marches through the surrounding hills. It was good training, for it taught the new soldiers how to endure boredom, and when that can be endured, there is nothing in war that cannot also be endured.

The acceptance of uniformity is one of the essential penalties the good soldier must pay, and by the end of November payment was being made willingly by most of the men. Off duty, on the streets of Picton, there was an acute individual awareness of the state of a man's clothes, the press in his trousers, the cleanliness of his web-equipment and for the lucky ones, the gleam of a cap-badge. Badges were a treasure. They were the one element which could distinguish a man of the Regiment from any other soldier in the Army, and they were almost unobtainable. A brisk trade in illicit copies went on, and three or four cents worth of stamped brass would fetch as high as ten dollars from some young fellow who hankered desperately for the distinction of the badge. It was a good sign.

The growth of the unit spirit, and the rising awareness of it at last reached a level where it needed something concrete to give it form. A mascot was required. The stag on the cap-badge suggested an interesting idea and forthwith a detachment of Bancroft men, bush dwellers all, were packed off with orders to capture a buck deer alive. Somewhere in Hastings, beyond the rock cleft known as The Hole In The Wall, they found their buck, but an old excitement overcame the hunters, and the stag proved unable to absorb half a dozen bullets.

The hunger for a mascot gained force, but it was to remain unsatisfied until the day before the Regiment left Picton for the east.

That day was fast approaching. In early December there were new and stricter medical examinations, and many of those who had grown into the Regiment so that they believed they had always been a part of it, were suddenly cast out to return to their civilian homes, and their lost jobs, and to face a bleak eternity of cold regrets. Theirs was a great tragedy, greater because it was so seldom recognized.

Those who passed the final tests were subjected to the endless assaults of hypodermic needles, and the stuff injected into their arms must have been the stuff of which rumours are made. December drew on and the Regiment seethed with speculation.

On Saturday night, December 16, George Ponsford, who was later to become a living legend in the Regiment, came to a personal decision on the mascot question. For days he had been eyeing a huge pewter statue of an Indian, probably Tecumseh himself, that stood in somewhat faded majesty on the roof of the canning factory. On Saturday afternoon George laid his plans and procured a long ladder which be secreted behind the building. Close on midnight, he recovered his ladder and, with the help of another man, made his way up to the roof.

The Indian was securely fixed in place, for he had stood at his post through three decades. It took much labour with a huge pipe wrench to free him, and when he was liberated at last, he slowly keeled over, almost crushing his kidnappers, and thoroughly drenching them in rain water which spilled out of a number of bullet holes, the legacies of many local Nimrods over the long years.

The kidnapping was further complicated by the unexpected arrival of a third soldier, very much the worse for wear, who stumbled against the ladder, and with proper Hastings spirit accepted the challenge and clawed his way up to the roof. He was very, very drunk, and the two men with their trophy were hard put to it to prevent first the Indian, then the drunk, from plunging over the parapet. They sweated blood as they lowered their two charges to the ground.

The possession of the Indian was one thing, his disposal quite another. But Ponsford was always a man of wit. Having bribed the sentry to look the other way, he and his companion dragged the Chief, complete with spear, to the doorway of the Sergeant's Mess, and there they set him up with a bottle of good whisky cradled in his arms. It was an enlistment credential that could not be denied.

In the morning the Indian was found, and the same morning the long-awaited word arrived from Ottawa. The Regiment was ordered to entrain that night. Its destination, Halifax – and after that, no man could say.

There was never any doubt about the Indian. That same day he was officially taken on strength, issued with his identification tags, and secreted in the battalion baggage.

He was a fit emblem in a Regiment which boasted many original inhabitants of North America amongst its soldiers. They named him Little Chief, in defiance of his great stature and formidable weight, and he became much more than a mere mascot, for in the end the Regimental Indian became an institution.

TWO

The Tiger in Their Midst

O N THE morning of New Year's day, 1940, a convoy fresh in from the Atlantic made its way up the Clyde to Greenoch. On the decks of H.M.T. *Ormande* the men of the Regiment thronged the rails.

The crossing had been a trying one. The wet and piercing cold of northern seas had penetrated the crowded troop decks with their make-shift bunks and seamen's hammocks; for while *Ormande* possessed air-conditioning to guard against the equatorial sun, she had no heating arrangements whatsoever. Neither did she have an easy motion, and the seas had been unruly. Most of her passengers had become seasick the first day out from Canada, and had remained in that condition all the way across.

Such prolonged bodily discomfort had had its effects upon the new soldiers. There had been near-riots when the English cooks served herrings at each succeeding breakfast – herrings whose sunken eyes stared balefully up from the heaving tables of the mess decks. Frozen mutton and rabbit from Australia had been greeted with mutters of outrage and there were many men who drew the whole of their sustenance during that voyage from what confections could be purchased at the ship's meagre canteen.

It was not a happy crossing. The new regiment was unprepared to accept these approximations to wartime conditions, for as yet the men had no real understanding of what war could be. Each new hardship imposed by the 'Limeys' who ran the ship was taken as a personal affront.

There was more to it. This was the first time that many of the men had ever been outside the confines of the two counties, and individually they were unprepared for new and inexplicable experiences.

There was a man, nick-named 'Toby Tanglefoot', who one morning found he could not face the kippers, and made an urgent dash up the companionway. But Toby was met, head-on, by a large, cold sea on its way down. He was literally washed back into the mess deck, bellowing with the desperation of a man who sees the Lord approaching.

"Take out, boys, take out! The son of a bitch has sunk!"

It was a time not only of incomprehensible experiences, but of incredible sights. On the horizon the mighty hulls of the battleships *Revenge* and *Dunquerque*, surrounded by the lesser vessels of the escort fleet, gave an impression of incalculable power that was strong enough to remain in men's memories even after actual contact with battle had destroyed the illusion. Distance itself became a baffling thing as for twelve days and nights *Ormande* drove through grey seas. And then when land was sighted, it too was out of joint with all the troops had known before. The loom of the lovely cliffs of Scotland was an unreal thing.

Grousing and grumbling steadily the troops had become something approaching a mob by the time the anchor dropped off Greenoch. It was Hogmanay Day, and there were a good many men of Scots descent aboard who could see no reason why the purgatory of ship-board life should be prolonged for another twenty-four miserable hours. Several strenuous attempts to make off with the ship's life-boats were reluctantly frustrated by officers who felt themselves fully in accord with the men's mood. The signs that pointed to the shape of the Regiment's future seemed dubious on that January day.

Disembarkation was completed the next morning and, still resentful and filled with their own uncertainty, the troops streamed into a railroad station, laughing mockingly at the diminutive train that waited for them. During the journey south, soldiers yelled boastfully to women, old men and children who leaned out of the back windows of tenement buildings to wish the Canadians Godspeed. A land compressed and concentrated into unbelievably small dimensions passed before the soldiers' eyes in the hours of a single day. They were amazed and at the same time contemptuous. There was open condescension in the replies they shouted to the crowds who greeted them at wayside stations. It was an attitude of bravado, born of ignorance and the sense of not belonging, and of first loneliness.

It took a long time before the misconceptions gathered on that journey were dispelled. Maida Barracks in Aldershot, the Regiment's destination, did little to dispel them.

Aldershot has held the heart of the British Army through many centuries. During two world wars it has also held Canadian contingents, and for them it has been a place of mixed memories, most of them sombre. In January of 1940 the Regiment found Aldershot a city of frigid barrack blocks with the smell of antiquity about them, and an atmosphere almost as bleak as the hutments of Depression labour camps. It was an unusually cold winter and there were no provisions to defeat the cold save for tiny open fireplaces – for which there was no coal. Those barracks were places where experienced soldiers might have made themselves at home, after their fashion, and after applying all their soldiering initiative to the task. But the Regiment was not yet a unit of experienced soldiers.

The men found the place quite unacceptable. It might do for the 'Limeys', but not for the Canadians. It was not nearly good enough for volunteers who had come of their own free will to succour the old Country.

During the second day many of the men straggled into the town of Aldershot to gape, and comment acidly on its oddities. They found the pubs at once, and in their naivety thought that these were comparable with Canadian beer

parlours, which are designed solely as alcoholic filling
stations. The art of making proper use of the English pub
came by degrees to most of them, but it took time. On
that first day in town the innocents were also faced by the
unexpected phenomenon of the blackout; and the combination of pitch darkness, a strange land, and far too much
English beer, resulted in a large part of the battalion being
absent without leave from the next morning's parade.

The first month in England was a dark one for the unit.
Had the officers and N.C.O.s been able to take firm hold
and force their men into the beginning of a pattern, all
would perhaps have been well. But the senior ranks were
almost as much at a loss as were their men. The officers
were not trained to cope with the realities of this kind of
soldiering. The hectic, happy days of mobilization were at
an end. The sometimes sombre and always laborious days
of learning the hardest trade in the world were now upon
all ranks.

There were, perhaps, too many other things with which
to cope. There were the problems of women who acted as
no county woman had ever acted and who could not at
once be understood. There was the great loneliness which
men of little experience must feel when they are thrust
into the outer world.

At Maida Barracks there were worse problems. If the
administration within the Regiment was disorganized,
then the whole military situation in England was chaotic.
Shortages of everything from paper to trucks were so
chronic that they had become the accepted way of things.
A single typewriter was issued to the battalion for all its
staff work. Three ancient civilian cars became the Regimental transport. A handful of Bren guns became the
main armament. There were insufficient clothes and
boots, and the weather was frigid. Sickness was epidemic
so that at one time three hundred men were ill with
influenza, and with what became known as 'Aldershot
Cough'. The food was abominable and men who had
taken the good victuals of Picton days for granted were

revolted by the musty-tasting frozen mutton, by the inevitable brussels sprouts, and by the sausages which contained so much bread that men wondered whether they should put mustard or marmalade on them.

The Regiment came to Maida Barracks in its unformed youth; callow, though of good heart. It lacked the fibre of knowledge, and the spine of inner discipline. Its officers, who should have supplied the restraint of maturity, were largely unable to do so. Officers, N.C.O.s and men shared a common grudge, a common resentment against the existing state of things.

Things grew worse. Many of the good N.C.O.s became embittered at the lack of support and some of them threw in their hands. Mail failed to arrive from Canada. Morale dropped lower. Men began to go A.W.L. There was a garrison Church Parade at which the unit appeared to such poor advantage that the Divisional Commander called the C.O. on the carpet for it. There were ugly rumours that the unit was slated to be used as a work battalion, or turned into a Pioneer Battalion – the bottom of the scale.

Like an unhappy adolescent, sullen, confused and miserable, the Regiment needed a strong man's hand.

January 30 saw the lowest point to which it descended, and on that date its recovery began. That initial rescue from a condition of near disintegration was largely the work of a single individual.

He was an outsider; Lt.-Col. Harry Salmon, a Permanent Force soldier who might well have been insulted by the order to take over a militia battalion. Certainly the Regiment was grossly insulted by his appointment. Nevertheless, this man possessed the catalyst which was needed to transform the magnificent promise of the Regiment into reality. He knew the way, and he was ruthless.

Heads rolled at once. A number of officers and senior N.C.O.s found themselves on their way back to Canada within a week of the new C.O.'s arrival. There was cruelty in their treatment, but cruelty was needed. Hard as a headsman, and as implacable, Salmon impressed his will upon the unformed human material of the unit. Fear was one of his weapons, used deliberately. Officers and N.C.O.s hated him at first because they feared him, but they did what he said – either that, or they were out.

Salmon's guiding principle was a simple one. He believed that the private soldier was never wrong. If the soldier got in trouble, it was the fault of his officers or his N.C.O.s. If, in battle, the officers were to expect the support of their troops, then they would have to give the men service during training, and give it so unstintingly that they would become little more than slaves to their men's needs. It was no new thesis, but Salmon made it a living fact.

The stories about him are legend. And now that he is gone, they have an affectionate overcast of memory about them. Grudgingly at first, but in the end wholeheartedly, the soldiers of those days gave him his due. He took the Regiment which other men had roughly shaped, and gave it fighting form.

Even Salmon's bitterest enemies came to admit that there was reason for his savage ukases concerning the niceties of military discipline; for the critics remembered incidents such as an early encounter between Lt. Ruttan and one of his men, in Salmon's presence.

The incident occurred the day after Salmon took command. Ruttan, a portly and amiable youth, was to escort the new C.O. through the transport lines, and the young lieutenant had been foresighted enough to speak to his men the night before, warning them that Salmon was reputed to be a fire-eater, and begging them to play the part of parade-ground soldiers for a while at least. The inspection tour proceeded well at first, and if Salmon did not like all that he saw he gave no immediate indication of dissatisfaction. With the tour almost completed Ruttan beheld one of his drivers approaching up the road between the barracks. Anticipating a smart salute, Ruttan's right hand began to twitch, ready to return it just as smartly.

The twitch was transferred visibly to Ruttan's face as

the private, both hands thrust deep into his pockets, ambled up to the two officers and stopped. "Say, Fats. You got a match on you?" he asked.

Within five minutes the entire Regiment recognized the tiger in its midst.

There is a certain humour in the comments that men made in their letters home during the first weeks of the new regime. One sergeant writing of the new impermanence of a sergeant's rank, had this to say. "It's so bad now that the first thing we do each morning is to read the daily orders to see if we're still entitled to eat in the sergeants' mess!" In more forceful language, the words of a private writing to a friend: "Before that b...came we'd have thought any guy was nuts if he moved at the double. Now if anyone just says your name above a whisper you start to run like you had a bayonet in your rear – just in case old 'Iron Guts' happens to come by!"

But Salmon was not only a breaker, he was a maker of men as well. The regimental sergeant major, Angus Duffy, the youngest Class 1 Warrant Officer in the Canadian Army, was dubious about his own abilities under the new master. Salmon, recognizing his worth, rode him unmercifully until Duffy was ready to resign and seek a posting as a private. And at that critical juncture the C.O. changed his tactics and each day, for weeks, made a point of lecturing the young man. He would always begin: "Remember Duffy – this is *your* Regiment. These are *your* men. God help you if you let them down!" Duffy, angry and on his mettle, rose to the challenge and in so doing he duplicated the reactions of most of the men. The first resentment changed to sullen resignation, and then, under the never-ending tickle of the lash, quickened to a stubborn refusal to be beaten by this new martinet; and this was followed in due course by an awakening pride, a new kind of pride, in the miracle that was taking place.

As the Regiment began to improve, the C.O. allowed himself occasional lapses from his inflexible stand.

The immense Aldershot parade ground served an entire

brigade and on a day in early March the square was crowded to capacity with half a hundred squads and platoons, marching and countermarching. To add to the confusion, a dozen tyro motorcyclists were practising their trade at one end of the square while at the other end a football match was in progress.

The harassed instructors had no hope of controlling their men in this melee, except by galloping alongside their platoons and bellowing the orders directly into their collective ears.

The outraged feelings of the instructors can be appreciated when, in the middle of the morning, a message from the C.O. was delivered to each officer and N.C.O. informing him that, henceforward, he would stand at a given spot and control his moving squad while himself remaining perfectly immobile.

Sgt.-Maj. Manley Yearwood spat expressively when he heard the order, but he kept his thoughts to himself, for the C.O. had appeared beside Yearwood's momentarily halted platoon.

"Now, Sergeant Major," Salmon said, "let's see what you can do."

Yearwood did his best. He began with close order drill and all went well; then when he could think of no more movements he reluctantly set the platoon to marching drill. Again all went well as the platoon swung back and forth within the narrow range of his voice. Then, to his horror, Yearwood beheld an entire company column bearing down to pass between him and his retreating squad. His order to the platoon to halt was never heard. There was nothing for him to do but wait until the company had passed, and so he stood rooted to his given spot, the cold sweat standing on his brow.

After an interminable time the intruding company withdrew and the sergeant major raised his cracking voice in one last despairing effort and sent it after his vanishing platoon.

"Aibo-o-o-o-t TURN!" he bellowed.

The last six men in the platoon heard him correctly and swung smartly about. The next six men were sure they had heard 'Right Turn' – and they obeyed. Three or four others were equally sure that they had heard 'Left Turn'. The rest heard nothing and marched straight on.

And Yearwood, with visions of his disappearing rank as real as the sight of his disappearing platoon, was stricken by a final blow, he lost his voice.

He did not regain it when the tiger sauntered up to him, smiled easily and said, "Well, Sergeant Major, I suppose you'll want that platoon back again some day. You might try telegrams."

The resurgence of regimental spirit began within a few weeks of Salmon's arrival, and it gained momentum rapidly. The setback had been temporary, and good for men's souls. The adolescent battalion had felt the iron and was conscious of a hunger for self-respect. It was ready now to learn its trade.

Spit and polish were no longer impositions, but once again had become matters of individual pride and concern as they had been in Picton. Men growled threats at slackers who showed up badly on parade. The mascot, Little Chief, who had stood at the prow of the troop-ship crossing the Atlantic, and who had sustained severe abdominal injuries from the heavy seas, was taken to a metal-smith and repaired. Resplendent in a new coat of paint he stood on a dais and critically accepted the salutes of the passing members of his Regiment.

Coming of age meant a good deal more for the unit than the hardening of its spirit. The time had come for it to learn how to co-ordinate its myriad parts into a smoothly functioning entity, capable of giving battle and of winning.

To those who have not served in an infantry battalion, the complexities of its internal organization must remain largely unsuspected. Superficially it appears to be a mass of undifferentiated muscle. In actuality a Regiment is an organism of complex internal intricacy.

A Canadian regiment was composed of roughly nine hundred men and officers. There were four rifle companies, each consisting of three platoons; each platoon composed of three sections of ten men led by a corporal. These companies were called Able, Baker, Charlie and Dog, and they were the striking force, the reason for the Regiment's existence. Their sole function was fighting and all their training was devoted to this end. The infantry soldier was required to be proficient in the handling of such weapons as his rifle and bayonet, the Bren light machine gun; the two-inch mortar; the .55 anti-tank rifle (and later the anti-tank projector); the Thompson submachine gun; the Sten, and five varieties of hand grenades. These were his basic weapons and learning how to use and maintain them was a major task. Beyond these were harder lessons. Each man had to be carefully versed in elementary tactics, in battle drills, in map reading, in field craft; in co-operation with other arms such as tanks, artillery, and the air force; in gas defence; in the rudiments of military law, field hygiene, patrol techniques, enemy methods and equipment, and a score of other vital subjects. The total requirements for an ordinary infantry soldier were in the end more demanding than those required of many 'specialists' who flew in aircraft, served in navy ships or handled artillery pieces.

This complex training was required of *every* man in an infantry regiment, but the unit's requirements went much further. In addition to the rifle companies there were eventually two others; Support, and Headquarters companies. Support was what its name implied, a pool of specially trained men equipped to support the rifle companies with special weapons. Initially it included an anti-aircraft platoon armed with light machine guns. Then there was the signals platoon, equipped with three types of short-wave radios, with telephone systems, with visual signalling devices, and with all the material required for intercommunication within the Regiment. There was the mortar platoon, in essence the Regimental artillery, equipped with three-inch mortars that threw ten-pound shells for a distance of a mile. There was the carrier platoon; the Regimental 'cavalry' eventually equipped with ten armoured, tracked Bren-gun carriers. There was the pioneer platoon, the unit's engineers, equipped for mine laying, mine detection and removal, demolitions, and field construction work. Later in the war there was also the anti-tank platoon, at first equipped with two-pounder high velocity cannon, and later with six-pounder guns.

Support and the rifle companies comprised the fighting group known as 'F' or fighting echelon, but behind them were 'A' and 'B' echelons controlled by Headquarters company, and concerned with internal administration. Headquarters company consisted of a transport section which, in later stages of the war, maintained and operated more than a dozen types of vehicles numbering as many as fifty trucks, fifteen motorcycles, and a number of jeeps and staff vehicles. It also included the quartermaster's section, which was responsible for the supply of all the thousand items of equipment needed by the Regiment. This company was a tremendously complicated organization that included butchers, mechanics, drivers, storemen, technical repairmen, instrument repairmen, batmen, cooks, postal clerks, sanitary men, water men and many others. Most of these soldiers (all infantry trained) seldom had an opportunity to fire a shot in anger, but they were often the recipients of the enemy's shelling, and, in many cases, of his machine-gun fire as well. Without them, fighting echelon could not have survived a single battle, and their importance to the Regiment was not to be assessed on the basis of the number of medals which they won.

Finally, there was Battalion Headquarters (B.H.Q.), the directing force in battle. It was not simple either, for it contained not only the executive officers, the C.O., the second-in-command and the adjutant, but a fully equipped medical section including a doctor and stretcher bearers; a chaplain; a military police section; a pay detachment; a staff section concerned with the administration of personnel; patrol and sniping sections; and an intelligence section whose job it was to know all that was knowable about the enemy.

March and April became the growing months in truth. The basic training that had been so haphazardly attempted in Canada was begun anew and a never-ending schedule of hard work was each man's lot. Men learned for the second time – and this time in a way that stuck – the principles of soldiering. But they learned little of how to fight a war in this year of 1940. The combat training of every regiment in England was still a deplorable farce. Troops that would soon be committed to battle were already paying for the blindness of politicians, and for the absurdities of a staff that had not changed a major thought in its collective head since 1918 brought the First War to an end. The year 1940 saw the 'phony war', and a bumbling military optimism based on nothing but conceit. The peacetime mentality that had brought about the débâcle at Munich still ordered the plans and preparations.

It was as well that the fighting soldiers had no intimations of the execrable quality of the high-level leadership. Within the battalion in these months there was no sense of foreboding, only a rising satisfaction springing out of the new-found pride of the Regiment in itself. Men worked too hard to think. Salmon maintained the pressure to the very limits of physical endurance, and few had time or energy to speculate on the antiquated type of training they were receiving, or on the strange lack of weapons and equipment for an army that might have to fight a battle on the morrow.

Constantly strengthened in their own opinion of themselves, and of their unit, the troops lost much of the nervous intolerance for English ways that they had earlier adopted. The large number of pubs about Aldershot became familiar places, and men began to appreciate them for what they were – the entry ports into the English way of life.

Although most of the married men in the unit were feeling an increasing strength in the pull of home affections, the single men were already experiencing a waning in the power of the emotional links that bound them to Canada. Before March ended there were few single men in the Regiment who had not found friends of one sort or another, depending on their appetites, among the English populace.

In late March, men had their first actual sight of the enemy when a German reconnaissance plane circled high above Aldershot, caught in the scintillating cones of searchlights. The nerve-tingling sound of the sirens was heard for the first time.

Aldershot was soon alive with rumours that seemed to spring full-blown into life with the advent of warm weather. The Regiment was slated for Egypt. In a week it would be off to France. The war was coming to an end and within the month the unit would be heading back to Canada – someone had even seen the movement orders for this journey in the Orderly Room.

Training progressed from the basic squad drills to field training. Each day the companies marched out to the broad plains beyond Aldershot where they learned about war – as it had been. The 1918 Pamphlet of Field Engineering was the Bible in those spring days. Fascines, fire-steps, revetments, traverses, communication trenches – these were the key-words in the military vocabulary. Miles of trenches grew and spread across Salisbury Plain and the pathetic futility of it went quite unnoticed. No voice cried out against that monumental folly.

April drew to its close and there were signs, for those who cared to see, of the cataclysm that would soon inundate a world. In England the signs went unheeded and the troops went on practising night trench reliefs in the tradition of the Somme.

And then May came.

With a stupefied incredulity the West watched as the blitzkrieg exploded over France and the Low Countries. There was near panic amongst the military staff in England. Hasty schemes to repel invasion were formulated overnight. In Aldershot the whole of the garrison was ordered to stand by to counterattack the enemy upon the English beaches on receipt of the code-word, *Julius Caesar*.

At midnight of May 10, the Regiment's orderly officer, sleepily propped up on a lounge in the Officers' Mess, heard the phone ring. Wearily he reached out an arm. For several moments he listened uncomprehendingly as a distant voice repeated a seemingly senseless phrase over and over again. The bemused orderly officer tried mumbling it aloud. "Julius Caesar? Julius Caesar – JESUS CHRIST!" he cried in a voice that wakened half the camp.

The flap that followed turned Aldershot into a bedlam, but there was no invasion and this was only the first of a series of false alarms that would continue to be sounded well into the following year.

But though the Western Front had disintegrated and the doctrine of static defence had crumbled into dust beneath Hitler's armour, understanding of the truth was slow in penetrating into the dusty crevices of the directing minds in England. On May 11, the Regiment moved into a full-scale 1918 trench system and there, during the days that saw the end in Europe, the troops practised trench warfare.

Then, abruptly the unit was ordered to proceed to France and in a mood of unparalleled excitement actually got as far as Dover before being turned back once more to Aldershot. It was only another portent of the state of nervous indecision which gripped the High Command.

The confusion at staff levels became even more impressive in the days that followed and orders and counter orders arrived so hard upon each other's heels that the Regiment at last grew impervious to them and took refuge from the uncertainty by returning to its normal life of drills and training.

On May 30 the unit was ordered to move to a concentration area from which it could be ready to repel an invasion. The place chosen was the little country village of Finedon, far from any area of military activity, and in a countryside that had never seen soldiers in the mass before. The troops were billeted in private homes for the first time, and the people of Finedon took them to their hearts. The Regiment remained here only a week, but in that short period it grew into England to a depth that was astonishing. From that brief stay a love of England which became a part of almost every man took root. The Regiment marched in ceremonial parades behind the red-coated town band, and felt a kinship with the civilians that it had not known since leaving Picton, and perhaps not even there. Finedon brought the unit its first unobstructed view of England. It was a view that memory harbours still.

THREE

"Cook's Tour"

BY JUNE 12, the 'Phony War' was done. Dunkirk was history. The whole of northern France was in German hands and the Panzer columns were driving southwest, almost unopposed by the disintegrating remnants of the French Army. Even to the most sanguine eye it must have been apparent that the Continent was doomed. But on June 13, the First Brigade of the First Canadian Division was ordered to proceed to France.

The story of that journey is the story of a child who walks unhesitatingly into the path of Juggernaut, so strengthened by the invincible ignorance of youth that in the end Juggernaut is cheated. That the Regiment should have escaped destruction is just comprehensible in these terms; but that the High Command in England should have ordered that excursion is beyond all understanding. Nevertheless, the thing was done. To make matters even worse, the staff so managed the affair that during the excursion the Regiment was deprived of its entire administrative arm, its heavy weapons, and its food and ammunition.

Three days before the rifle companies entrained, the unit transport had been ordered to proceed independently to France. It was a proud convoy that moved to the embarkation port – more than fifty bright new trucks, just received from Canada, together with ten Bren carriers and a dozen motorcycles. The transport carried with it the unit's two precious heavy mortars; most of the Regiment's records and files, its battle scale of ammunition, its reserve rations, the quartermaster's stores, and nearly a hundred men. It also carried the intelligence files, and the unit's entire stock of French maps.

Three days later when the rifle companies boarded a troop train in Aldershot each soldier was equipped with fifty rounds of rifle ammunition, and with rations for two days. So they went off to war.

On the morning of June 13, the spring sun beat pleasantly down on the port of Plymouth, while the Regiment formed up in companies on the station platform in the centre of a wildly enthusiastic crowd of civilians. The atmosphere was feverish with the intensity of the false optimism of the moment; that optimism which so desperately resisted the impact of truth.

Two ships were lying at the jetty. One was a decrepit French passenger boat, the *Ville d' Angier*, and the other was a dirty French freighter, unloading crates of ripe strawberries destined for the London luxury trade – while almost within sound and sight, France shuddered in the agony of death.

There was indescribable confusion at the docks. The master of the *Ville d' Angier*, an irascible Breton who spoke no English, was not at all certain that he wanted a load of soldiers aboard his vessel. A long and acrimonious argument developed between him and the regimental officers. Meanwhile the men, dispersed about the docks, filched crates of strawberries and smeared faces and uniforms with juice. The scene began to take on some of the aspects of a comic opera, and there were even some supporting players.

Lady Astor arrived and bustled about dispensing comforts to the Empire's troops. Pausing beside one young soldier, she demanded to know his age, and on being told that he was just nineteen she raised her voice indignantly, "Such children being sent to war," she cried. "I will not have it, I shall see that it is stopped at once!" And the 'child' in question squirmed uneasily, knowing full well that from this day onward he would bear the sobriquet of 'Junior'.

After some hours the captain of the *Ville d' Angier* was persuaded to allow the troops on board, but his attitude remained that of a master whose ship has been chartered for an excursion of Sunday trippers. Perhaps he should not be blamed, for in truth the atmosphere was one of carnival.

It was a quiet crossing. At 0130 hours a lookout reported seeing a torpedo slip past under the ship's stern, and at once every soldier aboard rushed to line the rails, hoping for at least a glimpse of the submarine to enliven the monotony of the voyage. These innocents abroad were honestly distressed at having missed the show.

At dawn they came to Brest.

What had been confusion in Plymouth, was chaos here. The town was already filling with refugees from the east and it was cluttered with slovenly groups of French soldiers, amiable, and completely without discipline; utterly careless of their war that was already drawing to a close. Marching up the dusty streets, the men of the Regiment were appalled by the demoralization of the French. It was an unforgivable blow to the mood of the moment. Where were the brave *poilus*? No flags waved, no bands played. In the streets the civilians went about their petty business, or eyed their saviours with disdain.

The military organization was beyond confusion, and it was more luck than anything which led the Regiment aboard its train bound for Sable, 200 miles inland, where the First Brigade was to concentrate in preparation for battle.

On the afternoon of June 14, the troop train puffed hesitantly forward, making short dashes between stations and then halting as if to regain its courage. No doubt the engineer knew a great deal more about the facts of the situation than did the soldiers.

In the crowded compartments men chafed at the heat,

and drank the cheap wine which flowed like water at each halting place. Hour by hour, but unknowingly, they approached the thrusting columns of the Panzer Divisions. No one gave much thought to the details of the intended purpose of the journey. Each man had fifty rounds of ammunition, and there were several cases of blank training cartridges in the baggage car.

The ignorance of the real situation was appalling, but it was not the fault of any man aboard the train. No one had bothered to inform the Regiment that the Germans had already by-passed Paris, which was even then entering a state of siege.

The train crawled on and at first light of dawn it came into the town of Laval, almost 200 miles inland, where it was halted by a frenzied station master. He was beside himself. "Are you Canadians insane?" he cried. "Do you not know that Paris has fallen and that all resistance is at an end? Do you not know that *les boches* are only forty miles away?"

The Canadians did not know, and the shock of the discovery was so great that at first it could not be believed. France had capitulated. The Panzers were even then bearing down on the channel ports. The C.O. held a brief conference. The engineer hurriedly uncoupled his engine, ran it to the rear of the train, and coupled up again.

It is to the credit of the Regiment that in this shattering moment when fantasy ended, there was no confusion and no dismay. In this, the first vital emergency of its career, the unit responded well.

But the holiday mood was certainly at an end. As the train retreated coastward, the face of the country underwent a terrifying change. Every little station was jammed with refugees, fleeing west in a state of unreasoning panic. A mob of men, women and children, crowded against the train at every halt. Laden with the most absurd articles of household furniture, most of them had neglected to think of food; and so the troops brought out their emergency rations and gave them to the hungry civilians. Salmon attempted to stop this dangerous generosity, but his command carried little weight when the soldiers saw him pass his own tin of bully-beef to an old farmer and his hungry daughter.

With the suddenness of a summer storm the atmosphere had changed. Soldiers now manned their Bren guns on the train roof to repel the air attacks which seemed inevitable. They stared back down the tracks as if to catch the first glimpse of the armoured spearheads of the German pursuit.

The situation in Brest, when they reached it at last, was one of hopeless muddle. By dint of good luck the train reached the docks and the men were unloaded along the harbour shore while the officers tried to find shipping. There was nothing for the men to do but wait in the hot sun. Many of them stripped off their clothes and swam, until a German plane swung over the harbour and the shrapnel from anti-aircraft shells began to hiss into the placid water.

Towards evening the companies were assembled and marched aboard a little channel pleasure steamer, the *Canterbury Belle*. She had been designed to carry seven hundred passengers but as the night wore on new troops swarmed aboard until, by dawn, she was laden with more than three thousand men, including wounded Belgians, fragments of French units, and two thirds of the First Brigade.

Now a strange inertia seemed to settle over the harbour. The war in France was finished, and it seemed that this retreating fragment of an army had lost the volition to make the final move to safety. All that day the *Canterbury Belle* lay in Brest and men waited for a new Dunkirk to begin.

Then, in late afternoon, there came an opportunity to release the accumulated tension and frustrations all in one wild moment. A German reconnaissance plane glided arrogantly over the harbour at five hundred feet. One moment the *Canterbury Belle* was a somnolent and peaceful old ship, the next she had exploded as if by spontaneous combustion.

Fifty or more Bren guns had been mounted about the ship in case of air attack. These opened up as one. They were joined almost instantly by every rifle, pistol, anti-tank rifle, or other weapon upon which three thousand men could lay their hands. There were some navy gunners aboard with an anti-aircraft cannon, but they could not get near it because of the wall of lead that the unleashed soldiery was flinging into the sky.

The startled German plane turned and fled without firing a shot. It climbed steeply for a moment, then levelled out with smoke trailing from one engine.

The captain, surveying his ship after the battle was momentarily speechless. He shook his fists in impotent fury at the soldiers who encrusted his vessel like brown moss. He wept as he looked at the perforated funnels, the lifeboats that had become sieves, the rigging hanging in shreds from masts that were studded with bullet holes. Later, when his voice returned, he spoke hard words.

In the evening the ship made steam for home, and at dawn of June 17 the Regiment entrained at Plymouth for those grim barracks on the plains of Aldershot.

The transport section meanwhile remained unaccounted for. On June 18, Sergeant Art Storms appeared at Aldershot driving the C.O.'s station wagon. The sergeant could give no news of the rest of the transport column and so preparations were sadly made to strike a hundred men off strength as missing, believed prisoners-of-war.

The story of what actually happened to the column is best told in the words of Basil Smith, the transport sergeant.

"We left Aldershot on June 10," Smith's account begins, "and arrived in Falmouth the next day. I remember the town was already teeming with Dutch, Norwegian and French seamen who had no home port any more. We sailed to Brest and when we landed the confusion was terrific, but quite in harmony with everything else concerned in this fiasco.

"When the stores truck came off the boat they looked for the driver, but he was missing. So the transport officer says to me, 'get in and wheel her'. I had never driven a truck before but this was no time to quibble. I took off into France in a cloud of gravel, literally driving blind. A bunch of us met by accident that night about fifty miles inland, and slept under the stars near a farmhouse, where we got some eggs and about a yard of that French bread. The old farmer rolled out the barrel and we had a happy evening, though the only intelligible conversation to both parties was '*Vive la France*' and '*morte Hitler*'.

"The morning of the second day we pulled inland, on our own, and soon got lost. Not seeing any other army vehicles we stopped at a village and made enquiries from the local schoolmaster, who spoke good English. He gave us dinner in a lovely little house with white table linen, beautiful glassware and silver service. After Calvados and cigars he remarked: 'I can't understand why you chaps have come over here. The Germans entered Paris this morning without a shot being fired, and the war is over.'

"Well, it was a cinch *we* didn't know why we were there, but as far as we were concerned the war hadn't even started. We found our way back to the route and pushed on inland till we reached the outskirts of Sable. Most of our vehicles miraculously turned up; but Bob Creighton, of Bancroft, who had been riding convoy duty on his motorcycle, cracked up and went to a French Hospital. Bob spent the next five years as a P.O.W.

"About midnight Lt. 'Fats' Ruttan got the order to return to Brest. We grabbed a quick breakfast and the 'skipper' organized his convoy. None of us will forget that drive. We passed thousands of refugees, in fact most of the roads were choked with them, poor devils. I don't know where they wanted to go; anywhere away from the Germans, I suppose. They were all ages, and all were carrying bundles.

"Another thing we noticed was the different attitude of the people since the preceding day when we were cheered as conquering heroes. That was yesterday. The only greetings we received now were black scowls and an occasional expectoration.

"We arrived in the outskirts of Brest at 1030 and there must have been a solid mile of British vehicles ahead of us, bumper to bumper. We joined them, and in a little while there was a mile of them behind us too. What the Luftwaffe was doing on that day I'll never know, but we sure expected the same treatment the boys got at Dunkirk.

"Finally all our vehicles were moved off to a small town 14 kilometres from Brest. For our parking lot we had a little wood in the grounds of a chateau. We dispersed the trucks and settled in for thirty-six of the most nervous hours I can recall. The tension was worse than being under shell-fire later in the war. We were momentarily expecting a Panzer column to come sweeping down the road.

"We sat there waiting for shipping space, with nothing to break the monotony except a turn of sentry duty.

"Even the worst hours have their humour though. At a time when everyone had pretty well taken it for granted that death or captivity was going to be our fate, one driver spent the whole afternoon servicing his truck. He went over it all with a grease gun, then tightened every nut and bolt with a spanner. Finally, conscious of a job well done, he approached the 'Skipper'. 'Sir', he said, 'I've just went all over my truck, greased her, filled the gas tanks, and she's in first rate shape.' Then he stands there beaming with righteous pride.

"The 'Skipper' stared at him as if he hadn't heard right, and finally replied, 'Jesus! the Germans *will* be pleased!'

"On Monday morning the order came to destroy all vehicles by fire. But we couldn't burn the trucks because it would have set the wood and chateau alight and drawn every German plane for a hundred miles, so we did the next best. We went to work on all those lovely new trucks with pickaxes; punctured the tires, gas tanks and radiators; jammed up the bodies, sheared off engine parts and cracked the blocks. Then we destroyed the equipment in them; the whole Regiment's equipment.

"It was here that we lost Little Chief. He had come over to France with us because he was too heavy to go with the fighting troops. Since he was made of pewter and weighed five hundred pounds, we knew we could never get him back to England. Rather than have him taken prisoner, we buried him in a roadside ditch.

"Back at Brest we waited in a dockyard shed. A Cockney sailor finally stuck his head in the door and yelled, 'Anybody 'ere for Blighty?' and with that we climbed on a little channel pleasure craft, the *Brighton Belle*. She was built to carry about fifty, and there were three hundred aboard and no room even to complain as we crossed to Falmouth harbour.

"That was about the end. But at least we saw a bit of France on our Cook's tour."

FOUR

"The Waiting Years"

T HE RE-UNITED regiment had undergone shock treatment, but it was not alone. In a matter of ten days Britain's polite dalliance with war had been rudely terminated.

Facing England's shores from Bergen in the North to Cherbourg in the South, the German Army ranged along the narrow sea; and it was now clear even to the most myopic politician that Hitler would not be content to halt for long.

The First Canadian Division, under General McNaughton, was the only infantry division left in Britain that was whole, and still fairly well equipped. Now it was given the task of multiplying itself into an army for the benefit of German intelligence. The marching and countermarching across southern England which followed was intended to give the illusion of vast forces on the move. The foot-weary men soon came to call their division "McNaughton's Flying Circus".

It was a time of ominous expectation, but above all it was a time of invigorating ferment. It was a time when all sensations were sharpened to an almost unbearable edge by the common threat. There was no drawing back from danger; on the contrary, soldiers and civilians alike went out to it, welcoming it as a drugged man, waking suddenly from suffocation, welcomes the sharp impact of sun and air.

For a full month the Regiment remained at Aldershot, but gone were the days of fantasy. The tactics of the old war went back into their coffins. The phrase 'static defence' became anathema, and the new slogans were 'flexible defence' and 'counter-attack'. The countryside erupted in a rash of tank-traps, road blocks, machine gun nests, pill boxes and barbed wire obstacles. The whole shape of infantry training changed with the new emphasis on air defence, dispersal and the use of one-man slit-trenches instead of elaborate trench systems. It was a time of improvisation. Molotov cocktails – beer bottles filled with gasoline and fitted with a wick – were devised to deal with German tanks. Weird land torpedoes – explosive charges tied to children's wagons that could be released down steep slopes against enemy vehicles – were built in backyard workshops. Weapons of other wars that were hardly more than museum pieces were renovated and emplaced along the coasts. The Home Guard became a reality, and in its enthusiasm turned southern Britain into an embattled camp.

On June 26, the first enemy bombs were dropped near Maida Barracks, and a few days later the famous Aldershot parade ground sprouted a forest of steel posts, intended to destroy enemy gliders which might attempt to land upon it. The parade square, most sacred possession of a peacetime army, had been sacrificed to the reality of war. It was a fitting sign of the change that had come over Britain.

There were other signs. In late June, ration scales were severely cut but at the same time munitions began to arrive. On June 28 the two-inch mortars were fired in practice, for the first time since the war began.

The lovely days of that summer were filled with incident, but heavy with labour. Working parties slaved at digging defence works. Companies stood-to at dawn, for weeks on end, to be ready to repel the anticipated para-troop invasions. Twenty civilian buses from the streets of London, painted khaki now, were attached to the Regiment so that it could move quickly to any threatened point.

In mid-July the Regiment gladly abandoned Aldershot forever and moved eastward into the gentle hills of Surrey, where it went under canvas in a countryside of sunken roads running under ancient oaks; of verdant fields and mellowed buildings, with not far away, the towns of Dorking, Reigate and Redhill.

Sharing the common urgency and mood, the soldiers and the civilians were soon one. Differences which would have been a matter for harsh resentment in other times, were overlooked or never noticed. The experience at Finedon was repeated, but intensified. Within a few months of the Regiment's arrival in the area, many of the men had been adopted into English families, and, in the words of one sergeant, "There wasn't a single girl under sixty in the area who wasn't going steady with one of us". This was much more than the soldiers' usual and rather casual interest in women. There were to be more than a hundred marriages in the Reigate and Redhill area between men of the Regiment and local girls before the war was over.

Sharing all fears, hardships and the few felicities with the civilians, the unit was putting down new roots. As the years passed the roots would grow until in the end England would become the familiar home for many of the men.

Through the summer the fine weather gave an illusion of beauty to conceal the stark shape of the future. The Regiment trained as it had never done before. Battle exercises became the day's routine. The troops fought imaginary battles in the English fields and lanes until they grew numb with fatigue. In the evenings they wandered to the country pubs, the 'Barley Mow' and many others, and drank their pints in company with the enthusiasts of the Home Guard, or with the local farmers.

But the expectation of battle was being maintained at too high a level and the lack of real action began to have its inevitable effects. The unit was on permanent call, so that there could be no complete escape from tension. One night a section guarding the ammunition trucks heard suspicious noises. Challenges were given, and ignored. A burst of fire shattered the calm Surrey night and in the morning the interloper was found, quite dead. That horse cost the Regiment a hundred and sixty pounds sterling since, naturally, it was the finest horse in England.

August brought with it a change in command as Salmon left the unit, his task done, to take over a brigade. The new C.O. displayed his character on his first day in command. That night a soldier happened upon his company commander in a pub. The officer was accompanied by a stranger in civilian clothes. The soldier was feeling convivial. Sauntering up to the pair he threw his arms affectionately around his captain's shoulders, and insisted on buying drinks all round until, at length, he ceased to have much further interest in the world. It was the stranger who eventually drove the intoxicated one back to his company lines and the soldier had just sufficient consciousness remaining to press a half-crown on his obliging, but unknown, benefactor.

He was a shaken man the following morning on battalion parade when the new commanding officer, Lt.-Col. Howard Graham, paused in his inspection of the ranks, produced the half-crown, and pressed it on the private with the dry remark: "I think perhaps your need is greater than my own".

Lt.-Col. Graham had been second-in-command of the Regiment since Picton days. It had always been his Regiment as far back as the 1920s, and now he devoted himself to maintaining the exacting standards that Salmon had set. During Graham's tenure of command the unit attained its full pre-battle maturity.

In the middle of August there came a break in the stultifying monotony of training. During August 15, the Luftwaffe came in force to England and at one moment on that day the troops counted more than a hundred aircraft weaving and fading in the harsh blue skies. It seemed to be a prelude for invasion, and the presence of those high-flying squadrons gave a new incentive to the work in hand.

London began to feel the weight of war. Men going to the great city for week-end leaves returned to tell of the prodigies of bravery they had seen amongst civilians. They took part in what they saw, for they could love these people who would not turn away from death. There is a record of two Hastings N.C.O.s who entered a burning and collapsing building to rescue a wounded child when it seemed certain that they could accomplish nothing except their own destruction. The incident was witnessed by a Civil Defense officer who hastened to ask the men for their names so that they might be recommended for the George Cross. The sergeants were unco-operative, not out of modesty, but because they happened to be two days over their allotted leave.

The tempo mounted as September drew near, for then, if ever, the invasion must come. Training grew more intense and the men found surcease from strain in their contacts with civilians. The good ladies of the nearby village of Rusper gave dances at the slightest provocation and there was a memorable time when several of the soldiers displaced the English orchestra, borrowed their instruments, and played the music of a proper hoe-down. For hours the English girls were churned about in the unfamiliar intricacies of the square-dance.

And there were the countless evenings when soldiers made their way quietly to English homes to share the slim rations of the family meals and to talk largely of the spacious wealth of Canada.

The air activity grew steadily until it was almost continuous. The tent camp was on the direct German route to London, and air raid warnings were sounded so often they became commonplace. There was some actual contact with the enemy when three Germans bailed out of a flaming Dornier and landed in the Regimental area. Men stared at the prisoners with surprise and did their best to feel hatred of these innocuous-looking youths in tattered flying clothes.

Then, on September 8, the Regiment heard the code word that England had been waiting for. CROMWELL. The signal that the invasion was about to come. Now the effect of the long training showed. Within the hour the Regiment stood ready by its buses, fully equipped for war. But the waiting dragged on interminably through ten taut days, and then the threat was gone. A mood of depression followed, for the troops had been desperately anxious to try themselves against the enemy.

The weather worsened and the tent camps became quagmires until at the end of the month the unit moved into billets in the vicinity of Betchworth. It was indicative of the way soldier-civilian relations had developed, that despite its own urgent needs, the unit refused to dispossess several elderly couples who were occupying homes capable of sheltering many men. To billet almost nine hundred soldiers in the countryside without causing friction seemed an impossible task, yet it was done. One platoon became the guest of J. Arthur Rank, the film magnate, and somewhat to its amazement found itself taking tea with Mrs. Rank.

For the most part the men were billeted in smaller homes where they were often asked to share the family meals, or pressed to share the owner's minute rations of tobacco. One company was billeted with the Earl of Winterton, and a sergeant wrote to his wife of an evening spent in His Lordship's dining room. "Tonight the butler is having a beer with us, and someone is playing the guitar while the old boy sings us Limey songs. Do you suppose that ever before in English history a Lord's butler sang and drank in the great dining hall?"

The autumn passed and the danger of invasion faded, but the air war was always present. Bombs, jettisoned by German aircraft on their way to London, fell frequently in the area. There was real anger the day the 'Barley Mow' was hit and the incident was taken as a personal affront. Apart from this, there was little damage, although a heavy raid in October scored a direct hit on Charlie company's new latrine, and dug a bigger hole than the sanitary squad had contemplated.

The men were becoming old soldiers now and they had learned many of the old soldiers' tricks. Circumventing a too inflexible authority became a major occupation. At this time civilian petrol was so severely rationed as to be almost non-existent, and the Army had dyed its own supply bright yellow so that its use by civilian vehicles could be readily detected. Many of the officers and men of the Regiment had purchased old cars or motorcycles, and it was an inspired lieutenant of Charlie company who discovered that the dye in Army petrol could be removed by straining it through the filter of a gas mask.

On December 8, the unit moved out of its billets to take its turn manning the coast defences around Brighton. For a month the companies lived at battle stations, guarding mine-fields and manning pill-box emplacements. It was a tedious duty, and the weather was foul.

Christmas, the second away from Canada, found the Regiment still on coastal watch, but it was a vastly different unit from the one that had looked out over Greenoch harbour almost a year before.

Although it had as yet seen no real action, it was now a veteran unit. Most important of all, it was a completely integrated whole. As the months of separation from Canada grew longer, the men came more and more to turn their hunger for a home inward to the Regiment. The unit had become far more than simply an organized group of soldiers. Within it every man now knew his comrades as he had perhaps never known his own brothers. The Regiment had become the home of the spirit and of the flesh, and after a week's leave in London a man would return to it with the same subdued anticipation that is in the heart of the labourer returning to his home at night.

Trained, toughened and moderately well equipped, it

was ready now to do the job for which it had been created. It had matured in the preceding year and found its balance. But there was to be no chance for it to play its destined role for a long time to come.

More than two years of waiting remained before the guns would sound in earnest. It was as well that the men did not know this when, in January of 1941, they returned to Betchworth and to the beginning of a new phase in their lives.

With the end of the invasion threat in 1940, the offensive spirit began to gain slow headway in the military thinking of the High Command and, as it filtered down to infantry regiments, it took the form of exercises, schemes and interminable battle games. The impact of the commando idea began to be felt as well, and a toughening-up program was instituted that sent the men out on what they came to call the 'rat races'. One of these, and a memorable one, was a sixty-mile route march in January that lasted three days and that put a large part of the battalion on the sick roll as a result of the long hours spent clambering about the countryside in the cold winter rains.

In the spring of 1941 the first of the gigantic battle schemes which would convulse whole counties, began. It was called Exercise 'Bulldog' and it resulted in an entire division being shuffled about the map of England for the education of the senior commanders; while the soldiers involved were left without the slightest idea of the purpose, or design. 'Bulldog' set a pattern, and for the remaining years in England the coming of spring was not heralded so much by the arriving robins, as it was by the immense exercises which, for weeks, would disrupt the normal existence of the Regiment without having, from the men's point of view, the slightest value. There is no doubt that the command staffs benefited from these manoeuvres but, on the whole, the fighting troops found them only boring.

Training, and schemes, were not the really important elements in men's lives. Within the unit the major part of every man's day was devoured by routine. For sixty hours a week there was no idle moment. The steady demands for fatigue parties to build roads, drain fields, do kitchen chores and a thousand other tasks made their insistent call. And for each soldier there were the multitudinous personal tasks; sewing on buttons, doing laundry, keeping equipment in repair, or taking turn as orderly to keep the billets clean. There were the routine parades; bath parade once a week, pay parade once a month, church parade each Sunday, inspection parades each day. There were the extra duties, guard duty, detached duty to build barbed-wire obstacles along the coast, or to dig defence positions at nearby aerodromes.

For the transport men there was an endless round of daily vehicle maintenance. For the medical section, the morning sick parades. For the signallers the long night hours on telephone duty. For the regimental clerks a ceaseless flood of queries from the higher staff that needed immediate answers in triplicate at least.

To complicate administrative matters further, there was a constant movement of small groups of men from one part of the Regiment to the other through transfers; or to one of a thousand special courses that were being run in every part of England, dealing with every conceivable aspect of military life from the digging of latrines, to the deployment of tanks. The Regiment was in a constant state of flux, and at the same time it was required to retain a smooth efficiency in its complex interior economy.

This aspect of a unit's life, dealt with so briefly here, is too often ignored. But in truth, actual fighting consumes only a minute fragment of the total hours that span a regiment's existence even when it is in contact with the enemy. The vast majority of those hours and the greatest portions of men's energies must be expended in the monotonous and mundane duties which alone can maintain the body of a regiment in health and fighting trim.

For the next two years the soldiers' lives were to be compounded largely of this normal daily drudgery, sometimes spiced, sometimes further stultified by war games and special training. The sole antidote was what could be found in civilian relations, and in the increasingly tenuous ties with Canada. These ties were becoming strained, not only by time but by the vagaries of the mails which were suffering severely from the increased U-boat activity in the Atlantic. Perhaps time was the most insidious and destructive of these strains. Many marriages, made in haste before the unit sailed for England, were already foundering. Many others that had lasted while habit and propinquity were strong, were approaching dissolution as women at home, or husbands overseas, reacted to the long separation and to the freedom from old mores, which the atmosphere of war brought with it. There were bitter words in the barracks at night when a letter from a 'friend' in Canada would shatter the illusions so painfully maintained in a soldier's mind. As early as 1941, the padre was busy writing to the Canadian civil authorities, in a usually fruitless effort to resolve the individual domestic betrayals which had become commonplace. It was by no means a universal condition, of course, and there were a good many wives and husbands who bore that seemingly endless separation in good faith. But there were many who did not.

As for the single men, their ties of affection to parents and family remained strong enough, but almost without exception they found new, more vital ties of love in England or in Scotland. During the spring of 1940 the first marriages were celebrated in the Betchworth area, and before the two years' wait was over, there were nearly as many men with wives and homes in England, as there were with wives and homes in Canada.

The troops were often called upon to help the local civilians face the bombing aftermath. Soldiers worked in the fields filling bomb craters, and in the villages, helping remove rubble and repairing smashed homes. The sense of unity with the English grew steadily stronger. Soldiers who had been farmers all their lives before the war watched the Surrey farmers sow the spring crops, and often they could not resist the hunger to go to the land themselves. Gardens were planted on English soil. Lads from the fertile fields of Prince Edward and south Hastings found opportunity to grip the plough again; to drive the cattle into the English barns; to do the things that are not labour, but which are the abiding pleasures of those who love the land.

In the evening there were the pubs, good talk, too much beer sometimes, but comradeship. For those who hungered for more sophisticated pleasure, there was always London, an hour away, and offering herself to any man in uniform – though at a fancy price. Canada was becoming an almost forgotten way of life, and an almost forgotten land. England was here and now.

Through the summer of 1941 the unit was becoming more and more a world apart, giving its prime allegiance increasingly to itself and taking what hold it needed on the solid earth from England, not from Canada.

In September there were drafts of reinforcements from Canada and these outlanders were coldly received at first by the men who had become a closed corporation. There was heartbreak in this, but it did not last, for as time passed the newcomers became old soldiers too.

One of the reinforcements deserves special mention. He was an Indian chief, standing seven feet high, whose powerful and ferocious face was said to be capable of stopping a Messerschmidt at ten thousand feet. His name was Chief Petawawa-much and he was the missing 'Little Chief's' replacement.

His story is also the story of a forgotten unit, the second battalion of the Regiment; it was the reserve battalion, officered by the men who had built the Hastings and Prince Edward Regiment in time of peace, and who had then by reason of age or sickness been denied the reward of accompanying it overseas. In the armouries at Picton, in Trenton, Bancroft, Madoc, and the other county towns, these men still laboured unremittingly that the Regiment which they could never join on service would remain strong. To them came boys too young by a year or so for active service, and men suffering from some medical defect that might in time be rectified. They trained as no active service Regiment had ever trained, on their own time, with equipment they made for themselves, and with an enthusiasm that was fabulous. And they cried out for places on the reinforcements drafts. In the years of the war the unsung second battalion contributed nearly two thousand men to the first battalion in Europe. It was the one strong link with home. It was the hidden reserve of strength for the fighting companies.

When news reached Picton of the loss of 'Little Chief' in France, no time was spent in mourning. The second battalion scoured the country to find a wood-carver competent to produce a replacement and, when they found him, he was commissioned to carve an Indian fit for the Regiment.

So Chief Petawawa-much (Petawawa for his birthplace, and 'much' for his immense proportions) came into existence. At a fire-lit ceremony on a stormy winter night in Trenton he was sworn in, documented and started on his journey overseas. His passage was not easy. On his first venture he accompanied a new Canadian corvette bound down the St. Lawrence and, when this ship came to grief on a shoal, the Chief was nearly drowned. He survived to reach Halifax but there he disappeared. The correspondence which flowed from headquarters to headquarters about him contains this letter from the Chief Naval Officer at Halifax.

"On receipt of orders I made enquiries regarding disposal of stores removed from the damaged corvette. The assistance of a light-crane operator was given me to help locate the Chief and I explained to the operator that I was looking for a big crate containing an Indian. The operator immediately replied that there could be no such Indian on the docks as he would have smelled him long ago. I explained that this was a carved Indian and we set to work and eventually uncovered him.

"I then approached the very British captain of an armed merchantman and asked him if he would take an Indian overseas and dispatch him to the Hastings and Prince Edward Regiment in England. The captain's reception of the request was chilly and he informed me that it was asking too much to allow any damn man to stow away on his ship, particularly an Indian.

"I pointed out that this was a cigar-store Indian, but the captain replied that he did not give a continental where the fellow had worked before the war, he wasn't stowing away on a British ship. I managed to collect my wits and finally explain that he was a *wooden* Indian.

"That made it all right, and the Chief sailed from Halifax."

After the Chief's arrival at Betchworth he was taken on strength, paraded in front of the full battalion and accepted as a worthy recruit. He took his stand on a dais by the entrance to the unit area, and there he received the smart salutes which were his due. Small boys sometimes came to stare at him in awe, but there was – and is – a dignity about the Chief that precludes levity, even amongst the comrades whom he came to know so well.

FIVE

The Hour Strikes

A NOTHER winter began on the south coast and once more there was a change in training. Battle drill, that ferocious invention of the Eighth Army in Egypt, had come into favour. In practice, the teaching of battle drill involved a process of driving that could, and did, kill men. To top it all, the drill was combined with what came to be known as assault course training, a brand of physical torture intended to make men into supermen. Assault training demanded ten-mile runs, belly-crawls through collapsing earth tunnels, swimming in freezing rivers in full battle-order, and even, under certain sadists, wading through the open sewage tanks which are a feature of the English countryside.

The spring again brought its wave of schemes. But schemes had some compensations, notably the opportunity for scrounging extra rations.

Chickens appeared in most unlikely places, often of their own volition. One morning an officer happened to peer into the driver's compartment of one of the carriers and his glance was met by the beady gaze of a large rooster. The carrier driver became aware of the unwelcome presence of the officer at that moment and with magnificent *savoir-faire* turned on the bird beside him and exclaimed in aggrieved tones: "Why you little feathered bastard – how did *you* get in here?"

The First Division had now come under indirect command of a little-known martinet named General Bernard Montgomery, and within a few weeks the men had come to think of him with a strange mixture of respect and downright malevolence. South-East Command was Monty's domain, but it soon became known as South-East Commando, for the little man with the biblical tastes had strong opinions about infantry training. It was his contention, for instance, that every man and officer should be able to march twenty miles in five hours – and Monty's contention was tantamount to the will of God.

Exercise 'Tiger' was one of Monty's children and a fierce beast it was. The scheme lasted ten days and, at the end of it, the troops who took part were careless of death and destruction alike. Under Monty's command the illusion of garrison life was icily dispelled, but he substituted imaginative training for the doldrums which had preceded 'Tiger'. Under his command the troops began carrying out schemes up to Brigade level with live ammunition. Platoons advanced over the South Downs to the thunder of very real artillery shells crashing a few hundred yards ahead of them in a rolling barrage. Mortar shells threw dirt in their faces, and their explosions could not hide the shrill whine of bullets passing only a few feet above men's heads. It was dangerous work, but of immense value for it shattered the monotony of ordinary war-games and at the same time gave the men a foretaste of the reality to come.

The summer passed and the Regiment moved inland again, this time into the lovely heart of Sussex, to the quiet valley of the Wal and the tiny, somnolent village of Horam with its Saxon church that has stood in tranquillity for a thousand years.

On August 19, the name Dieppe echoed from every radio in England and the news of the so-called 'reconnaissance in force' roused the Regiment to raging disappointment. Dieppe's tragic aftermath did nothing to dispel the bitterness of men who had waited in England for three long years for action – and who had been displaced by men of the newer Second Canadian Division for the

Dieppe raid. For a brief moment morale dropped to rock bottom but soon recovered and began to soar to new heights as latrine rumours spread that at long last the First Division was to seek its destiny in battle.

By the autumn of 1942 the armed camp that was England had ceased to lie under a state of siege, and there was a restiveness in the air that pervaded all aspects of life. 'Second Front Now' signs began to appear chalked on hoardings, and in every pub the question was no longer "will we attack?"but, "when does the attack begin?"

The Regiment's activities apparently belied the undertones. During all of that wet autumn the men were engaged in most unmilitary tasks, and normal training was almost abandoned. Whole companies were detached to help local farmers harvest the crops, and other companies laboured in the mud of a vast estate called Possingworth Park, building a permanent camp of Nisson huts. There was an atmosphere closely akin to peacetime in these activities, and the men gave themselves to the unwarlike tasks willingly, as if indeed they knew that this was the pause before the storm.

There were many changes. After two years as C.O., Lt.-Col. Graham reluctantly left the Regiment to take command of a brigade, and was replaced by Lt.-Col. Bruce Sutcliffe, who had also served the Regiment for many years before the war.

Changes in the regimental organization followed one another so quickly that at times the unit hardly knew which companies were which. Support company increased its strength by a full platoon of anti-tank gunners. The mortar platoon now boasted six three-inch mortars. The transport section burgeoned until it was very nearly capable of moving the entire Regiment on wheels.

Lavish issues of new equipment contributed to the feeling that the days of waiting were approaching an end. There was surprisingly little apparent reaction from the men. There was no wild enthusiasm. As the Regiment itself had matured, so had its individuals. They were ready to fight, and delighted at the prospect, but they kept their heads.

Leaves were granted but there was a difference in the way the leave-men acted. Married men spent every possible hour with their wives and children in the towns across South England. Single men were a little less jaunty in their approach to love, and a great many casual affections suddenly ripened into marriage or engagements. The time was drawing short.

Training began again, but this time there was no doubt as to what it presaged. It was assault landing training. The first preparations for an attack upon a defended enemy coast.

In mid-December the unit entrained for Scotland and for two exhausting weeks learned about combined operations. By day, men scurried up and down scramble nets on the sides of ships; loaded and unloaded from the heaving little cockle-shells known as assault landing craft, and learned the battle drills for crossing beaches under fire. By night, under driving winter rains, they practised what they had learned, flowing over the sides of landing ships into waiting barges; moving in through black night and dark seas to fling themselves on Scottish shores that crackled with rifle fire and glared in the light of bursting flares. Day after day, night after night, the work went on at a pace keyed to the limit of human endurance. The third Christmas Eve away from Canada found the Regiment fighting its way through the rain-soaked Highlands against an intangible enemy who would soon enough be real.

There were interludes. The camp was on the estate of the Duke of Argyll, and the presence of the Duke's deer proved too much for the long-repressed instincts of the hunters from the Bancroft hills. There were trout fishermen amongst the men as well, but their equipment consisted of Mills grenades – far more efficient than fly rods. There were parties, attended by Wrens from the naval establishments, when kegs of beer vanished mysteriously from the NAAFI canteen, and as a result whole companies groaned in unison the following day as they raced over assault courses in full kit.

Returning in January to Possingworth, the Regiment supplied working parties to help tear down the formidable defences erected in the preceding years against a German invasion. Defences were no longer needed. The steel could be reshaped into the weapons of offence.

In April there was a further flurry of secret and inscrutable preparations, orders and counter-orders. The month ended and in early May the Regiment moved back to Scotland to the quiet and delightful town of Darvel in the lowland country.

Expectation, so long contained, now burst its bonds. Tropical kits were issued to all ranks, and a wave of speculation mounted. Was it to be Africa then? Or the Far East? Air recognition roundels were painted on the bonnets of the vehicles. Companies rode up and down the roads on collapsible bicycles that had appeared along with countless tons of other oddities intended for invasion. The magnificent Scottish spring was an intoxication, but its effects were lost in the intoxication that filled the hearts of men who had waited three long years for their fulfilment.

The troops moved to the coast and carried out a full-scale combined operations landing from HMT *Derbyshire*. Embarkation leaves were granted, and there was the certain knowledge that these would be the last. For the second time in a single war, the Regiment bade farewell to its homes.

On June 13, the unit embarked at Greenoch, the port that had seen its arrival in England on New Year's Day of 1940.

From this date until battle was joined, the ships were home – but battle was not yet. Through a full two weeks the vessels of the swelling invasion fleet lingered in Scottish ports. HMS *Glengyle*, a converted freighter, carried the balance of the rifle companies. Able company was detached and placed aboard HMT *Derbyshire* with the 48th Highlanders. Able company was most displeased, for rivalry with the Toronto regiment had always been intense. The Regiment's transport had been loaded some days earlier aboard ships of another convoy which were due to join the invasion forces off the beaches of the enemy coast on D-Day.

As yet there were no indications of where that coast would be. There was little leisure time for speculation. Life aboard the invasion ship was complex. Platoons spent long hours practising the involved loading drills which, on D-Day, would bring them out of the bowels of a darkened ship in perfect order, and dispatch them shoreward through congested waters. Festooning the upperworks of each ship were rows of square and ugly iron boxes, the assault craft, each capable of transporting thirty men, and each bearing a serial number. For each landing craft there was, somewhere in the ship, a human serial to match. When the time was ripe that number, repeated monotonously over the ship's loudspeaker system, would bring men and boat together into one unit.

On the afternoon of June 28, ten troopships sailed from Greenoch escorted by a dozen destroyers and cruisers, and the summer sun shone on the crowded decks, and on the glitter of a mighty harbour. In the dockyards along the shore workmen paused to watch, and to raise their fists with thumbs extended in a gesture of good luck. Overhead a squadron of Spitfires bound south on patrol, swerved from its course to salute the stately line of great ships making steam towards the open sea.

Eire was passed on June 30, and with that threat of treachery safely behind, the men were told the name of their objective. Sicily. Operation 'Husky' – the first land assault upon the European enemy was under way.

It was a ten-day journey, north far into the Atlantic, then south again into warms seas, under a sun that struck the unsuspecting and turned half the Regiment into parboiled agonies. There was no monotony. The Regiment now belonged to the Eighth Army, Montgomery's army, and men found out at once what this could mean. Monty had long believed that every soldier down to the rear-rank private in the last platoon should know not only every detail of his own part in the battle, but should also know the general plan. Information that was denied to colonels in other armies, was the right of every private who served Montgomery.

Plaster models of the Sicilian coast were unveiled and men spent hours memorizing the details of their particular objectives. Maps were issued and studied not only by officers, but by the men as well. Briefing lectures swallowed hours of every day. In the evenings there were concert parties and aboard the *Derbyshire* at least, long hours with copious amounts of beer in the wet canteen.

On July 6, Gibraltar loomed to port and that night the troops stared across the calm sea to the north and beheld, with a sense of shock, the brilliant lights of Algeciras naked under the Mediterranean sky. Other convoys steamed over the horizon, ahead, astern, and on both flanks, until it began to seem that the entire sea was filled by one great argosy. Daylight, and in the south the hot yellow sands of Africa shimmered in a brutal heat.

On July 8, there was sudden flurry of confusion. A daring British submarine had examined the beach which the Regiment was destined to assault and reported a false beach a hundred yards off-shore that would prevent the assault craft from reaching land. A spate of new orders was issued. Then, on the ninth, the *mistral*, wind of ill fame, roared across the calm seas and in a few hours had churned them into angry breakers that threatened to swamp the smaller vessels of the fleet. The gale howled, and each man knew that if it held strong the invasion must be halted. That in itself would mean no more than a prolongation of the strain that always comes before a battle, but there was another implication. So far and almost incredibly, the operation had remained a secret from the enemy. Now the convoys were converging close on the Sicilian shores, and nothing could prevent them from discovery in the next dawn.

That night the men sat at rough tables in the mess decks. The dim and naked bulbs above them glowed through a hot haze of sweaty air. Beneath their feet the oily steel plates throbbed with the slow pulsation of the engines. The ships rolled heavily and oddments of men's equipment came adrift and slithered across the iron decks. There was very little talk. Here and there a section leader discussed some minor problem with his sergeant. Shadowed, and already withdrawn from the world about them, men sat motionless with their rifles between their knees – waiting, waiting. The groups at the mess tables played endless games of poker and the sweat dripped on their knuckles, and rolled between their fingers.

Everything was in readiness. It would be only the work of a moment to pick up the weapons, the web equipment, the steel helmets. The ship pitched, slowly, sickeningly, and men waited for the word.

It came at 2000 hours. Platoon commanders clattered down the companionway stairs to the troop decks. The men looked up, watching, saying nothing. The officers spoke briefly, and in every man's belly there was a tightening of the inner flesh. The show was on.

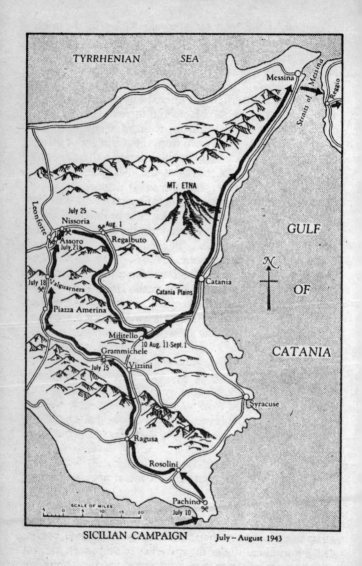

SICILIAN CAMPAIGN   July – August 1943

SIX

The Sands of Sicily

THE OPERATION order for the Regiment in the Sicilian invasion was a monument to meticulous and detailed staff work. It covered every eventuality of which the planners could conceive.

Shorn of its endless minutiae, the plan instructed Baker, Charlie and Dog companies from *Glengyle* to attack and capture two narrow segments of beach called Roger Green and Roger Amber. Able company, from *Derbyshire*, was to wait offshore in the role of floating reserve ready to exploit the first success. Thus far, the operation plan. Beyond it in the dark hours before battle lay reality.

Shortly before midnight, in the rank depths of the invasion ships lying at anchor some ten miles from the shore, there was a remarkable and unnatural silence eased only by the thin murmur of men's voices. It was a waiting silence that at ten minutes to the hour was shattered as the voice of the troop dispatcher burst raucously from the loudspeakers.

"Do you hear there? Do you hear there? Serial one! Serial one! To your boat-stations move now. Serial two! Serial two! Stand by."

The silence returned, more intense, and then the dispatcher's voice was echoed by a harsh and sibilant sighing that came not from men's mouths but from their bodies. Like iron filings under the influence of an unseen magnet the human particles began to draw together, shuffling across the congested mess decks, forming serpentine lines that wound behind stanchions and around obstructions. Each gripped the web-belt of the man ahead with hands tightly clenched. The serial leaders began the slow progress upward through black passageways where the dim glow of blue-hooded flashlights gave a brief and charnel illumination to the sweating faces under their steel helmets. When the lights flicked off the darkness became so thick that it was palpable. Men lurched as heavy swells caught the ships; and ripples as of wind in August grain ran down the shuffling lines.

On deck it was a night of nights. The gale had passed, leaving only a soft breeze laden with the warm land smells of Sicily. Scattered clouds hung in a luminous sky. It was very still and very lovely; but there was an undertone, something felt rather than heard – the hidden surge of a beginning motion on a hundred unseen vessels.

Until this moment the plan had guided every action made by men. But from this moment on the unforeseeable ripped at that careful blueprint. From this moment men acted largely out of their own resources, their own knowledge and their own strength.

Aboard *Glengyle*, Baker, Charlie and Dog companies stood ready to embark. The plans for Baker had suffered a sea change due to the submarine's discovery of the offshore bar; and a tank-landing craft, laden with amphibious trucks called DUKWs, had been ordered up from Gibraltar to meet the fleet at the 'release point' and ferry Baker to the bar. Beyond the bar, the DUKWs would take the troops on to the beach.

The tank landing craft was late, and lost. For hours it felt its way through the blacked-out armada seeking *Glengyle*, and during that interminable wait zero hour was relentlessly approaching. Charlie and Dog were also delayed by this prime delay.

Along the rails of *Derbyshire* the assault landing craft cavorted wildly in their davits as the men of Able company followed one another into these queasy cradles and jammed themselves on the narrow benches. Suddenly there was an appalling outburst of sound. Aboard a dozen of the great ships a myriad steam winches clattered into life and the landing craft plummeted down into the heaving sea ... the angry sea that was not in the plans.

Some of the little craft were flung back against their mother ships with such fury they were crushed like eggshells. Others hung helplessly in their falls with the cables fouled, banging against the steel walls of the ships with a nightmare clangour that made men recoil in fear that the noise must be clearly audible not only to the defenders on the shore, but north to Rome itself.

Of the Regiment's four companies, Able was the first to embark and by 0100 hours it was drifting through the heaving darkness in its three little cockle-shells. The sea was violent enough to make the transports roll heavily, and it played with the landing craft as if they were chips caught in a spring spate. Stomachs were soon in sympathy with the rolling turmoil under the thin decks. Nausea spared no one, not even the massive bulk of Capt. Alex Campbell crouched behind the square landing ramp in the bows of the lead craft. Alex was Able company commander, a fire-eating hulk of a man who had lost his father in one war with the Germans, and who had lost his brother in this one. Now in an interval between retchings he turned and voiced the battle slogan of his company. "*Nil carborundum illegitimo*" – "Don't let the bastards grind you down!"

Aboard *Glengyle* the remaining three companies were at last embarked. The night was no longer quiet but had a voice, a sibilant, muted, threatening cry like the sound of a great mob that, in darkness, contemplates riot and destruction. The combined putter of four hundred little motor craft was like the uneasy rumble of an awakening ocean giant. The landing craft pitched and heaved and yawed from crest to crest seeking, usually with no success, to find the dim blue-glowing buoys that were to be their points of rendezvous. The phosphorescent water gleamed with a thousand wakes that curved across the belly of the sea in aimless patterns.

The chaos of the night grew greater. Communications between the lost and the lost-from were non-existent since radio silence was still being maintained. Most of the naval coxswains and sub-lieutenants in command of the assault craft were as seasick as the soldiers and, with the sinking of the moon, the navigators could no longer hope to find the meticulously chosen points of landing.

Indecision rode aboard most of the landing craft until, as the promise of the dawn grew green in the East, each company commander reacted to the common urgency and turned his flotilla shoreward, his objective no longer a hundred-yard strip of beach – but Sicily itself.

Only one company ever found its predestined target, and that was Dog. The rest? They landed where they could.

But the landing was not quite yet. First there was the prelude to this battle, and the prelude to war itself. The first intimation of the passions which were about to engulf the Regiment's world was a delicately traced parabola of crimson specks that lifted from the unseen shore, hung for a moment, then vanished. These were the first shots; a stream of tracer fired by a startled Italian shore post. There was a breathless pause.

And then the vast conclave of battleships, cruisers, destroyers and monitors opened fire simultaneously. In a great arc the entire south horizon thundered and flamed, and the grave roar of shells rolling through echoing tunnels of air filled the dying night.

In that cataclysmic dawn of battle the soldiers forgot even the pressing urgency of their revolting stomachs. This was their moment of absolute awe – a moment that comes once with the first battle and that never comes again. In the flicker of the gun flashes they saw the outlines of a hundred anchored ships; they saw the countless assault craft that, like schools of water beetles, scurried past on every side. To the north they saw the faery flicker of the bursting shells outlining the low Sicilian shore. Zero hour, that instant of beginning and of ending, had come and gone.

The activity upon the sea which until this moment had been tremendous but subdued, now became clamorous and desperate. Each landing craft sought for a leader and for direction. Some spurted purposefully towards the distant shore then hesitated apologetically and circled back as if afraid of a rebuke. Far to the left the little flotilla that was Able company could bear the hesitation no longer. The square prows turned shoreward and the order went to the engines for full speed. Charlie and Dog were also heading in, while Baker, its three platoons double encased – first in the bowels of the DUKWS and the DUKWS themselves in the cavernous hold of the Tank Landing Craft, also went lumbering towards the battle.

Able's three craft came under sporadic shell and machine-gun fire a hundred yards from land and, as the pessimistic submarine had predicted, they ran aground on the outlying sand bank. Unwittingly Able had landed nearly three miles west of its correct beach on a sector that was due to be assaulted by British Commandos. Able did not know this, and had it known, would not have cared. After four hours of retching agony afloat, its men had but one desire, and that was to gain the solid land.

The ramps clattered down and the heavily laden soldiers leapt out into seven feet of water and somehow struggled ashore. Patterns of machine-gun fire from a white stone farm house laced the sea. The first to die was Sgt.-Maj. Nutley, a man who had spent twenty years in the peace-time militia and who had been allowed to accompany the Regiment into action only because he had so tenaciously insisted that his life of service would otherwise become a mockery. Perhaps this was the irony, perhaps it was the man's fulfilment that he should be the first.

In the canebrakes beyond the barbed wire of the beaches, the three platoons scurried about like over-burdened cattle. There was one overriding condition of those first moments – a vast urge for action that was still partly shackled by the confusion of the plans and by the fact that the intended objectives simply were not to be found. Alex Campbell, shot through the arm and bleeding like a pig, broke the impasse and freed his men. "Get on, you silly bastards!" he shouted. "Get on with it!"

It was the right order, though surely not one that had ever been heard on the field of battle-schemes.

A platoon commander galloped off through the canes in the direction of the white house with its stuttering and lethal voice. His platoon followed. A section fell as one man into a shallow ditch and brought its fire to bear on the house as cover for the other two sections which were already launched on their attack.

Heedless of the machine-gun fire (for this was an old and familiar sound, and no one quite understood or cared as yet that bullets could kill and maim) the two sections galloped up the slope, piled into a web of enemy barbed wire, surmounted it and rushed the house itself.

The defenders were Italians, and they were flabbergasted by this bull-headed and suicidal rush. They surrendered instantly, and the assault upon that beach was done.

It was full dawn now and far to the east the other companies had landed. But here, too, the facts were out of joint with the blue-print. Targets, objectives, roads and routes so clearly shown on the air photos and on the models did not exist, were lost, or could not be recognized. The confusion on the beach was tremendous but again it resolved itself into effective action once the stultifying obligations of the too-detailed plan went overboard. Baker and Charlie crashed through the beach defences with so much vigour that the Italian defenders, their morale already shaken by the sight of the thundering armada offshore, gave only token resistance.

Most of the Regiment was now ashore, but the balance of B.H.Q. was not. It, too, was lost and in a clumsy Motor Landing Craft was circling aimlessly off the western beaches. A somewhat academic argument about respective spheres of responsibility, between the adjutant and the naval commander, was terminated abruptly by the R.S.M. "Pick out any three landing craft," he ordered the coxswain, "and get us in behind them fast!" That, too, was a reasonable order. And BHQ, with the unit's three-inch mortars, came in upon the beach taken by Able company.

Able itself had vanished. Campbell had led it inland apparently intent on driving straight north to the Italian mainland.

Each company had by this time gone off on its own private rampage. Dog, rushing up from the beaches, met panic resistance from an Italian fortified hill and overran the position. The men paused only long enough to relieve the defenders of their boots – for the Regiment's boots had been ruined by too many salt-water immersions during the last Scottish exercises.

Able, in the meantime, was far off in the blue, steering its course northward at all speed. Marching headlong up a cactus-guarded road, raising clouds of white dust as it went, the company collided violently with an Italian artillery battery moving south to take up a defence position. The engagement was brief and, when it was done, Able possessed two horses, an unwieldy number of prisoners, and its own artillery. Three Italians lay in the ditch, their faces growing mud-coloured as their life blood ebbed. A soldier stopped to stare at them then turned quickly away, retching without results. Sea-sickness had drained him. Blood-sickness could produce no further token.

As the day aged, and the sun mounted, the heat grew intolerable. Massive dust clouds hung chokingly above the arid waste of farms. Shells from the naval guns beat overhead and aircraft droned with clean precision through the pallid sky. On the beaches, and in the beachhead, confusion multiplied as wave after wave of landing craft disgorged their loads of men, tanks, guns and vehicles.

The impetus of the assault had spent itself by now and slowly the fragments of the Regiment began to find their way towards the rendezvous. They straggled in, mortally weary and suffering from the sudden ebb of energy that had followed the enemy's collapse. Towing 'liberated' carts filled with melons, or riding phlegmatic little donkeys, they converged on a hill-top near Pachino where they threw themselves under the thin shade of gnarled old olive trees. The ingathering was not completed before night fell, when the Regiment took up a defence position on the perimeter of the bridgehead.

Meanwhile, on the beaches, the unloading of the transports had continued. The anti-tank platoon commander, Frank Hammond, fighting to free his weapons from the congestion, sent one of his men with a message for the second-in-command, Major Lord John Tweedsmuir. Lord Tweedsmuir had been unexpectedly posted to the Regiment during the last days in Scotland, and the unit had at first found it a little difficult to assimilate a British Lord into its county background. He was still much the stranger. When the uncertain messenger asked how he would recognize the second-in-command he was told, succinctly, to "Look for a God-damn Limey bloke about eight feet tall". It was no time for finesse.

It was incredible that anything orderly could have emerged from that confusion, but this was no longer 1940, and the long years of training paid their dividends. By nightfall all of the diverse parts of the Regiment, landed from more than a dozen ships on as many different beaches, had sorted themselves out and found their separate ways to the main body. The aura of chaos vanished as if it had never been. In the warm darkness of that first night ashore, the Regiment was again whole, competent and ready for the battles still to come.

It had been a remarkable day, a phenomenally successful one that might well have cost the Regiment much of its heart blood, but that had only scratched the outer skin instead. It was not quite real. There was a feeling of illusion about it, almost as if it had only been another in the great and bloodless schemes that had filled so many weeks in England. It left the men with an oddly discontented feeling, incongruously mingled with a superb self-confidence. Few of the soldiers put it into words, but one man spoke his mind. "Call this a war?" he asked. "Why, this is only fun and games. I wonder if it's all like this..."

In the morning, and with the rise of the destroying sun, some of the illusion of a battle practice passed away. Riflemen sat under the olive trees, and as they cleaned their weapons they gazed about them at another world. It was a tropic world, and an ancient one. Cacti flowered obscenely along the sunken tracks that served as roads. The sky was pale and unbearably brilliant and the sunlight glittered from the white stone farms that were scattered thickly through parched vineyards, looking like tombstones set in a particularly arid cemetery.

To the north, grey hills rose slowly from the coastal plain and the winding tracks leading to them were smoking arteries sending up dusty aerial projections of themselves as an army moved inland. Out to sea the Mediterranean glared in garish colour and in Pachino bay the hundred ships lay anchored while endless flotillas of landing craft moved from them to the beach. As the men watched, a flight of Italian dive bombers appeared and winged timidly about the edges of the fleet before jettisoning their bombs and fleeing through a multi-coloured tracery of antiaircraft shells.

The heat was suffocating. Water was a rare thing and what was available was soupy to the touch and rendered almost undrinkable by the addition of too many chlorine tablets. The soldiers sprawled, panting, in the meagre shade and waited for their orders.

The battle situation was confused. There had been few German troops in the landing areas and these had at once withdrawn into the hills leaving the unhappy Italians to hold the plains. The Italians took no pleasure in their role and almost all of the coast defence divisions had surrendered leaving only little groups of Blackshirt forces still showing some pugnaciousness. General Montgomery was faced with that abhorrent thing, a vacuum, between his beachhead troops and the real enemy. The vacuum had to be filled, and quickly, before the Germans in the mountains to the north could organize a new defensive line.

The men of the Regiment had enjoyed an easy battle on July 10, but they were to pay for it now in the agony of a forced march under appalling circumstances. They were not acclimatized to tropical conditions; they were in poor shape for marching, after nearly a month of shipboard life; but there was no alternative. The vacuum must be filled, and since no transport could be landed for at least three days to come, only the feet of the infantry remained.

The Regiment moved off from its olive grove at noon, turning its back on the sea. The heat was brutal and the dust rose so thickly that it became an almost palpable barrier through which men thrust their whitened bodies with an actual physical effort. It gathered thickly on their sweating faces and hardened into a heavy crust. Their feet sank ankle deep in dust as if in a tenuous slime. There was no water; the occasional foul well along the route dried up when the first few platoons fell upon it. The sun was an implacable enemy, and there was no escape from its brutality. Steel helmets became brain furnaces. The weight of the battle equipment, weapons and extra ammunition was one more agony. The marching troops straggled along the verges where there was no grass, but only dust, eternal dust. Occasional tanks rumbled past, obliterating whole companies in the hanging shroud. They marched.

Not least of the qualities of good fighting men is their ability to endure. Bravery, military knowledge and expert marksmanship – these things have their place in the making of a soldier, but they are as nothing if the man cannot endure the unendurable. The men of the Regiment were soldiers. They endured.

The attenuated column, strung out in single file over many miles, worked its way steadily inland, and upward into the hills. There were brief halts each hour, and in those intervals a few men looked back at the broad blue bay with its minute ship models. Most of them looked down at their feet. They dragged at the incomparably bad issue cigarettes that came with the 'compo ration' packs on which the fighting units subsisted; and the smoke was bitter and acrid in their parched mouths. They got to their feet and their boots slithered, clumped, and the dust clouds rose into the shimmering air.

Before dusk fell the column had passed the limit set for the third day of the invasion. There was no halt. Darkness brought some surcease from the heat, but none from the dust and thirst. The roads became steeper and exhaustion began to take its toll. Men slept on the move; an old habit learned in the English schemes, and they were guided by their companions. Here and there an N.C.O. shouldered extra rifles for those who had reached the apparent limit of their endurance. The troops marched on. Perhaps a dozen men could not go farther and were loaded on the backs of donkeys, to sit swaying with eyes shut.

At midnight the unit passed through its first Italian town, Rosolini, but the place left little impression on men's minds, and few have any memories of it except that in the central square there was a well.

A few miles beyond the town, and nearly thirty miles from the start point of the march, the Regiment was halted. Sections and platoons staggered into the open field and fell where they stopped. They were beyond caring even about food. They died on the hard ground, and three hours later they were dragged from their graves, and set upon the road once more.

It was noon of July 12 before they halted again. Men who had fainted during that morning march now came staggering up to join their sections. The rest lay in the ditches, stupefied, and simply waiting. In two and a half days they had fought a battle and then marched almost fifty miles. It was not credible that they could do more.

But the pursuit of the Germans could not wait. First Brigade now became the vanguard of the thrust and since its men could walk no farther a great effort was made to find transport for them. A squadron of Sherman tanks

from 12th Canadian Tank Regiment lumbered forward
and Able company, with part of Baker climbed on the
monsters' backs. Dog company loaded itself aboard artillery gun-tractors, jeeps, motorcycles and a handful of
trucks. There were none left for Charlie – and Charlie
marched. The vehicles were as heavenly chariots to the
multitudes. Burrowing through tunnels of thicker dust
they drove relentlessly forward. Giarratano lay ahead and
it was believed that the enemy would try to hold this hill-
top town. But the speed of the advance had been too rapid
and the Germans had not had time to fortify the place.
The Regiment rolled through the empty, stinking streets
and at midnight took up a position in the hills beyond.
And then at last the agonizing dash was at an end.

Men could be asked to do no more. The news was
passed that the unit had been granted a forty-eight hour
rest. It could not be a complete rest for there was only
empty space between the Germans and the Regiment and
the unit had of necessity to take up the posture of defence
and at the same time endeavour to gain contact by patrolling forward. These patrol duties were given to the carrier
platoon which, being mechanized, had been spared the
worst of the hardships of the forced march inland. The
carrier men were delighted. In sections of three, the little
armoured vehicles ground their way forward into no-
man's land, their crews enthusiastic and incautious.

One of these patrols, under command of Sgt. Jack
Milne, was ordered to locate a certain road junction and
discover if it was held by the enemy. There was something
remarkably stimulating in the idea of driving forward
over ground not yet taken by Allied troops. In a sense it
was very like the feelings of an explorer who sets foot for
the first time on virgin soil.

This probably explains why the patrol did not halt after
reaching its objective. It explains why Milne led his section on down a steep road into a mountain-guarded valley
towards the gleaming line of a distant railroad track.

There was a station where the road crossed the track,

and clustered by the roadside was a crowd of pretty girls who waved encouragingly. A wave is as good an invitation as any in war-time, and the men piled out of their armoured machines and strolled to meet the girls.

It was a brutal shock when three machine guns suddenly opened fire on the now defenceless section.

A company of Blackshirt Militia held the crossing, and they had waited until, whether by design or accident, the Canadians had been made to feel secure.

Caught in the open, the men dropped to the ground and hugged the hot, hard soil. But there was one exception. Pte. O. B. Thompson turned and ran across the open field towards the abandoned carriers.

As he ran, the machine-gun fire concentrated on him and he was hit in the stomach and in the thigh. Nevertheless he kept on his feet, reached the nearest vehicle, and levered his shattered body over the side. Although he was not a driver, he started the engine and turned the carrier broadside-on between the Italians and his own comrades. Under cover of this protection a gunner managed to race across the open space unhurt, and in a few moments was returning the enemy's fire from his Bren.

The remaining men of the section were now enabled to reach their vehicles. So the section withdrew, somewhat shaken, but having learned a vital lesson. The lesson was not without its cost, for Thompson died of his wounds shortly afterwards.

This was, of course, a very small and unimportant battle but it demonstrated the mood of those early days in Sicily. Men were hungry for action, and if they were unrealistic in their approach to battle, it was because they had not yet learned the meaning of fear. The illusion of war was still upon them.

Resilient in the extreme, the troops were themselves again after a single day of rest, and they looked about them for diversion. They found it in the railroad yard of Giarratano where an abandoned, but undamaged locomotive stood ready at hand.

For the whole of a blistering afternoon a dozen men worked on that engine, hauling water for its boilers in tin helmets, and expending as much energy upon an apparently pointless project as they would have done upon a battle. The fires were lit, and steam hissed into the cylinders. One man, a railroad fireman in civilian life, took charge and with the assistance of a most unwilling Italian driver, set the train in motion.

The train chugged doggedly north up an incredibly steep gradient into no-man's land and it was not for some time that the soldiers realized that they were practically unarmed. Reluctantly they decided to return.

The grade was steep enough to have allowed them to free-wheel back at a good pace, but the Italian engineer, convinced that he was travelling with madmen, had other ideas. The train came back to Giarratano at such speed that it could not be halted until it had retreated four miles to the rear.

That day there was a further diversion. The Regiment was mustered on the hills and out of the dust of the nearby road appeared an open car. General Montgomery, complete with his fly-switch, had come to call.

Monty plays his part in the story of the Regiment as does no other senior commander. There were those who hated him, but they were not amongst the fighting troops. There were a good many who were angered by him, but there were few men in the infantry who did not trust him, as they had never in the past, and would never in the future, trust another general officer.

Austere, withdrawn and coldly critical, he was a soldier's general for all of this. It was axiomatic that when Monty issued an order for an attack, that attack would inevitably succeed. He gave the fighting men the one really vital gift that is within a general's power to give – he gave them confidence.

Grouped informally about his car, the men watched and listened critically as this little 'Limey' stood on a seat and talked to them. Staccato and original, his words had meaning. When he left them, the soldiers were prepared to take him up on trust.

They were prepared to do the next job of work that he might give them. It was not long in coming.

SEVEN

Death Valley

IN LAUNCHING the Sicilian invasion, the Allied commanders had as their prime objective the capture of the
crossings to the mainland of Italy at the Straits of Messina.
Accordingly, Eighth Army had been instructed to go
directly for this objective up the eastern coastal route
while on the far left the American Seventh Army was
intended to contain and destroy the major German forces
which were then concentrated in the western and central
interior.

But as so often happened, the initial plan had to be
drastically modified as a result of the enemy's failure to
conform to it. Quickly disengaging the bulk of their forces
from the battles with the Americans in the west, the Germans abandoned most of Sicily and concentrated their
armour and their best divisions in the path of Eighth
Army's coastal thrust. Thirteenth Corps on the Catania
plains at once became involved in a series of savage and
exhausting battles of attrition that gained little ground,
and that took much precious time. Its role became that of
a holding force engaging the bulk of the German armour.
And it was left to someone else to force the path northward towards Messina.

Thirtieth Corps of Eighth Army, including First Canadian Division and Fifty-first Highland Division, had during the first few days been operating in a secondary role
through the interior mountains on an axis parallel to that

of Thirteenth Corps. Now Montgomery gave it the formidable task of making the major thrust northward and of opening up the front.

The Germans had anticipated such a change in plan and the Hermann Goering Division, Fifteenth Panzer-Grenadier Division, and a number of smaller units had been firmly established well south of Mount Etna in a vital hinge position based on the towns of Leonforte, Assoro and Enna. The enemy coast defence line could not be turned while these positions held and the whole Allied operation was in danger of being brought to a standstill.

The position of the defenders in the interior seemed almost impregnable. Crack troops all – including the best of the Afrika Corps evacuated by air from Tunisia – the enemy also had powerful natural allies in the exceedingly difficult terrain. The few tortuous roads leading through the mountainous interior to the north were already well guarded by defiles and pinnacles which seemed an almost certain barrier against attack. The enemy was not unreasonably confident that he could hold his ground.

His confidence was put to the test on July 15.

On the morning of that day the Regiment had again become the vanguard of the Division. It moved northward with part of a squadron of Shermans of the Three Rivers Regiment in the lead, and with Baker company clinging to the tanks. Close behind came the rest of the unit aboard a motley collection of transport, including the carriers, carrying most of Able company, which followed the tanks closely.

It was a glaring tropical day, but pleasant enough by contrast for men who now could ride to battle. The arid hills rose high on every side, and far to the north stood the dim cone of Etna, a distant majesty looming out of the central heart of the island. As the road looped and climbed men looked out over a wild landscape. On the crests of hills clung villages so ancient that their beginnings were lost in antiquity. On the scarps of rugged cliffs were decaying fortresses, memorials of wars that had raged through Sicily for three millennia. Along the whitened roads, brown fields burned under the beating sun and little groups of desiccated peasants straightened bent backs to watch impassively as the invaders passed.

The atmosphere was electric, and there was a tingling expectancy in the heart of every man. No one knew when or where the enemy would be encountered, but all were aware that the column must roll on until that moment came.

There was a sudden flurry of excitement when, at 0800 hours, the head of the column paused briefly under a single desolate tree at a crossroad and waited while an approaching pall of dust resolved itself into the shape of a truck of a strangely unfamiliar type. It came out of the north at full speed, only to slam on its brakes as it was about to collide with the leading tank. The dust hung in a moment of absolute immobility and then with a startled cry two German privates leapt down from their vehicle and threw their hands high in a panic-stricken gesture.

They had, it seemed, misread their map, and taken the wrong turn. In Sicily, that was not hard to do.

These first German prisoners were passed back down the line looking apologetic under the curious stares of the Canadians. Their truck, emptied of its load of ammunition, was turned about and took its place in the northbound column.

Now the tanks climbed slowly to a high saddle and here they were passed by a section of the unit's carriers which took the lead in company with a pair of armoured cars. The tanks paused, sniffing suspiciously as their guns swung from side to side. Below them lay a broad, flat plain and on its far side a ragged escarpment on whose crest hung the crenellated outline of a village.

That village and the world about it might have been quite dead. Only a pair of kites wheeled overhead. For the rest, no other living thing moved on the broad, parched plain or in the pallid sky.

Sensing no enemy, the tanks began lumbering down the

slope. Again the dust plumes rose into the still air. The vanguard spanned the silent valley and began the ascent of a switchback road leading to the high village on the far side. The carriers reached the outskirts and clattered into the cobbled streets, and they went scatheless under the hidden muzzles of unseen guns waiting for more important prey.

In defiance of the rules of war and of common sense, the mile-long line of vehicles crawled forward in the emptiness of the vast bowl. From the ramparts of Grammichele the watchers must have congratulated each other on an unprecedented stroke of luck, for it must have appeared certain that their trap would close upon the whole of that naked and unsuspecting force.

The leading tank reached the village and swung into the main street. Crouched behind the square shield of their gun the crew of a German 88 could wait no longer, and they sprang the trap.

An armour-piercing shell skewered the lead tank from end to end. Flames leapt from the engine. The officer in the turret threw open the hatch and struggled terribly to free himself; and failed, and hung there as the flames rose about him.

Not fifty feet ahead the appalled crew of a carrier saw the flash and were half-deafened by the explosion. But the driver, Cpl. Ernie Madden, spun his carrier on its tracks and with a courage born perhaps of desperation charged the gun headlong. The Germans were caught in the act of re-loading. The carrier crashed into the 88, and the gun crew died where they had stood.

But there were other guns, many of them; for the heights of Grammichele were held by parts of two battalions of the Hermann Goering Division equipped with artillery, tanks and a good supply of lighter weapons. As the echoing thunder of the first explosion died the Germans opened rapid fire from the whole length of the escarpment upon the column on the plain below. Mortar shells fluted overhead and plumped down in murderous coveys, and 20-mm., four-barrelled anti-aircraft cannons lowered their muzzles to sweep the plains with automatic fire. The dreaded 88s barked with excessive savagery, and from two-score well-concealed positions machine guns rippled into life.

If ever an enemy commander had reason to anticipate a crushing victory, this was the occasion. Despite the fact that the ambush had been sprung prematurely and before the Canadians were fully trapped, the odds for victory were still overwhelmingly on the side of the Germans. In the first moments of the action that victory must have seemed assured.

In the town's outskirts the infantry of Baker company threw themselves off the tanks with frantic haste, and none too soon, for within minutes two more tanks had been 'brewed up' and were sending ominous clouds of black smoke high into the sky.

Behind the vanguard the carriers bearing Able company came under such intense fire that the men abandoned them and leapt for cover in the shallow roadside ditches, even as the first carrier flamed skyward. Farther down the column Charlie and Dog companies hurriedly abandoned their vehicles as two ammunition trucks roared into a spectacular pyrotechnic display. Fully half of the column was now under intense small-arms fire, while the remaining half lay exposed to observed shelling from the 88s. There was little or no chance of extricating the leading vehicles and there seemed to be but one reasonable course of action open to the Regiment; to abandon what could not be saved, and to retreat in haste over the valley's eastern slopes.

That there was no retreat was due to two conflicting factors; a paradox of battle. First, was the fact that the inexperience of these men armoured them against any real comprehension of the true seriousness of their plight.

This was the negative element. The positive and paradoxical factor was their tremendous experience. They had been under fire in so many battle schemes, and had repeated the basic tactical manoeuvres so many times that now they automatically repeated them again with as little concern for the lethal reality of the enemy's fire, as if this had been only another exercise on the South Downs of England.

Able company, pinned down and unable to move, automatically took over the role of fire company to provide cover for the rest of the battalion. Naively heedless of the 20-mm. shells and the machine-gun bullets, the three platoons lay on their collective bellies on a flat plain bereft of shelter and fired back.

Baker, finding itself under the very muzzles of the German guns and in close contact, promptly did as it had been told to do so many times, and closed with the enemy.

In the command group, lying by the roadside, Lt.-Col. Sutcliffe acted out of the memories of a thousand schemes and quickly ordered his two remaining companies into a wide left flank attack to strike against the defended heights from the southwest.

Meanwhile the tanks of the vanguard which had escaped the initial ambush had forced their way into the town, dealing savagely with a number of MK. IV tanks that tried to stop them. Close behind the Shermans crowded the men of Baker company seeking the more secure shelter of the larger houses. By their impetuosity they were soon threatening the sole line of eventual withdrawal open to the enemy.

To add to the German commander's problems the gunnery of his troops was becoming deplorably bad, perhaps due to the inexplicable and stubborn refusal of the Canadians to withdraw in haste, but more probably due to the work of the balance of the Three Rivers tanks at the rear of the column, and to the work of a troop of self-propelled British 25-pounder guns. These heavy weapons had come into action almost at once, and with great vigour and effect.

At 1140 hours, the Hermann Goering commander suddenly lost his nerve and ordered a precipitate retreat.

It was indeed precipitate. In their anxiety to abandon a fortress that ought to have been easy to hold against twice the actual number of attackers, the Germans also abandoned seven artillery pieces, innumerable lighter weapons, six trucks in working order, four MK. IV tanks (some only slightly damaged) and – final disaster – their entire quartermaster's stores.

It was only a little after noon when the battle for Grammichele ended. In the shade of a stone wall the wounded men sat stoically and smoked their cigarettes. In the village, men of the infantry companies gazed happily at the piles of excellent German rations they had won, while drivers tentatively started up the German trucks which more than replaced the vehicle casualties suffered by the Regiment. Casualties had been incredibly light. Only three men in the Canadian force had been killed – none of them from the Regiment – and less than a dozen had been wounded.

The reward for victory was a day's rest in the baking plains below the village. For almost the first time the troops had an opportunity to assess the Sicilian countryside, and most of what they saw they did not like. The homes of the desperately poor farmers and villagers seemed hardly more than hovels and, as yet, the men had not begun to sense the bonds which bind together civilians and soldiers in a battle area. There was a rather brutal contempt for the Sicilians, but no sympathy. The people's meagre possessions seemed fair game and many a pitiful orchard or garden plot was casually looted of its slender store of fruits. The fruits did the thieves little good for the clouds of flies passing from manure pile to garden products had implanted dysentery germs in almost everything that came out of the ground. 'Gyppy gut', as it was called, was becoming an almost universal complaint; an unfortunate one when there were battles to be fought.

With the collapse of Grammichele, the Germans withdrew northward some fifty miles to the city of Piazza Amerina, guarding the approach to the main German bastion in the Enna-Leonforte-Assoro triangle. Here on July 16, the Loyal Edmonton Regiment found them and after a battle comparable to that at Grammichele, succeeded in forcing yet another withdrawal.

This time the enemy did not go far, but occupied an exceedingly strong natural position a few miles past the city, and six miles south of the town of Valguarnera. Here, at noon, on July 17, Third Brigade crashed into the outposts and recoiled to try again.

With this preliminary failure to crack the German position frontally, First Brigade was given the task of making a wide right hook through the mountains to outflank the town. It was already dusk on the 17th, when the Regiment received its orders to execute this grandiose manoeuvre.

Superficially the order seemed impossible of execution. Without prior reconnaissance, and in complete darkness, the Regiment was to cross ten miles of trackless mountain terrain, debouch upon a strongly defended town and force the enemy's withdrawal from his positions to the south. There could be no artillery or tank support and the men would only have what weapons and ammunition they could carry on their backs. Heroic in the best traditions of the Light Brigade, the plan was daring, but most uncertain.

As night fell, the rifle companies moved off in single file into the dark wilderness and at once encountered a maze of nearly impassable mountains and canyons. The maps were useless and Able company, in the lead, advanced by guess-work and with a sublime faith in the Gods of Infanteers. The going soon became so bad that the Regiment could not even maintain contact with its component parts. First Able, then Charlie, became detached and disappeared into the gloom. Baker and Dog, with the C.O., managed to stay together, but where they were going, or where they were at any given moment, no man could tell. Heavily laden (every man carried at least sixty pounds, and some carried nearly a hundred) they climbed cliff-faces and slithered down cactus-filled gulleys until they

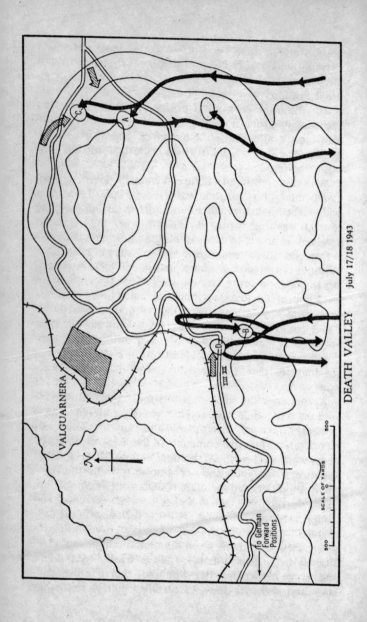

VALGUARNERA

To German Forward Positions

SCALE OF YARDS

500   0   500

DEATH VALLEY   July 17/18 1943

were so utterly fatigued that battle would have been welcome, if only for the fact that it would bring a halt to the mountain climbing.

All night that heart-bursting scramble continued. As dawn approached, the men of Able flopped down outside a tiny Italian shanty while the officers wakened the occupants in an attempt to locate themselves. The Sicilian family was terrified by this unexpected invasion of their mountain valley, and while an old woman screamed the night down, her shaking husband, as naked as a babe, pleaded for his life. They were far too frightened to give information, and wearily the company picked up its weapons and, steering by compass, moved doggedly north. The lead platoon had not gone a hundred yards when it became aware of dim shapes looming ahead of it. There was a breathless silence broken only by the sounds of tommyguns being cocked. But before the guns could fire, one of the dark approaching shapes was heard to complain bitterly that, "Nobody but a sick louse would want to live in this bleeding hole." Charlie and Able companies had found each other and now with infinite relief the two joined forces, and continued forward.

The other two companies had wandered farther to the west and as dawn broke they descended a steep slope to find themselves directly in front of the sleeping town of Valguarnera and between it and the enemy's main defence position to the south. There was no communication with Brigade, and none with the rest of the unit, so these two companies prepared to fight the war alone. Dog established a road block and settled down to await results, while Baker optimistically moved on towards the town.

Meanwhile, two N.C.O.s, Sgt. Ross McKnight and Cpl. Rusty Lawson, had gone off on a patrol of their own. When they discovered a German anti-aircraft position, its guns unmanned and its crews sleeping, the two were moved to act. Stealthily they went from gun to gun, opening breech blocks and removing bits of the firing gear until they had immobilized the entire troop. The alarm was finally given, but when the gun crews rushed out of their nearby barracks they were met with close-range bursts of tommygun fire, and the survivors fled.

The firing had roused the sleeping town and the enemy, incredulously observing the approach of Baker company, exploded into violent activity. Somewhat thoughtfully Baker decided to withdraw into the hills again.

In the town a veritable hornets' nest erupted, for this was a rear area and Allied soldiers had no business to be within miles of it. German troops rushed out in every direction, as yet unsure of the exact nature of the alarm, but mightily disturbed. A convoy of trucks, led by an armoured half-track dragging an 88-mm. gun, raced down the road towards the front, apparently under the impression that the Canadians had broken through from that direction. When the half-track was close upon the roadblock, Pte. Ralph Turner, sometime sanitary man of Dog company, raised himself out of the ditch and let fly a bomb from the Rube Goldberg weapon called the PIAT. The bomb smashed into the armoured radiator and the vehicle blew up.

As if unwilling to credit the facts, the Germans continued to send more vehicles along the road, some from the town, and some hurrying back from the front. As each arrived at the blazing pyre it too became added fuel until, in the end, there were more than a dozen vehicles of all types burning fiercely and surrounded by a satisfactory number of dead and wounded Germans. Dog company would have been content to remain at its post indefinitely had not its ammunition begun to run low, and had not a company of lorried German infantry launched a spirited counterattack, forcing Dog to make its withdrawal into the nearby hills.

Meanwhile Able and Charlie companies had been having adventures all their own. Towards dawn they had crossed a road that bore every sign of heavy military use. Not far away a small hill gave some promise of protection and here the two units dug in, in the company of half a hundred startled Sicilian refugees from the front areas. The soldiers were utterly fatigued and all but a few sentries dropped off to sleep.

Sleep was shattered, rudely, when a drowsy Bren gunner, peering out of his slit trench, beheld six enormous troop-carrying trucks, each laden with twenty or thirty German soldiers, moving sedately along the road below him. These were reinforcements going to the front, but the front was a long way off and it was early morning. The Germans were also sleepy, and indeed many of them were slumbering when a wave of gunfire enveloped them.

The range was less than a hundred yards – almost point blank – but it was not close enough for Alex Campbell. Seizing a Bren, Alex launched his huge bulk down the slope in a one-man charge, firing from the hip. He gripped a spare Bren magazine between his teeth, the while bellowing inarticulate challenges at the enemy. Campbell was one of the few men in the Regiment who, at that time, actively hated Germans. His hatred was almost a mania, but on this occasion he nearly satiated it, for when he was done, the truck that bore the brunt of his rage was silent and in its body, like sardines packed in tomato sauce, twenty of the enemy lay dead and dying.

Few of the grey-clad soldiers escaped. A handful managed to reach the ditches where they fought back courageously with rifles and automatic pistols. Later even these were forced to surrender and the two companies found themselves encumbered with eighteen prisoners.

Able and Charlie had arrived in the valley of Valguarnera some miles east of Baker and Dog, and almost behind the town. The road below them, which they now controlled, was the only eastward exit. So quite by accident the town had now been isolated, and the news of this calamity must soon have reached the German staff. The danger to the main forces who were at the moment staving off the renewed attacks of Third Brigade was obvious, and while the valley swirled with disconnected but bloody little actions, the Germans began to pull back their main force in order to deal with this totally unexpected threat upon their rear.

The Regiment had begun fighting its battle on the company level. Now it began to fight on the platoon, section and even on the individual level. The action developed into straight guerrilla warfare.

As Dog company withdrew from its position at the road-block it split up into several small groups. One platoon that had foolhardily 'tried to attack the town now found itself cut off. With commendable speed it went to ground in a culvert under the road where, out of ammunition, it stayed hidden for twelve hours while enemy transport and tanks retreated over its head.

A young lieutenant, Manley Yearwood, withdrawing in company with a captured German officer, faced a worse problem when the German suddenly attacked him. For long and savage minutes the two men fought desperately for possession of the Canadian's revolver. The German lost, and died where he had fought.

It was not all one-sided. Two men of Dog company, Ptes. Miller and Valencourt, who had been badly wounded, were taken prisoners in the early afternoon. A German officer, brandishing a pistol, approached and ordered them to their feet. Miller, who had been hit in the leg and abdomen and was almost unconscious, could not comply, but Valencourt, wounded only in the wrist and arm, staggered to his feet in time. Miller was murdered where he lay. Valencourt survived to tell the story, after being marched north through the streets of Rome where, he recalls, women emptied chamber pots over the heads of the ragged string of Allied prisoners being taken into captivity.

Eight Dog company men, withdrawing under command of Sgt. Major Turner, encountered the second-in-command of the R.C.R. coming forward on reconnaissance. This officer, Major Pope, insisted that the Hastings men accompany him and somewhat unwillingly they did so. It was nearly fatal to all of them. Turner was shot through the back by a sniper, but the survivors pushed forward into the inferno of the aroused valley. Reaching the road they came face to face with three MK. IV tanks supported by a platoon of German infantry.

With great personal bravery Major Pope attempted to engage the tanks with a PIAT, but the first bomb failed to explode and he was killed before he could reload.

The seven Hastings privates were now on their own. With their one Bren gun they engaged in a spirited exchange with the tanks and German infantry. The tank commander, foolish enough to thrust his head out of the turret, was shot by a rifleman, and for few precious minutes the German force was disorganized. The eight men ducked quickly into the ditch, through a culvert, and began belly-crawling up the hillside through a field of cactus. Tank shells and incendiary machine-gun bullets set the dry hill-side on fire. Preferring death by burning to shooting, the men lay doggo as the flaming grass scorched their bare legs and arms. After lying in the open sun for six hours they escaped at last when dusk had fallen.

The withdrawal of Able and Charlie companies was more orderly, but just as hard. After the massacre of the lorried infantry the two companies continued to deny the enemy the road. In due time the Germans moved up forces for a counterattack, including one or more companies of infantry, two armoured cars, and a number of heavy mortars. The infantry attack was met and thrown back, but the Canadians could not cope with the mortar fire and in any case their ammunition was now all but exhausted. Reluctantly the two companies retreated to the hills, leapfrogging backward under cover of each of other's fire. Several wounded men were carried with the retreating force and the German prisoners were herded ahead. A rearguard, left on a commanding knoll above the road, took the brunt of the Germans' fire for three hours and during this time Capt. Waugh and Pte. Langstaff risked their lives to descend again into the valley and rescue a man who had been badly hit during an attempt to get water for his wounded comrades.

During the whole of that night little groups straggled back through the weary miles of mountain country until by the next dawn the battalion was almost intact once more. Losses had again been incredibly low. Four men had been killed, three taken prisoner and fifteen wounded. The adjutant, who had been left out of the attack, was almost hysterical with relief to see the unit return and he confessed that he had been about to indent for one brand-new regiment.

Death Valley, as the Valguarnera action came to be called, had been a confused and savage struggle, but it too had been a victory and a solid one. Not less than eighty Germans had been killed and the figure may well have been twice the number. Probably a hundred more had been wounded. Twenty prisoners had been brought back and at least fourteen enemy vehicles had been destroyed. But this is only a box score. The real value of that incursion into the heart of the enemy's country had been that it so threatened his lines of communication that he was forced to abandon his strong defences in front of Valguarnera.

That night the 48th Highlanders occupied the town without real opposition, and the way was cleared for the final battles against the central fortress.

EIGHT

Montgomery's Mountain Goats

F IRST CANADIAN Division's thrust through the mountainous heart of Silicy, in its attempt to force the withdrawal of the strong German forces in the Catania plains, was approaching it climax. Catania itself already lay south of the line of the advanced Canadian units and it was nearly time for the Division to swing eastward and drive towards the coast. But before the turn could be made there was a most formidable gate to be opened.

The enemy had established himself on the Leonforte-Assoro base where the mountains swelled abruptly out of the bed of the Dittaino River and lifted steeply towards the peak of Etna to the east. Of the many almost impregnable positions available to the Germans, this was by far the strongest. Astride the two roads leading out of the valley the Assoro feature rose nearly three thousand feet from the dead river and thrust itself forward from the main mountain massifs like a titanic bastion. On the slope of the highest peak the village of Assoro clung precariously while a few miles westward the town of Leonforte guarded the back door to the citadel. As long as this position was held by the enemy there could be no further advance of Thirtieth Corps towards Messina; and the Germans had chosen the formidable Fifteenth Panzer-Grenadier Division to garrison this natural fortress.

By July 20 the forward Canadian unit (again the Edmontons) had reached the Dittaino and had established a bridgehead across it. From the valley floor men could now look up to the sheer cliffs of Assoro and to the narrow, tortuous road that climbed the crags.

The German defenders were unperturbed by the appearance of the Canadians. They had no reason to be worried, for it was obvious that any frontal attack must be suicidal. And they believed Assoro to be one bastion that could not be outflanked, since its only open side, upon the east, was a cliff face rising nine hundred feet to terminate in the ruins of an ancient Norman castle on the very peak of the mountain.

Brig. Howard Graham, entrusted with the assault of the fortress, believed differently. He knew as well as did the Germans that a frontal assault would be disastrous. But remembering Valguarnera, he found some faint hope in the prospects of an attack from the right flank and rear. The hope was very faint; nevertheless, he called Lt.-Col. Sutcliffe and asked him if the Regiment could do the job. Sutcliffe agreed to try.

With his Regiment committed, the c.o. immediately went forward across the Dittaino to the most advanced positions in order to estimate the chances of success. With him was the Intelligence Officer, 'Battle' Cockin. The two men crawled through an olive grove and far down the exposed northern slope, in their anxiety to get a clear view of the enemy position. Crouched beside a single tiny foxhole, too small to hold them both, they were soon engrossed in their study of the great mountain thrusting high out of the dun-coloured earth.

On the Assoro scarp the crew of an 88-mm. gun laid their weapon over open sights. And when the cloud of yellow dust rose clear of the foxhole, Sutcliffe was dead, and the I.O. lay dying.

Prior to this moment all of the soldiers of the Regiment who had been killed had died in the confusion and tumult of action. Their loss had not been deeply perceived as yet, and hatred had not grown from their graves. This new stroke of death was something else again.

The tragedy had a remarkable effect. It irrevocably and utterly destroyed the pale remainder of the illusion that war was only an exciting extension of the battle games of 1941 and 1942. The killing of the C.O. *before* the battle seemed to be an almost obscene act, and when the news came to the men it roused in them an ugly resentment. The emotions stirred by the first skirmishes with war were only awaiting crystallization, and now they hardened and took form. Hatred of the enemy was born.

One more element had been added to the moods of battle and with its acquisition the Regiment reached a new level of efficiency as an instrument of war.

With Sutcliffe's death the command passed to the Regiment's adopted Canadian, Major Lord John Tweedsmuir. Tweedsmuir took over at a moment when the Regiment was faced with the toughest battle problem that it had so far encountered. He reacted to the challenge by accepting and putting into effect a plan so daring that failure would have meant not only the end of his career, but probably the end of the Regiment as well.

It was his appreciation that only by a wide right-flanking sweep through the mountains, culminating in the scaling of the Assoro cliff, could the enemy's position be reduced. Therefore the Regiment would scale the cliff.

It was already late afternoon and preparations had to be hurried. Alex Campbell was ordered to form a special assault force, a volunteer unit, consisting of one platoon from each of the regular rifle companies. The men in this special group were stripped of all their gear except for essential arms and ammunition, for it was to be their task to lead the Regiment; to scale the cliffs, and before dawn broke clearly, to occupy the mountain crest.

The approach march began at dusk and it was the most difficult forced march the Regiment ever attempted, in training or in war. The going was foul; through a maze of sheer-sided gullys, knife-edged ridges and boulder-strewn water courses. There was the constant expectation of discovery, for it seemed certain that the enemy would at least have listening posts on his open flank. Absolute silence was each man's hope of survival – but silence on that nightmare march was almost impossible to maintain.

There were terrifying moments; once, when the scouts saw the loom of a parapet that could only be a masked machine-gun post. Incredibly it was deserted, but so recently that fragments of German bread upon the ground were still quite fresh. Hours later there was a faint sound of stones, disturbed by many feet, ahead of the assault company. Men sank into the shadows tensed for the explosion that never came. Instead a young Sicilian boy came sleepily out of the darkness driving his herd of goats. The youth stared unbelievingly at the motionless shapes of armed men that surrounded him on every side and then passed on, as in a dream.

There was a desperate urgency in that march for there were long miles to go, and at the end, the cliff to scale before the dawn light could reveal the Regiment to the enemy above. A donkey, laden with a wireless set, was literally dragged forward by its escort until it collapsed and died. The men went on.

By 0400 hours the assault company had scaled the last preliminary ridge and was appalled to find that the base of the mountain, looming through the pre-drawn greyness, was still separated from it by a gully a hundred feet deep, and nearly as sheer as an ancient moat. It was too late to turn back. Men scrambled down into the great natural ditch, crossed the bottom, and paused to draw breath. First light was just an hour away. Under the soldiers' hands were the cliff rocks towering a thousand feet into the dark skies.

Each man who made that climb performed his own private miracle. From ledge to ledge the dark figures made their way, hauling each other up, passing along their weapons and ammunition from hand to hand. A signaller made that climb with a heavy wireless set strapped to his back – a thing that in daylight was seen to be impossible. Yet no man slipped, no man dropped so much as a clip of ammunition. It was just as well, for any sound by one would have been fatal to all.

Dawn was breaking and the whole cliff face was encrusted with a moving growth that like some vast slime-mould oozed upward almost imperceptibly. This was the moment. If the alarm was given, nothing could save the unit from annihilation.

The alarm was never given. The two men at the head of the leading assault platoon reached the crest, dragged themselves up over a stone wall and for one stark moment stared into the eyes of three sleepy Germans manning an observation post. Pte. A.K. Long cut down one of the Germans who tried to flee. The remaining enemy soldiers stood motionless, staring as children might at an inexplicable apparition.

Ten minutes later, as the sun cleared the eastern hills, the Regiment had overrun the crest and the companies were in position on the western slopes overlooking the whole German front. Close below them the village of Assoro showed a few thin spirals of grey smoke as peasant women prepared the morning meal. Half a mile below, in the steep valley leading to the front, a peaceful convoy of a dozen German trucks carried the day's rations forward to the waiting grenadiers.

Twenty Bren gunners on Assoro's crest vied with one another to press the trigger first.

The appearance of the Canadians must have come as a shattering surprise to the enemy and had his troops been of a lesser calibre, a débâcle must have resulted. But the Germans here were of a fighting breed. Although they were now at a serious disadvantage, they had no thought of giving up.

From the ditches beside the burning trucks German drivers returned the Regiment's machine-gun fire with rifle shots. The crews of four light anti-aircraft pieces, sited beside the road, cranked down their guns to fire point-blank at the Canadians upon the crest. Machine-gun detachments, hurriedly withdrawn from the front,

Assoro and Nissoria

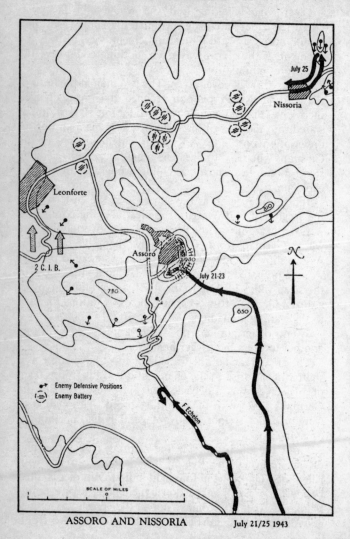

ASSORO AND NISSORIA   July 21/25 1943

scrambled up the road, flung themselves down behind the stone fences and engaged the Brens in a staccato duel. With commendable, but frightening efficiency, the enemy's batteries, which had been concentrating their fire on Second Brigade in front of Leonforte, slewed their guns around to bear upon Assoro. Within an hour after dawn the crest of the hill was almost hidden in the dust of volleying explosions.

The Regiment dug in. Able company and the assault company on the south and southwestern slopes; the balance of the unit on the north and northwestern side. A series of narrow terraces gave scant shelter but the men scraped shallow slit trenches in the stony soil, using their steel helmets as shovels. The enemy's fire grew steadily heavier, while that of the Regiment died away as realization dawned that this would be a long battle, and there would probably be no new supplies of ammunition until it ended.

But the surprises of that morning were not all one-sided. Before the infantry companies moved off it had been agreed that two green Verey flares, fired by the assault group, would indicate that the enemy position had been overrun and that it was safe for the unit's transport to move forward. Sometime after midnight, while the infantry was still struggling through the maze of hills and valleys far from the objective, a German in the positions overlooking the Dittaino sent a routine signal to his own artillery. The signal that he fired was two green flares.

Although there had been no sounds of battle as yet, the transport group accepted the evidence of its eyes and began moving north. Before dawn it had crossed the valley and the leading carriers had been halted by a crater blown in the road by German engineers some time earlier. Things were still quiet and some of the men of 'F' echelon got out of their vehicles and lay down on the gentle slopes to catch a little sleep.

The Panzer-grenadiers defending the road must have found it hard to credit their eyes as the grey light revealed thirty Canadian trucks and carriers drawn up in a neat line almost under the muzzles of the German guns.

The men of 'F' echelon were rudely awakened. Some of them, leaping up out of a pleasant sleep, yelled horrid threats at their comrades who, they believed, had gone mad and were firing upon them. Others, more alert, realized that they were in a most unhappy situation and did what they could to remedy things. While one of the three-inch mortars was hastily put into action, the drivers tried to turn their vehicles on the narrow road. Someone, thinking with great rapidity, began throwing smoke grenades around the leading vehicles and under this thin protection the carriers managed to turn and clatter wildly down the slopes. One of them was driven by a motor-cyclist who had lost his own mount. He missed a turn and his carrier skidded off the road and somersaulted all the way down to the valley floor. The driver was miraculously uninjured and when he had dragged himself to his feet he stood for several minutes, in full view of the enemy, cursing his steed as if it had been a horse that had thrown him, and angrily banging its steel flanks with his boot.

It was fortunate for the transport and carrier men that at this juncture the balance of the Regiment on Assoro's crest carried the battle to the enemy's rear. In the ensuing confusion, and not without casualties – four trucks destroyed and four men badly wounded – 'F' echelon managed to make good its retreat to the Dittaino and beyond. But it was in a chastened mood, and for some weeks afterwards it was notably suspicious of all orders to move forward to a 'captured' area.

Meanwhile the position of the men on Assoro was becoming critical. The five hundred infantrymen were almost completely surrounded on the three-acre crest of the mountain, and they could neither withdraw nor advance. Patrols were sent scuttling through the curtain of small-arms and shell-fire into the village. The place was cleared, but its capture brought little relief. The Regiment's threat against the enemy supply route could not be fully implemented, for already the scanty ammunition supplies carried on men's backs up the cliff, were growing perilously low. Confined to the congested area on the crest, the Regiment was exposed to an increasing fury of artillery shelling which was suddenly, and terrifyingly, supplemented by the fire of a number of German rocket batteries. This was the unit's first experience with the weapon nicknamed "The Moaning Minnie" and there was not a man who was not shaken by the initiation. The shells were nine inches in diameter and they were fired in salvos of five or six. The screaming of their rocket motors was an intolerable sound, as if the heavy shells were being forced through interminable rusty cylinders, slightly too small for their diameter. In addition there were single twelve-inch rockets, each containing a hundred and fifty pounds of high explosive, that screeched their way slowly overhead and burst with a tremendous blast. More than four hundred rocket and artillery shells crashed into the crest of Assoro in the first two hours of that bombardment.

But if the Regiment could not attack, it was not content to remain simply passive under this punishment. The Germans had decided that the crest of Assoro must be held by a very small number of Canadians and that, under cover of the shelling, it would be safe to withdraw the many vehicles which had been at the front. It was not safe. As the armoured half-trucks and open trucks came scuttling up the road the Regiment caught them in a withering small-arms fire and destroyed or forced the abandonment of almost a score of them. The Germans promptly reassessed the danger and prepared to counterattack the hill in force.

The Regiment's situation now became desperate. Unless it could somehow silence the enemy artillery it could not hope to hold on. Desperation sharpens men's wits, and in this extremity someone remembered the captured German observation post. It had been equipped with a fine pair of 20-power scissor telescopes and these were now hurriedly moved to the north end of the hill where Tweedsmuir and his second-in-command, Major Kennedy (who had originally trained as an artilleryman), could sweep almost the entire area from which the enemy guns were firing. There was only one radio – the short-range No. 56 set that had been miraculously carried up the cliff on a man's back. It sufficed to save the unit.

In the next hour the Regiment gave the distant Canadian artillery a series of dream targets. As each German gun fired up at Assoro, its position was radioed to the rear and within minutes salvos of Canadian shells fell upon it. There was no escape, for every movement of the German gunners could be seen. Methodically, carefully, the officers at the telescope directed the counter-battery fire until by noon well over half the enemy's artillery was out of action, and the rest was hurriedly withdrawing to safer sites.

But the vicious bombardment of the hill had added a new emotion to the battle mood. Men had discovered fear.

It was met by the beginning growth of a special type of fatalism, relieved by wit. The sort of thing that led one man to say: "When you dig a good slit-trench nothing can get you except a direct hit, and if it *is* a direct hit, it's because you teased your grandmother – or pulled the wings off flies." And another. "There's no use trying to hide out from a shell. If it's got your name on it, it'll chase you into the house, follow you upstairs, push the pot aside and get you under the bed." The humour was not uproarious – but it was adequate.

On the forward crest of the hill, pinned down behind a rock by a salvo of mortar bombs, Paddy Gahagen replied to the shout of his platoon commander who demanded to know what in the name of all the furies he was doing. "Looking for goddam four-leaf clovers with my nose" was the muffled reply.

Never had there been a greater need for the solace of humour than on Assoro. As the first day drew on, the heat grew worse and though the continuous heavy shelling had ceased, there were spasmodic outbursts from hour to hour. Water was a problem for there was only one well on the crest and those attempting to reach it were exposed to sniping fire. There was little food, for the emergency rations had long-since been consumed. In Charlie company, Pte. Greatrix became the hero of the moment when he produced a can of sardines that had been secreted in his haversack, and gravely offered each man in his platoon one fish.

A small cave near the well had been converted into a medical station and here the wounded lay in silent rows. The padre, Capt. Reg. Lane, a man of more than forty-five years of age, who was not equipped either by nature or by training for the hardships he had undergone, performed his own private miracle of endurance as he helped the stretcher bearers care for the living, or helped the living bury the dead.

In the late afternoon the C.O. gave up hope of a relief column breaking through to the Regiment that day, and called for two volunteers to return to the Canadian lines and attempt to guide a carrying party forward with rations and ammunition during the night. The R.S.M. and an officer accepted the task and set out down the great cliff, and across four miles of enemy dominated country, finally reaching safety in a state of complete exhaustion. But when darkness fell they were still able to guide a hundred men of the Royal Canadian Regiment laden with food and ammunition, back through the gorges to the foot of the mountain. The next morning the garrison received its first rations in thirty-six hours.

While the supply party was toiling over the hills and gulleys, the battle situation had reached its climax. The Germans were being fiercely attacked at Leonforte by Second Brigade and they could not stand firm there while the threat of Assoro lay on their supply routes. They understood that Assoro would have to be retaken or the whole position would have to be abandoned; so at 2200 hours the enemy counterattacked. They came through the north end of the town, two companies of grenadiers, under cover of an intense mortar and artillery barrage, and they met Dog company on the lower slopes. Dog had very little ammunition left, but when the attack broke and fell away, Dog company had not given any ground and had taken a heavy toll of the attackers. It was the Germans' last effort. As darkness fell, they began to withdraw both from Assoro and from Leonforte to the west. The gates were opening.

The ordeal of the men on the mountain was not yet at an end for the road up to Assoro had been so badly cratered that it was not until late on July 23 that the Regiment could be relieved.

At the precious well a group of a dozen soldiers relaxed contentedly, drinking to their hearts' content, and splashing cold water over their faces and arms. Below the town, supply trucks at last rumbled forward. Now the Regiment could rest.

And then, somewhere far to the north, the crew of a German rocket-launcher prepared to abandon their position. One 21-cm. rocket was set up for firing with its electric igniters wired and ready. And someone, in a last defiant gesture, paused for a moment to close the circuit and send the rocket screaming into the quiet sky.

The indecent shriek of the projectile drifted over the brown hills. The men by the well heard, but they had only time to stiffen warily before the rocket struck. It hit the curbing of the well, and when the black and acrid smoke had cleared, four dead men lay in the new crater, while five others moaned in mortal agony.

It was a brutal way to learn the grim lesson that in battle there can be no escape – until the war is done.

NINE

The Flavour of Defeat

W HILE IT was no great victory in terms of casualties
inflicted on the enemy, Assoro was nevertheless a
spectacular triumph of endurance and initiative, and the
spirit of the men, subdued temporarily by their first bap-
tism of heavy shell-fire, now rose to unprecedented
heights. Even the taste of fear was not too bitter in their
mouths, for it possessed an astringent flavour which made
the battle even more stimulating in retrospect. Men
looked forward, almost eagerly, to the renewal of the war
and to deeds that would surpass even the epic struggle just
completed.

They did not have long to wait, but the new battle,
when it came upon them, was to be a dark and harrowing
experience.

With the loss of the gates to the inner mountain stronghold, the Germans had withdrawn – but not nearly as far
as had been confidently predicted. The grenadiers were
stubborn soldiers and they elected to fight desperately for
each mile of ground which lay between them and their last
strong point below Mount Etna. It came as an almost
unbelievable surprise when the R.C.R. moving forward
with the Salso River twenty miles to the eastward as its
objective, was halted and flung bloodily back at the village
of Nissoria, less than five miles down the road.

It would appear now that either the staff was not fully
informed, or else did not credit the infantry reports that

the Germans were holding the Nissoria position in regimental strength, with the support of tanks. The optimism that followed Leonforte and Assoro seemed to have dazzled the commanders, for instead of accepting the fact that the Germans were disputing the road in great force, higher command continued to treat the enemy at Nissoria as no more than a small rearguard. There was no attempt to mount a proper assault. Instead the First Brigade was thrown in piecemeal.

Hardly had the R.C.R. withdrawn, having lost many of its supporting Sherman tanks, and many men – when the Regiment was ordered to renew the assault but with no tank support, no artillery support, and no prior reconnaissance for a battle to be waged in darkness. The lessons of Valguarnera and Assoro were ignored, and the Regiment was committed to a head-on assault against an aroused enemy.

Nissoria itself was an abject collection of stone hovels huddled on the road where it crossed a high col into the eastern range. Directly behind the village two massive hills rose north and south of the road, and on these the Germans waited in carefully prepared positions.

Untouched by the disaster which had befallen the R.C.R., and filled with a mood approaching blind confidence, the Hastings companies moved up to Nissoria on the night of July 24. There was a faint crescent moon, but in the shadows of the col there was complete darkness. The long lines of men were quiet, their excitement subdued by the silence of the night. They passed in single file, between the dead rows of houses in the deserted village, and a little after midnight climbed the col and became aware of the loom of the twin guardian hills.

Tweedsmuir halted the column while he attempted to gain some idea of the nature of the country about him, but in the darkness this was most difficult. The northern hill seemed to be the more imposing bastion so he sent for his company commanders and gave instructions for an attack on the northern feature. There was only a slight shuffling of equipment, and the muted rustle of boots on crusted grass as Baker company swung clear of the road and began to climb into an ominous silence.

The slope rose harshly up a long and rocky scree. Men made an intense and largely successful effort to be silent, for the enemy seemed as yet unsuspecting. Half the hill lay behind the leading platoon when suddenly the scouts dropped to their bellies and behind them the twisted line froze into immobility.

Thirty yards ahead, and almost invisible in the darkness, human figures moved uneasily and there were sounds of coughing and muttered words. For Baker company's commander it was a moment of taut indecision. He could not be sure whether these were his enemies, or whether they were stragglers from the R.C.R. attack. He did not dare order his men to open fire at once; instead he ordered two platoons to swing wide and surround the mysterious figures. The platoons moved off, crawling silently, and in a few moments they could identify the dim outlines of men against the sky-line. They were the enemy beyond all doubt.

It was the moment for a surprise blow that might have made the difference between success and defeat, but even as the platoons crawled the last few feet into battle positions fate played against them. Two men of another company, lost from their platoon, came stumbling up the slope and blundered into the German positions.

The night exploded. A star shell illuminated the attackers, caught without cover on the slopes. More than fifteen enemy machine guns immediately began to sweep the exposed ground with interlocking cones of yellow and red tracer. Close patterns of mortar bombs, previously ranged on all avenues of approach, began to thump wickedly into the shallow gulleys where the balance of the Regiment lay waiting. Three MK. IV tanks, dug-in to their turrets, sent their shells screaming over the low crest.

Baker company had penetrated into the advance posts of the German position, but now it paid for its temerity.

All three platoons were hopelessly pinned down, unable to advance or to retire, and under a merciless and sustained fire. There was nothing anyone could do for them.

The platoon officer of No. 12 platoon was wounded and Sgt. Johnson took his place. An enemy anti-tank gun was crashing almost within throwing distance of Johnson who leapt to his feet and attacked it with grenades, killing the crew and putting the gun out of action. A moment later he in turn was killed as he was giving orders to his men for a new assault.

Individual sections, cut off from their platoons, did what they could to survive. One section found a German outpost under the nose of its Bren gun and with a furious burst of fire persuaded the Germans to surrender. The grenadiers came out of their slit trenches – but with their weapons held in front of them, and at the last moment they tried to rush their captors. They were slaughtered where they stood. It was a confused, savage and terrifying battle, with Germans and Canadians inextricably mixed up in almost utter darkness. But the night was nearly done and as dawn broke over the great mound of Etna, it laid bare an entire Regiment under the guns of the enemy.

The Germans on the crest of the northern hill increased their fire, while from across the road the defenders of the southern hill poured their fire into the Regiment's back. Baker company was in a desperate plight, while the other companies were now hardly better off.

Still the sections fought their own independent actions. One section under Cpl. Freddy Punchard, a rangy, taciturn farm lad, was caught completely in the open. Punchard ordered his men to break away while he gave them cover, and they crawled through the appalling weight of machine-gun and mortar fire, most of them to reach safety in the end. The Germans moved in on Punchard and called on him to surrender, but there were still two wounded men of his section in danger and Punchard cried out "Not bloody likely!" and fired the last of his Bren magazines. When that was done he picked up a tommygun and waited for the ultimate attack. It came in a few moments. Punchard did not die alone, for when the position was finally cleared several days later, his body was found with those of seven grenadiers to bear him company.

There were many like him. There was Pte. A. K. Long of Able company, the first man to the top of Assoro only a few days earlier. Long was badly wounded by a mortar bomb but he would not allow his comrades to lessen their already slim chance of survival by trying to drag him back. He waved them off and when they saw him last he was sitting with his body braced against the shattered remnant of an olive tree, sucking on an empty pipe, and leafing through a pocket edition of *Macbeth*.

But guts and endurance alone could not save the battle. The unit's casualties were mounting fearfully and it was clear that the Regiment must move or be destroyed. Tweedsmuir was bracketed by four mortar bombs, and was severely wounded. The officer who succeeded him gave the order to retire, but it was easier said than done.

No man who was on the slopes that day will forget the frightful sensation of turning his naked back on the enemy as he ran his own private race with death. Scrambling from rock to rock, rolling down open stretches, or crawling down shallow ditches, the men who were still alive came back – all save a section of Baker under Cpl. Bulliard that could not retreat without inviting certain destruction. Bulliard's men, most of them stricken with dysentery, were forced to lie for another eighteen hours in a shallow depression only ten yards from the enemy. Without water, and unable to move or even whisper, they suffered the Sicilian sun all that day and having miraculously escaped detection, came back from the dead when night had fallen.

There were many who did not come back. In that brief and impassioned battle the unit had lost six officers and sixty-three other ranks dead and wounded – a savage blow. There was not much to show for it. A few enemy positions knocked out, and a handful of prisoners taken. Nissoria remained firmly with the enemy and, like the R.C.R., the Regiment withdrew westward to lick its wounds.

It was the unit's first experience of failure and retreat, and the effect on the men was incalculable. Those who survived the battle carried with them the knowledge of a new and terrible experience – panic. One of the most dreadful things about panic is its contagious power and the sight of what it can accomplish is enough to break the spirit of a man. There was one soldier, a lance-corporal in a section withdrawing through the streets of Nissoria under a deluge of enemy shells, who found the meaning of it. Seeking refuge from the shells, the lance-corporal dodged into an empty house, and discovered that it was not empty. Under the stairs was a human being, but not human in its abject terror. It was a soldier, crouched hard against the wall, and weeping bitterly and piercingly into cupped hands. In that instant of recognition, the lance-corporal's healthy fear of shelling turned into a more dreadful fear and he ran, heedless of the bursting shells, along that smoking street as if the devils which pursued him were more frightful than death itself.

He never forgot that moment and there were few men in the Regiment that day who did not experience something similar, and they, too, did not forget.

From Nissoria onward the men of the Regiment had to live not only with fear of death and inquiry, but they had to learn to live with, and to conquer, fear of themselves – the fear of fear. That they succeeded, for the most part, is a firm indication of their worth, for there is no greater strength, no greater courage, than to acknowledge fear, and to fight on despite that incubus.

The Regiment learned much at Nissoria, and it immediately began to develop the protective cynicism of the fighting man who really understands his trade. The men were learning to be skeptical of the infallibility of higher commanders. When, on the night of July 25, the men watched the 48th Highlanders march up to Nissoria to repeat, almost identically, their own experiences and those of the R.C.R., that scepticism was strongly reinforced.

These doubts of the infallibility of the staff were not necessarily bad things for they tended to isolate the infantryman and to make him turn inward in search of confidence and of something he could trust. The Regiment was the gainer as more and more it became the one sure thing in a world that must grow ever darker with continued disillusionment. It became each man's home and sanctuary, and its spirit grew large, not with love, for there is little love in war, but with the need for faith and a belief. There was no other sufficient source of these things. Even a faith in God could not suffice for the majority of men; and as for faith in the empty maxims of politicians – there was none and could be none. Even the old home ties, attenuated now by too many years and too much distance, could give little comfort to the men in need. Too often, instead, they irritated him and only served to emphasize his growing isolation. The chasm in experience which separated the soldier from his people in a distant land was unbridgeable. He could be understood by, and could understand, only the men who stood beside him. Only the Regiment made of these men could give him comfort in the days to come.

After a full-scale attack by Second Brigade, with massive artillery support, had finally cleared the Nissoria position, the Division thrust eastward to bitter fighting at Agira and at last to Regalbuto, the Germans' final holding to the west of the Salso River. On July 30 and 31, 231st British Infantry Brigade (attached at that time to First Canadian Division) fought hard to gain this town, but were unsuccessful. On August 1, First Brigade moved up to the attack and the R.C.R. clawed a foothold into the western outskirts of the shattered town.

Conditions here were not unlike those at Nissoria, for the real strength of Regalbuto lay in a commanding ridge beyond the town, and in two flanking hills to the south.

Here the enemy, this time units of the Hermann Goering Division, sat firmly in position and no amount of frontal battle could dislodge him.

When the R.C.R. could make no further progress the 48th Highlanders attempted to swing in from the north, but without success, and towards evening the R.C.R. had to be withdrawn from the town.

This was the situation when the Regiment moved forward to join the battle. But someone on the staff had learned a lesson from Nissoria, and when the Regiment was ordered to attack during the night of August 1, it was given a free hand to do the job in its own way. The Regiment, too, had learned a lesson and the new C.O., Major A. A. Kennedy, was a man to profit by experience.

Regalbuto was to be no buccaneering rush into the unknown – the sort of thing that had brought renown at Assoro, and disaster at Nissoria – but, as far as the C.O. could make it, this battle was to be a carefully calculated action. Kennedy began by sending long-distance patrols far to the east with orders to penetrate deeply into the enemy's flank and report his dispositions, and the best routes of approach. The C.O. himself, with his company commanders, then carried out a detailed reconnaissance, and laid the battle plans with care and caution. The operation was to be a wide right flank attack, but not a blind one. Nor would it be unsupported. The artillery F.O.O.s were ordered to travel with the C.O., and the mortar platoon was ordered to come along on foot, and manhandle its heavy weapons and ammunition over the five miles of the approach march.

It was already dusk when the companies moved off. The country was at least as difficult as any that had been traversed in the earlier days, but there was this difference – the patrols had done their task well and the long lines of marching men moved smoothly through the broken cliffs and canyons with guides leading them, and with scouts well in front.

The atmosphere in the marching columns was different,

too. There was no exhilaration in men's hearts. They went into this battle soberly and with full knowledge now of the consequences which could follow error. There was a new kind of tension that acted upon each man so that he was keyed to an almost mechanical pitch of efficiency. Controlled, fear can be a weapon of great strength and the unit had this weapon ready to its hand.

So the night hours passed and the companies followed the tortuous routes of the patrols until at last the heights of Mount Tiglio, the southern bastion of the enemy position, bulked large against the star-lit sky.

There was no delay, and both Able and Baker companies were on the crest within a quarter of an hour. They reported finding no enemy, but they found machine guns sited beside newly dug weapon pits and it was clear that the Germans had anticipated a flank attack. There was no explanation for the enemy's absence now, except that they had perhaps grown careless when in the first three days of battle no southern assault had developed. It seemed likely that this outpost was only manned at certain hours.

This much was luck. Now the Regiment faced the south slope of the main ridge behind Regalbuto, but dawn had broken and any premature attack might have been disastrous. Kennedy chose to wait until each company commander had time to assess the ground carefully, and until the three-inch mortars, manhandled across country by herculean effort, were in position to support the assault. The artillery F.O.O.s swept the ridge with their binoculars and picked the likely targets for their guns, radioing the information back over pack sets.

At noon the battle was 'laid-on' and Dog company swept forward into the broad valley to divert and focus the enemy's defence away from the main assault. The Germans reacted quickly, pouring their fire down upon the widely dispersed attackers from at least ten positions. Dog, its allotted part in the battle almost completed, went to ground and busied itself continuing to hold the Germans' attention.

REGALBUTO   Aug 1/2 1943

Now the battle plan bore fruit. The enemy had exposed his strong points and the three-inch mortars, supported by accurate fire from the distant Canadian guns rapidly neutralized these positions. Under cover of the barrage Baker and Charlie quickly crossed the valley almost unopposed and before the Germans on the crest could swing to meet the new threat, both companies were in amongst the enemy. Baker swept the high ground overlooking Regalbuto, clearing it within half an hour, while Charlie swung east and stormed down the length of the ridge. Many machine-gun posts were overrun and the remaining Germans dropped their equipment and fled as best they could.

The battle was over. Regalbuto itself was later occupied without opposition by patrols of the 48th Highlanders and the enemy's last stand west of the Salso was at an end. The action had gone so smoothly as to appear unremarkable. Its very excellence tended to obscure its real merits and as a result it has been denied its proper place in the official histories of the campaign. Nevertheless, it was probably the most important, if also the most colourless action fought by the Regiment in Sicily. It differed from all the previous battles in that it was fought by men who were at last fully aware of the meaning of war, and who fought with full understanding of it and with consequent skill. The capture of Regalbuto was a fitting conclusion to an arduous apprenticeship. It twenty days the unit had been well blooded and hardened into a superlative machine for battle. Now it had earned a rest.

When First Brigade was withdrawn from action a few days later it was relegated to a 'rest' area far to the south. On August 7, an incredibly hot and dusty convoy travelled back down the remembered roads to reach a high and desolate plateau not far from Catania. Here the Regiment was allotted an arid stretch of olive groves and vineyards and here it settled down to spend the remaining August days in nominal peace.

But peace is an elusive thing, and the men found little

peace at Militello. Temporarily the war with the Germans was at an end, but in its place there was a new round of hostilities with the rear echelons of an army stretching back to England and across the ocean to Canada itself. In Militello the fighting troops discovered yet another truth about war – and a distasteful one – that victories seldom earn the real victors any fruits. Hardly had the companies settled into their bivouacs, shelter tents and lean-to huts made of bamboo and thatch, when they were set upon by a horde of tormentors.

Many of these were non-combatant officers. They descended on the Regiment and subjected it to what seemed to the men to be a pointless persecution, beginning with detailed inspections of everything from carburettors to foreskins. When they grew tired of examining latrines and cook-houses, they arranged for ceremonial inspections of the troops – inspections that often called for days of preparation, terminating in long hours spent standing in the blinding sun while emissaries of the staff examined the sweating soldiers as if they were no more than parade-ground mannequins.

No one was exempt. The Regiment's administrative sections, the clerks and quartermasters, were equally harassed by deluges of paper work. It seemed that the rear echelons were possessed of such an insatiable curiosity that nothing short of a detailed report, in quintuplicate, on the state of every last button in the Regiment, would suffice.

These pin-pricks might have been borne more easily if the fighting troops had been allowed a few prerogatives of victory. They were allowed none. All towns were placed out of bounds and when the padre took a group to Catania on a sight-seeing tour, he was turned back by the Military Police on the General's orders. Once or twice, it is true, men were allowed a visit to the sea where they could briefly disport themselves in the blue waters – but only under supervision. There was a belief in the Regiment at this time that the higher Canadian echelons, unable to impose their will upon men actually engaged in battle under Eighth Army, jealously hastened to demonstrate their power once the fighting ended. There may have been no truth in the idea, but it was firmly believed by the fighting troops.

It is only fair to say that the Militello ordeal stemmed almost entirely from Canadian sources; for the rest of the Eighth Army had long ago gained a measure of personal freedom which was theirs by right of sacrifice. Most of the time at least, they were treated as men. But the Canadian staff was new to battle and perhaps it was only trying to mask its own uncertainty. In times to come the rear echelons would learn to mind their own affairs – but the time was not yet.

The troops, nevertheless, managed to extract some pleasure from the stay at Militello. Not far away was an immensely deep ravine along whose bed a small, cold torrent ran, and here a dam was built where swimming offered some relief from the destroying heat. Although all civilian contacts were forbidden, it became a point of honour to circumvent the regulations at every possible turn, and many of the men found opportunities to learn a little about the life of this age-old land. They could enjoy the novelties, the pomegranates ready to be plucked, the sweet green figs and the swollen melons. They could also enjoy the scraggly chickens and the dry and bitter native wines.

If the long years in England had taught the men anything, it had taught them the secret of adapting themselves to any conditions, anywhere. Even in the parched and blistered olive groves of Militello they made themselves at home. Some of their bamboo shacks were works of art, decorated with cacti and blossoms of exotic plants. There was nothing in the way of local materials that could not be put to a good use. The art of scrounging had been magnificently developed and now it was applied to every need of daily life, from food and drink to the more esoteric pleasures. Only women, alas, were not to be found in sufficient numbers, or of a sufficient degree of willingness.

At Militello the already tenuous links with Canada were further strained. Mails had begun to arrive and each bag brought its quota of 'Dear John' letters from wives and sweethearts for whom the links had parted. Far worse than these, which were to be expected, were the fragments of Canadian news. The continual evasion of the conscription issue by the Government and the anti-conscription riots in Quebec were bitterness distilled. The strikes of coal miners and labourers for even higher wages made sour reading to the men at Militello. The frequently infantile orations of Canadian politicians gave rise to a deep disgust amongst the soldiers who bothered to read about such things. Only the land was universally remembered with pride and pleasure – the good land of the counties, so far removed from the hot red dust of this Sicilian plateau. There were still men whose ties with home remained firm enough, for they were the lucky ones with wives of strength and understanding, but even these soldiers, while they loved their own people, and their own places, began to share a rising mood of resentment against their native country as a whole.

It was only one more step towards spiritual exile, and again the Regiment grew strong because of it; becoming more and more the living home.

TEN

A Trap Unsprung

O N THE morning of September 1, 1943, the Long Regimental convoy drew its route in dust from Militello to the coast, then northward through Catania towards the narrow Straits of Messina that separate the island from the mainland of the continent. The heavy trucks jounced through the hot little plains towns and across innumerable *torrentes* and *fiumares* (the dried and whitened gorges of rivers that live only for a few weeks in the spring and fall) while the peaked silhouette of Etna loomed large to the northwest. As the afternoon grew old, men stared out from the trucks across a glaring sea and faintly discerned the purple loom of distant land.

Across the narrow straits the continent of Europe waited and there was a new mood in the Regiment that evening as the trucks dispersed and the men clambered down into the sparse shelter of the banks of a *torrente* bed. For three long years that continent had stood abandoned to the enemy but now the time had come for the return. There was a pride in knowing that the Regiment would be amongst the first to breach the ramparts of the Fortress Europe.

The two days which followed the arrival at the concentration area were feverish ones devoted to the intricacies of a combined operations plan. But this was old stuff to the Regiment now, and things went smoothly. Vehicles and men were formed into their loading serials and briefed on the immediate tasks. The hour when the new battles would begin drew closer, and tension mounted. Across the straits the massive mountains of Calabria began to take upon themselves an aspect of menace.

When the hour came it brought its own anti-climax. All night on September 3, the guns of Eighth Army muttered and roared and in the dawn light the landing craft carrying the assault troops of Thirteenth Corps scuttled across the sunlit waters to the smoking land ahead – and found no hand raised against them. The Germans, having had warning of the projected landings far up the west coast of Italy, had hurriedly withdrawn from the south. The Italian coastal defence troops, never with much heart for this war, had also heard rumours – rumours of the impending surrender of Italy – and they were in no mood to die heroically, and futilely, with peace only a short time away.

The Regiment embarked in its landing craft at noon on September 3, and enjoyed a pleasant outing on a pleasant sea. For spice there were seven Fiat fighters that swept in from the east, danced prettily in the sky some miles away, dropped their bombs where they would do no harm, and flew off content with their gesture of defiance. The landing craft nosed into the Italian beaches and there were no difficulties to contend with other than heat, thirst, and overloaded haversacks.

These were old enemies by now, and ones to be ignored. The companies were torn between relief and disappointment that the human enemies were gone. But there was no time to weigh emotions. The unit turned from the sea and began a forced march up the black face of the mountains.

Like an attenuated khaki worm, the column climbed; while descending parallel to it on the white road was another worm, a broker one, of bluish-green. The Italian army units left by the Germans to defend the hills, were seeking their own peace. They came with an atmosphere of fiesta about them, marching raggedly by platoons, their personal belongings hanging from their weapons in little bundles, and the hot, still air, filled with their laughter and their singing. For the Regiment it was a bemusing experience and the men were inclined to be angrily resentful of these other soldiers who took the war so lightly.

The pursuit of an absent enemy had brought the unit into the heart of the Aspromonte mountains. For three days the Regiment sat down to wait events. It rained. Steadily, massively it rained. Rations were short since no transport could reach the mountain climbers. Fires could seldom be persuaded to burn. In their thin tropical shirts, men huddled in the scanty shelter of pine thickets and shivered through the cold nights. In daylight they dried their clothes so that they would be fully absorbent for the next night's downpour.

The pause in the mountains was not without its interesting moments for the stream of deserting Italians had swelled to a river, and there were excellent pickings to be had in Beretta automatics, wrist watches and binoculars. But the Italians were an infernal nuisance. They refused to take their capture seriously, and they showed a boundless desire to fraternize and to be amiable even to the extent of wishing to supply the addresses of their girl friends to the Canadians who would soon be going north. Their attitude seemed quite incomprehensible until at last the whole thing was explained. On September 8, the Regiment paraded to hear Kennedy announce that Italy had capitulated unconditionally.

Some of the Regiment's discontent and disappointment in the anti-climactic invasion of Italy evaporated with the news. On the next morning, when the unit stirred itself and began its long journey north, spirits were high and the fiasco of the invasion was forgotten.

While the unit was immured in the dripping forests of the Aspromonte, great events had been taking place elsewhere. At Salerno the U.S. Fifth Army had attempted to spring a gigantic trap. The Allied intention had been that Eighth Army, by landing at Reggio, would lure the bulk of the eleven divisions the Germans then possessed in Italy, into the foot of the peninsula. Then the Fifth, by landing high up on the coastline, would slice off the foot and the enemy would be caught, to be masticated at leisure. The enemy was not caught. Fifth Army made its landings and discovered that it was in grave danger of being driven back into the sea. Counterattacking fiercely the Germans turned their backs on Eighth Army, far away to the south, and concentrated on the task in hand. The situation was soon desperate for the Fifth, and it was apparent that this unfortunate army's only hope lay in the prompt arrival of help from Montgomery.

Later Montgomery was severely criticized in the United States because his army took some fourteen days to link up with the Fifth. The men who actually took part in that 400-mile race know, as do their comrades who waited at Salerno, that the dash up the southern spine of Italy was as remarkable a feat of arms as any roaring victory on the battlefield.

The Regiment's part in the race for Salerno was small and obscure. There was little active resistance from the enemy, but before they retreated the Germans did as thorough a job of demolition as has been seen in modern war. Not a bridge along the worn-gutted mountain tracks that was not blown. Not a culvert or an overhanging cliff that had not been converted into an obstacle. And everywhere, along the road verges, at blown bridges and road craters, in the entrances to roadside fields and in the fields themselves, were mines.

The Regiment went north along the east coast road and for a while could use its scanty vehicles. But as the forced advance continued vehicles without wings became useless. On September 11, the entire unit was afoot, crawling towards Catanzaro Marina.

Meanwhile, all through the country along the route of march, and far into the interior, the Italian army sat in its barracks or in its bivouacs. It was a well-armed force completely equipped to give battle, and although Marshall Badoglio had concluded his peace with the Allies, it was not a universally acceptable peace to some of the Italian militarists.

This ticklish situation produced strange incidents.

From Catanzaro Marina the unit was to turn inland and climb high into the pine-clad mountains to the city of Catanzaro. Kennedy sent his one mechanized element, a motorcycle driven by the Intelligence Officer, on ahead to carry out reconnaissance. The I.O. loaded Sgt. Bruce Richmond on the rear carrier and puttered off.

It was a fine fall day with clear skies, and a sun that warmed but did not burn. The motorcycle, a miniscule vanguard for an army, climbed steadily into the high places and every now and again it passed a road block manned by armed Italians. Both sides were startled by the sight of one another. The Italians uneasily fingered their weapons and were torn between scowls and grins.

The two Canadians crouched lower on their machine and fled onward, not daring to glance behind. Then there came a turn beyond which the road was completely blocked by a huge Italian truck. Rather than come to a halt beside this behemoth and its seething crew, the I.O. skidded his cycle on to a side-road and continued the wild ride. Both he and his sergeant had by this time reached a state of mind where they were afraid to halt, unable to turn back, and terrified of going on. But going on required no new decision, so on they went.

Thus it was that in due time they reached a barbed-wire road block in the centre of the Mantova division. The fields on both sides of the road were crowded with tents, with armed Italians, with artillery pieces and with transport.

A sentry lowered his rifle and pointed it at the newcomers and there was nothing left to do but bluff. The sergeant in his best Vino Italian, gruffly demanded to see the General. The startled sentry backed away and fetched his officer. The two Canadians found themselves under escort, being taken to a large farm house, and in the reckless mood inspired by sheer nerves, they not only demanded to see the General (masquerading as emissaries of Montgomery) but having met this fat and sweating gentleman, they demanded his entire divisional transport column, at once, with which to move the Regiment up the mountain road to Catanzaro.

There was some argument, but the Canadians were firm, albeit stating their demands in voices pitched an octave higher than normal. The Italians finally capitulated to confusion, and so it came to pass that the Regiment completed its journey to Catanzaro aboard a concourse of Italian trucks, driven by the world's most suicidal drivers who, a bare three days earlier, had been the declared enemies of the soldiers whom they now hauled into their own heartland.

At Catanzaro there was a vitally essential halt while the administrative elements of the army caught up. A platoon of Able company under Lt. Al Park and accompanied by some armoured cars was sent to capture and occupy the port of Crotone some 70 kilometers to the north. The adventurers found the town deserted by the enemy, and here Park ran his private army for almost a week.

As the Regiment waited in the cool comfort of the pine-clad slopes, there was a growing feeling that the war had blown itself wide open and that the remaining fragments were only comic opera. The Mantova Division proved to be not only neutral, but after some consideration of the situation, downright amiable. The Italian division's transport drivers insisted on attaching themselves to the Regiment and becoming Hasty P's. The Regiment's auxiliary service officer successfully arranged a first-rate football match between the soldiers of the two armies. There were some excellent parties held at a lower level, between enlisted men. Photos of girl friends and wives were mutually admired and the atmosphere of unreality grew to the point where it even affected the C.O.

Kennedy reacted in a manner that did not endear him to his battalion headquarters officers. It became his habit to set out in his jeep, with himself at the wheel, to make hundred-mile excursions into unknown country. The sole concession he would make to the efforts of the German rearguard was to have one of his subalterns perch precariously on the jeep's bonnet, his feet dangling between the wheels, to look for mines. The jeep seldom travelled less than fifty miles an hour, and it would have required X-ray vision to detect the inconspicuous disturbances in the dust where mines were buried. Those who were privileged to perform this service for Kennedy recall those expeditions with recurrent shudders and with the faint memory of Italian voices screaming after the speeding vehicle, *"Minata! Pericolo! Minata!"*

On September 16, the unit moved again, this time by a sketchy mountain route, to the vicinity of Terranova, 160 miles farther north. From this place the balance of the Division swung inland towards the key city of Potenza, leaving First Brigade to continue north to guard the Army's unprotected right flank against possible counterattacks.

It was an eery experience. Established on flat, deserted plains near Montalbano, the unit dug in for all-round defence aware that the rest of the Division was out of radio contact, and that there was an undefended front of sixty miles between Potenza and the elements of Eighth Army which had just landed at Taranto under the Italian heel. Reconnaissance patrols scouring the hills ahead encountered the enemy in brief skirmishes, but no major action developed.

On September 27, the Regiment again moved on, this time in comfort and in rear of the advance units. When the column halted at Gravina, the month had ended, and with it had come the end of yet another phase of the Regiment's war. Ahead lay the high ridges of the central Apennines and a German army that had halted, dug in its feet and was prepared to fight.

There was a three-day pause in the flat plains near Foggia and during this time Lt.-Col. Tweedsmuir returned to the unit and resumed command.

The month-long prelude to the real Italian battles had been a fairly bloodless time. There had been only a few casualties to the enemy mines and booby traps, but disease had wasted the unit. Jaundice, malaria and dysentery had been unrelenting enemies. They had sent a heavy toll of men back down the long lines of communication, through the field hospitals to Sicily, across the Mediterranean and to the hell-holes of North Africa that were euphemistically called convalescent camps. Here, soldiers who had survived long years with the unit, had seen the war in Sicily, and had finally fallen to disease, received their own reward. Doomed for weeks to the blistering heat and boredom of the camps, many of them were at last sent forward again – not to their own unit – but as reinforcements for battalions scattered throughout the Division. It was a cruel way to treat them, but perhaps it was not entirely the fault of the staff, for already the anti-conscription policy of the Government at home was drying up the trickle of volunteer reinforcements from Canada. There were not enough reinforcements to go around, even in those last months of 1943, and when a forward unit suffered casualties, these had to be made up from what sources were available in the field. So the Regiment lost many of its good men; many of the old timers who had grown so deeply into the unit. There was a legacy of resentment in this that was not forgotten even when the war was done.

Not all the companies suffered equally from disease; and Baker company seemed relatively immune. It was not until the Auxiliary Service officer became suspicious at the phenomenal run on his stock of health salts that the company's secret was exposed. Baking powder was in very short supply in southern Italy and the company cook, one Pte. Jack Potter, had been inspired to substitute health salts instead. Not only was Baker able to gorge on food denied the other companies, but it also seemed to be miraculously armoured against any disease bacillus Italy could produce. The explanation, forced from the reluctant company after all was known, was that no bacteria could remain in the innards of a Baker company man long enough to get established.

On October 2, the unit moved forward across the Foggia plains towards the looming ridges of the central Apennines.

The actions that followed were for the most part of an inconclusive nature. The enemy was fighting a rearguard war and carrying out a planned withdrawal. His outposts consistently brought the Regiment under fire, forcing it to deploy – but when the battle was mounted, the enemy was gone. Frustrating and confusing, the actions leading up to Campobasso and the Biferno did not shine with military splendour. But since these were the last battles to be touched by comedy, they are not forgotten.

On the edge of the mountainous plateau bounding the Foggia plains, the village of Motta guarded the road north. On October 1, the men of the R.C.R. moved up to attack this town. Through the night they struggled and by dawn were in the streets, but the Germans still held the high ground farther north.

The road across the plain was clotted with transport, parked nose to tail, waiting for the Germans ahead to be dislodged. Weeks of freedom from enemy air attack had made men careless. When three ME 109s suddenly appeared at tree-top level to strafe the hapless column, most of the Canadians at first failed to recognize the enemy. But the German planes roared past so close that the pilots could be clearly seen and in that sudden shock of recognition men did strange things. One slender olive tree became the shelter for thirteen men, each standing hard against the man in front, while the whole long line swung like a clock hand about the axis of the tree as the Messerschmidts approached, whipped past and vanished. Lt. Cliff Broad of Baker company was startled into a good north county rage. Blaspheming with a will, he drew his .38 revolver and went galloping across the olive grove firing at the retreating enemy. There was little damage to either side. The Germans had been in too much of a hurry to take aim, and the Canadians had been too incredulous of this appearance of the Luftwaffe to defend themselves.

At noon the Regiment received instructions for one of its famous flank approaches, and promptly set out in single file toward a cavernous gulley that reached upward to the east of Motta. The approach was arduous but uneventful until the leading companies clambered out of the head of the gulley and began to scuttle across a narrow opening towards the shelter of an oak forest. Instantly the waiting Germans opened fire from both flanks and the front, and the two forward companies dropped into what cover they could find. It was uncomfortable, and frustrating. The enemy lay concealed in the forest only a few hundred yards ahead, but could not be dislodged. Smoke was called for, and under its cover the rest of the unit attempted to come forward, but was soon halted. Individuals exchanged fire with their opposite numbers or crawled snake-wise amongst the rocks. The heat was heavy and the dust was acrid. The day drew on, bringing a chill darkness and a driving rain that saturated the men in their makeshift fox-holes. Scrambling through the dripping underbrush, firing at shadows, nervous and wet and cold, the unit edged forward and the enemy withdrew. Dawn broke at last as the Regiment reached its objective, feeling exhausted and disgruntled.

There was more to come. Towards evening of that same day there were new orders for another flanking march across the mountains but this time with a much more distant objective – and in darkness. It was a devilish night, heavy with mist and rain, and the unit, attempting to find its way over the rough terrain without any real knowledge of its own position, grew morose. Men cursed their fellows and their loads. At the head of the long column the scouts sniffed and cast about like fox-hounds who have lost the scent. Men stumbled into gulleys and fell over rock outcrops. It was a dank nightmare, and the enemy was temporarily forgotten in the struggle with the wilderness.

ACTIONS IN THE APENNINES   Oct. 3–Nov. 2 1943

When, unexpectedly, the scouts encountered the road they should have been paralleling, there was a new decision born of rashness. "The hell with this," the unit might have said. "We'll stick to the bloody road and see what happens."

The Germans guarding the road must have been incredulous that attackers could be so foolish or so bold. In the stillness of the hanging mist a German voice was heard to shout one startled phrase. There was the metallic rattle of a machine gun being cocked. Silence. And then the night exploded.

The enemy had sighted his guns along the high ground to the north of the road, covering the logical approach. He had not bothered to sight on the road itself, and now he could only fire blindly at the Regiment. Nevertheless, the Germans made up in volume of fire what they lacked in accuracy. Companies and platoons lost contact and milled about. Direction was lost in the darkness and the C.O. could do nothing else but order a withdrawal to the next hill slope to the east.

Reorganized once more, the Regiment prepared for an attack at dawn – and when dawn came, the enemy, as usual, was gone.

There was still more to come.

Before the day was out, orders arrived for an even bigger, more ambitious right flank march through even bigger mountains, to Celenza, eighteen miles away, Resignedly the unit turned away from roads and again headed into the tortuous maze of hills and broken valleys.

What followed makes a tale to tell over beer mugs, but to forget on days when men stand on patriotic platforms holding forth on the heroic deeds of war.

For two solid days and nights the Regiment wandered in the wilderness. Sometimes it was lost. Frequently the rear communications were lost and the distant Brigadier (still Howard Graham) must have chewed his nails. There was seldom an enemy to be seen, only new hills to climb, new rains to shudder under. Food was a dream, and so was sleep. There were some memories that stand out in men's minds, and one of these is of a tiny one-room shanty in a hidden valley where an aged Italian peasant stood at his door freely giving of his own poor supply of bread and milk to the straggling soldiers who had so recently been his country's enemies. There was the incident of an Italian doctor, also lost, who joined the column and became its muleteer, rounding up three scraggly beasts with which to equip a forlorn patrol. And there was the patrol itself, mule mounted and mule tired, making its way brazenly across the intervening plain below Mt. Miano, careless of death or bullets and in a daze of boredom and fatigue.

The patrol reached the crest of the mountain at noon on October 6. It found Miano heavily populated with unidentified soldiery, so it slunk cautiously over the crest, its spirits quickened by the possibility of action. On the far slope the patrol took up an ambush position along the lateral road and fingered the triggers of its guns as the roar of a motorcycle approached it from the south.

No shots were fired. The motorcycle was driven by one of the Dispatch Riders of the Regiment, left far behind with the transport section days before. And the 'enemy' on Mt. Miano turned out to be the cooks, the clerks, the drivers and the storemen of the unit, quietly preparing lunch against the hour when the Regiment would choose to emerge from its long pilgrimage into the hills.

The story was told boisterously by the men of the rear echelons of the Regiment, the troops who so seldom had a chance to show their mettle. Impatient at the long silence of the unit, the transport men had moved forward to occupy Miano on their own. Then, fired by their own daring, they dispatched a force – they called it the Odds and Sods Hussars – another ten miles to the town of Carlantino. Here the Hussars met an outpost of the enemy, but the cooks were in no mood to halt. Heavily fortified with *vino* they attacked, routed the Germans and killed a brace of them.

It was a long and weary time before the men of the rifle companies were allowed to put Miano out of mind.

During the four-day halt that followed, two of the scouts, Lyall Emigh and Keith Close, were ordered to reconnoitre across the Fortore River immediately ahead.

Close and Emigh were intimate friends – both young, both enthusiasts and both of high intelligence. They accepted the patrol assignment contentedly and set out in the heat of noon.

The river was low, and the scouts crossed easily and unmolested and cautiously approached the hill town of Macchia. Their entry was the signal for an outburst of great excitement from the civilians who explained that the Germans had vacated the place that morning. Close and Emigh were greeted as the advance guard of the liberation and were seized upon as the central figures for a celebration such as only the Italians know how to stage. Up and down the cobbled streets the two men were carried on the shoulders of their hosts. Vino, and vintage vino at that, was thrust upon them as if they were two vast and empty hogsheads. Men, women and children swarmed about them with gifts of flowers, figs and pomegranates. They were taken to the village hall and speeched-upon by all the local dignitaries. They were treated to a formal banquet, and at the end of the day were laid tenderly on the broad bed of the best room in the local *albergo* – to sleep it off.

They woke, bemused but happy, and convinced that this was the way to fight the war; but their paradise was spoiled in the morning hours by the arrival of a platoon of British Recce. troops, and the two scouts were lost in the melee.

They had tasted the fruit, and they wanted more. Instead of returning to the unit, they continued their patrol, heading hungrily for the next town to the north – and not bothering to follow the serpentine road, but puffing a straight course over the intervening mountains.

It was with deep disappointment that they surmounted the final crest to see a khaki-clad figure waving to them in a broad open stretch of unharvested grain. They had been forestalled. Nevertheless, they walked towards the stranger to pass the time of day, and perhaps to learn if there were any other unliberated towns around.

As it happened, the Afrika Korps to which the Hermann Goering Division had belonged, was fond of khaki instead of the blue-grey drab common to the rest of the German Army. The Canadian scouts knew this, but they had forgotten. It was not until they were a hundred yards from the unknown one that Close felt doubts.

"Lyall!" he said sharply, coming to a sudden halt. "Doesn't that guy's uniform look queer to you?"

It looked very queer to Emigh.

"Maybe we ought to start shooting," he replied.

Both men dropped to their bellies and hastily fired a few rounds from their rifles, but at that, "what sounded like a million Spandaus" opened up from every side. As Close recalled the incident he described the fire as heavy. "It trimmed the grain over our heads as neatly as any mowing machine," he said.

Embracing the hard earth Close muttered plaintively to his companion, "What the hell do we do now?"

"You still got your map-case?" Emigh asked. "Then wave the damn thing overhead – and do it quick!"

The Germans interpreted the signal correctly and the firing stopped. A voice yelled "*Komm*" and the would-be liberators got warily to their feet.

They were greeted by a jovial German Company Sgt. Major who thought the whole episode was the most delightful joke and for the balance of the day the two captives were his guests. They were well treated and the enemy chatted with them at length, in broken English, about the futility of war in general, and of this war in particular. Close and Emigh were strongly inclined to agree, and their mood was not lightened when in the late afternoon they were dispatched to the rear. They did not go with dignity. Instead they were placed in command of the outpost's ration mule, a singularly stubborn beast.

Close hauled at the beast's head, while Emigh pushed from the rear – and the German guards convulsed themselves with merriment. The patience of the two Canadians was wearing conspicuously thin when at last they were bundled into a motorcycle side-car. The driver, a burly type, was armed with a rifle slung across his back and a pistol at his belt. The guard, riding pilion, carried a machine-carbine cradled in his arm.

The road was bad and the journey slow. The guard could understand schoolboy English if it was spoken slowly enough, so Close and Emigh talked to him at intervals. Occasionally one of them would risk a rapid-fire remark in vernacular, and when the guard appeared suspicious the scouts would hastily apologize for forgetting that he could not understand. So, bit by bit, they laid the plans for an escape. But opportunity arrived before the plans were ready.

A crater in the road brought the motorcycle almost to a halt, and Close seized the chance and jumped the driver. Emigh responded by tackling the guard, and all four men fell from the machine.

It was a near thing. Close's man was too big for him to handle, and the German succeeded in getting his pistol free. It was no time for niceties. Desperate, Close snatched at the muzzle of the rifle, still slung on the enemy's back, and pulled it down with such force that the butt flew between the enemy's legs and dealt him a blow that left him with little further interest in the battle. Emigh, meanwhile, had narrowly escaped being shot by the guard's carbine, and only the timely intervention of Close, swinging the driver's pistol as a club, saved his life.

There was no time to gloat. An armoured half-track chose that moment to rumble around the bend, and the two scouts fled up the nearest hill while behind them enraged shouts were the prelude to a fusillade.

Beyond the hill lay a narrow valley with a small stream running down its centre. The fugitives knew they would have no time to scale the far slopes, so they leapt into the stream, crouched down and scurried hopelessly along. Then Close caught a glimpse of a dark shadow under the river bank. He yanked at Emigh's arm, and the two dived into the shelter of a small cave.

It was no natural cave. Crawling into the gloom the scouts were horrified to find the cavity stuffed with crates of chickens – and the chickens looked as if they would resent the intrusion with a wild alarum. Neither Close nor Emigh dared to move, to speak, hardly to breathe. They shut their eyes and prayed.

The Germans must have been nonplussed by the disappearance of the fugitives, and they were loath to give up the search. Three times Close saw jackboots pass the entrance of the cave and each time he swivelled his eyes to stare in fascinated horror at the restless chickens. But the chickens kept the secret.

Dusk came and the scouts still dared not move. Once more they heard approaching footsteps and a hairy face appeared suddenly at the cave entrance. As one man they raised captured weapons, but the face belonged to an aged Italian farmer who, being far-sighted and knowing the habits of *Tedesci*, had carefully contrived this sanctuary for his precious flock of hens. Each night he came to feed them. Now he found himself the prisoner of two wild-eyed Canadians.

Emigh and Close were at a loss what to do next. They dared not let the old man go for fear he would inform on them. They did not trust him to act as a guide. Emigh finally hit on a solution. Fiercely he instructed the old man to make his way to the Allied lines and to bring back a British patrol. And if he failed, or if he betrayed the scouts, he could be sure that every single chicken would be massacred. No more effective form of blackmail could have been devised and, weeping copiously, the old fellow went off into the night.

Incredibly he did manage to cross the lines; did find a British officer, and did tell his story. But the officer, not unnaturally, would have none of it. So, laden with his sorrows and his fears the old man came back alone. It was past midnight by this time, and in desperation, Close and Emigh chose to risk him as a guide. Poking him along with their pistols they made their way back over the Fortore and reported safely home. It is recorded that when the Italian returned to his chickens and his *casa*, he was so laden with tins of bully-beef and Canadian cigarettes that he could hardly stagger.

ELEVEN

Interlude in the Apennines

O N OCTOBER 13, the troops clambered aboard their vehicles and the convoy moved up over craters and diversions to the attack upon the central mountain city of Campobasso. Once more it was an advance with no real battles; only a succession of skirmishes against an enemy with whom one could not come to grips. The R.C.R. and 48th led the advance into the outskirts of the city with the Regiment following in reserve.

At midnight the unit was ordered westward to occupy a fantastic hill-top town called Ferrazzano that, like so many of the mountain villages, clung to the very tip of a high crag.

Ferrazzano itself offered no opposition. A company of the 48th Highlanders had occupied the eastern portion, and as the Regiment moved through the narrow, curving streets, the enemy evacuated the remaining western part. Two companies were detached to follow him down the abrupt slope along a narrow tongue of land that pointed towards the white city of Campobasso, four miles distant. There was a sharp skirmish and an exchange of machine-gin fire that caused several casualties. Outflanked by Baker company the enemy withdrew again, and doggedly the infantry moved after him. Reaching the end of the tongue, the companies deployed and, as dawn broke, they opened fire on the still-distant town.

As the morning light broke clear the R.C.R. walked into

Campobasso as the enemy walked out and shortly after-wards the Regiment moved eastward through the city to the right flank of the brigade.

The centre of the new position was at a paint factory on the edge of the plateau south of the Biferno River. To the north lay the enemy. On a steep spine out-thrust from the plateau, the town of Montagano overlooked the broad and rugged river valley and here Able company took up posi-tion after exchanging the usual desultory fire with the retreating enemy rearguards. A patrol of the carrier pla-toon rumbled eastward along a deserted road for fifty miles until at last it made contact with British troops moving inland from the Adriatic coast.

Directly ahead of B.H.Q. and only two miles from it, another carrier patrol confidently rattled down the valley slopes to visit the hamlet of San Stefano – and came under such intense machine-gun fire that it was forced to make a hasty withdrawal. Less than a mile from San Stefano, in the village of Ripalimosani, the church bells pealed and the entire populace stood in the streets to overwhelm a jeep load of Canadians who were out sight-seeing.

Things were further confused by the arrival of numbers of Allied war prisoners, released by the Italians at the time of the capitulation, and pursued southward by the Ger-mans ever since. These men, hungry, very dirty and very shabby, drifted across the Biferno in ones and twos, accompanied and guided by Italian civilians. Their relief at being again inside the Allied lines was pitiful. But there was not one of them who did not find time to sing paeans of praise to the Italian peasants who had helped in the escapes.

Partly due to this concrete example of the friendliness of the local people, and partly due to an accumulation of small experiences during the two months on the Conti-nent, the attitude of the Canadians towards the Italians had begun to undergo a marked change. Soldiers who were forced to spend most of their time in a chronic state of uncleanliness no longer sneered at the Italian standards of sanitation. The earlier contemptuous and half-pitying attitude towards civilians dissolved as individual soldiers found friendship offered with sincerity and warmth by the peasant families and by the town-folk as well. And too, soldiers can always appreciate bravery in others. It was not difficult to appreciate that quality in one little man, a notary of sixty years of age, who approached one of the Regiment's patrols near Montagano. The old man carried a wicker-work basket, and, from the tender way in which he held it out to them, the patrol hoped it might contain eggs. The contents of that basket were far more delicate than any eggs. It was filled with igniter assemblies from half a hundred German Teller mines.

Beaming with pleasure the old man explained how he had watched the enemy engineers mining the road below Montagano. He had waited until the Germans withdrew, then with consummate courage (for he knew little about mines) he had descended to the road, dug up the deadly weapons and carefully removed the detonators.

Then too, there was a tall, saturnine mountaineer with a great eagle nose, who called himself Giovanni, and who attached himself to the Regiment during its stay in the Campobasso area. Giovanni was a Marxist who had been variously an anti-Fascist and an anti-German guerilla, leading a tiny band of his fellows through the crags and valleys of the high Apennines. Twice he had been captured and tortured extensively, as his livid scars bore witness. Yet he had continued with his desperate game. Now he became chief of a completely unofficial intelligence section operated by the Regiment; and Giovanni and three of his associates made a total of twenty-six incursions into the enemy lines to bring back information that was of inestimable value. Giovanni never came back empty-handed. If he did not bring a German prisoner, then he had a couple of American airmen, or a British survivor of the fall of Tobruk, in tow behind him. He took no money, and asked for none. Even the most racially bigoted soldiers in the Regiment could not hide their admiration for him.

But a growing respect for the Italians was perhaps not as vital in breaking down the barriers between the soldiers and the civilians as was another emotion. Envy. It has been called by other names, but at heart it was envy that led these soldier-exiles to spend their evenings sitting beside the charcoal fires in tiny farmhouses, treating the Italian children to hard candies out of Compo rations, passing Victory cigarettes to the older men and women, and drinking vino with the family. It was a soft, pathetic envy; a hunger to recapture memories dimmed by five years of absence. And the Italians recognized it for what it was, and with the understanding of those who live hard lives on the rim of existence they responded to it.

Many friendships were made in the Campobasso area that would endure for a long time – and some of them are strong to this day. Later when the Regiment was far to the north, involved in the savage struggles of the following year, men with a few days of leave would make their way back to the mountains of Campobasso and spend the precious hours with these Italians for whom they were adopted sons. Hungry to find a substitute for old roots in which the sap was drying fast, the Regiment was becoming as much a part of the Italian scene as strangers ever could become. The men could not identify themselves intimately with the land itself, nor with a nationality whose religion, language, and social structure were so utterly strange to most of them. However, they could, and did, identify themselves with the essential human attributes of the Italian people.

From October 14 to 22, the Regiment remained in a static role. Nominally it was resting, but in point of fact it was continually engaged in minor actions. Able company remained detached to hold Montagano against a possible counterattack from across the Biferno, and it was shelled heavily for eight successive days.

Charlie company, meanwhile, was attempting to capture San Stefano. This enemy outpost on the south side of the river appeared at first to be a minor holding, and yet it was five days before the Germans were driven out. Beginning with attempts by small patrols the action built up daily until in the end it required a full-scale assault supported by artillery and tanks to reduce the outpost. Baker and Dog companies were committed in this final battle, and when they had at length taken the village, they were subjected to heavy and accurate mortar and shell fire for the remainder of their stay.

It was a period of trivial and painful operations, that represented no real achievement. Probably the only people who extracted any sense of satisfaction from the military activities at Campobasso were the patrols. The Regiment had a particular genius for this kind of thing. It appealed because so many of the men had been backwoodsmen, either by trade or by inclination. It appealed to them, too, because it was relatively free of control from higher up. Once committed to a patrol, the men involved were able to make their own rules, and there was room for considerable individualism. The patrols were usually long-range reconnaissance expeditions across the river and deep into enemy territory. Typical of these was one carried out by Sgt. Leroux and three scouts.

Leroux's crew crossed the Biferno in darkness and having avoided the advance enemy positions, headed inland at a good pace. Morning found them hidden in a vineyard in the B.H.Q. area of a Panzer Grenadier Regiment, only a stone's throw from an outbuilding that served as an N.C.O.s mess. Leroux and his men crawled up to the building in full daylight, leapt in through the open door and surprised the German orderly room sergeant taking his morning cup of coffee. The Canadians drank the coffee, then removed the sergeant whom they carried back across the river the following night. It was a startling coup, but one that was equalled by the daring of another of the regimental scouts, Pte. George Langstaff.

Langstaff was a remarkable character, lean and soft spo-

ken, with penetrating eyes and a flair for guerrilla operations. He preferred to operate alone on patrol and on this
occasion he spent the day beside a German company H.Q.
making notes on the enemy's activity. At dusk, his primary task completed, he calmly walked into the enemy
billets, shot the German company commander dead, and
walked away again.

There is no doubt that these activities produced a most
uneasy state of mind amongst the enemy outposts, and it
was at Campobasso that First Division achieved its early
reputation for phenomenal skill at long-range patrolling.
It was a reputation destined to last.

The 'rest' in Campobasso was cut short on October 23,
when the Regiment moved to the west of the city in
preparation for the jump across the Biferno River.

The general situation in Italy was relatively static by this
time. The first impetus of the Salerno breakout was spent
and Fifth Army was halted before Venafro. Winter was
near and the weather was deteriorating. In the central
mountains the enemy had established his winter-line
along the Biferno. To the east he held the line of the
Sangro River in great strength. Monty was doggedly pushing north from Termoli towards the Sangro line, and to
assist him in the central Apennines the Canadians were
now given the task of thrusting forward across the Biferno
to the headwaters of the Sangro.

First Brigade led off on October 23, when the R.C.R.
crossed the Biferno and took the nearby town of Castropignano. Then on the night of October 25, the Regiment
crossed the now swollen torrent on a booby-trapped
power dam and struck inland for the mountain village of
Molise, some twelve miles distant.

Apart from rain and miserable marching conditions,
there was little opposition. Molise was reached and taken
at dawn on October 27. The carrier platoon, on foot, was
then detached and sent to seize the town of Frosolone to
the west, a mission that it accomplished without difficulty.

Then for a week the Regiment sat in Molise and Frosolone enduring a remorseless and continuous artillery bombardment. The accuracy of the enemy guns seemed uncanny. Six men were killed and fourteen wounded in the first few hours. It was not until Giovanni had spent some time testing the under-currents of the place that the Regiment discovered it was living in a Fascist hot-bed. Both the mayor, and the owner of the house that B.H.Q. had occupied, were informing the Germans of the unit's movements. Giovanni administered rough justice, and though the shelling continued to be extremely heavy, it became far less accurate.

The five days that followed were singularly unpleasant. Any movement in daylight drew heavy fire, and the companies, dispersed on the forward slopes of the hill, lived in their slit trenches. The inhabitants of the town were unlike any civilians the men had so far encountered, being shifty and sullen. The town itself was indescribably dirty and the steep streets were sodden with debris and filth.

It was a war of patrols and agents. Each day Giovanni's men disappeared into the deep valleys to the front, and often enough one- or two-man patrols from the rifle companies followed them out. They would come in again at dusk bearing the location of the German guns and troop positions, and through the nights, the Canadian artillery would pound away at the new targets. With dawn, the tables turned. The enemy picked out his targets in the town and pounded them through the daylight hours.

Yet even this grim situation had its lighter moments. A section of four men of the carrier platoon, dismounted and acting as infantry, had been placed well forward on the slopes where they came in for more than their share of shelling. One morning it was decided to withdraw them, but every movement in that area brought a fresh blast of shell-fire, and the four appeared to be trapped till darkness fell.

Anxious to escape, the section solved the problem for itself. Two of the men had once acted in amateur theatricals and they knew all about stage horses. So, they reasoned, why not a stage mule? Draping themselves with blankets and using two wicker baskets from a shattered shed to represent mule-panniers, they made their way out into the open ground led by a third man (also blanket draped to look like a farmer) while the fourth soldier scuttled along on hands and knees in the lee of the pseudo mule. A Canadian artillery observer spotted the weird cavalcade approaching, and was so astonished that he nearly fell from his high perch in the church steeple. But he was close enough to see the details. The Germans were deceived and not a shot was wasted on the mule and its pathetic owner.

The routine incidents of those days were less amusing. In the evening, the padre went forward to bury the dead, and on occasion was sniped at by German patrols. His task was a grim one on those nights, for the steady shelling would sometimes send the burial party to cover a dozen times before each meagre service was completed.

Rations were short and only mule trains and the occasional jeep could reach the village, under cover of darkness. One company, dug in beside an apiary, discovered that it had a beekeeper in one of its sergeants, and for a while the issue hard tack dripped with honey. The weather worsened, and heavy rains made the Molise position even more abominable. The valleys steamed in the occasional pallid bursts of autumnal sunlight. Soldiers huddled in the pools of water that were their slit-trenches or crouched uneasily by the lips of these water holes listening intently for the warning whine of an approaching shell.

The unit was relieved on November 2, and sent south to Castropignano. Now, for the first time since leaving England, the men went into billets. They were not palaces, but the little town of Castropignano – familiarly known as Castropigface – nevertheless gave of its best. Badly damaged by artillery, and worse damaged by the attentions of the Kittyhawks of the Desert Air Force, the battered village offered at least some protection from the biting rain squalls that swept down from the high mountains almost daily. The face of the country was changing, becoming dour and sullen as winter approached. The rivers rose and washed away the Bailey bridges over the Biferno, cutting the unit off from the rear areas for a week. Winter clothing was slow in coming, and each soldier added to his own kit from what local sources he could find. Army blankets began to appear in the guise of short coats, fetchingly tailored by the Castropignano civilian artisans. A naturally strong feeling for individual eccentricities in dress became more pronounced, and the Regiment began to take on the outward look of a band of mercenaries.

Schools were established for junior N.C.O.s who had taken their promotions in the field. Angus Duffy paraded his senior N.C.O.s in rain and mud on a 'smartening-up' course that would have led to open mutiny had not Angus's personality been so strong. Training became the daily routine within the rifle companies, and an essential one, for the great gaps opened in the unit's nominal rolls by disease and battle were now being filled with new reinforcements, most of whom had received woefully inadequate training in Canada. The staff of the unit was changing too, as officers left for other tasks and were replaced. Capt. Essex, a padre whose work had endeared him in all truth to the regiment, left the unit, to be replaced by Capt. Goforth, a slight young man whose air of gentleness at first made his a hard lot.

One morning a strange Italian forced his way past the indignant guards at B.H.Q. and presented himself to an astounded adjutant. Filthy, thin as a refugee, and clad in disintegrating civilian clothes, Major Bert Kennedy had returned to the unit out of the limbo of the missing. Kennedy had a tale to tell.

A month earlier while the Regiment waited for the attack on Campobasso, Kennedy had gone forward to contact the R.C.R., then in the vanguard of the battle. In company with two privates, Bert had been making his way cautiously up a road when he came under heavy mortar fire. It seemed wise to detour around the noisy area, so the three Canadians swung into an open field and up along a hedgerow. Unfortunately they were not the only ones using that hedge. A German infantry platoon, moving down it for a counterattack, came full upon the unsuspecting three and took them prisoners.

Kennedy found himself headed for Germany. Four days later he was aboard a truck approaching Rome. The road led through the central mountains near Avezzano, and the many curves forced the truck to move with caution. A heavy rain was falling and the German guards huddled forward under the canvas hood for shelter while Kennedy managed to work himself close to the tailgate. There were five other prisoners aboard but only Kennedy sensed the opportunity. He waited until the vehicle slowed for a sharp bend, and then he leapt.

He landed hard, rolled to his feet and dived headlong through a heavy hedge with, as he remembered, "some damage to my bald pate". Beyond the hedge there was a little stream. Kennedy threw himself into this freshet and lay doggo while the guards fired a few wild shots in his direction. Evidently it did not occur to them that their man could still be lying close at hand, when a hundred yards away a forest beckoned. Their search was perfunctory and after a time the truck ground away up the slope, and Kennedy was free.

Freedom was an easy thing to obtain, comparatively. To maintain it was another matter. For the next three days he made his way slowly south down the very spine of the Apennines, avoiding all roads and tracks and climbing goatlike amongst the crags. Weary almost unto death, he at last dared to crawl into a tiny stone barn and rest amongst the straw.

Here, in the morning, he was discovered by a very frightened peasant farmer. In pidgin Italian Kennedy calmed his host and explained that he was a *Commandante Canadesi*. The Italian may or may not have understood, but this he knew; the ragged, hungry man in his barn was a fugitive from *Tedesci* and therefore deserving of help.

The help he gave demanded a calculated courage that few of us could find even for ourselves in time of need, and that fewer still could find on behalf of another man – a stranger and a one-time enemy. The farmer took Kennedy into his own house, dressed and fed him, and when twenty minutes later a German motorcyclist unexpectedly banged on the door, Kennedy was hidden under a bed while the Italian bribed the enemy with gifts of eggs and poultry to forego a search. Had Kennedy been found the little farm would have vanished beneath the torch and the occupants with it. All this the farmer knew, but he was master of his fear.

Two days later he led Kennedy into the third-class compartment of a southbound train, and guided him and protected him on the forty-mile journey to Sora, half way to the front. He could do no more. The land ahead was strange to him. But he pressed further food on his guest and wept as he saw him off into the friendly hills. Diminutive, weak in body, terrified by the audacity of what he was doing, that farmer was possessed of a spirit such as few men can boast. Yet he typified the true heart of the Italian peasant. Kennedy was to discover just how typical the little man had been, during the rest of his twenty-five-day ordeal in the mountains. No longer suspicious of the civilians, he sought them out and without exception they gave him freely of their friendship and of their pitifully meagre goods. Passing him on from family to family, they saw him southward to within sound of the battle line and here he joined a group of seven other escapees under the protection of the local people. By this time he was in an exhausted condition, having lost fifteen pounds from what was at best a lean and sinewy frame. His shoes had long since disintegrated and he wore makeshifts made of rags and cardboard given him by the Italians. His condition appeared so shocking that other members of the escape group tried to persuade him to remain hidden until the

Allies drove north. He would have none of it. Leading a British lieutenant who had lost his glasses, and was blind without them, Kennedy made his way through the German lines in daylight. That night, it was November 6, he delivered himself and his charge into the hands of an American patrol at Venafro.

By the usages of war Kennedy should have been returned to Canada, or at least to a back area job. Kennedy did not see it this way. Borrowing a jeep from the Americans he headed back to his home, back to the Regiment, and once returned he resolutely refused to budge away even when the Brigadier endeavoured to cajole him into a well-earned holiday in England. The day after his return he again became acting commander of the Regiment when John Tweedsmuir was evacuated with jaundice.

The long rest at 'Castropigface' came at a time of foul weather, yet on the whole it was a good time for the Regiment. Campobasso had been turned into a leave centre, called Canada Town, and here a man could relax on forty-eight-hour leave, see ENSA shows, drink abundantly of local vino, initiate the local girls into the peculiarly Canadian approach to romance, and even do a little souvenir buying. In 'Castropigface' itself, there was time for a variety of personal pursuits and there was a relative freedom from staff irritations. Divisional Headquarters had shaken down and had adopted the more reasonable Eighth Army attitude towards the fighting troops – allowing them adult status at last. The Regiment itself had settled into a comfortable unanimity of spirit and comradeship, the fruits of the long years in England, and of the fighting since July.

Home had become more than a spiritual affair. Knowing that tomorrow might bring another battle, each man had developed the faculty of living for the day, and of finding his physical home in whatever cellar, windowless room or half-shattered shed might be his temporary lot. In the first few hours at Castropignano the village became a familiar place and as the days lengthened, men came to know it almost as well as they had known the little towns in Hastings and Prince Edward counties. Matchless scroungers and improvisers as they were, they made their quarters into sanctuaries of real permanence, ignoring the sure knowledge that here was nothing permanent, for the war was waiting still.

Expeditions to exchange *scarpe* (shoes) and bully-beef for eggs, vegetables and vino were daily routine. In the evenings men gathered in the homes of Italian families for stultifying feeds of spaghetti.

The collector's instinct – it is not really fair to call it looting – had a chance to flower and it led to some strange incidents. There was a man whose first name was Alf, and Alf was billeted in the ruins of what had been a chapel. Two beautiful candlesticks standing on the altar had escaped destruction, and for ten days Alf stared at these fine trophies and tried to control temptation. He fought a good fight, but a losing one. Jumping to his feet one day he snatched the candlesticks and was stowing them in his kit when an old friend, an Irishman and a good Catholic, chose to visit Alf and caught him in the act. Lightning flew, and under the tirade that followed, poor Alf wilted and reluctantly dragged the candlesticks out of his bag and set them on the altar. Thoroughly chastened he left the billet to seek solace in vino.

He returned half an hour later to discover that the entire roof of the chapel had collapsed in his absence. Shaken to the core, Alf took it as a stern warning from on high, and for at least a month he was one of the most devoted followers the padre had in all the Regiment. But he back-slid. His teeth had been bothering him and a visit to the dentist resulted in the removal of the lot and the substitution of dentures. The following day the whole unit went on a diet of hard-tack instead of bread and Alf incontinently decided that Heaven had carried his punishment one step too far. He turned his back upon the Church from that time forth.

The new padre, coming to the unit fresh from the elite Black Watch, was in a position to assess the Regiment with clear eyes and his first impressions are worth recording.

"I joined the Regiment at Castropignano," he wrote, "and it was late at night when I reported to B.H.Q. A poker game was in progress, and although I was a complete newcomer, and a padre, I was at once invited to sit in. It was the day after an officers' party at Campobasso and several of the senior officers were nursing wounds. One captain had a broken arm, and several of the rest sported black eyes. My first impression of the Regiment was that it had a pretty 'down-to-earth' character and, after the Black Watch, I hardly knew what to expect. But I will always remember the way the unit took me in. There were no cold down-the-nose stares and no questions asked. From that first day I was The Padre, as if I had been born in the unit. I understood that here were chaps who were getting on with the job with no unnecessary palaver and no drum beating. They were fighting men."

TWELVE

The River of Blood

B Y THE end of November winter had reached the Adriatic coast. In the mountains to the west the new snows built up on the flaring peaks, and on the coastal plain the snow fell into grey valleys, wetly and endlessly. The sleeping *torrentes* wakened and rumbled towards the sea; their waters, heavily laden with yellow muck, sucking at the creaking underpinnings of the army's Bailey bridges. From the coasts of Yugoslavia the infamous *bora* gales drove the heavy clouds down to the level of the ground, and brought dark mists that were as cold as death itself. Everything that was not rock became fluid mud. The lines of olive trees, gnarled by a hundred winters, stood gaunt upon the shrouded ridges. The vineyards became morasses, deep with slime. In the villages, the sad stone houses seemed to draw yet closer together as the unceasing rains beat down upon them.

It was a time for plants to die, for birds to flee, for animals to shelter in the deep sleep of hibernation, and for men to huddle by charcoal braziers and wait the winter out. It was surely no time for war, and yet in the last days of November a great convoy began to roll eastward from the Campobasso mountains bearing First Canadian Division to a new battle.

The journey was agonizing, of the kind that can reduce men to unfeeling clods. Precipitous roads, innumerable diversions, mud, endless delays, chill rain and mounting fatigue were the lot of drivers and passengers alike. Yet battle called, and could not be gainsaid.

The battle had already commenced when First Division began its move. In the last days of November, Eighth Army had struck a staggering blow against the enemy's winter line on the Adriatic sector. This line, named for the Sangro River which marked its geographical position, had been most carefully prepared by the Germans who were convinced that the autumn rains would bring an end to active fighting for the year. All along the high north bank of the broad valley the enemy had constructed emplacements and into these fortifications had gone the best troops that the Germans could command in Italy. The enemy considered the line impregnable. Montgomery did not.

In a week of the most ferocious and bloody battle, Fifth British Corps crossed the river and smashed a great rent in the Sangro line. Pushing relentlessly forward in an effort to maintain the momentum of the break-through, 78th Division drove on up the coast, while behind it First Canadian Division moved to take over the pursuit. The German defence was broken for the moment, and Montgomery's grand design, to reach and capture Pescara and the lateral road across the mountains which leads to Rome, seemed destined to be realized. But there were other enemies ahead, more formidable ones than the German troops, and allied with them. These were the weather and the land.

The coastal plateau north of the Sangro is seldom more than a few miles in width, hemmed in between the high mountains on the west and the Adriatic on the east. At intervals of a mile or so it is deeply gashed from mountain to the sea by mighty gullies carved out by the seasonal *torrentes*. By December 1, all of these ravines had become impassable to vehicles, wheeled or tracked, except along the tenuous lines of the narrow and poorly surfaced roads. The bridges across the gullies were extremely vulnerable. As the Germans withdrew they had only to pause long enough to lay their demolition charges, and the bridges vanished. Even for men on foot most of the valleys were major barriers, for the *torrentes* were running deep and angry, and the steep slopes were slimed with mud. Each ravine in its turn could, and did, become a natural fortress line where the German forces could turn and stand, and force the pursuers to mount a major battle.

To make the attackers' lot even more difficult, the enemy still held the high mountains to the west and so had observation over the denuded olive groves and vineyards which – at their best – offered but little cover to the advancing troops.

The German High Command, shaken by the Sangro débâcle, rallied its reserves and sent them racing down from the north to stem the breakthrough. By December 4, when the advance elements of 78th Division had reached the line of the Moro River, a new enemy division had already arrived and stood ready to contest further advances. This was 90th Panzer-Grenadier Division, fresh from a long rest and refit. Its orders were to hold the Moro.

On December 5, First Division relieved the exhausted 78th before the Moro. At the coast the Regiment moved up to take over the positions of the Royal Irish Fusiliers on the high plains escarpment which fell abruptly some four hundred feet into the sea.

That relief was heavy with foreboding. Persistent shelling harassed the long files of soaked and muddy soldiers as they wound their way forward over the bleak highlands. And when the relief was completed, the advance platoons of the Regiment found themselves at the edge of the escarpment, looking out over a deep and shadowed valley at a landscape that seemed almost lunar in its desolation and its emptiness. But each man knew that the emptiness was an illusion.

The hollow feeling of dread anticipation that all soldiers know as they move up towards the rumble of the guns was now replaced and overlaid by the strange insulation of the mind that, to a detached observer, looks like insouciance, but that is in reality the armour of a soldier's soul. Squatting in their shallow trenches, or in the ruins of smashed buildings, the infantry waited in an outward state of apathy for the word that would send them forward down those forlorn slopes.

They had not long to wait.

General Vokes, the divisional commander, had already planned his battle. He had decided that his major thrust would not be at the coast, but some three miles inland along the main highway running through the village of San Leonardo. To mask his intentions and to divert the enemy's attention, Vokes ordered the Regiment to make an immediate feint attack across the river near its mouth.

There was no time for preparations; no time to arrange a covering artillery barrage, and hardly time for even the briefest reconnaissance of the river obstacle. However, a patrol, sent out hurriedly, accomplished a remarkable feat by making its way unobserved to the centre of the valley in daylight, and by finding a ford across the swollen river some three hundred yards above its mouth.

Kennedy chose Able company to attempt the crossing. The men knew the odds as they gathered near the lip of the escarpment and waited for darkness to mask their movements.

At 2100 hours, in the wet night and in a silence that was doubly ominous, the men of the lead platoon descended the slopes and felt their way across the muddy slough that was the valley floor. Luck was with them, and the absence of an artillery barrage played in their favour for the enemy received no warning of the attack. The platoon forded the stream and began moving painfully towards the black shadows of the northern slope while behind it, the remaining two platoons came forward.

Suddenly the tension snapped. A single enemy machine gun rippled into hysterical life and at once a dozen flares, some green, some blinding white, lifted and hung above Able company. The signal was instantly answered by the

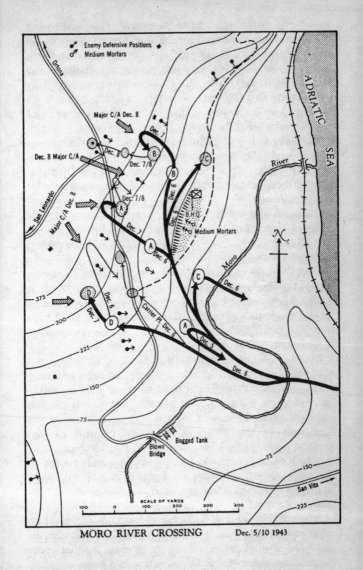

Enemy Defensive Positions
Medium Mortars

Ortona

Major C/A Dec. 8

Dec. 8

Dec. 8 Major C/A

Dec. 7/8

Dec. 7/8

Dec. 7

San Leonardo

Major C/A Dec. 8

Dec. 7

Dec. 6

Dec. 7

Dec. 6

River

ADRIATIC SEA

B.H.Q.

Medium Mortars

Moro

Dec. 6

N

375

300

Dec. 6

Dec. 7

Dec. 6

225

Carrier Pt. Dec. 6

Dec. 5

Dec. 6

150

Dec. 6

75

Bogged Tank

Blown Bridge

75

150

San Vito

225

SCALE OF YARDS
100   0   100   200   300   400

MORO RIVER CROSSING   Dec. 5/10 1943

muted and distant thunder of the enemy guns, and by the violent outcry of twenty or more machine guns emplaced on the high banks. A shimmering curtain of tracer swept the valley and within seconds the enemy artillery and mortar shells began to fall in thundering salvos, their flashes outlining the scene with terrifying clarity.

There was no cover on the valley floor. The pioneer platoon which had been sent down to the coastal road to try to build a diversion around the demolished bridge, was driven back. Able company was forced to seek a non-existent shelter in the deepening mud. The forward platoon, directly engaged with several enemy posts, was helpless to advance.

Back on the southern escarpment Kennedy felt the appalling weight of the enemy's defence, and understood that to prolong the battle would be to lose Able company. He gave the order to withdraw.

Shocked and exhausted, Able straggled back while the rest of the Regiment, watching that vicious concentration of fire, knew that it had not, before this time, seen war in its real magnitude. For the balance of that long night men manned their Brens and kept their minds away from thoughts about the morrow.

Meanwhile, the main assault at San Leonardo had not met with success, for the enemy there had been as strong and as vigilant as he had been at the river mouth. Vokes did not change his plan but ordered the assault on San Leonardo to be renewed. When this news reached the Regiment in the morning, Kennedy decided on the greatest gamble in his life. He went to Brigade Headquarters and asked permission to try to force a real crossing at the river mouth. Howard Graham, who was still commanding the Brigade that included his old Regiment, concurred. Zero was set for 1400 hours.

Now that Kennedy had committed the Regiment to what must surely be one of the most difficult and dangerous battles in its career, he set about ensuring that every conceivable aid to the fighting men would be on hand.

The battle of the Moro which began, for the Regiment, at 1400 hours on December 6, was a near miracle of co-operation between all arms. The 4.2-inch mortars of the Saskatoon Light Infantry Support Battalion were laid for twenty minutes on the known enemy positions which had been pinpointed during the feint assault of the previous night. On the crest of the south escarpment a squadron of British tanks and self-propelled guns stood ready to engage each enemy machine gun as it opened fire on the advancing infantry. The guns of the Second Field Regiment, given eyes by two forward observers who moved with the infantry, were prepared to bring down salvos upon each enemy strongpoint as it revealed itself.

Charlie company led the attack and when, in the exposed killing ground of the valley, it came under a withering enfilading fire, the 4.2 mortars, and the Regiment's own three-inch mortars immediately switched to smoke bombs and effectively curtained Charlie from the enemy. Under cover of the smoke, Dog company began swinging to the left into the centre of the enfilading fire before the blinded German gunners could recover their vision.

Kennedy, watching from a high knoll on the south bank, glimpsed victory ahead. But there was bad news with the good. A troop of tanks which had descended into the ravine hoping to cross the river near the demolished bridge and so support the infantry in their assault over the crest of the far bank, reported itself hopelessly bogged down. The loss of the tanks was catastrophic, for the enemy had many tanks and would assuredly use them for a counterattack against the naked infantry men if these should manage to scale the northern slopes.

In every battle there comes a moment when the certainty of the commander is shaken, when his doubts become agonizing, and when the weight of his responsibility becomes intolerable. The commander who thinks of his troops only as ciphers is sometimes spared this moment, but Kennedy was not spared.

From his observation knoll it appeared to him that Dog company had become too deeply involved on the left flank, and was in danger of being overwhelmed. The failure of the tanks to get across made it seem certain that any local success which might be won by the infantry would be transitory and liable to be turned into costly defeat. Charlie company, on the valley floor, was clearly unable to get forward to assist Dog, and the weight of the enemy defensive fire seemed to be increasing, rather than decreasing.

Remembering that this was not the major battle but still only a diversion, Kennedy gave in to his doubts and ordered the two companies to withdraw.

Charlie received the message and obeyed. Dog, with its radio out of order and all three platoons running hog-wild in the centre of a disorganized enemy position, neither heard nor could obey, and Kennedy found himself in a terrible dilemma. His choice was this: to sacrifice Dog in order to preserve the rest of the Regiment – or take up the battle again with all of his resources in order to extricate that unfortunate company. He hesitated for no more than five minutes.

The battle that had been declared over, began anew.

The carrier platoon, dismounted and acting as infantry, had been sent out to try to cover Dog company's retreat – now it was told to cross the valley and get astride of the road behind Dog. Baker and Able companies were ordered to take Charlie company's original objectives. Kennedy himself joined Able and crossed with it.

The enemy fire which had slackened somewhat after Charlie's withdrawal, now redoubled its efforts to wipe out the infantry in the valley. The artillery of two German divisions was concentrated on the fragile flesh of the companies and it was being thickened, minute by minute, by the fire of self-propelled guns and by a massive weight of mortar bombs and rocket projectiles. But the very massiveness of that bombardment defeated its purpose. The men of Able and Baker companies, once committed, had no choice but to struggle forward to the distant slopes, for there alone could they find protection from that shattering bombardment. To stay in the valley was to die. To attack was to have some faint hope of survival.

Within an hour Able and Baker were across, had climbed well up the enemy-held slopes, and had dug in with an unshakeable determination not to be driven back into the thundering inferno of the valley. And on the left, the carrier men had proved that they needed no armoured shields about them. They fought their way up along the climbing ribbon of the road and arrived in time to cover the somewhat precipitate withdrawal of a Dog company platoon that, flushed with victory, had made its way over the three-hundred-foot crest only to be met by a heavy enemy counterattack.

Striving to keep the enemy off balance, Kennedy now ordered Able and Baker to strike up to the crest; and went along himself. The crest was gained with little further fighting, but on the level plains above, the enemy was waiting with armour and fresh infantry reinforcements. Darkness had come, and Kennedy knew that his regiment could do no more without the support of tanks and anti-tank weapons. The companies withdrew just over the lip of the escarpment and dug in for the night.

It was the kind of night men dream about in after years, waking to a cold sweat and to a wild surge of gratitude that it is but a dream. The darkness was violent with sound, and chaotic with confusion. Small German outposts had been isolated and left behind all through the area of the bridgehead, and these, in hysterical dismay, were firing their automatic weapons at every shadow. The roar and grind of enemy tanks working their way along the crest was multiplied by echoes until it seemed that an entire Panzer Division was massing to descend upon the scattered units of the Regiment. Verey flares cut the darkness with sick radiance, and the insistent scream of 88-mm. shells rose high above the lumbering thunder of both the Canadian guns, and the heavier cannon of the enemy.

Mortar shells whumped over the crest, searching for the hurriedly dug slit-trenches of the bridgehead defenders, and patrols from both sides blundered through the vineyards while both sides shot at them with panicky impartiality. To make things worse, the night grew bitterly cold and wet.

Perhaps the greatest strain lay on the C.O. and his company commanders for they alone knew that the Regiment was now to all intents and purposes cut off in German territory. The engorged Sangro river had risen twenty feet in a few hours and had smashed the precious Bailey bridges, leaving the two advance brigades of the division isolated from the rest of the army. The Regiment itself was now holding a bridgehead perimeter of nearly half a mile, and it could expect no assistance, for the crossing at the Moro mouth had only been intended as a diversion and never as the main effort.

With the river of blood behind them, the infantry dug in and waited for the dawn.

December 7 dawned overcast with wild weather brewing, and both sides used the grey early hours to reorganize and sort themselves out preparatory to continuing the battle. Meanwhile, the whole situation on the Canadian front had undergone a change. Two small bridgeheads, established northwest of San Leonardo the previous night after grim fighting by Second Brigade, were now abandoned, leaving the Regiment holding the sole Canadian foothold on the north bank of the Moro. Intelligence sources reported that the Germans apparently believed the Hasting's bridgehead represented the point where the division would now make its major thrust, and German reinforcements and tanks were therefore massing near the coast. Because of this, General Vokes was further confirmed in his original plan for the main crossing to be made at San Leonardo, and while new preparations were maturing, the Regiment was given the task of drawing unto itself the full fury of the enemy counter-assault.

That the counterattack would come, in force, no one

doubted. During the day heroic efforts were made to provide the unit with some anti-tank defence, but the Sherman tanks again bogged in the river bed and the shellfire here was so heavy that the best efforts of the pioneers could not provide a diversion. Stan Walker's platoon (the anti-tank men), with the help of Charlie company, and with the ebullient example of C.S.M. George Ponsford, thereupon accomplished the impossible and *carried* two six-pounder guns across the valley and set them up in Able company area. In addition, two of the unit's three-inch mortars were carried over, together with a good supply of bombs, and set up in a gravel pit just below the lip of the valley.

Kennedy chose not to wait for the enemy attack, but as darkness fell he ordered a platoon each from Able and Baker to move forward. These two platoons successfully reached the crest and took up positions commanding not only the highway to the north, but the vital lateral road leading to San Leonardo as well.

At 0100 hours on December 8, the enemy launched his carefully prepared assault, designed to smash the bridgehead and sweep the Regiment off the north slopes. A vicious bombardment by heavy mortars, tanks, S.P. guns and artillery preceded the infantry attack. The advanced Able company platoon met the assault head-on and was forced to withdraw to save itself from annihilation. But it was a calculated withdrawal, and the enemy followed pell-mell, not realizing that he was being lured into a deep salient between Able and Baker. It was a deadly trap, and when the Germans were thirty yards away, the concealed weapons of the two companies caught the enemy on both his flanks. The minutes that followed brought a débâcle to the panzer grenadiers and when they had withdrawn, running in panic-stricken groups with no regard for cover, they left more than two-score dead men in the vineyards, and another twenty were taken prisoners. The German retreat was turned into a shambles by the unit's three-inch mortars, firing from a range of less than 200 yards – the first of the mighty work done by the smooth bore tubes in the bridgehead fight.

Baker company followed up the enemy's defeat and Sgt. Bill Nolan, with ten men attacked and overran a house controlling the road junction, capturing eighteen German paratroopers in the process.

The capture of the paratroopers was a disquieting event. It was the first indication that the enemy's finest formation, the First Paratroop Division, was arriving upon the scene, and it meant that the fighting ahead would be of unprecedented ferocity.

During the afternoon of December 8, the 48th crossed the river west of San Leonardo and established a local bridgehead. At 1500 hours the R.C.R. crossed into the Regiment's area and prepared to drive to the northwest along the lateral road to capture San Leonardo itself.

This was a ticklish operation, and doomed to failure. During the next twenty-four hours several heavy counterattacks launched by the newly arrived paratroops struck against the left flank of the Regiment's bridgehead and caromed off to spend their remaining strength against the R.C.R. column. Time and again the R.C.R. recoiled, reorganized and set out once more for San Leonardo – each time to find itself under attack from the open right flank. On the night of December 9, the R.C.R. was forced to give up and withdraw to the south side of the Moro.

The enemy counterattacks had been almost fanatical in their attempts to smash the bridgehead. On the circumference of the little pocket held by the Regiment there were not less than eleven separate German assaults during the thirty-six-hour period that ended on December 10. Most of these attacks were in company strength, but three at least were mounted on a battalion basis. They were supported by the most concentrated artillery fire, and by the S.P. guns and tanks which were patrolling the crest. Nevertheless, the bridgehead held. The newly arrived German reinforcements that were to have driven the Canadians back across the Moro expended the bulk of their strength in a useless effort to destroy the Regiment's foothold at the river mouth, while at San Leonardo the rest of the Division made good the crossing and was soon ready to strike north for the Ortona lateral road.

On December 10, belatedly, the enemy commander recognized the error of his concentration against the coastal bridgehead, and withdrew northward towards Ortona with the Regiment hard on his heels.

This then was the outward shape of the Moro battle. In the messages that pass from battalion to brigade and on down the line, a regiment in action consists not of its ultimate constituents – men who bear certain names, talk in a certain way, think in a certain strain, and feel with all the power of their living tissue – rather a regiment becomes only the sum total of its corporate acts. Those who direct the battle dare not think, or are prevented by the very nature of war from thinking, of the individuals who make the whole. And in aftertimes, when war is history, the men who write the histories tend to forget also that regiments are built of men, and that a regiment has real existence only as far as the multitudes within it live – and die.

In the valley of the River of Blood, men lived and died in many unremembered ways. For them the battle of the Moro held no coherent pattern, and that struggle was formless except in so far as events impinged directly on each man's eyes. No soldier amongst the five hundred who took part saw more than minute fragments of the picture that was sketched on the battle maps and written in the records. And yet these fragmentary glimpses which were the sole lot of the individual fighting man are truer things, have more to tell of war, than all the histories of battle compounded into one.

Few of these details deal with the efforts of men to kill each other. Rather they deal with the efforts of men to survive the struggle, and yet more important, to help the Regiment itself to go on living.

Men remember the Regimental Aid Post, for example.

It had been established in a low-roofed house on the south lip of the escarpment, and there, Capt. Charlie Krakauer, the Medical Officer, laboured in a welter of confusion and turmoil, and fretted because he could not move his Post across the river, closer to the places where the wounded lay. Krakauer and his sergeant, Charlie Reid, worked in a dimly lit room, cluttered with stretchers, with smashed fragments of furniture, and heavy with the smell of blood. A section of British engineer troops, who became Cockney angels of mercy in these terrible days and nights, brewed endless gallons of black tea to give the wounded warmth, and to give the unwounded new strength.

And the regimental stretcher bearers, many of whom, originally in England, had been sent away unwanted from the rifle companies, now showed themselves peers in bravery and strength to any rifleman who ever wore the decorations of courage on his breast. By day and by night these men made their way across the valley, going forward to the lead platoons, and beyond if necessary, to bring in their wounded comrades. There was no transport to help them. Men's muscles served alone until they stiffened into outright disobedience. Fighting the mud, the slimy slopes, the river and the tangle of shell-torn debris, the bearers made their agonizing passages, some of them ten times in a single night. For them there was no rest, and no refuge in a slit trench when the enemy guns spoke out. For them there were only the unending journeys into danger, and return to momentary sanctuary before once more setting forth. Perhaps the hardest thing to bear was the constant change of tension, for this is one of the most destroying strains that a soldier may face. Those who are constantly under fire can armour themselves with apathy. But those who must come and go, knowing a steady sequence of relief, followed by exposure to new terror, those are the ones who pay the greatest price.

The regimental stretcher bearers were not alone in the Moro battle. A section of bearers from the 4th Field Ambulance was always attached to the Regiment during action. The duty of this section (equipped with jeep ambulances) was to evacuate the badly wounded from the R.A.P. to the hospitals in the rear. At the Moro, the men of the 4th Field section saw their duty differently, and they spent their time working *forward* from the R.A.P. on foot, helping to carry the wounded back from the very perimeter of the bridgehead. Their courage, though not flamboyant, was of a sort to make men wonder at them. One stands out in memory, a coloured lad, who suffered the most obvious attacks of terror each time his duty called him forward; and yet he never failed in his self-imposed task. During the five days in the bridgehead the men of the 4th Field Ambulance earned a place within the Regiment, and no soldier in the infantry would have denied it to them.

Amongst those who used the river valley for their promenades were the signallers. Their task in battle was never easy. Attached to each company were the wireless men and telephone men, and the moment that a company stopped moving, the wire was laid. It was laid, and laid and laid again, for hardly an hour passed without that thin metallic contact to the rear being ripped apart by shells, or cut by enemy patrols. Communications had never been so vital, or so difficult to maintain, as at the Moro battle. Cpl. Jess Garrison and his section laid the first line across the Moro within the hour that the bridgehead was established, and when the line began to go 'out' Cpl. 'Mick' Mulvale and his men mended it. Prowling through the darkness they spliced the broken ends, leapt to the shelter of swollen ditches while barrages thundered down, then crawled out to repair the new damage. There was no end to the struggles of the signallers while the battle raged and many of them saw the end of all their battles on the Moro front.

Daylight crossings of the river were almost suicidal since the valley was enfiladed from the left, and under full enemy observation. Nevertheless, daylight crossings were made almost continuously. Signallers and stretcher bearers made no distinction between night and day. The men of the pioneer platoon performed prodigies of valour as they tried to build a tank diversion over the swollen river, under direct mortar and machine-gun fire.

And other men were there as well.

Rations and ammunition had to go forward and this was the task of the company quartermaster sergeants and the drivers of the unit's trucks. Jeeps brought the supplies up to the south bank of the river, but from there they were carried on men's backs, or on the backs of mules. A dozen mules had been attached to the Regiment, some of them complete with Indian muleteers, who understood no word of English but who were possessed of great understanding and courage. On many occasions, muleteers and quarter-masters traversed that blighted valley on their bellies, dragging the mules behind. Casualties were heavy both to the animals and men, but the soldiers of the fighting companies never went short. Even mail, that precious stuff from England and from Canada, was carried forward – and with it an even more precious commodity, the issue rum. The Regiment gained a reputation at the Moro in connection with its rum. Some irate staff officer in a far distant base later reported that the Hastings and Prince Edward Regiment had managed to draw, and presumably to consume, as much rum as the rest of the division.

Support company fought at the Moro, too. The carrier platoon served as infantry and served well. The mortar platoon fired eleven tons of three-inch high explosive, most of this from the pits at the gravel quarry; and every round – each weighing ten pounds – came across the valley on men's backs. The anti-tank platoon accomplished the impossible in manhandling two guns over the river, and in so doing, greatly aided the Regiment in pushing forward out of its tank-proof locality for the drive inland. The sense of security given to the infantry soldiers by the presence of those two guns can hardly be exaggerated.

Without exception, every element of the Regiment played its part. From the cooks who stayed over the stoves during heavy barrages so that the men up front would have hot food, to the padre who spent the entire week moving about amongst the forward companies, getting in the wounded, and generally doing those essential tasks that the fighting men had no time for; from bat-men-runners to the senior officers, each man did his job. There was 'Junior' Mansfield, an eighteen-year-old jeep driver who knew that the unit was desperately in need of some kind of transport in the bridgehead. On December 8, Mansfield quietly got into his little vehicle, drove across the river through the shell-torn diversion just established at San Leonardo, and came roaring down the lateral road through the enemy positions and under constant fire to arrive somewhat shaken but intact within the regimental perimeter. There Mansfield remained until the action ended, and his jeep moved ammunition forward and brought the wounded back under conditions that seemed to guarantee his early destruction.

But these selfless efforts of the men in the unit were matched by the efforts of those arms placed in support. The massacre of the attacking Germans was in large part due to the assistance of the F.O.O.s and the gunners of the Second Field Regiment and of the 4.2 mortars. The F.O.O.s also became Hasty P's at the Moro battle. Men like 'Trapper' Elliot, Frank Fullerton and Roscoe Zavitz wore the Artillery badges, but their loyalties belonged equally to the Regiment – and they served the Regiment as well as any man who was upon its official rolls. Moving forward to the very edge of the perimeter, these men controlled the guns so closely and so accurately that they could bring shell fire down within one hundred yards of their own troops, and full upon the assault waves of the enemy. Often enough infantry soldiers take a superior attitude with artillery men, considering them a necessary evil. After the Moro the Regiment thought of the Second Field as its good foster brother whose strong hand could always be called upon to smite the Hun; and the same feeling applied equally to the men of the S.L.I. mortar company.

At this distance in time most of the individual moments that remain alive in memory deal with illogical events, with the anomalies.

There was Cpl. Doug Ruttan of Dog company who gave his life in a quixotic attempt to save the life of a mule that had served the company valiantly through the long days. Caught under a sudden enemy barrage the mule was standing helplessly in an open field until Ruttan, abandoning the shelter of a crumbled house, ran out to save it. He caught the distrait animal by the halter and had dragged it almost to the safety of the building when a shell dropped close beside him, and Ruttan died. Perhaps his action was not quixotic after all, for it was the expression of a humanity that was a rare thing in the places where men let each other's blood.

Memories of the tragic survive in odd juxtaposition with the ridiculous, for this is how things were.

Charlie company suffered severely in its initial crossing of the river and many of its officers and senior N.C.O.s were killed and wounded; yet the particular incident that sticks in the memories of this company is not tragic, but absurd. The company had made good its crossing and was crouching in the shelter of the far bank when it began to run out of ammunition. Someone became a little panicky at the prospect of being left defenceless on the enemy's side of the valley, and called out to the acting company commander, "We're out of ammo on the Bren, what the hell do we do now?"

Lyall Carr, who had taken over Charlie company after Capt. Les Yates was mortally wounded, racked his brain for a reassuring answer but before he could find one, an unidentified voice boomed out from a platoon off to the left.

"What do we do? Why, you stupid bastard – make military noises!"

It was a long way back to the English schemes when Military Noises were an essential part of every battle game. But every man remembered, and Charlie company found itself grimly amused at its own predicament.

The men of the carrier platoon remember little enough of the agonies of their experience, but none has forgotten a moment during that first night when tension had mounted to a pitch almost beyond human endurance. They remember the private who went under the joyous name of Three-star Hennessey.

Hennessey always strove to live up to his name and in the midst of that dark battle he went off on the prowl and uncovered a supply of particularly excellent vino. Coming back through the vineyards in pitch darkness he announced himself by screaming at lung-top "The Germans are coming!"

The effect upon the overstrained men of his platoon was indescribable and the momentary paralysis was so complete that no one even raised his hand to clobber Hennessey when he at length crawled into the platoon area, stood up, and announced in his slow drawl: "Relax fellows. I just found the best damn bug juice in Italy, and I wanted you to be in the mood to enjoy it some!"

Dog company men remember the wild frustration of Pte. Greene, a Huron Indian who was one of the company Bren gunners, and avid for blood. Greene wore heavy glasses, without which he was almost blind, but this handicap did not normally disturb him and he kept the glasses polished to perfection against the day when he could lay his gun upon the enemy. His opportunity came on the night of the crossing, when his platoon found itself amongst a company of thoroughly disorganized Germans. It was Greene's moment and he dropped to the ground, cocked his gun and then discovered that his glasses were so steamed up from the heat of his own excitement, that he could see nothing save a blur. Hurling the glasses from him with a curse that was half a sob, he emptied the magazine blindly, then turned to his companions and pleaded, "Did I get one? Tell me I got one!"

But the fragments that remain are not all of this nature.

One of the sharpest concerns a bath parade held at San Vito while the Regiment was still engaged in battle. The bridgehead had been firmly established by this time, and the C.O. had arranged that each forward platoon should be withdrawn in rotation and sent to the rear area for a bath, clean clothes, hot food and a night's rest. This brief surcease from battle had a fabulous importance in men's lives and the chosen platoon that each day crossed the river to the rear was filled with the knowledge that for the space of twenty-four hours it would be immune from death. The shock then, when the enemy dropped a salvo of heavy shells full on the mobile bath at San Vito on December 16, was shattering. Five men died and fifteen more were injured in a single platoon. In terms of the total casualties suffered by the Regiment during the Moro battle, these figures are lost to sight. They have their importance because of circumstance alone. As it had been at Assoro, when a stray rocket shell killed as many men, after battle was done, so in this case there was a feeling in the Regiment that this was a particularly abhorrent thing. It unnerved even those who had become almost immune to the sight of violent death upon the battle field, for it told them that nowhere in the world they knew was there a haven.

THIRTEEN

Battle of the Bulge

T HERE WAS no respite after the enemy's withdrawal
from the immediate area of the bridgehead. Accompanied by a troop of tanks that had crossed at San
Leonardo, the Regiment drove north towards Ortona
keeping pace with, and sometimes ahead of, the main
advance up the inland road. Until December 19, the unit
remained in constant action, striving with its depleted
companies to push the enemy back to the grey ramparts
of the city that huddled high above the sea on the verge of
the plateau. It was a time of continuous effort and of
mounting exhaustion. The paratroopers gave no ground
that was not marked by death. Along the cratered track
leading back to the Moro the ambulance jeeps wove a
steady pattern and the attrition of the Regiment's flesh
and blood continued unabated.

By December 19, it had become clear that Ortona was
the key to any further advance towards Pescara. On that
day, the R.C.R. and 48th established a firm hold on the
Ortona-Orsogna lateral highway, on the heels of an attack
by Third Brigade. The Loyal Edmontons at once moved
through, turning east towards the coast. By evening of the
following day, the Eddies were in the outskirts of the city
and the savage street fighting which was to make the name
Ortona known to the world, had begun. Resisting with the
same fanatical tenacity which they later demonstrated at
Cassino, the paratroopers contested every house and every

alley and General Vokes realized that Ortona would not fall to direct assault without an agonizing and protracted effort. A new plan was devised to assist Second Brigade.

First Brigade was ordered to by-pass the city to the west and drive a long salient deep into the enemy lines, hooking east again towards the coast so that Ortona would be out-flanked and isolated.

Orders for the new attack reached the Regiment on December 22, as it rested in an olive grove near San Leonardo. On December 19, the unit had been withdrawn from its own coastal salient and the desperately weary soldiers had assured themselves of some days' escape from battle. There was to be no escape – only a brief interlude with its own particular horrors.

On the morning of December 22, the sun broke wanly through the grey rain scud. As the platoons picked up their mess kits and gathered about the cook-tents there were some who remembered that Christmas was just three days away. It was a time to think of the giving of presents, and of the receiving of them. One came. At 1000 hours a shell from a 21-cm. gun moaned over the scraggly olive trees and buried itself in the centre of the battalion area.

The concussion seemed of unprecedented violence and the blast tossed men about as if they were shocks of corn. A dark cone of mud thrust upward from the sodden ground and the acrid, filthy smell of explosives lay across the grove. Men some distance from the blast stood half stunned, staring at the crater where, moments before, the Regimental Aid Post had been. Now there remained only fragments of the equipment which alone in war's panoply is intended to heal rather than to destroy. And there remained only fragments of the doctor, Charlie Krakauer, of medical sergeant Charlie Reid, and of the medical orderly. It was a grim pre-Christmas gift, but only a token of what would follow.

The divisional plan directed the Regiment to 'burst out' from the front that had been established along the lateral highway, and to drive on for a mile to take the base of a

THE MORO AND THE WINTER BATTLES   Dec. 5 1943 – Jan. 30 1944 long thumb-like feature that ran northeast towards the coast road beyond Ortona. When the base of the ridge had been captured the rest of the brigade was to follow through, to reach the sea.

In its early stages the battle went well. Able company on the left and Charlie on the right advanced three quarters of a mile, behind a barrage, against intense machine-gun, mortar and artillery fire. By 1030 hours, both companies were within a few hundred yards of their objectives, but now the artillery could no longer help them, and the weight of the enemy fire increased. A squadron of tanks, held up by enemy mine fields, failed to arrive as planned, and Baker, swinging to the right of the enemy strong-points, attempted an assault without armoured support. The attempt failed, bloodily, but when two tanks belatedly appeared, the attack was renewed, this time with success. Overrunning the opposition, the forward platoon and the two tanks slaughtered the paratroopers where they stood, and only a few of the Germans remained alive to be herded to the rear as prisoners.

Dusk had fallen by this time and the impetus of the assault was gone. Thrusting far into the enemy lines, the Regiment was now exposed to attack from three sides, but though the Germans probed angrily all night long, they failed to break into the salient. They did, however, succeed in preventing the pioneer platoon from clearing paths through a second mine field in order that the tanks could assist in the next day's operations.

The day before Christmas was a cacophony of shell fire and destruction. The Regiment was on the feature which was its objective, but the enemy was still there, too, and could not be entirely dislodged. Able company, reduced to about a platoon in strength, was still chewing stubbornly at the machine-gun positions upon the left flank. The company knew a momentary elation when up from the muddy ditches to the rear loomed a huge and familiar figure. It was Alex Campbell, back from a long siege in hospital, and bellowing for action.

All four companies were now committed. Dog on the extreme right was waging its own private war. Baker had pushed well forward but was nearly surrounded by obstinate enemy posts that refused to be quieted until each man in them had been killed. Charlie, having suffered heavy losses the previous day, was somewhat in rear but still in contact.

It was time now for the 48th Highlanders to carry out their part of the attack. They came up through Baker company and by a combination of luck and good management, were able to move forward half a mile through a gap in the German defences without the enemy apparently becoming aware of their presence.

The brief spell of wan sunshine had ended on the 23rd, and the 24th was wet and bitterly cold with fine sleet driving into the shallow slit-trenches and into the gaping ruins where men huddled over their weapons. The few remaining areas of stable soil now relapsed into slimy wallows. The only transport was by mule; for tanks and jeeps alike became hopelessly mired. The salient was more than a mile deep, and its entire length was swept by sustained shell-fire. Carrying parties bringing food and ammunition forward staggered in the slime and slumped into water-filled ditches to escape the shelling. The new M.O., Homer Eshoo, carrying on Krakauer's tradition, moved his R.A.P. so far forward that it was under small-arms fire for a time, but Eshoo's audacity saved many men. That long and sombre journey to the base of the salient would have drained the last of life from the seriously wounded. Eshoo, although afflicted with a violent stomach ailment, worked continuously in his shell-pocked ruin of a house for forty hours, and took time off only to step outside the door and retch when his stomach rebelled completely. The padre and the stretcher bearers wandered about the confused front area, sometimes being trapped for hours at a time under crossfire or sustained mortar 'stonks'. With indefatigable patience and calmness, Kennedy moved from company to company, reassuring the uncertain, and reiterating his thematic phrase: "Take it easy lads! No matter what happens we'll look after you." By 'we' he meant the Regiment – and so great was the spirit of the Regiment that no man doubted him.

As Christmas Eve fell upon the field, the 48th found itself cut off in the enemy back area; still undiscovered but short of food and ammunition. In the rain-drenched darkness of that night, the R.C.R. moved forward to relieve them. Those who saw that long snake-line of men, soaked to the skin, drugged by fatigue, shorn of all desires save to drop and lie in oblivion in the yellow mud, saw the essence of what the Battle of the Bulge meant to all the infantry. In the morning the R.C.R. went a few hundred yards beyond Baker company's position but was so savaged by the enemy that it could not continue.

The Regiment remained in active contact on two sides through Christmas Eve. In Dog company area men crouched beside their silent weapons and listened half incredulously to the sounds of singing from the enemy trenches a few yards to the front. "*Stille Nacht...heilige Nacht...*" the words came clear, but there was horror in them, for they were a grotesque travesty on truth.

There was another episode of that day which cannot be forgotten. In the early hours a reinforcement draft, one hundred and sixty men strong, marched up into the salient to fill partially the gaps opened in the Regiment by the long battles. Many of these reinforcements were youths recently volunteered, and shipped overseas with hardly a modicum of training. They came up through the frightful chaos from San Leonardo to the Bulge, and at one place on the way, they saw the bodies of a full platoon of Canadian infantry lying beside their waiting graves by the roadside. But nothing had prepared them for the salient itself, and as they moved forward a heavy enemy barrage dropped full upon them causing heavy casualties. Strangers in hell, they had no one to give them strength, for they were not yet able to draw upon the spirit of the Regiment.

In the shattered ruin where the C.O. had established his forward H.Q. were fifteen Italians; men, women and young children. There was no time for gentleness. Abruptly they were herded out and sent towards the rear and safety – all but one man. He was the patriarch of the family, very old and blind. He sat in his carved chair, his hands clutching the worn wooden arms with an unbreakable tenacity, and would not be removed. Tears followed the corrugations in his cheeks, and his whole body trembled, yet he would not go. Men looking at him remembered that the crumbled piles of stone where they sought shelter from the blast of fire had once been homes; had sheltered other, gentler, people.

With the next dawn Christmas came to the salient.

At Able company headquarters, Bill Graydon came in to report. The H.Q. was in an old house, and a blasted one. As Graydon said his piece, a German quietly lobbed a grenade through the window. There was the white flash, the intolerable bang. Miraculously no one was hurt, but a huge vino cask in the corner was punctured in several places and the red wine ran freely out the door. The occupants of the building staggered outside to find the company mule, legs spread for better balance, sucking up the wine as it appeared. In that moment when the world was a crashing discord, the watchers forgot the war to gaze in fascination as the mule's legs spread out to broader angles and its eyes began to glaze. Not until several gallons of good red wine had vanished down its gullet did it collapse with a contented gurgle.

Later that morning what was left of Able company renewed its attack upon the Germans to the left. Alex Campbell led the company as he had done so many times before, and led it full into the heart of the German position before he crumpled and his great bulk fell motionless.

Christmas day of 1943 was any day for the men of the Regiment, any day to be survived and forgotten if luck and the Gods of war were on your side. There were many who did not survive it and when the bitter night had fallen and the rain swept again in driven sheets over the glistening mud, the guns cried out their mockery of Christmas Day.

There was but little place for love upon this field. Yet love was there. The love of comrades for each other, the sole redeeming element in the dark morass of human degradation which is war. It is a love too little known, too soon forgotten, yet of an incalculable power. In the battle which had begun at the edge of the Moro valley and which would go on into the long months ahead, this curious affection would become a vital shield against all things save death itself. Unwatched, often unrecognized, it grew in each man's heart to succour him during the days of his enforced bestiality.

For the Regiment, the Battle of the Bulge lasted until December 29. The drive to cut the Ortona highway north of the city did not achieve success, but the Regiment had done its part and during the ordeal in the salient it held the Bulge as a firm base in the face of a never-ending artillery and mortar barrage, and in the face of winter weather that was enough to melt the last strength out of men's bones. Then on December 29, Third Brigade passed through and there was a brief respite.

Until January 9, the unit remained in its positions subject to relatively light but steady shell-fire, yet able to feel that – by comparison with what had gone before – this was a holiday. The water filled slit trenches were abandoned and shelter of a sort was found for most of the platoons in the ruins of scattered farm houses. By companies the unit went back to San Vito for clean clothes, a few hours of relaxation and a bath. With that ability for adaptation which was now an integral part of them, men turned the ruins into homes. A few old blankets draped over shell holes; piles of straw spread in convenient corners; a blackened petrol stove made from a perforated can half filled with sand; and such oddments of Italian furniture as had survived the battle – these were the raw materials. Sufficient food, a little warmth, occasional dry clothes –

and above all, the knowledge that sleep was theirs – these were the things that mattered.

With the failure of the Eighth Army to reach Pescara, the pattern of the campaign on the eastern sector underwent another change. As the winter progressed, more and more effort was diverted to the western front and to the attempt to crash into the Liri Valley past the ramparts of Cassino. So, for a time, the Adriatic became the forgotten sector. It was doubly forgotten, for the whole Italian theatre was now beginning to suffer from the burgeoning preparations being made for the Second Front. There was a dwindling of supplies and of new formations to relieve the hard-pressed Allied troops in Italy; while the Germans on the other side of the line continued to reinforce. Early in the winter the enemy had twenty-seven divisions in the Italian struggle, far more than the attacking forces could muster; and the German High Command was being lavish with supplies for its troops. South of the line of battle the Allied commander was forced to suck the eastern front almost dry in order to strengthen his assault upon the western sector. So it happened that through the winter and the early spring of 1944, Eighth Army was reduced to a mere skeleton force, so overtaxed that half-strength battalions were holding fronts of two or three miles. This meant, of course, that the troops were forced to do the work of three or four times their actual numbers. In terms of the infantry, it meant that individual soldiers could expect no release from the exhaustion and danger of the battle line. And not only was there no release from battle, but the forward units had to be trebly energetic in order to delude the enemy into thinking that the threat of new offensive operations still existed.

From the opening of the Moro battle on December 5, until April 20, 1944, the Regiment was seldom out of close touch with the enemy, and never out of reach of the enemy guns. For five months it existed under the most adverse conditions of war. During this period there were more than four hundred battle casualties from a unit whose fighting strength was seldom much above six hundred. It was a time when each man believed that he and his unit had been utterly abandoned and forgotten, left to dwell in the filthy limbo of the Ortona battlefield forever. It was a time of shortages, when the guns of the supporting artillery were rationed to three shells per day, when mortars sometimes could not be fired because there were no bombs; when even some types of small-arms ammunition had to be conserved. Tanks could seldom be used because of the weather and terrain and so the full onus for maintaining pressure on the enemy fell on the back of the infantry soldier. For five months that pressure was maintained, and though there was no great victory to celebrate the results of this protracted period of attrition, the bare survival of First Canadian Division was surely victory enough. As for the Regiment, not only did it survive physically but the spirit too survived, outwardly undamaged and perhaps even strengthened by the long purgatory.

FOURTEEN

Winter Front

O N JANUARY 9, the unit moved forward to relieve the
48th Highlanders in the twin villages of San Tommaso and San Nicola. These little hamlets overlooked the
deep valley of the Arielli River – a valley which had
become no-man's land. In early January the villages still
bore the shape they had known for a thousand years. The
low stone houses with their red-tiled roofs crouched close
to one another on the crest of the valley wall. The narrow
streets, rough with old cobbles, still carried the stench of
mules and pigs and household refuse. There were even a
few civilians left, leading mouse-lives, it is true, but at least
living in their own homes.

Three times during the long winter the Regiment found
itself occupying the two hamlets, and as the months
passed men saw the villages gradually disintegrate; withdraw into the multilated earth and disappear. The old
walls crumbled. The roofs collapsed. The cobble street,
deep in mud now, was shattered and destroyed. The very
smells changed, for now there was only the stench of death
and of the death-bringers – the shells. Buildings of any
kind grew few and far between on the Arielli front, for the
location of each farm house, or village home, was known
to the enemy artillery. The enemy also knew – for he too
was suffering from the weather – that soldiers would risk
their lives to exchange their water-logged slit trenches for
the dubious shelter of a broken roof. The Germans

suffered from no such shortage of ammunition as plagued the Canadians, and they set out, methodically as is their nature, to destroy every building their guns could reach.

It was during this winter that the men of the unit developed to an acute degree the capacity to estimate the relative strength of a building at a single glance. Without conscious thought a new arrival would note the wall thickness, the firmness of the mortar, the number of rooms between him and the enemy, the number of rooms over his head. It became routine to approach *any* building with caution, paying attention to the number of fresh shell craters that surrounded it and to the proximity of a crossroad, bridge or other obvious aiming point for the enemy guns. The last fifty or a hundred yards of open ground leading to a building were frequently covered at a dogtrot, and if it was not always a physical sprint, it was at least a mental one. In many cases the men were compelled to keep indoors during daylight, for any movement outside would bring an inevitable 'stonk', as a sudden salvo of enemy was called. Minor tasks, like getting a pail of water, or performing a natural function, tended to be highly exciting during daylight, and in the Regimental files there is one really virulent tirade by a quartermaster sergeant who was three times mortared off the make-shift seat of a make-shift back-house, and who wished the Authorities to know that he was going to apply for a post-war pension for a condition of enforced and permanent constipation.

Visitors were seldom welcomed at the *casas* of the forward troops, but they came nevertheless. Officers from Brigade or Division would rumble up in their jeeps, which they would sometimes leave parked in full view of the enemy. These officers seldom stayed long enough to reap the inevitable whirlwind, and they could not seem to understand why they were greeted so dourly.

Another unhappy pastime engaged in by certain higher commanders consisted of sending a few tanks, a troop of anti-aircraft guns, or a section of heavy mortars, into the forward area of some infantry company. The guns or tanks would fire a hasty salvo at the enemy and hurriedly withdraw. A few minutes later Jerry would retaliate with a thundering flight of shells, full upon the unfortunate infantry who owned the place.

No matter how long a man is exposed to shell-fire, he never develops an immunity to the fear of it. Machine-gun or rifle fire can be terrifying, but it cannot compare with the sensations that fill the heart at the sound of the high throbbing whistle of an approaching shell or mortar bomb. On the Ortona front there was a period of five months when the Regiment was never out of reach of these sounds.

This constant shelling affected men in odd ways. Cpl. Jack Hill had worked out a game to play when under shell-fire, a game that helped him bear the brutal strain of wondering when his turn would come. Crouched in his slit-trench he would take a leaf from a note-book and sketch in the positions of the trenches of his section. Then he would listen to the howl of the approaching shells and try to guess where they would drop. A pencil point upon the paper was his marker, and after the explosion he would poke his head up to see how closely he had guessed the point of impact. He called his little game 'Dots and Spots'. One day on the San Tommaso front the point of his pencil fell close to the slit-trench of one of his men. Hill's guess had been accurate. When the fumes lifted, the man lay buried under the debris of the explosion with a broken back.

Several soldiers raced to help him, but they had not yet uncovered him when a second salvo forced them to throw themselves on top of the wounded man. They were packed into the tiny trench in layers, and the man on top was exposed to the full blast of three explosions. For him it was the breaking point, and he leapt up to run crying across the bleak and muddy fields while the contagion of his panic gripped the soldiers who still cringed in the slit-trench.

There was not a man in the forward companies, and

few enough in the rear echelons, who did not have a similar experience – sometimes repeated a dozen times over – during the winter. But these were the routine events. There were others that stood out above the rest for the special quality of the horror which they brought.

On one occasion the enemy brought down a heavy barrage of phosphorus shells. These are amongst the most savage weapons known. The shells, on impact, fling flaming pieces of white phosphorus about for yards, and any of these fragments that strikes a man will cling and burn through flesh and blood and bone with equal ease.

One such shell fell on the slit-trench of Sgt. 'Holly' Hollingsworth. The platoon runner 'Sucker' Towns died mercifully in the instant. But 'Holly', though frightfully burned, and burning still, remained alive. Others of his men ran to help him, but the sergeant held them off crying "Don't come near me, boys; don't let this stuff get on you!" They did what they could with buckets of water, but the smouldering thing before them could not again become a man despite the strength of his spirit. Hollingsworth died in agony, and left behind him in the Regiment a memory of great horror, but of greater courage.

Yet most of those who remained alive were able somehow to withstand the never ending strain. They joked about the shelling or grumbled about it in the same way they grumbled about the quality of the food – which was atrocious. They did not become immune to fear, but they drew upon their own strength to the uttermost limit, and when that failed they drew on the strength of the Regiment itself. Not many broke, though many died.

Men did their jobs. There was Bill Fuller, a driver in the carrier platoon, who set out on foot one day, carrying the heavy dixie filled with hot soup up to his comrades in a forward post. They tell how Bill came stumbling into the broken house his eyes filled with tears of helpless rage. He was so angry that he was incoherent and it was some time before the rest of the crew could get his tale. All the way forward, with the dixie lashed firmly to his back, Bill had been sniped at by an 88-mm. S.P. gun. As each shell arrived Bill had been forced to duck. The dixy had a loose lid, and every shell-burst sent a cascade of scalding hot soup down his bent back. It took strong arms to keep Fuller from dashing out of the house and staging a one-man attack upon the enemy.

Another incident concerns the Palm Sunday church parade in April. Ortona boasted a huge theatre and here the church-going Protestants of the Brigade gathered on Palm Sunday morning. The theatre was crowded to capacity by perhaps a thousand men. The service was about to begin when a heavy shell came crashing through the roof.

For long minutes it was impossible to see or hear. Clouds of plaster dust whitened the air and blinded those who crawled about amongst the falling debris. But when the confusion was resolved, it was found that no one had died, and of the thousand men, less than thirty had been badly wounded. The incident would have seemed miraculous had it not been for the fact that each soldier knew how unpredictable the effects of a shell can be. The aftermath came when Goforth met his opposite number, the Brigade's Catholic padre, at lunch that day. Goforth, still somewhat shaken, asked the priest how *his* service had fared, and whether he had 'heard anything unusual' (the Catholic church was only a stone's throw from the theatre). The priest was Irish, and with a smile, he replied that his service had gone smoothly enough, and that he had heard nothing out of the ordinary, except, perhaps, a faint suggestion of the sound of angels' wings!

In the last days of January the Regiment was committed to a tragic action that cost it as many casualties as any battle fought during the war, and that accomplished nothing useful that could be comprehended by most of the soldiers who took part.

On January 22 the Anzio landings had been made in an attempt to bring about the long-deferred fall of Rome. But once more the enemy had met the sea-borne forces in such strength that the landings were not only ineffective, but the landing forces were in grave danger of being driven back into the sea. At the same time Fifth Army was again attempting to break into the Liri Valley and drive north to link up with the Anzio landing; but the Germans at Cassino stood solidly and could not be dislodged. The entire campaign on the west coast, involving the major strength of the Allied armies in Italy, was stalemated.

On the east coast the enemy had become aware of the weakness of the remaining Eighth Army units, and German divisions were preparing to withdraw from the Adriatic area and move west to break the stalemate. It was imperative that these formations should not appear at Anzio and so it was decided that the overstrained troops on the east coast must make a superhuman effort to hold the enemy in position. On First Canadian Corps front the job fell to the Hastings and Prince Edward Regiment. On January 30 the unit moved out of the gullys before San Tommaso, to launch a daylight attack across the 2000-yard-wide flats of the Arielli plain, towards distant Tollo village.

From the start, those who took part in it were aware of the hopelessness of the battle. A single battalion attacking on a divisional front against at least a full enemy division was obviously doomed. Nevertheless, the attack was made with great courage and élan. Some of the tanks of the supporting squadron actually reached the enemy advance positions and for a short while ran wild amongst them, but before the battle had lasted many minutes, the enemy retaliated with one of the most massive German artillery concentrations seen until this time in Italy. Intelligence reports showed later that the full fire of at least two enemy divisional artillery groups was brought to bear upon the advancing infantry. The shelling was further thickened by the fire of dozens of mortars and rocket projectors, and the whole of the flat 'killing ground' before the enemy's commanding positions was crisscrossed by the fire of at least fifty machines guns sited on fixed lines, or on observed targets.

Considering the circumstances it was incredible that any of the attacking infantry managed to escape, but many of them did, and by nightfall they had crawled back to the relative shelter of a complex of narrow gullys near their starting point. It was a Regiment of shaken men who waited that night out while the whole of Support company, assisted by Goforth and the stretcher bearers, worked until midnight evacuating the casualties.

The enemy believing reasonably enough that this insane attack had been completely crushed, celebrated the victory by a heavy shelling of all the forward positions and of the routes along which the wounded were being removed. It was a night of turmoil and agony, but the morning brought with it the incomprehensible order that the attack must be repeated – again in daylight, and over the same ground!

Although this was in many ways one of the Regiment's most terrible hours, it was also one of its greatest. By this time every man in the unit recognized the suicidal futility of renewing the battle, for every man had already been exposed to the destroying weight of the enemy's defence. Nevertheless, the Regiment went out again into that flat arena of destruction, and no man held back though all understood what the inevitable results must be.

The enemy must have watched incredulously as the attack began. But he had ample time to repeat his performance of the previous day and to amplify it. Mortar bombs fell so thickly amongst the advancing troops that their movements were obscured in the rolling dust of the explosions. The few remaining tanks fell early victims to anti-tank mines, to 88-mm. gun fire, and some even to ordinary shell-fire.

Still the infantry struggled forward in an inferno that cannot be adequately described. The lead platoons made good two or three hundred yards across the flats before Kennedy, watching in agony from an observation post as his Regiment was destroyed piecemeal, refused to carry on the murderous farce and issued orders for withdrawal.

Under cover of smoke the men came back – those who survived. And again, all that night, the stretcher bearers and carrying parties moved towards the rear with their burdens of mutilated and dying men. The battle of Tollo Road was over.

It cost the Regiment one hundred and twenty-two casualties from the rifle companies which had already been reduced by the long pre-Christmas battles to less than three hundred and fifty fighting men. Physically it broke the Regiment's back, yet that sacrificial and futile battle did not shake the spirit of the unit nor weaken its morale. There was a bitter pride in the fact that the Regiment had been chosen to make the sacrifice, but it was a twisted and feverish pride. It focused the eyes of the unit inward upon itself, for there was the certain knowledge that the outer world would see this episode only as a routine defeat, and would never know nor understand, how great a battle it had been. Far from destroying the Regiment, Tollo Road lead directly to the greatest victory the unit ever won – but that battle was still far ahead.

Meanwhile the battalion returned to the routine of the long winter. It went back to the business of being shelled and not being able to reply. It went on with the task of pretending to be three or four regiments, instead of the skeleton of one.

Reinforcements came forward slowly, and in inadequate numbers. In February a band of sixty arrived at San Vito and were initiated into the new life by a barrage that killed several of them and wounded many more before they even saw the Regiment. Support was reorganized as an infantry company in order to ease the growing strain on the survivors of the rifle companies. The strain grew daily heavier for every day more and more patrols were sent out in an effort to convince the Germans that Eighth Army in the east remained a threat. The seriousness of the real position could be recognized from the fact that, behind the thinly held front line, strong-points were being built so that if the Germans ever realized how weak the opposition was and attacked in force, there would be some faint hope of slowing them when they broke through.

During the first three months of 1944, it was the patrols that carried the heaviest load, and the patrols were made up of men from all the rifle companies and from Support as well. Day by day, night by night they went out. Fighting patrols, reconnaissance patrols, ambush patrols, standing patrols – there was no end to the patrol duties.

There were hundreds of these little actions that were casually reported in the press of the world during that winter with the laconic words: "The Adriatic sector remains quiet, with only local patrol activity."

"I remember an officer who was sent out one night with a patrol to have a look at an enemy strong-point across the Arielli, called 'Bluebell'," runs an account written by the padre. "It was a horrible night, rain and sleet and mud, and pitch dark, and the patrol couldn't even find its way across the mile of no-man's land. It came back without having achieved success, and was ordered to do it all again the next night, and to get results. I went along this time, part way. Just after dark we made our way through the outposts and out to a deserted farm building where we were to wait until midnight. I spent most of the waiting period talking to the officer. He was absolutely certain that he was going to be killed, but he was quite calm and matter-of-fact about it.

"At last they went on, leaving me and a stretcher bearer in the empty house to wait. We spent the time getting our bandages ready and trying not to think about the others. It was only an hour until the patrol returned. They had run smack into a German ambush about half-way over the valley and the officer had been killed instantly. Several of our lads were wounded, one of them very seriously. He was a chap called Thomas, only eighteen years old and the pet of his company. Mike Gahagan, that tough old character, carried Thomas all the way in on his back. The lad was suffering horribly. When we stripped him at the farm building we found a bullet hole in each shoulder, but he kept complaining of a terrible pain in his stomach, and it wasn't till later we found one bullet had been deflected by the bones and had passed down the full length of his body.

"It was a mile back to the nearest R.A.P. and still pitch dark, with several deep ravines between us and safety. We couldn't get him out until first light. I don't think I ever felt quite so helpless as I did that night, waiting for dawn and trying to help the boy. He was such a kid. From time to time, the pain would come over him again in a great wave and he would scream 'I can't stand it! I can't stand it!' Tough old sweats like Gahagan and Jack Hill stood by helpless, looking as if Tommy had been their own son. We got him back at dawn, but it was no use. He died at the Field Ambulance."

Goforth's account could be the story of many of the infantry patrols. There were minor differences. Sometimes there were no casualties, sometimes it was the enemy whose blood ran in the night. But there was always the tension, the never ending tension.

On March 5, a message from Brigade ordered the Regiment to bring back a prisoner that night, and the scout platoon drew the assignment. The patrol, fifteen men strong, started after dark and wound its way down into the trough of the Arielli.

Their leader was Jimmie Fraser, known affectionately as 'Fearless' Fraser. Jimmie led the way across the broad valley while the artillery fired a rolling barrage to keep the Germans in their trenches. The darkness, and the closeness of the barrage resulted in confusion, and when the shelling ceased, Fraser and Sgts. Lusk, 'Punchy' Davis and Ray Lapalm found themselves isolated in what appeared to be an abandoned garden. The enemy was close at hand, perturbed by the shelling and suspicious. The four men huddled close to the ground as a German section opened fire on the shadows and began hurling grenades at imaginary intruders. Cross-fire from two machine guns swept the garden and the bullets seemed so close that Lusk automatically turned his head sideways to give them clearance. It was no place to linger, but as the four slithered away, one of them caught his foot on a trip wire and the party was instantly bathed in the sick radiance of a flare. They froze, and went miraculously undetected as the flare burned out.

Clear at last of the cross-fire they huddled in a shell hole within six feet of an unoccupied enemy slit trench. Dimly visible some twenty feet away was a stone shack and beside it a nervous German sentry who kept firing quick bursts from his automatic carbine. Fraser decided that this was the man to suit Brigade and was about to give the signal for a four-man charge when Lusk, glancing over his shoulder, was horrified to see two Germans standing by the empty slit trench staring down at him in the momentary hesitation of complete surprise. Lusk's reactions were instantaneous and he cut the Germans down before they could raise their weapons.

The dead men were too heavy to bring back across that valley, so the patrol contented itself with searching the corpses for papers, and removing the tunics with their identification markings. So the patrol withdrew, its mission done. No one had been killed, and with only two men wounded, the scouts felt that they had made an adequate bargain for the night's work.

After a single day's rest, they were again sent out. This time a sergeant and three men were ordered to penetrate the enemy lines in darkness and to lie up in a house in the German rear area, from which they could observe and record the routes and times of the enemy supply parties. It was not an attractive assignment and the three platoon sergeants drew cards to see who got it. Lusk was the unlucky one. Darkness came all too soon, and Lusk with his three companions set out accompanied by Fraser and a small protective group.

Artillery support had been arranged if it was needed, but Fraser, with unpleasant memories of the previous night, chose to do things differently. In absolute silence he led his men down the gulley to the coast. The beach was known to be heavily mined, but the patrol crawled along the line of low tide mark, reasoning that no explosives would have been placed so near the water. In pitch darkness they made their way, yard by yard, under the guns of the enemy coast positions. When Lusk estimated they were well through the lines, he bade good-bye to Fraser's group, and with his three men set off inland. Dawn was threatening when the four found the skeleton of a house, almost roofless and badly holed by shell-fire. Into it they went, and up a rickety ladder to the remaining fragment of a loft. First light came, and the patrol discovered itself only thirty yards from a larger building occupied by a platoon of Germans. To the south, Lusk and his men could look down at the backs of the enemy defences on the Arielli.

There was a long day ahead and Lusk issued his orders. "If *Tedesci* come in here," he said, "count how many there are. If there's only three or four, let 'em have it. If there's more than that, get out your handkerchiefs and wave like hell!"

As the light came clear the four got busy at their tasks, pinpointing enemy machine-gun and mortar positions on a large-scale map. They kept a close eye on the Germans nearby, but this platoon appeared singularly slothful – probably because it was in a reserve position. Occasionally a German would saunter out, relieve himself, and wander back into the building. Once, one of them came seeking firewood and prowled about the ruined shack where the four lay. He did not enter, and the fingers on four tommy-guns relaxed – if briefly.

Canadian mortaring began and the watchers experienced the singularly unpleasant sensation of being under their own fire – but the only casualties were to the German occupants of a nearby slit-trench which sustained a direct hit.

So the day passed, and only those four can say how long

it was. Dusk came and with it the problem of the return. As the darkness deepened, an enemy mule-train of four beasts and five drivers came forward and it inspired Lusk with an idea that, for sheer audacity, can have had few equals. He hustled his men out of the shack and, as non-chalantly as possible, the four joined the procession, some ten yards behind the mules, and ambled forward as if they were reinforcements going up the line. Unhindered, they followed the mules until they were out of sight of the German road posts and then they broke for the beach. Gaining it, they repeated the long and tortuous crawl to the mouth of the Arielli, and here, as the new dawn was making, they found Jimmie Fraser waiting to take them home.

The enemy patrolled as well but with nothing like the frequency of the Canadians, and when the Germans did cross to the Regiment's lines they were roughly handled. Several of the county men, deer hunters all, had become justly famous for their prowess as snipers. Men like Bernie Crawford, Don Stoughton, George Langstaff, and 'Rambler' Nobes, were in constant demand, for their abilities to wage war single-handed were phenomenal. The snipers were men of considerable individuality. Most of them were frankly eccentric, yet their eccentricities were probably only reflections of the tremendous strain which was their lot. New officers sometimes failed to understand and make allowances. There was the case of an Able company officer, Wayne King, who once sent back an urgent request for two snipers to deal with infiltrating enemy on his flank. The company was in extremely close contact with the Germans and it was in a jumpy state of mind, almost afraid to breathe for fear of drawing an enemy attack.

The reaction of King and his men can be imagined when up the dark trail from the rear there came a great booming voice in full song, and the clump, clump, clump of heavy boots.

The sounds came to a stop outside the company H.Q.

house. The sentry whispered the night's challenge in a taut and stricken voice. He did not get the password in reply. Instead there was a somewhat alcoholic shout. "That Able company? Well where the hell is 'Cowboy' King? He sent for me."

King was furious and arrested the sniper, 'Rambler' Nobes, only to find that he could spare no one to escort him to the rear. There was nothing for it but to make Rambler his own guard, and send him on his way. Rambler took the incident as a supreme insult, for it was well known that he could kill more Germans when he was drunk than when he was sober, so he allowed himself to escape from his own custody and went on a three-day bender that was memorable even for Nobes.

Another excellent marksman was Sgt. Mike Gahagan. Major Carr, commanding Charlie company, once had occasion to call on Gahagan to deal with a troublesome German sniper. When Gahagan arrived, Carr was stretched out in undignified proximity to the ground by the edge of a field while the enemy sniper whanged away at him. Mike got into position nearby, then bellowed "Hey sir! Stick your ass up and draw his fire!" Meekly Major Carr obeyed and a bullet whizzed close over his posterior. "I think I saw him. Not sure." Mike yelled. "Do it again!" Once more Carr obeyed and this time Mike's rifle echoed the enemy sniper's shot – and the duel was at an end.

Eccentric types like these were the Regiment's own secret, for they were not appreciated in higher quarters. General Crerar's First Canadian Corps had now taken over command of First Division – and a reluctant First Division it was. The Corps personnel – most of whom had never heard a shot fired in anger – at once tried to make their weight felt. A deluge of trivial commands poured down on the fighting troops from the 'New Boys' – as Corps staff were called. Orders became filled with such gems of higher wisdom and authority as this:

"The hair on the head of all troops will be cut short. It will not be permitted to wear sideburns."

Winter dragged on and even late March saw no improvement in the weather. Mud, snow and driving rains remained each man's lot. Occasionally the Germans would fire propaganda pamphlets over the lines and these gaily coloured cards, showing lovely women on a golden beach, were labelled "Come to Sunny Italy". With a heavy Teutonic effort at subtleness the message on the other side read: "Well Fellows, it *is* nice here in Italy, isn't it? Much nicer than in Canada where Limeys and Yanks are stealing your girl friends."

The German propaganda experts would have been hurt and bemused at the laughter their attempts evoked. It had been a long, long time since most of the men of the Regiment had thought very much of girls at home. They were pleasant enough subjects for vague dreams, but no longer real enough to be of use to the enemy in his propaganda efforts. As for the Italian weather, it was only something to be endured without much comment, and without much conscious recognition of its vileness. And as one man said: "Who cares, so long as the Wops remember how to bottle sunshine for us?"

The Italians had bottled a good deal of liquid sunshine. Almost every house and farm had its hogshead of red wine in the cellar and for those who desired a finer product, there were the caches hidden by Fascists who had fled. One of the most memorable of these, discovered by the scout platoon in a manure pile, consisted of two hundred and forty bottles of vintage wines and old liquors. For a few weeks the scout platoon men would have won any popularity poll in First Division. But ordinary vino remained as the prime salvation of men's spirits, and the ruin of their stomachs. There was a thriving business in illicit distilling and the resultant brew was known as 'Steam'. One of the most able producers of this beverage was a Mohawk Indian, known inevitably as C.N.R. because, of course, he was a steam injun.

Occasionally someone in authority felt compelled to wage a temperance campaign. At an earlier date Angus

Duffy had made himself somewhat unpopular by visiting the buildings occupied by forward troops and turning his tommygun on the vino casks. It was said that after the R.S.M. had done his worst the gutters ran red with wine for two full days.

There was little else save vino to give life savour. Attempts to establish rest hostels at Ortona were not very successful, since the town was under steady shell-fire and the infantry preferred to stay home and be shelled where there were slit-trenches at hand. Leaves were a sad fiasco. The official leave camps at Bari were the most depressing and dismal places in South Italy. A leave consisted of a jolting hungry ride for hundreds of miles down the shattered coastal roads, enlivened by brief stops at British transit hostels. These were slightly better than the Italian refugee camps, but not much. And at Bari there was little enough to do. The Americans from the Foggia airfields had rounded up what female talent did exist and had bought up the few shoddy souvenirs. Most of the men who went to Bari returned early, and thankfully. Many of them had not realized before how vital a part of them the Regiment had become; how much it had become their home. Only when they were away from it, did they know from the depths of their nostalgia, how much that home had come to mean.

FIFTEEN

The Road to Rome

S PRING came late to the Adriatic sector, but when it
arrived it brought an almost miraculous transition.
During the first weeks of April the fabled Italian sun
returned to its rightful place and the seas of saffron mud
began to harden. The olive trees put out their first silvered
leaves and the shattered vineyards covered their scars with
new growth. Far to the west the snows on the great
Maiella massif began to withdraw into the clouds and the
winds that blew across the Adriatic were gentled by the
spring.

In the line positions in front of Ortona, men sat in the
sunny shelter behind the houses and idled in the spring
days. The war seemed to have become a victim of the
ennui of April and there was little activity on either side.
Sporadic shelling, a few patrols, the occasional soaring
flight of a group of Kittyhawks of the Desert Air Force –
these were the only remaining indications of the war that
had laid such an intolerable weight upon men's backs
through the long winter. The current had stilled itself and
the Ortona sector had become a backwater, disturbed only
by the mechanical actions of men who could not entirely
abandon the habits of long months.

Spring found great changes in the Regiment. The faces
that had been the unit's in Sicily had largely vanished, and
many of those that had replaced them had vanished in
their turn. Not more than two hundred of the men who

had sailed from England the preceding year were still with the battalion and for the most part these were of the administrative staff which, while it, too, had suffered casualties, had not been decimated, as had the infantry companies. The R.S.M. Angus Duffy was gone, and to replace him there was a different sort of man, Harry Fox – another outsider who had to make his way into the family. Fox was not alone. Officers, N.C.O.s and private soldiers from a score of other units had found their way to the Regiment during those desperate days when reinforcements were the vital need of First Division. These were strangers, come from their own regimental homes, each with its own background and atmosphere. They came to the Regiment and in a few weeks at the most, were Hasty P's. A few came with chips on their shoulders, from elite battalions of peace-time fame. Some came from ill-disciplined units that had been torn apart to fill the reinforcement quotas. Some came from fighting units as good as the Regiment. Many of them initially resented the fate which had taken them from their own comrades and familiar formations, and sent them holus bolus to this obscure farmer regiment in the mud of the Ortona battlefield. They came, some of them, with an ill-concealed attitude of disdain for the 'plough jockeys' as the men of the Regiment had been nicknamed by the R.C.R. and the 48th Highlanders. But they changed.

There was but one criterion for acceptance – that the stranger be a man. And if he was, then he was accepted without question, without reservation. Negroes, Jews, Indians, Ukrainians, Germans, even Italians, they came and they were taken in. They gave their loyalty and their love without stint, without limit. And so it was that though the human face of the Regiment was constantly changing, the spirit and the heart remained the same, for the newcomers gave what they themselves had received from the hands of those whom they replaced.

Bert Kennedy was originally a foreigner from the Grey and Simcoe Foresters and when, during the last days at

Ortona, he was badly wounded by a German 'S' mine, he was replaced by yet another outlander.

Major Don Cameron had come to the unit shortly after the Moro battle. He had been transferred from Third Division, then in England, at his own request in order to help fill the gaps created by the heavy officer casualties in First Division.

Cameron found full acceptance within a few days after his arrival. Posted to command Dog company, he spent his first day with it by taking out a three-man patrol and liquidating a German position that had been making a nuisance of itself for some time past. Returning to his company H.Q., dishevelled and a little thirsty, he found Angus Duffy, that arbiter of men's destinies, waiting in the little farmhouse. Duffy eyed the major critically, listened without expression to Cameron's casual account of the patrol, then made his decision. "You'll do" was all he said as he produced a water-bottle full of rum.

That was a masterpiece of understatement.

Cameron was in command when, on April 21, the Regiment left the Ortona lines for the last time. Back down the familiar roads again, past the burned-out tanks, the crumbled houses, and across the tortured land, the convoy rolled. The sun shone and the smells of spring were strong, yet not strong enough to obscure completely the sickly stench of rotting flesh from a thousand shallow graves.

The convoy rolled westward, then south, and those who had survived that winter felt an incomparable sense of release, almost of new birth. Now there was the quietude of bird songs, of laughter, of the soft syllables of peasant women standing by the roadside. It was a kind of silence after the fading and disappearance of the last hollow rolls of gunfire. It was the silence of life, after the cacophony of death.

Southward the convoy rolled. Across the Sangro down the route that had carried the unit into battle five months earlier.

It was a time of movement, and the battalion stretched

its muscles joyfully. A few days here, a few days there, and the transports fell into line and there was movement. The sun grew hotter. The mud on the roads caked, was pulverized and turned to the thick penetrating dust that had been so achingly familiar in Sicily. The troops wore handkerchiefs across their months and travelled stripped to the waist – their white bodies reddening in the welcome heat. There was gaiety and ribaldry and the vehemence of life which condemned men, pardoned when hope is past, can alone know. Even the staff contributed to the entertainment, though unwittingly, when one morning the Part One Orders bore a most remarkable entry in the stilted argot of staff language. Some typist had not been equal to the need.

LATRINES: All troops will ensure that faces are covered with soil after each person has deprecated.

After a week at Campobasso the unit moved on to Lucera in the Foggia plains. Here it went under canvas and the first mood of release began to wear off as it became clear that there was to be no long rest period, but only preparation for a new battle.

Rumour became the king of the hour and the rumours were wild. The battalion was going to the Pacific. It was to attack the coast of Greece; it was to do an assault landing above Rome. But if there is one thing a soldier does grow used to in war, it is rumour. The old sweats ignored the talk, and laughed it off. Time enough to worry on the day. Meanwhile they enjoyed the unaccustomed pleasures of the Lucera interlude. They went out on tank-cum-infantry exercises designed to give the green reinforcements battle training. At night they sneaked past the guard pickets and explored the scant delights of the countryside. Off parade, in daylight, they sat in the shade of newly leafing trees and somnolently yarned the hours away.

On May 5, there was a further move, this time across the mountains and for the first time to the western side of Italy. At Limatola on the Volturno River, a short thirty miles from Naples, the Regiment settled down to a week of intensive river-crossing schemes. Rumours had begun to jell, and it was becoming apparent that the Regiment was to take part in the new assault upon the fortress of Cassino, and upon the Gustav and Hitler Lines which blocked the Liri Valley and the approach to Rome.

Once more the pre-battle tension began to mount, yet this time it was overlaid by the intense excitement that came with change, with spring, and with the prospects of what was to be the greatest battle fought in Italy to this date. There were other alleviating factors – primarily the proximity of Naples and of the large cities of Avellino and Caserta. For troops who had been denied the entertainments of cities ever since leaving England, this was an opportunity to be exploited to the hilt. The fact that these cities were overcrowded with base troops did not make much difference, for the men of the Regiment were now adept at finding what they wanted.

During this period the unit acquired several new jeeps, urgently needed, since Canadian replacements of lost or damaged vehicles had become painfully slow. Officers en route to Naples supplied themselves with distributor rotor-arms for jeeps, the object being to return them with the rest of the machine attached. The methods used were various, ranging from outright theft to the inspired application of bottles of Canadian rye whiskey to the dry palates of American base officers. This was scrounging in the grand manner, and free of all stigma, for it was abundantly clear that the fighting troops had far more need of jeeps than did the pampered troops of base.

The Limatola interlude was a time of hectic activity for the chief regimental scroungers, the quartermasters. Despite the fact that most items of military equipment were in short supply, or not available, the unit was quickly re-equipped. Reinforcements, too, were brought up from the holding units at Avellino and though the Regiment was not up to war strength, it was much stronger in man power than it had been for half a year.

Never in its history was it in finer fettle than on the May

day when it made ready to move forward towards the battle line again. There was an effervescence in those days, and an unreasoned optimism that the war was on its last legs. The massive preparations that had been made for this new battle could not help but impress the troops from the Adriatic who for so long had fought their battles with so little.

On the night of May 11, Eighth Army launched its mighty attack upon the hitherto impregnable Gustav Line and on Cassino. Twelve hundred guns spoke out as one, and the distant roll of the almost continuous thunder echoed back to Limatola where men listened in the darkness, and gazed at the flickering northern sky in wonderment.

Reports of the success of the first assault began to arrive at once. On May 14, the convoy moved to battle.

The Gari River at the mouth of the Liri Valley had already been crossed and the troops of Thirteenth Corps had fought their way into and through the formidable Gustav Line. On Cassino mountain the Poles were suffering incredible casualties, but they were going ahead, and the German First Paratroop Division, so long the victor of Cassino, was giving bloody ground. The great assault was making headway as the second wave of Eighth Army, including First Canadian Division, prepared to take over and carry through.

On May 16, the Regiment moved out of the Gari River bridgehead through the town of Pignataro, just captured by the Indians. Supported by a squadron of tanks from the British 142 Tank Regiment, the unit was ordered to strike north into the disorganized enemy and fight its way to the great obstacle ahead, the Hitler Line.

Standing in the rubble heap that was Pignataro, it was hard for men to understand how any attacking force could have gone so far, or could hope to continue. Off to the right, and well to the rear of the advanced Allied troops, towered the crest of Cassino mountain with its battered monastery overlooking the entire valley of the Liri. Far-

LIRI VALLEY CAMPAIGN

May 17/25 1944

Cassino
Gari
River
GUSTAV LINE
Monte Cassino
2nd Polish Corps
May 18 Monastery
Piedimonte
Route 6
XIII British Corps
May 18
Airfield
Aquino
F. d'Aquino
May 23
2 C.I.B.
May 23
3 C.I.B.
May 23
Pontecorvo
5th Canadian Armoured Div.
May 24
To Rome
SCALE OF MILES

First Canadian Division
Pignataro
River
May 17
Balance of I C.I.B.
Hastings and P.E.R.
48th Highlanders
LINE
HITLER
May 23
Liri
MT. D'ORO
MT. MANDRONE
May 22
French Corps

ther north the mountains rose to the 8000-foot heights of Mt. Cairo, and then continued north, a ragged wall on the right flank of the attackers. To the left another wall of mountains rose between the Liri and the sea. Ahead there was only a flat expanse of farm lands, bisected by frequent gulleys and defended by the formidable Hitler Line. It seemed an impossible pathway into enemy country, overlooked on both sides by the towering cliffs still in German hands. It was little wonder that Cassino and the Liri Valley had, for generations, been used by half the military staff colleges of Europe, as the ideal example of an impregnable defence position. Impregnable it looked. Impregnable it had proved during the six months when Fifth Army threw its weight against it. Impregnable it should have remained...but it did not.

It was a variegated assembly of troops that had massed for the attack. In the western mountains the Free French Corps struck with regiments of Moroccan Goums, clad in flowing robes and anxious to remove as many German ears as possible with their long knives. In the centre an English division and an Indian division shattered the Gustav Line, while two Canadian divisions waited in reserve. On the right, the Polish Corps assaulted the famous monastery itself.

The breakthrough of the Gustav Line by 8th Indian and 4th British Divisions had produced a deep salient at the mouth of the long valley, but it was a most exposed and dangerous salient as long as the Germans controlled Cassino and could look down at the backs of the attackers. With a desperation and ferocity only matched by their opponents the Poles, the German paratroopers held Cassino hill until May 18 and during the two days between the 16th and the 18th, First Brigade was thrusting far forward out of the salient into a valley dominated by enemy observation posts.

The battalion's first contact with the enemy came almost at once. Clouds of dust combined with protective smoke screens to obliterate objectives and confuse direction. The battle quickly degenerated to the platoon and company level, and became a savage melee of infantry against infantry. Dog company, sent off to the left flank, got itself lost and finished the day fighting its own private war under the eyes of the 48th Highlanders. Charlie company, driving forward up a covered lane got so far in advance of the balance of the Regiment, that it was in danger of being cut off. German and Canadian sub-units became intermingled. Regimental jeeps and stretcher bearers hurrying forward to evacuate the wounded wandered into the enemy lines, then out again unscathed.

The Germans appeared to have unlimited supplies of shells and mortar bombs and they had complete observation from the hills to the east although Cassino itself was now partly obscured by Allied smoke screens. Any movement of the forward troops drew massive bombardments, and the Regiment suffered forty killed, or seriously wounded, in the first few hours.

The shapelessness of this battle resulted from the breakdown of communications. Wireless communications became largely impossible, not through mechanical difficulties, but due to frequency congestion resulting from the great number of units engaged in the operation. At one time both a German unit and the Regiment were simultaneously attempting to use the same frequency, and at all times several Allied units could be found on any given wavelength.

So the Battle of the Woods followed its own chaotic pattern and even after it was done, no man had a clear impression of its form. One thing only was certain, by nightfall the enemy had been forced off the wooded ridge behind Pignataro, and was again in full retreat. When dawn broke there was no contact and the unit marched on through the dusty haze in close pursuit.

The confusion of the running battle did not lessen until early on May 19, when the scout platoon, feeling its way through the heavy cover of dense vineyards and olive groves, came under intense machine-gun fire. A report came back at once to B.H.Q. "Have bumped the Hitler Line."

A great deal was contained in that succinct sentence. The Regiment had reached the final obstacle that blocked the Liri Valley and the approach to Rome. It was an obstacle that had loomed large in Intelligence reports all winter. Air photo reconnaissance and prisoner interrogations had built up a formidable picture of the defences that bore Hitler's name. For six months the enemy had laboured on that line, utilizing not only corps of local labour, but the best brains and man-power of the famous Todt Organization which had built the Siegfried Line and the Atlantic Wall. Neither expense nor material had been spared to make the Hitler Line impregnable. The full strength of the defences was not to be known until the battle ended, but enough was known on May 19 to give hesitation to the attackers as, all along the line from Pontecorvo in the west to Piedimonte in the east, the advance units of the pursuit reached the line and halted.

There was a pause in battle.

Behind the forward units, road-building bulldozers ground through the dry soil sending streamers of dust high into the sky. The transport of an army moved up toward the front along narrow, sunken trails, whose ditches were filled with the bodies of men, and the debris of defeat. Spring lay on the land, but it was overlaid with the autumnal wreckage of war. Hawks hung in the warm air and shifted uneasily in flight as unseen projectiles drilled tunnels of turbulence about them. On the ground, the corn fields were green and peaceful about the smoking ruins of houses and the stinking craters left by bombs and shells. The smell of death and the smell of life were inextricably intermingled.

The lull lasted from May 19 until May 23, and during that time Eighth Army gathered its strength for the next blow. Behind the lines the guns moved up and convoys carried forward supplies and ammunition. In the line itself the forward infantry lived through four tense and exhausting days.

The Regiment had reached the enemy defences just east of the road leading into Pontecorvo, the western pivot of the Hitler Line. A long, low tongue of land stretched out to the south from the high ground behind Pontecorvo, and in its first rush the Regiment gained a foothold on the tip of this tongue. Charlie company had pushed forward until its advance platoons were within thirty yards of the enemy barbed wire on the right. These forward platoons were under direct enemy observation and heavy machine-gun fire, but they consolidated their position and held their little salient. Dog company then went forward on the left, almost as close to the wire, and took shelter in the battered remnants of a group of farm buildings on the edge of the enemy's 'killing ground'. This well-named strip extended right across the front and had been swept clean of all cover. Houses had been dynamited into rubble, trees had been cut, and vineyards flattened. Every inch of the desolate strip was covered by a cross-fire pattern so designated that nothing could hope to cross it with much chance of survival.

As darkness fell on the first night, Jim Fraser and some of his scouts went out towards the wire. Crawling through a mine field, the six men reached the heavy forest of double-apron fence, crawled under it and moved close in upon a German machine-gun post.

The patrol's task was reconnaissance and it was not looking for a fight, but chance decided otherwise. Tom O'Brien, one of the ablest of the scouts, chose to rest his back against the wall of the concrete pill-box and at this moment one of the occupants stepped outside to relieve himself. As an aggrieved O'Brien explained later, "I had to shoot the...or he would have wet me down!" In the excitement that followed, the enemy post was wiped out and the scouts retired. They brought back with them vital information about the wire and its defences.

The Regiment lay under a venomous hail of mortar and

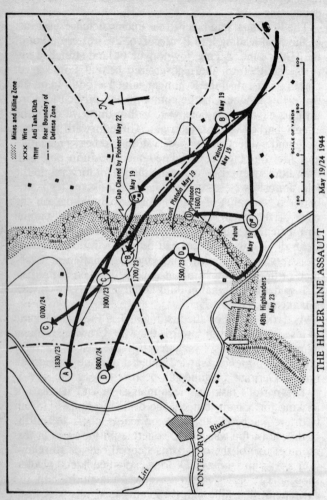

THE HITLER LINE ASSAULT   May 19/24 1944

Mines and Killing Zone
xxx Wire
Anti Tank Ditch
Rear Boundary of Defense Zone

SCALE OF YARDS
0   250   500

Gap Cleared by Pioneers May 22
May 19
B May 19
Patrols May 19
Scout Platoon May 19
D-Platoon 1600/23
Patrol
May 19
B 1700/23
C 1900/23
D 1500/23
C 0700/24
A 1830/23
D 0800/24
48th Highlanders May 23
PONTECORVO
Liri River

artillery fire – but it did not lie quiescent. The pioneer platoon reconnoitred and swept a tank route through the mine fields up to the enemy wire and past it, on Charlie company front – a remarkable feat, for it was done literally under the noses of the Germans, but without their knowledge. The Regimental snipers were the busiest men in the unit and the enemy in his permanent dug-out positions hardly dared raise his head by daylight.

On May 22, the plans for the great attack arrived. With some relief, and yet with disappointment, the Regiment found that it was not to take part in the initial assault. The main breakthrough was to take place on May 23, to the right and on the front of Second and Third Brigades. Meanwhile the 48th Highlanders, of First Brigade front, were to mount an immediate attack near Pontecorvo as a preliminary diversion, or, if it was successful, to provide a potential break-out point.

The 48th Highlanders' attack began at 1000 hours on the 22nd, but after a good start, lost its momentum. From their positions on the high ground, Dog company's platoons gave what help they could with covering fire, but it soon became apparent that the Highlanders were in serious trouble. The Regiment watched the battle anxiously for the Brigade plan called for the unit to move through the Highlanders' bridgehead and strike into the Hitler Line the following day. By nightfall it was clear that the bridgehead of the 48th could not be consolidated and the Highlanders needed help to hold what they had taken.

With dawn of the next day, the entire front exploded into action. On the right, Second and Third Brigade's assaults went in bloodily and with mixed success. On the left, the 48th were reported badly cut up and urgently in need of relief. The plan changed. At noon the Brigadier ordered the Regiment into action to relieve the 48th.

Cameron issued his orders for an attack that had already been well planned, and that had been thoroughly prepared. Dog company was told to relieve the 48th forward companies by striking directly along the Pontecorvo road until it was through the wire, then swinging right to capture the high ground which blocked the Highlanders. Meanwhile, Baker was to move up through Charlie, and with tanks in support, was to pour through the gap made by the pioneers and drive north along the ridge. Charlie was to provide fire support for the attack, while Able stood ready to exploit initial success on whichever company front this might be achieved. It was a simple plan and a good one, but there was a complication. Dog company's attack had to be made without benefit of tank, mortar or artillery support, since the 48th positions were obscure and the Highlanders might have been endangered by tank or artillery fire.

At 1400 hours Dog company moved. One platoon was sent up to the wire to give covering fire while a second platoon made the dash across the 'killing ground'. This assault platoon stood an excellent chance of being annihilated. While two sections went to ground and tried to keep the enemy quiet with Bren and rifle fire, the third section raced for the gap and plunged through it to fall into a narrow ditch where it took over the job of giving cover. So the sections went up, leapfrogging each other, and miraculously passed through. Once inside the wire, the platoon turned sharply right to find a commanding position from which it could assist the 48th. But the only commanding spot was already occupied by the enemy in company strength. It consisted of a heavily fortified group of farm buildings supported by steel machine-gun turrets in sunken emplacements.

The attacking platoon, commanded with great verve by Lt. Don Kennedy, had no time to assess its chances. There was no time to regret the absence of supporting tanks. The platoon was alone on the enemy side of the wire, and it could go nowhere but ahead. Firing Brens, rifles and tommyguns from the hip, the platoon went up the slope through the waving grass and was in the heart of the strong point almost before the enemy could react. The infighting was brief but savage – grenades and small arms at point-blank range; and then with an almost unbearable suddenness it was done. Thirty-two prisoners were gathered in and the victors took over the enemy's own deep fire-trenches in company with many of the defenders whose blood still ran red but whose faces were beginning to turn the ashen grey that marks the dead.

Dog company's reserve platoon came forward at once and the position was made secure. Contact was established with the 48th on the left, and that regiment's precarious situation was eased.

Meanwhile, to the right, Baker had attacked on schedule at 1500 hours supported by Churchill tanks from 142 British Tank Regiment. Here too, the attack went with almost perfect coordination. Storming through the gap in the wire, the infantry cleared the way for the tanks and when the lead platoon was forced to ground by heavy machine-gun fire, the tanks lumbered up and blasted the concrete and steel pill-boxes at point-blank range. The second Baker company platoon then leapfrogged ahead, supported by another troop of Churchills and in its turn, the second row of strong-points cracked and fell. By 1700 hours after only two hours of battle, the vaunted Hitler Line was pierced and Able moving swiftly up, passed through Baker and on to the height of ground behind the line.

It was a clean breakthrough, and as far as the higher command was concerned, a totally unexpected one. It was probably the most brilliant single action fought by the Regiment in the entire course of the war. For a total cost of eight men killed and twenty-two wounded, the Regiment had smashed through the Hitler Line, taken more than three hundred prisoners, and had killed or seriously wounded another hundred Germans. Later, looking over the enemy fortifications with their pre-fabricated steel pill-boxes, 75-mm. cannon in ground-mounted steel turrets, mine fields, wire entanglements, camouflaged mortar and machine-gun positions and concrete emplacements, the achievement took on new lustre. The lustre was not dimmed by the fact that farther to the right, Third Brigade had also penetrated the line, after the most severe and painful struggles, and with heavy casualties.

That night there was jubilation in the unit and a sense of pride so strong that it needed no overt demonstration. The British tank men who had shared the victory were equally stirred and from this battle there came a new tradition in the 142 Regiment – the wearing on its tanks of a small red patch bearing a Maple Leaf – the emblem of the Canadians. It was well won.

This was the shape of the Regiment's battle in its over-all scope, but there were a hundred other smaller battles – the struggles of the individual infantryman.

There was the story of a brand-new platoon commander riding into this, his first action, on a tank and firing his tommygun with juvenile abandonment. Careless of danger (he did not yet know that war was dangerous) he charged over the field and when he had exhausted his tommygun he did not bother to reload, but heaved it away and sent his batman to the rear to get another. Three times this happened, and at company headquarters an irate quartermaster handed out the third gun and with it a message. "You tell that silly bastard," the Q.M. roared, "that if he asks me for another gun I'll bring it up myself and shoot him with it!"

And there was Ken Smith, bespectacled, small and scholarly and strictly temperance, who took his platoon forward in the first passage of the wire and was cut down by a long burst of fire. Lying helplessly in a ditch he sent his sections on and would not have them stop to help him. When, hours later, he was evacuated to the R.A.P. he was near unconsciousness from loss of blood. Padre Goforth, striving to ease Smith's pain, prevailed upon him to take a mouthful of rum. Close enough to death to know it, Smith spat out the liquor muttering "My God! And people drink that stuff for fun!"

And there was the smallest man in Charlie company, a miniscule soldier inevitably called 'Tiny' who suffered for his size and who bore a grudge against the world because of it. 'Tiny' was detailed to escort a batch of eighty Germans to the rear and grumbling mightily that he was being discriminated against, he set off with his surprisingly willing charges. He did not take them far. Half a mile from the front, he found a secluded gulley and settled down to work off his resentments. It was a senior officer who found him. The officer came down the gully and was appalled to discover four-score Germans grouped in a tight circle, and in the centre of the ring a diminutive Canadian beating the tar out of an equally diminutive enemy soldier. When the fight had been stopped and the Geneva Convention explained to 'Tiny', he was asked for an explanation. "Shucks, sir," he said. "That's the first *Tedesci* I've ever found who was whittled down to my size. It was too damn good a chance to miss!"

For the R.A.P. the battle was a long red sequence. Homer Eshoo worked in his farm house hospital with a steady devotion to the wounded that knew no distinction between Canadian and German. The stretcher bearers laboured in their endless task. When a German sniper killed the lead man of the first assault section of Dog company and the rest went to ground, a stretcher bearer ran forward to the dying man, unarmed and unprotected and making no effort to find cover for himself. The sniper shot him through the head so that he fell upon the man he would have succoured.

And there was a signaller attached to a rifle company who had his radio in the room of a tiny house that had been heavily and continuously mortared and shelled for three days. On this last day an armour-piercing shell crashed into the front wall of the room and passed through the back one with a terrifying burst of sound and dust. The signaller leapt to his feet and in his ungovernable terror pulled an old newspaper over his head and wept. But, ten minutes later, he was back on his set passing the first reports of the battle. It was to men of his calibre, men who could endure what for them was unendurable, that victories belonged. It was men like this who broke the Hitler Line.

SIXTEEN

The Regiment at Rest

WITH THE shattering of the Liri fortresses and the destruction of seven first-line German divisions, the Italian front began to collapse. At Anzio the beleaguered garrison smashed out of the weakened ring, and on the coast the American Fifth Army moved north to link up with the Anzio defenders. In the Liri Valley, Fifth Canadian Armoured and the British Guards Division took up the pursuit and drove north towards the gates of Rome. For a few days the Regiment rested on the remnants of the Hitler Line.

There were strange things to see. There was the turret of a MK. V Panther tank sunk in a steel and concrete emplacement with its gun pointing to three dead Sherman tanks that it had killed. In the turret, fly-clouded and stinking, was the body of the German lieutenant who had laid the gun, and who had taken a direct hit from the armour-piercing shell of a fourth Sherman. There were the deep bunkers that Dog company had overrun, complete with underground chicken-pens and even with domestic items such as brassieres and women's underpants. There was a chapel on a little hill, gutted and almost utterly destroyed, and in it the bodies of a score of civilians, old men and women and young children. Death had been merciful to them. When the flames charred their bodies they had felt no pain, for they were already riddled with the bullets of German machine pistols. The tableau of the three dead tanks and the Panther turret had made sense in a horrible way; but this tableau made no sense. There was a bestiality here that was beyond comprehension.

There was much to see. The unused belts of machine-gun ammunition lying beside dead German gunners in the slit-trenches that had not been deep enough. The pathetic litter of old letters, and photographs of remembered faces scattered about the body of a youth whose bowels stretched from him like green and scarlet rope. It was a place of strange visions, for the war had passed on and the birds sang, and the green crops grew straight and lovely, their roots about the hidden evil of forgotten mines.

The mail arrived. One man sat on the ruined wall of an Italian house and near his feet were three Lee-Enfield rifles, up-ended on their bayonets in the dirt, with three helmets hanging from their butts. Three graves. And he read of the amusements of some onetime friends of his, men and women his own age, who had spent a happy Sunday in a maple bush in Ontario at a sugaring-off bee. He read, and tore the letter up and let the fragments settle at his feet. And in his diary he wrote with incoherent bitterness of the things he felt.

There were many men in the Regiment who shared that bitterness, for it was growing as the years passed.

Men deliberately turned away from thoughts of home, and listened to the world of fighting men instead. There was a message from the Russians to the effect that the Canadian First Division was the finest unit the Allies possessed. Heady stuff from Uncle Joe. There were mutual congratulations between the Brigade and the French; from generals all the way up the line to Allied Force Headquarters. The 8th Battery of Second Field Regiment which had for so long and so well supported the battalion, now fired a twenty-one gun salute in its honour. The Plough Jockeys took their pride and held it high, for this alone had meaning in those days. It was well they took it while they could, for within a week or two the Second Front would roar into headlines the world over, and for the rest of the war Italy would become the forgotten battleground.

On May 30, the unit moved forward through elements of the Fifth Armoured Division and took up the pursuit. The Germans were demoralized and anxious to withdraw before the road to the north was cut behind them. There were some brushes with rear-guards, but the greatest enemies were heat, dust and mines. The pioneer platoon and a detachment of Royal Canadian Engineers did yeoman's work during the advance, and suffered several casualties.

On June 3, Anagni, a hillside town under the eastern mountains, was occupied by the vehicles of 'F' echelon; and so the campaign came to a close. For almost two months the unit was to hear no guns fired in earnest.

Sitting under the olives of Anagni, avoiding the heat, and loath to move about because of the ever-present mines, men listened with resentment to the publicity given to the Americans for the liberation of Rome. They felt, and rightly, that they had done as much to free Rome, as had been done by anyone. Nevertheless, there were political considerations, and because of these, First Division and indeed, all of Eighth Army was once more denied the fruits of victory. Rome was placed strictly out of bounds to the Canadians but this did not prevent surreptitious jeeps and trucks from making the journey up Route Six to the eternal city.

Perhaps rumours of the fact that the forward troops were enjoying life a little reached the ears of High Command. At any rate, on June 9, the unit moved south to one of the most isolated and barren regions to be found in central Italy. Piedimonte d'Alife was the nearest village, a scrofulous and ancient hamlet lying in white exhaustion under a merciless sun. Here First Brigade was incarcerated for six weeks.

The Regiment went under canvas and at once began a rigorous training program. This in itself was not resented for constant training was an essential condition of active service, and if it was particularly demanding at Piedimonte men understood the reason. The new reinforcements who were arriving to fill some of the gaps left by the Liri battles had received totally inadequate training in Canada and had they been committed to battle in that condition, their lives, and those of their comrades, would have been risked needlessly. Cameron, much as he may have wished to give his men the rest and freedom they deserved, dared not relax the pressure.

There was no corresponding excuse, however, for those in higher echelons who further burdened the resting troops with elaborate ceremonial parades and other arbitrary demands upon the men's scant hours of surcease from duty.

For the first time absenteeism became a problem as men took it on themselves to find their own compensation for a year of battle. Those who were caught suffered severely, in many cases receiving penal servitude. Perhaps the punishment was just but the number of these cases would have been drastically reduced had the fighting men been treated a little less like insensate automatons.

Much of the harassment bordered on the absurd. Alarmed at the fact that men were drinking vino in an effort to escape from the monotony, some careful statistician in the rear, issued a memorandum pointing out that a liter of Italian red wine had the same alcoholic content as a bottle of Canadian rye whiskey. Intended, evidently, as a deterrent to drink, this piece of news was received with great enthusiasm and *vino rosso* rose much higher in men's esteem.

Lack of imagination and an unfortunate sense of its own importance had already brought much of the administrative staff into bad repute with the forward troops. At Piedimonte the good work done by staff, and the regulations imposed for the real good of the men, were largely nullified by the fact that the base troops, under direct staff control, lived in freedom from most of the restrictions inflicted on the fighting men. Base units invariably established themselves in the largest and most attractive cities they could find and appropriated to themselves all available pleasures. They could hardly be blamed for this, but when the fighting troops showed signs of the same appetites and desires they were hurriedly banished out of temptation's way. To the men it was an old story. The infantry, the artillery, the tanks and the engineers fought the battles and did the dying. The base troops and the staff reaped the rewards. And if this belief was not wholly justified, there was quite sufficient truth in it.

Piedimonte d'Alife had few pleasures to offer. The Regiment organized its own swimming trips to the Volturno River and a few supervised 'educational' tours to Rome and Pompeii. These were pleasant interludes, but hardly the release men yearned to know after five years of close regimentation. When the staff finally organized an excursion to a 'rest beach' near Naples, it was a complete fiasco. The soldiers arrived at the beach, very hot and very dusty, and were promptly driven out of the water by an American assault force, practising with live ammunition.

The common dislike and distrust of the rear organizations continued to help weld the Regiment into an even tighter unity. When one man was wounded on a training exercise, he hid for three days to give the wound time to heal a little, rather than report to the new M.O., Max Lerner, and risk being sent away from the Regiment to a hospital and the subsequent miseries of a reinforcement camp. Daily, at Piedimonte, wounded members of the Regiment hitch-hiked up from the base depots at Avellino and pleaded with the adjutant to be rescued from that hated place where only the permanent staff had claims to being human. They hung wistfully about with their old sections and platoons, and at nightfall went sadly down the mountain again, still hoping for a miraculous release, and a fulfilment of their great desire to come home.

While at Piedimonte another restriction came close to causing real trouble. For a year the troops had done business with the Italian civilians using cigarettes as money –

the only medium of exchange that had real value. Both soldiers and civilians profited by the trading, and fresh fruits, vegetables, vino and a score of other little pleasures could be had in exchange for cigarettes. The cigarettes were the men's own property, sent to them from Canada by friends and relatives. Now the staff ruled that no man would be allowed to receive more than nine hundred cigarettes a month. Soldiers smoke heavily if they smoke at all, and this was barely enough to meet each man's private needs. There was little left over for trading. One of the few remaining methods of obtaining pleasure in the midst of war was now denied the fighting troops. Perhaps there was a good and sufficient reason for the ruling, but it gave rise to a new resentment towards the staff, particularly when it was reported that base troops in Naples and elsewhere were obtaining apparently unlimited quantities of cigarettes that had, perhaps, been stolen from the stocks held back from the fighting men. The fighting soldiers reacted by selling their boots, or anything else of Government issue, which the Italians would buy. It seemed only fair.

For the officers, things were better. Transport was available, and in Naples, there was the fabulous Orange Grove club (for officers only), and there was the beauty of the Amalfi coast where several officers' rest hostels had been established. It was only human nature that the officers should make use of their opportunities, and it is significant of the real unity of the Regiment that the disparity in opportunities did not lead to bitterness. Perhaps the men accepted the situation more readily because most of them had come from the same levels of life as had their officers.

On July 25, the Regiment left Piedimonte unmourned, on a long, slow trip northward towards an unknown destination. It was the first of several involved moves designed to hoodwink the enemy as a prelude to an assault upon the new German positions that had been firmly established across the wide part of the Italian leg from Pisa on the west to Pesaro on the east coast. The troops took down all their Canadian flashes and Regimental insignia, and covered up the unit markings on the trucks. And at each stop, one or more civilians would cheerfully inquire if the *Canadesi* would like to trade some cigarettes for vino. It seemed unlikely that any one was being fooled.

Like a gigantic tourist caravan the convoy rolled over central Italy seeing Rome (from the backs of rapidly moving trucks), Perugia, Assisi, Lake Trasimene, Siena and Florence. The Regiment moved in fits and starts, sometimes stopping for a day, sometimes for a week. It was a pleasant time, and despite the stern restrictions on all contacts with civilians, men saw much of an ancient land that was still good to see. The hills of Tuscany brought forth their flagons of Chianti and the regimental quartermaster quickly found himself very short of boots.

In Florence, for the first time and the last, the Regiment was quartered in a city. It was hardly a place for unrestrained revelry for the Germans held that part of Florence north of the River Arno – the major portion – while the Canadians held the southern bank. Florence was an open city and so the north bank was respected by the Allied artillery. The south bank was not. Steadily, heavily, the Germans bombarded the cluttered streets and in many places to move in daylight was to invite the fire of a sniper, an 88-mm. gun, a machine gun – or all three. All this was confusing to new reinforcements, and one of them had himself paraded to his company commander to register a formal complaint.

"Pardon me sir," he said, "but isn't Florence an open city?"

"It is, in theory anyway," was the reply.

"Well, something's wrong," the aggrieved one complained, "Yesterday I started across the bridge (the Ponte Vecchio remained undamaged at that time), and those damn Germans shot at me. Not only that, but when I came back to this side and sat under a tree to smoke a cigarette, some bastard fired a machine gun into the branches overhead."

Not many of the men were quite so ingenuous, and before the first day was out, a sharp and savage little war was being waged across the muddy river. In one day the Regiment's snipers bagged seven of the enemy in retaliation for one of their own who had been killed by long-range rifle fire. Occupying houses separated only by the narrow water, the troops of both sides became adept at shooting, without being a shot at. A favourite trick was to set up a machine gun aimed on fixed lines at a likely target; tie a string to the trigger, then sit out of sight and stare into a mirror. When an enemy appeared, one had only to twitch the trigger to shoot while still remaining safely hidden.

The stay in Florence was all too brief, and no opportunities were wasted. One of Able company's platoon sergeants accosted an attractive *signorina* who was carrying a bouquet of roses, and made some hungry comments in English. The rest of the platoon joined in with variations on a theme, until the girl turned, smiled sweetly and in excellent English said quietly, "Would any of you gentlemen care for a rose?" The silence that followed was marred only by the usual distant chatter of machine-gun fire.

Charlie company found itself billeted in a hat factory, and within hours the whole company had shed its regulation head-gear and was dodging shellfire in boaters, panamas, rakish fedoras, and some particularly fetching examples of ladies' millinery.

The company sergeants' mess was established in the palace of a bishop and here a table was set that would have been difficult to duplicate in the ancestral halls of any English Lord. Each day the sergeants returned from their skirmishes with the Germans to sit a snowy linen while they were served their meals on silver plate, and drank their wines from fine Italian crystal. This was worth fighting for. Florence was a lovely place to live.

For once there were things to 'liberate', apart from the usual litter of the enemy's battle gear. There was a minor orgy of liberating – not to be confused with looting – and kit bags bulged with weird oddments ranging from a stone statue of an Ancient Roman to colour photographs of Mussolini, signed by that gentleman himself.

In point of time the Regiment spent only a few days in Florence, but in weight of memories Florence stands out brilliantly against an otherwise bleak back-drop.

On August 8, all identification marks came down again and the Regiment, once more incognito, moved south and east. Its ultimate destination was not known, officially, but few of the men had little doubt about it. The Adriatic coastline beckoned, and memories of the winter at Ortona came to chill the lovely late summer days.

In effect, Italy had already been abandoned as an active battleground by the Allies. Most of the American Fifth Army, and the French Corps, now withdrawn from the line, were preparing for the sea-borne invasion of southern France. Most of the tactical air force had already gone. Eighth Army had been weakened by the dispatch of several divisions to join the Second Front in northern France. Patched up with scratch formations including some reconstituted divisions of the defeated Italian forces, the Eighth suddenly became the pauper army. Starved of men and weapons and ammunition, its new task was to hold the line and somehow to persuade the enemy not to weaken the defending force of twenty-five divisions which Kesselring still commanded in North Italy. It was to be a thankless, bloody, but vitally important task, for those German divisions, had they been free to move to France might well have turned the tide of battle there. But Kesselring's army could only be held in Italy if Hitler was convinced that Eighth Army posed a real threat to Austria or southern Germany. The only way that Hitler could be convinced was for the Eighth to attack, attack again and yet again.

With a force numbering little more than half that of the

defending enemy, General Leese (now commanding Eighth Army) was forced to substitute guile for man-power. His troops were already so thin on the ground that the Allied line could not have stood against a determined enemy counter-thrust. Nevertheless, Leese had to thin out the general line still further in order to mass some sort of striking force with which to carry on the grand deception.

There was but one sector of the new German defence line across Italy where an attack would be practicable. This was on the east coast where there was a narrow gap, less than ten miles wide, between the shoulders of the Apennines and the Adriatic sea. To the west the moun-tains raised an almost impassable barrier all the way across the peninsula.

Leese knew this, but so did Kesselring, and the German had barred the gate. Profiting from the lessons of the Hitler Line, Kesselring had built the new defence system (which came to be called the Gothic Line) not as one wall but as a defence in depth.

The coast plain at the gateway to the Lombard plains was like that at Ortona, cut by a myriad of steep ravines and *torrentes*, while in between rose steep finger-ridges running down almost to the sea from the mountain mass inland. The Gothic Line embraced a strip of this coastal complex some thirty miles in depth from south to north. Its outlying defences began at the Metauro River and were echeloned back all the way to Rimini. And it was manned by the best troops the Germans had in Italy.

Leese could do nothing to circumvent the natural obsta-cles, but he did what he could to weaken the enemy defence force.

The visit of the Canadians to Florence had been intended to convince Kesselring that the next major thrust would be directed through the mountains beyond that city, and to persuade him to attenuate the Gothic defence as a result.

For the scheme to succeed, it was essential that the Canadians then be secretly withdrawn from Florence and moved east to the real battleground. Such an operation, in a country filled with spies and with ex-Fascist informers, seemed doomed to failure. It was a long and desperate gamble.

The Allied troops concerned knew little of the real situation. They did not know that they were the unwitting pawns in a gigantic bluff. They did not know that for the next eight months they would be committed to a desperate and largely hopeless battle.

On August 22, when the roar of gunfire came clearly to them from the ridges of the eastern plains, they may have guessed some of the truth at least. Nevertheless, First Division went forward with high heart.

SEVENTEEN

The Gothic Line

FROM THE town of Fano, on the Adriatic coast, the *Via Flaminia* runs southwestward up the deep valley of the Metauro River to climb at last over the high passes in the Apennines. North and south of the river and of the old Roman highway, great mounding ridges push down almost to the coast. They are ancient ridges encrusted with innumerable little villages, and filigreed with tangles of trails and tracks. Their slopes and plateaux have been deeply scarred by a multitude of gullys that in the summer are no more than muddy-bottomed canyons, but that in the fall and spring roar angrily in flood. The ridges are sturdy sanctuaries, and have been so for countless centuries, and it is because of this that the villages cluster in their hidden places.

In the last days of August, fields were golden with ripe grain and the vines were heavy with dark grapes; and in those days the sanctuary was invaded.

The Germans came, up from the south, and turned and stood. Before them the Metaura ran sluggishly and from their eyries they could look far southward over the lower ridges running to the sea. They dug their weapon pits, machine-gun posts and dugouts and prepared to give battle.

On August 23, Eighth Army reached the Metauro and on August 25, three hundred guns thundered along the front and First Canadian Division crossed the river valley six miles inland while, near the sea, the Polish Corps struck up the coastal highway to the north.

The divisional plan called for a two brigade assault with Second Brigade on the left and First Brigade on the right. First Brigade was to make two bridgeheads over the river with the 48th on the left, the R.C.R. on the right, and the Regiment in reserve.

The opening of the battle on First Brigade's front seemed remarkably auspicious. Both forward regiments crossed confidently and easily and were soon climbing the slopes of the massif. On the morning of August 26, when the sun stood hot in the high sky and the day was already heavy with the somnolence that comes at summer's end, the Regiment moved forward, following the leading battalions, until it reached a gentle ridge where an old church tower cast a long shadow on the warm ground. Here the companies dispersed and men lay down to rest in shade and sunlight. The first phase of the battle was over and it had been hardly worse than the training schemes at Piedemonte. In the haze of that fine summer day the human mind could not accept the fact that this was all illusion.

Relaxed and not yet aware, the men of the Regiment had not bothered to direct their eyes to the north and to draw the obvious inferences from the high ridges in that direction. It had not occurred to them that the church ridge was completely over-looked. The Germans had been more alert. With an unheard-of target before them, the enemy observers concentrated at least thirty guns, including several of 21-cm. calibre, on the unsuspecting Regiment and at a given signal opened fire. The first flight of shells landed in a single obliterating salvo – and instantly the peaceful ridge was buried under a swirling curtain of grey dust and yellow smoke.

The awakening was savage. When the roar of detonations died away at last, the ridge appeared to have been swept clean of life. Hiding in hastily dug shelter holes, in pig-styes or in the nearest buildings, the companies counted up their losses and understood that the interlude of peace was done, and war was with them once again.

A few miles ahead, and to the right, the 48th meanwhile had come under heavy fire and their advance company had been pinned down and cut off. Occupying a looming hill to the west, the Germans looked down upon the unfortunate Highlanders, and the vindictive crackle of MG 42s greeted any attempt to break free from the trap. Hurriedly Brigade instructed the Regiment to by-pass the 48th and take the lead.

The obvious route for such a move involved a wide swing to the right of both the 48th and the enemy strong-point, but this would have meant moving into open ground under full enemy observation. The C.O. went forward with his company commanders and after a long look, made a bold decision. Dog company, supported by a troop of Churchill tanks, was ordered to assault the German strong-point and destroy it.

What followed was a small masterpiece of infantry and tank co-operation and was a further proof that fighting men, in small formations and given a free hand, can accomplish marvels. With consummate skill Dog company, under command of Major Alan Ross, moved swiftly forward, covering the tanks and protecting them from the hidden enemy armed with close-range *Faustpatronen* (Bazooka-like anti-tank weapons). The tanks, lumbering in the rear, engaged and silenced the machine guns on the crest of the defended outcrop. When a German anti-tank gun was spotted, an infantry platoon rushed it, firing from the hip, and so protected the armoured friends behind.

Scrambling up the slope the men of Dog company were on top of the enemy positions before the Germans could sense their fate. Within an hour of the time the orders had been given, the strong-point was gone and the 48th company had been extricated. The enemy had suffered twelve men killed or wounded, and twenty-six taken prisoner. In addition, Dog company captured – intact – a 75-mm. gun with its towing vehicle, two heavy trucks, a self-

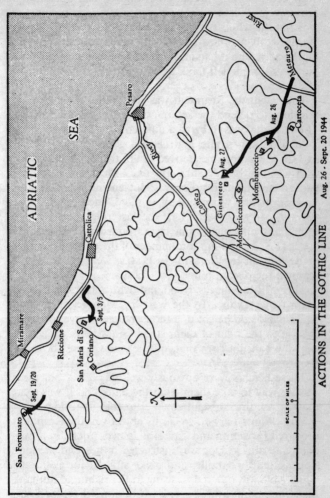

ACTIONS IN THE GOTHIC LINE   Aug. 26 - Sept. 20 1944

propelled 20-mm. cannon, an armoured half-track and a motorcycle. It had been only a minor action within the scope of the whole battle, yet it had been executed almost faultlessly. It had cleared the way that had been blocked for the 48th, and it had also materially assisted in enabling the R.C.R. on the left flank to move up and take the town of Mombaroccio.

That night the Regiment was content, as it took up its positions to defend the armour against night infiltrations. The next day was to bring a different sort of battle.

At 0300 hours, after patrols had gone forward, Baker and Charlie companies moved out of the defence position with a squadron of tanks. By 1600 hours the Regiment had advanced three miles, without encountering serious opposition, and was overlooking the divided valley of the *Torrente Arzilla*. Beyond it, the last ridge between the Canadians and the Foglia lay shrouded in the evening haze. The C.O. and the commander of the tanks, accompanied as usual by the artillery F.O.O.s, went forward and scanned the distant hill.

Three little villages stood out white and crenellated against the skyline. To the west lay Monteciccardo and San Angelo at a height of a thousand feet above sea-level. A mile to the right of them stood Ginestreto and near it were two abrupt rises that, on the maps, were shown as Points 268 and 146.

These heights were obviously well defended, but there was no way to take them from the flank and it was clear that only a direct assault could clear that final ridge.

With Points 146 and 268 as its objectives, the Regiment prepared for action and Cameron issued orders for a two-company attack. Dog was instructed to descend the long slope, cross the Arzilla, and make straight for Point 268 while Able was ordered to swing to the right and outflank the strong-point from a group of buildings that stood out, distant and unclear, in the evening light. The British tank squadron was ordered to accompany and support the infantry while the F.O.O.s arranged a covering barrage.

Within the hour, the action had begun. Down that long exposed slope the infantry made their way while the tanks grumbled along behind. When the ravine of the Arzilla was reached it was found to be steep-sided and bog-bottomed – an impassable tank trap. There was no time to change the plans. The infantry companies scrambled across and pushed on alone.

Enemy mortar and artillery fire was becoming intense as Dog moved steadily up the slope, forcing its way to within two-hundred yards of its final objective. Then a torrent of small-arms fire from the front and from two flanks made further progress suicidal and Dog dug in and fought back from the meagre shelter of slit-trenches and ditches.

Able company had even less success. The first building was reached and the lead platoon burst in the door and found the place empty of the enemy.

And then a whistle blew, sounding incongruous and somehow childish in that place. The men behind the lead scout thought the whistle was a joke played by one of their own. It was no joke. Caught neatly in ambush, the platoon was suddenly blasted from three sides by well-sited machine guns.

Able company's ordeal had just begun. Retiring into the houses, the company dug in to face a counterattack, and shortly found itself surrounded by a ring of machine-gun fire. The company commander called by wireless for artillery support, but the enemy positions were so close to Able that the shells dropped on the company position. The situation was already desperate, but it became worse when some Churchill tanks far off to the right and under command of another unit, concluded that Able company's house was held by Germans and opened fire on it. Under fire from the Germans, from their own artillery and from the English tanks, the company very nearly received its *coup de grâce* from two Spitfire fighter-bombers that rolled lazily overhead intent on joining in the fun. In the nick of time, an officer threw out a canister of yellow air-recognition smoke and the Spitfires veered off to find another target. The tanks also recognized the meaning of the smoke and ceased their firing. Then, as if to make amends, they rumbled on to catch and destroy two Tiger tanks that were coming down the ridge towards the survivors of Able company.

The Regiment's own supporting tanks had meanwhile made valiant efforts to cross the Arzilla. One of the tank officers threw open his hatch in order to see the ground better, heedless of a heavy mortar and artillery fire upon his vehicle. A mortar bomb fell through the open hatch and exploded in the confined coffin of the tank.

Darkness brought little relief to the two forward companies, for in the valley behind them confusion had begun to multiply. Elements of the R.C.R. were wandering about in the darkness, intermixed with Baker and Charlie companies of the Regiment, while off to the right, the 48th appeared to have become lost. The C.O. of another unit coming up to Lt.-Col. Cameron in the angry darkness inquired in a matter-of-fact manner, if Cameron had "seen his battalion anywhere". It was easy enough to lose a battalion that night.

Men of both sides took to wandering in unforeseen directions and as a result B.H.Q. became the scene of one of the most peculiar encounters of the war. Cameron had established his H.Q. in a farm outbuilding already occupied by a pair of bullocks. A blanket had been hung over the door as a blackout precaution. A table had been procured and on it a candle guttered in an empty bully-beef can. Stew had just been served and the B.H.Q. officers were getting down to it when Cameron heard a deprecatory cough behind him. Thinking that it was one of his men, he turned to see.

The newcomer was a complete stranger. He stood six feet in height and he was wearing the uniform of a corporal in the German army, with the insignia of a paratrooper to boot.

The rest of the B.H.Q. officers were fairly paralyzed, but

Cameron had had a hard day and he was in no mood for nonsense.

"You," he said abruptly to the large German, "are in the wrong camp. Go away."

The German looked startled. "But I'm lost!" he explained apologetically.

Cameron was not impressed. "That's easily rectified," he said. "Just go out that door, turn right and follow the footpath. You'll find your people on the hillside four hundred yards away."

The German stood open-mouthed as Cameron belatedly remembered the duties of hospitality. "Have you eaten?" he inquired. The corporal admitted that he had not seen food in twenty-four hours. Whereupon he was invited to sit down, and he accepted after politely excusing himself while he washed his face and hands.

During the meal, the other officers, still bemused, fell into an academic argument about the provisions of the Geneva Convention on prisoners as it related to social affairs. The German listened with interest, and then with his belly full of excellent stew, decided that he had had enough of war. With a sigh of satisfaction he pushed back his chair and announced that he now considered himself a *bona fide* P.O.W. Cameron turned on him at once.

"Nonsense!" he said brusquely, "you've already admitted that you wandered in here by mistake. And since we've already taken quite enough prisoners today, one more would simply be an administrative nuisance."

The German, thoroughly caught up in the Alice-in-Wonderland atmosphere, waxed indignant. He pounded the table.

"But I tell you," he insisted vehemently, "I *am* your prisoner. The Geneva Convention says I am!"

Cameron, not to be outdone, banged the table in his turn.

"Now see here!" he said sternly. "You are a soldier absent without leave from his unit, and your C.O. will be looking for you. You may even be charged with desertion.

You go along, and when you get back, tell your C.O. that we're going to beat the hell out of him come dawn."

It is conceivable that the argument would have lasted far into the night, and who can tell what improbable results it might have had, but at this juncture Cameron was called back to duty and reluctantly he agreed to accept the corporal's surrender.

On August 28, confusion still held its ground. Cameron had planned a new assault in the morning but this was cancelled by higher authority and a full-scale Brigade plan was devised which called for the 48th to attack to the right of Point 146 while the R.C.R. attacked on the left to gain the lateral road along the ridge. Delay followed delay and the battle did not begin until 1830 hours when, under cover of a heavy artillery barrage, the 48th moved off. By 2200 hours the attack had bogged down in a welter of mortar and shell-fire, and not until dawn did the R.C.R. pass through the rear companies of the Regiment and move forward. There was little further resistance. The P.P.C.L.I. had cleared Ginestreto during the night, and First Brigade moved up almost unopposed. The Regiment occupied Point 268 at last, and the battle for the approaches to the Foglia River was at an end.

It had been a confused and inconclusive struggle, in sharp contrast to the incisive little victory of Dog company a few days earlier.

On the morning of August 30, First Brigade went into reserve after four days of movement and fire, and Third Brigade took over the next phase of the attack, across the Foglia.

The Regiment rested and reflected. The dream of a quick breakthrough to the Lombardy Plains was no longer an assured vision. Each man considered thoughtfully the fact that the Germans he had faced during the past four days were old acquaintances – the men of the First Paratroop Division, and the toughest soldiers in the *Wehrmacht*.

During the next few days the war slowly retreated northward as Third Brigade and the newly formed Twelfth Infantry Brigade of Fifth Armoured Division performed valiantly in the destruction of the central core of the Gothic Line, between the Foglia and the Conca rivers. The men of the Regiment made good use of their rest, with the sure knowledge of old soldiers that it would be too short. They took time to wash their clothing in nearby streams or at the wells of farm houses. Scrounging expeditions scoured the countryside for eggs, chickens, fruit and vino – always with due regard for the legacy of hidden mines left behind by the enemy.

Each man fought his own private battle with the hordes of dung beetles and lice-like creatures that appeared out of the ground each night and swarmed into the little shelter tents; but these were relatively bloodless battles and DDT in quantity ensured eventual victory. Mail came, was read and answered, and the quartermasters did what they could to repair the ravages of battle. Little groups gathered about the signals truck and listened to the news reports, first on the German radio, then on the B.B.C. A year of conflict had taught them that neither source could be relied upon. The Allied news was good. In the west, the Second Front was rolling forward, and in South France Seventh Army was half-way up the valley of the Rhône. The Russians too came in for their share of the glory – but there was no mention on the B.B.C. of Italy, except for a brief statement now and then that "operations were proceeding without difficulty". It was a little irritating to be so completely neglected, and so soon after the great victory at the Hitler Line. But it was an irritation that would become so chronic that it would be forgotten before many months were out. Meanwhile, the German radio was more concerned with the Italian front.

The Germans had some reason for their concern. By September 1, the core of the Gothic Line had passed under the feet of the infantry of Third and Twelfth Brigades and the Canadians had driven half-way through the barrier towards Rimini and the entrance to the Lombardy Plain.

On September 2, the Conca River was reached and crossed, and on the coast, First Brigade once more led the van. This time the Regiment approached the battle with caution even though it was again the reserve battalion. When the unit was allotted a large house at a crossroad for its B.H.Q., the C.O. took one look and blasphemously refused it, for it was too good, and too obvious, a target for the German guns. A decrepit farmhouse was chosen instead and in due course of time troops of another unit who had happily moved into the spurned mansion were thoroughly pounded by the enemy artillery. They had not yet developed the sixth sense that functioned almost automatically in close proximity to the enemy – the sense that enabled men to assess instantly and unconsciously the magnetism for shell-fire possessed by any given piece of real estate.

Before dawn on September 3, First Brigade moved up the coastal road to take over the pursuit of the enemy from Second Brigade. The R.C.R. and 48th led off, to right and left, but before long it became clear that mines, demolitions and the attention of the enemy gunners, were going to slow a straight infantry pursuit to a crawl. Accordingly, at 0630 hours, the Regiment was ordered to load Baker and Charlie companies on the tanks of a British armoured regiment and this mobile striking force was told to drive quickly northward, through the two other infantry units, and to make for Rimini some fifteen miles distant. It was a desperate effort to keep the front fluid and prevent the paratroopers from digging in their toes and making another stand. And it was doomed to failure. The mobile force had little better luck than that which had attended the 48th and R.C.R., and by 1500 hours the tanks were halted and unable to proceed.

From the enemy's point of view, the Canadian thrust had to be stopped between the coastal towns of Cattolica and Riccione since this was the only area before San

Fortunato ridge (the last real barrier to the Po Valley) where a stand could be made on favourable ground. Inland a complex of finger ridges surrounding the town of Coriano made a formidable obstacle to Fifth Armoured Division's progress – but Coriano could be turned by First Division, unless the enemy could retain control of the Riccione-Cattolica sector. To help the paratroopers there was a long out-thrust spine of the Coriano ridge complex that came down almost to the sea, passing through the village of San Maria di Scacciano only four miles inland from Highway 16.

Here on September 3, the First Paratrooper Division took its stand and from this eminence attempted to halt the coastal drive on Rimini.

EIGHTEEN

Gateway to the Plains

BEFORE day dawned on September 3, San Maria and its ridge had been recognized for what it was – the key to the whole coastal sector.

At 1600 hours on that day, the Regiment was told to give up its attempts along the coastal road and swing inland to assault and clear the ridge. Supported by a squadron of the British 48th Royal Tank Regiment, Dog company took the lead and turned its back upon the sea. Close behind came Baker, while the balance of the Regiment moved up in rear.

By 1800 hours Dog company and the tanks had moved three miles inland and had turned north towards the village of San Maria which could now be clearly seen huddled in typical confusion on the long crest of the ridge. Speed was clearly the essence of a successful attack upon the feature, and the assault group pushed forward without pause for detailed reconnaissance. Then, at 1900 hours, the tanks reached a blown bridge across a deep gully and their part in the battle came temporarily to an end. Dog company continued the advance, beginning to climb the long swell of the forward slope even as the sun closed with the horizon.

It was not good country for an assault. Vineyards, olive groves and fruit trees stood close and heavy, and brush hedges intersected each other every few yards. The waiting enemy had everything on his side and the feelings of the men of Dog were unenviable as the three platoons leap-frogged through the tangle expecting at each instant to hear the fierce whip of machine guns from ambush. But there are times when speed can succeed ahead of caution. Dog company's dash for San Maria almost succeeded. The appearance of the Canadians was sudden enough to confuse the paratroopers and catch them slightly off balance, and Dog company was within three hundred yards of the village before the Germans were able to halt the advance. The preliminary enemy fire was heavy, but it was clear that the paratroopers had not yet had time either to prepare the San Maria position fully or to man it with sufficient troops. Nevertheless, Dog company, alone and deprived of its armoured support, could not take full advantage of the enemy's unreadiness. Dusk had come and the attack was not pushed home.

Under heavy shell-fire the balance of the Regiment moved forward at its best pace and at 2200 hours the scout platoon was sent out in darkness to by-pass Dog and find a covered route into the village from the left. By midnight, Lt. Charlie Case and his scouts had penetrated, unseen by the enemy, into the western outskirts of the village. Guides led Baker forward, and before dawn Baker and the scouts were established in a group of farm buildings within easy striking distance of the little town. Preparing to attack, the company had complete surprise upon its side until the moment when two German soldiers came walking down the road chatting to each other, and quite oblivious to the presence of the Canadians so close upon them.

Then Baker fumbled. Someone called to the Germans to halt while they were still a hundred yards away. The Germans, startled into instinctive action, dropped their weapons and scuttled for the cover of the nearest village house. A scattering of small-arms fire followed them. The enemy, alerted now to the new threat upon his flank, was soon ready to receive it.

While the Regiment had made good use of darkness, so had the Germans. Reinforcements had come up during the night and the whole crest of the ridge was now occupied in force by determined and courageous men.

En route to its new position, Baker company had detached one of its three platoons to protect a group of tanks that had become lost and were in fear of enemy infantry attacks in darkness. This platoon had not rejoined the company by dawn, and with first light it could no longer do so since the exposed slope was completely dominated by enemy fire. A troop of tanks that had managed to by-pass the blown bridge lumbered up the rise to assist Baker, but before they were in useful range two of them were hit by anti-tank fire and the third went out of action from mechanical troubles. The two platoons of Baker, and the scout platoon, were now completely on their own and having lost surprise, found themselves in a most unpleasant situation. Heavy artillery fire from both sides was falling on the group of farm buildings, and if a man so much as exposed the top of his helmet, it was greeted with a withering blast of machine-gun fire from three directions.

At 0730, Able was ordered to divert the enemy's attention by swinging far to the right and assaulting the most commanding height – known as Point 83 – a mile eastward of the village. As Bill Graydon led his company off he was prey to some inner doubts, for little was known of the enemy positions to the right, and both Dog and Baker company's exact locations were obscure. Unexpectedly, Graydon came upon two tank officers who had escaped from their burning vehicles, and these two were able to prevent Able from walking straight into an ambush where a dug-in and camouflaged German MK. IV tank was waiting hopefully. Swinging even wider to the right, Able reached and cleared the buildings on a little secondary ridge and here, with a Besa heavy machine gun taken from a dead tank, the troops turned one building into a fortress and from the upper window cleared the enemy from two nearby positions. But to the left, the Germans held yet another house and their fire effectively prevented

SAN MARIA DI SCACCIANO

Sept. 3/5 1944

SCALE OF YARDS
0   100   200   300   400

➤ Enemy Defensive Positions

▤ = TANK

Able from moving farther forward. Two English tanks now appeared from the right, and Graydon realized that these alone could help his company on. Dashing from shelter he ran to the nearest tank across an exposed field of fire, but as he was trying to make contact with the crew inside, he was hit and fell to the ground while unwittingly the tanks moved away. With six bullets through his leg Graydon managed to crawl back to the buildings where he lay in agony for two more hours, directing the company's struggle, and refusing to be evacuated. But neither the courage of the company commander nor that of his men could help at this juncture, and Able was bogged down some two hundred yards short of the crest of the ridge and its final objective.

With three companies committed, the C.O. now made a hard decision. He decided to throw his sole remaining reserve – Charlie – into one more attempt to gain control of the ridge, by sending it in between Able and Dog to a group of houses on the crest. Charlie moved up behind three tanks, and in part due to the tanks, but also due to the fact that the paratroopers were now thoroughly engaged at three other points on the front, Charlie managed to reach its objective in less than an hour. From the shelter of the houses, the company pushed east to within a few hundred yards of Point 83 but here it was fiercely counterattacked and was soon engaged in a bitter survival battle of its own.

Meanwhile Baker was being slowly decimated by snipers, machine guns and concentrated artillery fire. Rather than stay put and be destroyed piecemeal, the company at noon launched an attack of desperation.

The two platoons and the scouts scurried from their scant shelter through a virtual shroud of fire and reached the row of houses on the edge of the town. The fighting became indescribably confused. Within an hour, both platoon commanders were dead and the surviving men were split up into sections, fighting their own independent battles from house to house. Germans and Canadians fought hand to hand or shot at each other through the floors and walls. The muted roar of hand grenades eclipsed even the thunder of artillery fire. The enemy defenders were the same who had held Cassino through an entire winter of savage street fighting, and they had lost none of their skill or courage – or their arrogance. A German officer under cover of a white flag approached a beleaguered section of Baker company and called upon it in these words: "Surrender you English gentlemen – you are surrounded and will only die." Pte. 'Slim' Sanford, a sniper and a man famed for his tongue, bellowed back a classic rejoinder. "We *ain't* English. We *ain't* gentlemen – and be God-damned if we'll surrender!"

In the hamlet of San Maria it was kill or be killed – and yet it was, within the limits of the meaning of war – a clean battle. At one time there was an actual truce between the combatants to allow the evacuation of the wounded; and a German medical N.C.O. came forward and treated the badly wounded Canadians who had no medical aid of their own.

All of that long and bloody afternoon the surviving soldiers of Baker company held the houses they had taken; and both they and the Germans were in a state of complete exhaustion when darkness began to fall. It was a stalemate. The C.O. could do little to change the course of the action now, for the whole Regiment was committed and there were no new reserves. There remained only one thing to do.

At 2100 hours Baker company received orders to withdraw out of the town so that an artillery concentration could be brought to bear on the tenacious defenders. Dog company was also pulled back at the same time.

The concentration went in as planned, and it was too much for the remnants of the paratroop defence force. When, at 0600 hours, the Regiment attacked for the final time, the enemy withdrew before it and as the dawn broke clear, the battle for San Maria ridge was at an end.

Much of the inner nature of the battle, as it appeared to

the eyes of individual soldiers, has been preserved in the story of R.S.M. Harry Fox. Fox's words accurately reflect the real emotions of men in battle, and so they are given here, as they were written.

"Together with C.S.M. Ponsford of Charlie company I had gone up to Able about noon to see what was going on and we got there just in time to see Captain Graydon shot. There was little we could do here, but Ponsford pointed out to me a big house in the distance, on the hill crest by the village, where Baker was marooned. Seeing as I did not have much to do right then I took a notion to go up to Baker.

"I cut down a road past Charlie and hiked along. There were no friendly troops here since the division on the left had not been able to keep up with our advance. It gave me a nice feeling to be walking over those sunny fields munching some figs I had picked. Breakfast had been quick, skimpy and long ago. I crossed a deep drainage ditch and went along for a peaceful mile, as if there wasn't any war at all, through vineyards, orchards and ploughed fields. Finally I reached the foot of the hill from the far left and I started up it, keeping my head down to look for mines. Then CRACK and a bullet snapped by my head so close I smelled it. I did not wait to see if I was hit, but made a flying leap for a deep ditch fifteen yards away. I landed crawling and must have looked comical, all arms and legs, tommygun dangling about my neck, jumping along like a bear with a burned backside. It was comical for the joker who had fired, and he whanged away four more rounds but missed with all of them. I laid low for a spell, and he started to chuck mortar bombs at me and the 'canaries' whistling and sizzling about did not reassure me at all.

"Finally I moved off up that ditch and pretty soon found two lost men from Baker company. I pointed them to the rear and crawled on, to bump into four nuns. They had pillow cases full of stuff slung over their backs, and boy, were they excited! Chattering away a mile a minute, they lost no time in social visiting but disappeared down the hill.

"For a while I crawled on the road, on my belly, checking it for mines, then I cut off straight up the hill and ran for it through an old orchard. I carried on, huffing and puffing and wondering where the house was when a Jerry popped out of a bush and ducked behind another one. He had an MG 42 in his hand but his back was to me. I dropped behind a convenient tree and started to breathe again.

"As I lay there wondering if it was any use praying, a voice in unmistakable Canadian Army language hailed me, so I upped and ran to the left to a seven-foot stone fence that I cleared without touching anything but the top row of stones. I landed in a lean-to at the back of the Baker company house, and the guy who had yelled at me gave me almighty hell. He said he was one of the few men still standing, and would I please not call attention to the fact by wandering around that hill and getting Jerry to start the war up all over again. At the house I found Capt. Lazier and C.S.M. Forshee. They were somewhat surprised to see me and borrowed my water bottle. While they were drinking, a Jerry stretcher-bearer came bustling round the corner waving his Red Cross flag. I was startled, but everyone else seemed unconcerned. They told me he had been around most of the day and had arranged a kind of truce at the moment, and was making sure everybody abided by it. The situation was such that the Jerries couldn't throw Baker out of its houses, and Baker couldn't move the Jerries with the few men it had left in one piece.

"I walked over to the Jerry and asked him if I could bring up a vehicle to evacuate our wounded, but he wouldn't hear of it. It was a pretty wild conversation since I spoke no German and he spoke no English; all we had was vino-Italian. While we argued, a broken-down Sherman tank about a hundred and fifty yards off, cut loose with its machine gun.

"Everyone cursed and got a horrified look on their

faces, particularly the Jerry. Then there was an almighty BANG as a *Faustpatrone* exploded on the tank and two Jerries popped out of a bush and charged the tank head-on, firing machine pistols. One of them hopped on top and emptied his mag down the hatch, then the two hauled a wounded man out, and still at the double, carried him fire-man fashion over to us and plopped him down before dashing back to their bush. The Englishman was badly hit, with a shattered left knee and eye amongst other things. I can still see his ginger hair and the way he tried to grin as we and the Jerry tried to help him.

"The place was full of our wounded and there was no time to waste so I said good-bye, and took off down the hill, staying under cover pretty well, and getting back at last to B.H.Q. I told Colonel Cameron the story and he suggested I might borrow an armoured half-truck from the tank medical section and try to rescue the wounded.

"Off I went again, and bumped into a platoon of the 48th Highlanders under Sgt. Jim Harker. He and his platoon razzed me cheerfully for going the wrong way, but I told them that was the usual thing for an R.S.M. and when we parted they wished me the best. Too bad they couldn't have used it for themselves; they ran into trouble that night and Jim and most of his men never came back.

"A flock of 75-mm. shells straddled the road, and I dived into the ditch again. Something banged me on the shoulder and I grunted, sure I had bought it. Then a very haughty Limey voice asked what I was grunting for. The voice belonged to a tank officer who had leapt for the same ditch, gouging my shoulder nicely with his big boot.

"He told me where his R.A.P. was and when I got there and explained my needs, the Limeys jumped to help. Only they insisted on stripping me of my weapons and equipment and tying a Red Cross brassard on my arm before we started.

"The trip back up that hill was pretty quick. I rode on the outside to con the way and wave the Red Cross flag. I held it in my teeth and it at least kept my teeth from chattering as we approached the place where I had seen the Jerry machine-gunner. He was still there holding a *Faustpatrone* in his hand at the 'ready' position and staring at us as if he didn't believe his eyes. We went past fast, and he never even budged. We swung into the village and up the main street to the Baker company house.

"In no time we had a load and were heading down the hill, feeling a little naked with our back to the Jerries. But nothing happened so we unloaded and came back up, this time with an ordinary ambulance following.

"We were met at the top of the hill by a Jerry corporal looking very mad, and waving his gun at us and yelling 'kaput!' It was pretty clear we weren't welcome, but our driver had a spare pack of cigarettes and I passed these to the corporal. He was looking at my rank badges the way all corporals always do, in that 'you've-got-nothing-on-me-*this*-time' sort of way. The cigarettes mellowed him a bit and he let me look into the big house, but what was left of Baker company seemed to have vanished. There was a dead lieutenant, but we could do him no good so we left him.

"We could hear tanks rumbling in the distance, and it was getting dark so the driver suggested we get out before an attack began and we got caught in the barrage.

"At that the German pricked up his ears and wanted to know if there was going to be a shoot. We said, 'Damn right – we're going to blow this village off the map!' He frowned and began to look really peeved, so we got the hell out of there.

"It hadn't been a bad day. We had evacuated twenty-six of our men and the Limey tank men. Max Lerner, our own M.O., bawled me out for not bringing the wounded to him, but he said it with a smile. He had a busy enough day as it was. He was always busy for he kept the most forward R.A.P. of any unit in the Div."

The battle for San Maria cost the Regiment eighty-seven casualties. Many men died, and yet the soldiers on that day retained some hold on the fragile fabric of humanity. It had been a battle without hatred, and in the intervals between attempts to destroy one another, men on opposing sides had served each other. And this perhaps makes the battle for San Maria even more terrible in retrospect.

With San Maria taken, the front again rolled slowly forward in the face of steady shelling and mortaring. The weather which had remained so fair gave signs of breaking and on September 6, a heavy downpour caught the tired troops and gave them an unheeded warning of what the months ahead would bring.

For three days following San Maria the companies moved on, dodging shell-fire when they could and sending out patrols that brushed against the machine-gun hedge of the retreating enemy. Then on September 8, the Regiment was relieved and ordered into rest near Cattolica.

Once a seaside resort, the little town seemed a haven of repose and quietude. The pioneers hastened to the beach with their mine detectors and cleared a short stretch of the white sands so that the men could bathe in the warm green waters and absorb the last of the summer sun. It was a strange sensation to lie at peace upon that beach while out to sea the miniature silhouettes of three destroyers lethargically shelled the city of Rimini, in full view of Cattolica and only fifteen miles away.

Again the resting men clustered about radios to listen to the news from other fronts. Everywhere the war seemed to be raging towards a near conclusion – and only on the Adriatic plains was there a need for the slow, dogged grinding-up of a persevering enemy. That the Italian front was being necessarily starved to make the victories elsewhere was poor consolation. The starvation was too obvious, not only in battle but in rest as well. The regular issue of soldiers' 'comforts' gave each man a single bottle of beer, a package of gum and three chocolate bars as his share of luxury after a month of battle. Scrounging was no longer a hobby, but a virtual necessity.

There were the usual importunities of the rear echelons.

When the Regiment sailed for Sicily it had carried with it the sum of twenty pounds, the residue of the Officers' Mess Fund. During the year since then there had been neither the time nor the inclination for anyone to comply with the tedious regulations which demand a monthly accounting of such funds and, as a result, whenever the battalion withdrew from action, it was invariably met by a bespectacled major from the Regimental Funds Board. This major, a conscientious type, would seek out the C.O. and demand an immediate accounting of the twenty pounds. His visits became almost a rite, for he refused to be pacified by the simple explanation that the money had been long since spent.

At Cattolica the major appeared as usual, and this time Cameron lost his patience. A meeting of the officers was called and a collection totalling twenty pounds was made. The money was immediately invested in alcohol and there was a party of monumental proportions. The following day the adjutant prepared a statement, witnessed, signed and in quadruplicate, to the effect that the elusive money had finally been accounted for. The major went happily away, and was not seen again.

The Regiment was learning how to circumvent or to ignore this kind of nonsense. It was harder to ignore the plague of fleas and lice that swarmed in the denuded buildings where the troops were quartered.

Nevertheless Cattolica was a pleasant interlude and when Coriano Ridge fell to Fifth Division on September 13, and the way was opened for the final attack upon the last bastion of the Gothic Line, the unit marched out of its billets with regrets.

The old spine-tingling feeling of apprehension came alive again as the companies marched inland and turned northward over the battlefields just taken by Third Brigade. The sights were enough to perturb even hardened veterans. Here, by the roadside, lay five men of the Van Doos (the Royal 22nd Regiment) twisted into incredible contortions by the blast of a heavy shell. Burned-out tanks littered the countryside. Death lay everywhere and friends and enemies, bloated slightly in the September sun, lay amongst the bodies of the lesser beasts, horses, cattle and hogs. The roads were cluttered with a stream of civilian refugees blank-eyed and somnambulistic in their distress.

As for the Gothic Line, it was now no more than one thin remaining wall. For thirty miles its defences lay empty of defenders so that First Division stood at the very entrance to the valley of the Po. Not far ahead lay Caesar's Rubicon, but, in between, one final ridge ran steeply from the mountains to the sea. The ridge was called San Fortunato.

The approach to San Fortunato was bitterly contested by the Germans and the task of driving them back towards their final stronghold fell largely on Second Brigade. Meanwhile the Regiment was pushed far out to the left flank, which was now completely open and the obvious place for an enemy counterattack.

The divisional plan called for the attached Greek Brigade to strike up the coast road towards Rimini while the R.C.R. and 48th drove across the flats under the nose of the ridge to take Rimini airfield. Neither of these attacks could succeed, however, until the ridge itself was captured, and on September 19, this heavy task fell to Third Brigade.

At that time the Regiment was still on flank protection duty off in the western 'blue' and was not expecting to take part in the assault. But Third Brigade had been seriously weakened by the previous fighting, as had most other units in the Division, and so it was decided at the last moment to commit the Regiment in the initial assault against the stubborn ridge under Third Brigade's command.

Cameron hurried forward and had a quick look at the ground. He must have been appalled by what he saw, but neither then nor later did be betray uneasiness.

From the Third Brigade observation post on San Martino hill, a two-mile-wide valley stretched before him, flat

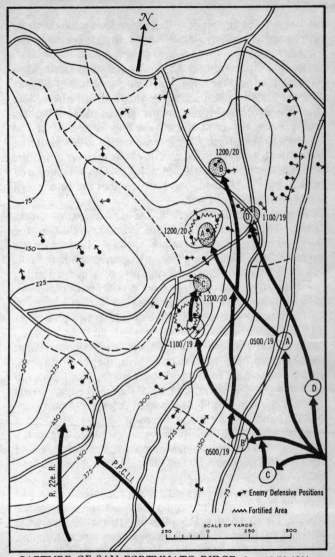

CAPTURE OF SAN FORTUNATO RIDGE Sept. 19/20 1944

as a desert and almost devoid of cover. Down the centre of it, ran the meandering Ausa River, swollen now with the first fall rains.

Beyond lay Fortunato; a looming and steep-sided ridge, well clothed in vineyards, and rising to a height of four hundred and fifty feet above the valley floor. Looking like the ramparts on old battlements, groups of stone houses clung along the crest to provide fine fortresses for the defenders. And from the crest the entire valley could be swept with observed cones of fire. On that far ridge the C.O. knew that the First Paratroop Division was prepared to make its final stand; and he knew that the veterans of Cassino would stand well.

Returning to the Regiment, the C.O. called his orders group. The plan was this: Third Brigade would take the ridge by means of a night attack, with the Hastings on the right and the West Nova Scotia Regiment upon the left. The Carleton and Yorks having first obtained a footing over the river, the two assaulting regiments would move through some time after midnight.

The battalion's attack would be made in two phases. At H-Hour, Able and Baker companies would cross the open ground and capture a base on the lower slopes. Then, before dawn light could expose them, the remaining two companies would follow and strike up the steep slopes to gain the crest. A squadron of tanks from the 48th Royal Tank Regiment would also cross at dawn and 'marry up' with the infantry for the final assault.

It was dark before the plans were completed and as the C.O. gave his orders one new company commander could not control his doubts. "Sir!" he said, "we'll never make it."

Cameron showed his mettle. As if the interruption had not taken place he continued in his quiet voice to give the details for the battle. His placidity, in the face of what seemed to most of his officers to be a suicidal action, perhaps made the difference between defeat and victory.

In the darkness, the Regiment moved forward to attack

a ridge the men had never seen. There was no reconnaissance. The attack had to be made over completely unfamiliar ground with only compasses as guides. Reaching the forward slopes of San Martino hill the companies found what shelter they could and waited through the long, tense hours. Word came at last that the Carleton and Yorks had made their bridgehead against light opposition. The time for H-Hour was now set. It was to be 0400 hours.

There was precious little time before the dawn.

The paratroopers had evidently not expected a night attack and so most of their troops were concentrated on the crest itself where, in daylight, they could control the valley. When H-Hour struck and the two attacking companies moved out across the dark valley they encountered only the futile resistance of advance posts and standing patrols and in the darkness they by-passed these, taking a few prisoners along the way.

No one lingered in the valley crossing. By 0530 hours the radio at B.H.Q. was receiving the message of a first success, and at once the two remaining companies began to cross, while in their lagers the crews of the Churchill tanks started up their engines and eyed the thin glimmer of the approaching dawn.

Able and Baker were now on the main lateral road below the ridge and in close contact with the defenders. But the course of battle was confused and at length the enemy, unsure of the situation, withdrew his remaining outposts to the higher slopes. Charlie and Dog company then passed through the forward companies and prepared for their assault of the ridge proper.

The light was clear by now, and the tank squadron, grinding across the plain to join the infantry, received the full attention of the enemy anti-tank guns upon the crest. A Churchill slewed suddenly and halted with smoke rising from its turret. Another and yet another was hit, but still the rest came on.

With the dawn the paratroopers' resistance became

further headway. They were now too close to the enemy for artillery support to help them, yet only heavy shell-fire could make the paratroopers keep their heads down long enough for the final assault to stand a chance. At 1030, after a confused and violent action, the lead companies went to cover and let the artillery have its way. All along the slopes the smoke mushrooms lifted and slowly dissipated in the morning sun.

Then Dog and Charlie attacked again. Up through mangled vineyards and orchards the platoons clawed their ways to reach their objectives under the lee of the last slope. Here, engaged in bitter hand-to-hand fighting they dug in to hold the ground.

Meanwhile things had not gone as well on the flanks, and the Regiment's position soon became precarious in the extreme. Radio communications had been blanketed by a wave of heavy interference and it was almost impossible to communicate with the forward companies. The tanks, reduced by shell-fire and breakdown to a single trio, were out of ammunition.

Cameron urgently requested fresh tanks with which to launch a new assault and help his infantry to clear the final crest beyond the original objectives.

Division refused permission. Having done its intended job, the Regiment was not to be asked to continue on. A new plan was already in preparation, one calling for an intense artillery bombardment of the crest, to be followed by a night infiltration through the advance positions by Third Brigade.

The order went to the companies, stubbornly clinging to the high slopes. "Retire three hundred yards in preparation for barrage."

Not all received the message. No. 14 platoon of Charlie, isolated in the heart of the enemy positions, spent a lonely and violent night under the Canadian barrage, and under the ceaseless fire of the enemy.

The withdrawal had bloody consequences. Baker company was caught by German mortars in its new positions and suffered particularly heavily.

It was here that Cpl. Alfred Maddick found an end. Maddick, a man of thirty-five, had been a C.S.M. with the medical corps at Ortona, and he had been dissatisfied. When he saw the wounded infantry brought in to his care he had felt that he was doing too little. And so he gave up his rank and came forward to join the Regiment as a private soldier. Now, for his reward, Alf Maddick died.

Night fell and the barrage began. To the left, the Princess Patricia Light Infantry and the Royal 22nd Regiment worked up the central spine of the ridge through the West Nova Scotia Regiment while the forward companies of the Hasty P's returned to their temporarily abandoned positions and thrust forward on their own. Success upon the left decided the battle and before dawn resistance on the whole of Fortunato had been broken.

By the end of the day the victory was won and the last mountain barrier athwart the gateway to the Lombardy Plains was passed. From the high crest of the ridge, men looked out over the widening angle of the level plains, and they were jubilant. In this last battle the unit had taken one hundred and twelve of the famed paratroopers prisoner and had killed forty more.

The final battle of the Gothic Line was done and now the future seemed as bright and open as was that fine September day. Tomorrow the pursuit across the plains would begin, and in a week or so Eighth Army would be driving a beaten enemy back to his home borders, even as the other Allied armies were smashing in the outer ring of the *Festung Europa*. So thought the Regiment. Tails were up, and the infantry felt themselves at the summit of the war. In the days to come they could visualize only the swift certainty of an end to battle.

NINETEEN

Across the Rubicon

ON SEPTEMBER 22, the Regiment joined the rest of the Brigade in reserve and moved down to the one-time resort town of Miramare, while other units of the Army prepared for the pursuit across the plains.

Hopes for that pursuit were high. The weather was fair and it seemed certain that only a few days would intervene before the welcome news of the breakthrough to the Po could be announced.

The billets at Miramare were square white villas that had known the dignitaries of the Fascist Party in the days before 1943. But they had long been in the hands of the *Tedesci* and the Germans had stripped them to their plaster walls and tiled floors. Doors and windows had vanished along with all the furniture, and the incoming troops made haste to rectify the losses. Scrounging trips took vehicles to Rimini which was not yet in the hands of base troops, and returned with truck-loads of mattresses, bed springs, tables and chairs. With the matchless ingenuity hard won over the years, the infantry made homes out of the bare white boxes and with the rare mood of holiday upon them, prepared to make the most of the rest period.

The holiday mood was destined to be short-lived.

First the weather changed. The infamous *bora* gale came thrusting out of the Jugoslav mountains and drove across the Adriatic. The winds howled through nights that were black with beating rain.

The driven walls of water poured into gaping windows and made light of the protective blankets that were nailed across the openings. The parched soils of the uplands glistened with moisture and turned liquid, slipping into the flooded *torrentes* and staining them an ugly yellow. The mud grew deeper each succeeding day. The temperature dropped sharply and the cold sea gales seemed unrelenting.

The weather alone could not have materially lowered the high spirits of the fighting troops, but its effects were tragic to their hopes. Out in the narrow triangle of flatland that led from Rimini towards the open plains, the ploughed fields turned to gumbo. The countless little irrigation ditches swelled to minor rivers. The steep sided canals and *fiumares* became livid torrents. First the tanks began to bog down, and then all vehicles became helpless except upon the congested and deteriorating roads and tracks. Inevitably the pursuit and the attempt to break out into the Lombardy plains slowed, hesitated and came to a muddy halt.

At Miramare men waited with growing impatience for the news that could not come. Slowly the hopes died. Slowly the infantry recognized the shape of the months ahead; remembering the bleak winter spent outside Ortona.

First the weather, and then the end of the hopes for a quick stroke across the Po and northward. There was more to follow. From Canada came the mutterings of the politicians, uneasily aware of the great undercurrent of resentment that was stirring through the Army against them. Rumours began to flow as heavily as the *torrentes* on the Italian slopes. It was said that all family men with five years' service overseas would be returned to Canada within a month. The 39ers were to be asked to make no further sacrifices. Reinforcements were to be found amongst the Zombies, the Canadian conscripts, who *en masse* had been excused overseas service. Now those 'living dead' were to be packed abroad to a duty that they would not accept voluntarily. So ran the rumours.

It would be impossible to describe adequately the emotions of the men who were directly affected by these tales. There were men with children four and five years old, whom they had never seen. There were men who had lost their wives and their homes to the long years of separation, but who had clung to a faint and desperate hope that their personal return might restore that which had been shattered. There were men who had served through five years of active service and a year and a half of continuous battle and whose nerves were now only empty sheaths – men who had given of their reserves to the last dregs and who were afraid that one more battle would see them smashed into palpitating inner dust.

The rumours were false.

A string of important people arrived at Miramare to explain matters to the troops. First there was the Divisional Commander, bluff and earthy Chris Vokes, who had his faults, but was at least a fighting man. The unit paraded to hear him try to dispel the clouds. The clouds remained. Then the Corps Commander who, perhaps unaware of what the fighting men felt about things, attempted to produce an aura of confidence by appealing to the soldier's sense of duty and painting rosy pictures of future operations. What the men thought of that can be summed up in a sergeant's succinct comment.

"Listened to the Corps Commander this p.m. giving us the guff. I prefer Vokes. At least you get a little honest entertainment watching his moustaches waggle!"

Then finally Col. Ralston, the Canadian Minister of National Defence, arrived. For some time Ralston had suspected that the reinforcement situation was far worse than the Government was willing to admit. But he had been badly advised in Canada, and much had been kept from him. Now he came to see for himself. He saw and understood. He talked earnestly to the men, but they had little enough faith in his ability to sway the Government at home to a just action.

Meanwhile, to still the growing outcry from the relatives of the fighting men, the Government had announced with considerable hullabaloo, a plan to solve the problems of the long-service men. It was called the Triwound scheme and it provided that any man who had been wounded *on three separate occasions* was now eligible for return to Canada.

This was the sop. For the Regiment it actually meant that six men who had come very close to death three times, were released from further duty at the front.

Thirty-four reinforcements reached the unit, which was, as usual, far below its fighting strength. For the most part these reinforcements were old-timers who had been wounded only once or twice, and who could still be used in battle. In Canada almost 100,000 Zombie conscripts lived a comfortable and pleasant life, secure in the knowledge that they would never be asked to face the enemy.

As the days at Miramare drew on, awareness of the full scope of the betrayal on the home front wore deeply into men's souls. There was only one antidote for it. The infantry scrubbed their khaki gaiters, pressed their worn uniforms, polished their cap badges and did what they could to keep the Regiment – *their* Regiment, their only home – as a living focus for their lives. It was the sole remaining source of strength for most of them and as it had not failed them in the past, it did not fail them now.

The days of rest passed by. Forty-eight hour 'leaves' were granted at the nearby town of Riccione where a so-called rest centre had been established. But this was just another phase of army life with the difference that men could sleep a little longer and were not called out for parades.

The officers fared slightly better, for Cameron believed, and rightly so, that it was the platoon and company commanders who bore the brunt of battle. He kept a keen eye on his company officers and when he saw the tell-tale signs – the vacant eyes, the slowed reactions, the heavily nicotine-stained fingers – he sent these men away to find some change of scene, some hope of rest, before the battle came anew. Yet it was hard for the other ranks to watch their officers go off to Rome or Florence, and there was a widening of the gap that must always exist to some extent between the officers and men.

The private soldiers lived their own lives. Daily, and illegally, scrounging parties in borrowed trucks scoured the countryside and the rear areas with boots, carefully hoarded cigarettes and army rations, to trade for fresh meat, eggs, wine and fruit. For over a year the unit had been living on British Army rations – never of high quality – and now made even worse by the fact that the Italian theatre had become only a side-show. Interminable bully beef and Australian dehydrated mutton with dehydrated vegetables and inedible margarine – these were the staples. At home in Canada people complained because fresh meat and butter were rationed. They said, sometimes with rancour, that they "hoped the troops appreciated the sacrifice". But the troops in Italy did not appreciate it for they gained nothing by it.

On October 10, the stay at Miramare ended when the inevitable word for which men waited with dread certainty, came that the unit was to go into action once again.

On a wet, cold morning the troops moved north and as they went some of them sang a peculiarly sardonic little song to the tune of Lili Marlene.

> We shall 'debouch' into the Valley of the Po,
> Jump off from the Gothic Line and smash the cringing foe,
> We shall 'debouch' into the Po,
> And this we know,
> Cause Corps says so!
> So onward to Bologna – drive onward to the Po!
>
> Six and twenty Panther tanks are waiting on the shore,

But Corps Intelligence has sworn there's only four.
We must believe there are no more,
The information
Comes from Corps.
So onward to Bologna – drive onward to the Po!

There were other verses but they all expressed one
thing – the growing disillusionment with all authority that
lay immediately beyond the boundaries of the Regiment.

The pathway into the Lombardy plains from the gates
of Rimini and San Fortunato was a level one, but narrow.
A long wedge of land, reclaimed from the marshes less
than a century before, broadened gradually out to the
northeast. This sodden angle was criss-crossed by a myriad of drainage ditches; and on the left the out-thrust
bastions of the Apennines stood harsh and scarred. To the
right, the land grew increasingly boggy and was hemmed
in by a series of immense marshes and swampy lakes
extending beyond Ravenna almost to the distant city of
Ferrara. There was no other path. Beginning at the Rimini
apex, the wedge had to be cleared of an enemy who was
now much assisted by the autumn floods.

The one relatively dry route down the angle was along
the *Via Emilia* – Route 9 – the highway to Bologna that
ran close under the shadows of the mountain ridges. During the two weeks while the Regiment rested, attempts
had been made to force this road toward Cesena. But by
October 10, the forward units of the British division which
carried the brunt of this assault had reached only as far as
the town of Savignano standing on the south banks of a
famous little river called the Rubicon.

Here, on October 10, the Regiment relieved the 44th
British Recce. Regiment as the spearhead of First Division
in the attempt to carry the battle to Bologna and to the
freedom of the open plains. Close on the right of the
Regiment, the Second New Zealand Division was to
attack simultaneously while far to the left in the high
mountains which were already snow-covered, Fifth

British Corps was to attempt an almost impossible scramble through the crags. The Regiment had as its axis of advance the *Via Emilia* while the boundary between it and the New Zealanders was a railway embankment that paralleled the highway a mile to the northwest.

In front of Savignano the flat grey landscape was heavily enclosed by the inevitable olive groves, orchards and vineyards; with here and there the squat silhouette of a peasant's hut, or the untidy outline of a straggling little hamlet. The raised banks of ditches covered the low land like worm-casts, and water stood or flowed almost everywhere, turning the rich soil into heavy muck. It was a depressing spectacle that greeted the Regiment at dawn on October 11 as it crossed the Rubicon.

There was no immediate resistance as the platoons moved cautiously through the tangled vines. Only the ubiquitous attention of mortars and artillery signified the Germans' will to resist. By 1000 hours the unit had formed a bridgehead 2000 yards deep and only then did Baker company patrols contact the enemy at a strongpoint covering a blown culvert in the road. After a fierce little battle the Germans were driven off with the loss of four prisoners and as many killed.

The battalion's operation was now well ahead of schedule, while the flanking units were far behind. On the left there were no friendly troops on the high complex of swelling mountains. On the right the New Zealanders had run into stubborn opposition and had been halted.

The C.O. now had a difficult decision to make; whether to take advantage of this apparent soft spot in the enemy's front and push forward, quite unprotected on either side, or whether to consolidate and await progress on the flanks. Cameron chose the riskier course. The battalion went forward into a long exposed salient of its own making.

A squadron of Lord Strathcona tanks gave comforting support as far as the blown culvert, but beyond it they could no go. The infantry went on. With the lead company went the artillery representatives, and the unit's three-inch mortars moved close behind.

From the mountains on the left, and from the strongly fortified town of Gambettola on the right, the Regiment was now under full enemy observation, as the increasing fury and accuracy of his shell-fire testified. Anything that moved brought down heavy fire and the highway itself became a lane of death. Each company when it halted at its objective, immediately sent protective patrols far out to its flanks, for there was no knowing where the enemy might strike a counter-blow, and there was reason to suspect that this apparent vacuum in the front might be a trap.

Not far ahead lay the Rigosa River, Baker approached a cluster of houses on the southern bank and found them to be in enemy hands. Another minor battle raged until the Germans were driven back across the swollen river; retreating in such a hurry that they failed to complete the demolition of the road bridge.

On the road between the culvert and the Rigosa, the enemy had left several massive concrete tank obstacles, each protected by mines and booby-traps. The pioneers at once attacked these obstacles in a strenuous effort to clear the way for tanks.

The Rigosa was clearly the enemys' main line, and so Dog and Able companies deployed. Able struck off to the west and came to within a few hundred yards of the river before darkness, small-arms fire and a blistering fall of shells and mortar bombs drove it to cover.

Dog company, half a mile off the highway to the right, ran into severe resistance at a group of buildings controlling a lateral road leading across the railway embankment into Gambettola and here again, darkness brought the battle to an end.

The salient was now a mile deep and a mile wide, and there was only the one battalion, widely dispersed in the entire area. It was no pleasant night. Baker and Dog engaged in incessant small-arms duels with the enemy

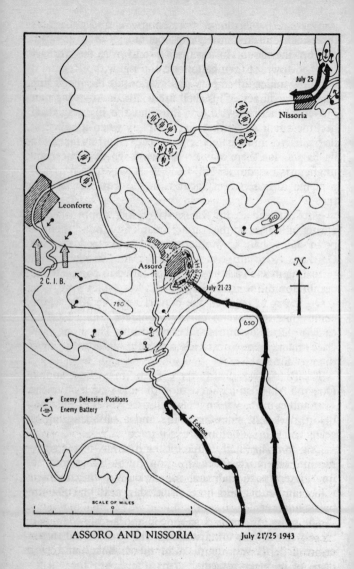

July 25

Nissoria

Leonforte

Assoro

July 21-23

N.

810

980

650

750

2 C. I. B.

F Echelon

- Enemy Defensive Positions
- Enemy Battery

SCALE OF MILES
0

ASSORO AND NISSORIA   July 21/25 1943

immediately in front of them. Elsewhere, the Germans threw a tremendous weight of bombs and shells upon the approaches to the salient itself – striving to recover with fire-power what they had already lost.

Baker managed to get patrols across the river, but these were forced back, to report that the Rigosa was a formidable obstacle to men, and an impassable one for tanks.

Nevertheless, the C.O. would not give up the advantage of initiative and during the dark hours plans were made to cross the river even though the tanks had not yet been able to get around the culvert, now far to the rear.

That night the company quartermasters carried on as usual. In darkness, over unknown ground, under incessant fire, they saw to it that hot food was cooked and brought forward to reach the fighting troops wherever they might be. The men who took the rations forwards will not easily or quickly be forgotten. Driving in open jeeps, and deafened by the sound of the engines, to the scant warning whistle of shells and bombs, they traversed the flaming *Via Emilia* several times that night so that the rifle companies would know the benison of hot food and drink before the morning's battle.

The attack began at 0900 when Dog company, led by Don Kennedy and No. 16 platoon, and with the help of an artillery barrage, assaulted the enemy-held houses one by one. The fighting lasted most of the morning, but when it was done the company had taken four enemy strongpoints and had sent twenty-three prisoners marching sullenly to the rear. The attack could not be pressed forward to the river here, for the enemy in Gambettola had too great an advantage of observation and field of fire.

Able, on the far left, attacked at the same time and after silencing two German posts at the river bank, the platoons waded the swollen river and dug in with a small but secure holding on the enemy's shore. Being the only company across the Rigosa, Able received the most violent attention of the German guns – a bombardment that grew in fury as the hours passed.

It was imperative to move the tanks forward now, and for the rest of the day, although subjected to a steady pounding from the German artillery, the engineers worked to build diversions at the culvert, and to demolish the remaining road blocks.

B.H.Q. had moved forward close behind Baker company and established itself in a tiny *casa* close to a German army cemetery where more than five hundred of the enemy lay buried. Men coming back to B.H.Q. glanced at the lines of Gothic crosses and some smiled grimly, finding here a solace for the murderous barrage they were enduring.

Back at the base of the salient a quartermaster bringing up supplies in his jeep was halted by a terrified Italian girl who screamed the words *'similari Tedesci'* as she pointed at her home where two officers from a rear echelon unit, one of them of senior rank, stood watching intently. The quartermaster attempted to calm the girl, but the unknown officers brusquely ordered him to go about his business. It was not until several hours later that he could return with an Italian interpreter and interview a weeping girl and a stone-faced older woman. The story of the rape went forward that night, and there was a corrosive anger in the hearts of most of those who heard, for a deep and protective sympathy had grown within the Regiment for the people of the little farms and villages, who alone shared the world of the fighting soldier.

Before dawn on October 13, the tanks managed to close up on the Rigosa but there was still no crossing place for them. The C.O. would wait no longer. At 0500 hours Charlie company came forward and forced an infantry crossing on the right of the highway, driving on for almost a thousand yards until it was halted by fire from a straggling group of houses, called Bulgaria. The upper stories of the stone buildings, emerging from the thick cover of olive groves, were heavily manned and each house held at least one machine gun sited to sweep the intervening spaces. It was readily apparent why Bulgaria should be tenaciously defended, for the hamlet controlled the German supply routes into the town of Gambettola which lay just across the railroad embankment and which was still effectively resisting the onslaughts of the New Zealanders. The fate of Gambettola, which was the central strong-point of the enemy's line, now rested on the ability of the Germans in Bulgaria to stave off the threatened flank attack.

The Bulgaria defenders belonged to a different unit from those in Gambettola and the embankment formed their inter-unit boundary. Had the Gambettola garrison been in command of both sides of the embankment, the outcome of the ensuing battle might have been quite different. But there appears to have been a singular lack of liaison between these two enemy battalions. The unit on the Gambettola side seems to have relied completely and unquestioningly on its neighbour to the south, and it was evidently ignorant of the depth of the Regiment's penetration. Had it wished to do so it could easily have counterattacked across the embankment near the base of the salient, where only a handful of drivers and clerks from rear B.H.Q. stood in the way.

Cameron could not know of the enemy's decision to adhere strictly to the boundary, and he was vitally aware of the threat of being cut off. But he had not so much as a platoon to spare for rear-flank protection since the Regiment was already spread dangerously thin across the front of the salient. Any counterattack at this juncture might well have been fatal and it was Cameron's task to prevent such an attack by deception, since he had not the physical force to do so. The projected attack on Bulgaria could not be attempted until the tanks arrived. During those vulnerable intervening hours it was essential that the enemy be kept on the defensive.

This was achieved largely through the efforts of the gunners. Throughout the whole of that day the Second Field Regiment kept its gun barrels hot as it brought down 'stonks' on every known or suspected enemy position. It laid smoke screens here and there across the front to add to the confusion, and to keep the Germans in the tense expectation of an infantry assault. To help the guns a squadron of Desert Air Force fighter-bombers was called up. These aircraft, known as 'Cab Rank', functioned in an unusual manner. They had direct wireless communications with an air-liaison officer at Brigade and could be called down on targets within five minutes of a request being sent from the forward infantry companies. They did yeoman service on this day, strafing and rocket-bombing every position that the enemy might have hoped to use as the spring-board for an assault.

The efforts of the air force and the artillery had the required effect, but there were subsidiary results. Deluded into a panicky conviction that the Canadians were about to attack in force, the enemy guns responded in full measure. For the balance of the day the salient lay under a rolling, crashing fall of German shells.

As darkness came Cameron completed his battle plan. This was to be a set-piece battle in two phases, and it was completely dependent upon the arrival of the tanks. In the first phase, Baker and the tanks were to break out of the salient along the *Via Emilia* to assault and capture an unnamed hamlet opposite Bulgaria and a mile southwest of it. Charlie company was then to launch the main attack by swinging across the front from the captured hamlet; supported by the tanks, all three field artillery regiments, a regiment of medium guns, and a battery of 4.2 mortars.

It was a bold plan, well conceived, but risky; for during the battle the salient would be most vulnerable to counter-attack. Cameron tried to minimize the risk by leaving no detail to chance.

Chance nevertheless played its part early in the game. Word came before dawn that the tank crossing just completed over the Rigosa by the engineers had collapsed. The entire plan was in jeopardy until the men of the Lord Strathcona's Horse assayed the impossible and began edging their ponderous vehicles over the ruins of the partially demolished road bridge. No one gave them any hope of success, but by consummate skill and with great courage, they made the crossing, and ninety minutes later the battle began.

There has seldom been more perfect co-operation between tanks and infantry than in the struggle which followed. Operating as if they could read each others' minds, the tanks and Baker company went forward to the highway hamlet with such precision and speed that by 1100 hours the village had been cleared, the last enemy killed or driven out, and the tanks were ready to join Charlie company for the major thrust.

At 1130 hours, with only half an hour's delay to allow the tanks to replenish their ammunition, the assault was renewed. The enemy, knowing full well what Bulgaria was worth, resisted savagely. Under the superb leadership of Capt. Max Porritt, the attacking tanks and infantry moved and fought almost as one organism. Surrounding the armoured machines to protect them from the deadly *Faustpatronen* of the enemy infantry, the men of Charlie company at the same time found vital protection in the covering fire of the tank guns. When an enemy-held house halted the lead platoon, the tanks engaged it, firing armour-piercing shells through the thick walls, then following these with high explosive shells that burst inside the rooms. When the surviving defenders rushed out to gain the security of their dugouts, the tank Besas and the infantry Brens cut them down. Moving in close, the tanks covered the infantry as the sections crawled the last few yards to reach the Germans in their deep trenches with grenades and small-arms fire.

It was a slow, methodical process of annihilation, and it was not all one-sided. Huron Brant, a Mohawk Indian who had won the Military Medal in Sicily, was killed with his entire section when the six men were caught by enfilading machine-gun fire in a narrow ditch. Enemy mortar and shell-fire spattered the fields in destroying patterns despite the sharp retaliation of the Canadian guns.

For seven hours the battle raged and at the end of it, at 1630 hours, the last battered house in Bulgaria was in Charlie Company's hands and there came a lull.

If there is merit in success in war, the action of Charlie company and the Lord Strathcona's tanks upon this day must stand high among the deeds done by the Canadian army. The company and the tanks had not only fought a major engagement against heavy odds, but the victory had materially affected the whole course of battle on the Army front. The importance of the victory is not to be measured in statistical records, but it is worth noting that in the Bulgaria action fifty-five Germans were taken prisoners while an even larger number were reported killed. Of the eighty Canadian infantrymen and the two troops of tanks in the attack, no tanks were lost and Charlie company suffered less than thirty casualties in all.

Now, when it was too late, the German staff (which could blunder as gravely as any staff) realized the error of the inviolate boundary line, and attempted to launch a counterattack on Bulgaria from the Gambettola strong-point.

At 1730 hours five Panther tanks closed on the embankment and began to cross into Charlie company's area with supporting infantry behind them. It was a moment when the whole course of the action could easily have been reversed, and for long minutes it seemed almost certain that the enemy would take a full-blooded revenge upon the Regiment. Utterly exhausted, the survivors of Charlie company pinned their faith upon the lightly armoured Shermans that had been such good companions all that day. The Lord Strathcona's tanks merited that faith. The first Panther had hardly reached the outskirts of Bulgaria when it was hit and destroyed by an ambushing Sherman. Then, as the Lord Strathcona troopers watched in disappointment, the counterattack faltered, and the surviving Panthers turned and ran.

It was the end of the struggle and the end of the fortress of Gambettola. That night the enemy evacuated the town and Charlie company patrols, thrusting far forward, went almost a mile before locating the German rearguards.

The next morning Baker moved half a mile farther up the *Via Emilia* towards Cesena. For a time it too was threatened by a counterattack but artillery fire and the presence of the Strathcona's tanks again discouraged the enemy who again retreated. In mid-afternoon the R.C.R. passed through to take over the pursuit.

Back over the battleground the padre took his sombre duty and gave burial to the dead. The rains, beginning once more their autumn tasks, drove down to fill the shell craters, to obliterate the tracks of men and tanks, and to rust the litter of a war that had passed on.

Full awareness that battle was at an end came on October 18, when a captain from brigade came forward and incontinently ordered the B.H.Q. cooks out of their shelter in a relatively undamaged house, to make way for the Headquarters staffs.

TWENTY

Betrayal

WITHDRAWING to a reserve area at Santarcangelo, the unit went under canvas in the sodden fields beyond the little town. Here for two weeks the troops endured the vilest of the Italian autumnal weather. They existed in two-man shelter tents that were designed for summer use in tropical climates and that had hardly enough room in them for two recumbent forms. The tents were without floors, and only a small man could sit upright.

The rains returned in earnest on October 21, and continued almost without pause until November 9. They were the hard driven, frigid walls of water that the Adriatic spawns in the dark months. On two occasions they brought full-scale floods with such a weight of water that nearby roads were inundated two feet deep.

In the entire Regiment hardly a man knew what it was to be even momentarily dry, free of the clogging mud, or moderately warm. No training or other activities could take place and for the most part the soldiers huddled in their sodden blankets, under the meagre tents.

There was no overt demonstration of resentment, and the whole incident was simply taken as a further proof of the 'bloody-mindedness' of all authority. Men wrote about it in these words. "It looks as if they're trying to drown the lot of us. But we've had worse than this, and if they think the Regiment can't take it, then they'd better guess again."

And – "So help me, it's so Goddamn wet out here that

even our hair is rusting. Somebody seems to have it in for us for fair."

The weeks at Santarcangelo went slowly. But they were not without that vital saving grace, the touch of humour.

From a diary of those days comes this small incident.

"Tried to play a round of Hearts in the tent, but it was too wet and cramped even for that. It rained again soon after dark, and I mean *rained*. Never faltered all night long. We weren't the only ones afloat. A mother mouse who couldn't find another dry spot in all of Italy hatched her family under my pillow in the night. Bet the young have flippers. If they have, we'll make them Hasty P's."

Finally in the first week of November after endless false starts, the companies began to move into billets at Miramare.

The villas had now been occupied for several weeks and the ingenuity of many temporary Canadian inhabitants had accomplished wonders. The gaping doorways and windows had been largely filled with oddly assorted doors and sash scrounged from several hundred square miles of countryside. Even stained glass from shattered chapels stood out resplendently in the dour walls of squalid shanties. Furniture, much of it mildewed, and damaged both by war and by the rough handling of its 'liberators' gave a semblance of luxury to the stone rooms with their tiled floors. Bounteous piles of straw served as beds for the unlucky ones who had not 'scored' a mattress on a scrounging trip. For heat, there were a hundred improvisations of gasoline-can stoves, or homemade braziers.

As always when things looked brighter, rumours became optimistic. There were so many rumours that only the most naive soldiers believed them. The unit was booked for France. The Germans had withdrawn across the Po. Hitler was seeking peace at any cost. These were the stock ones.

Few men listened. There were better things to do. At last, and for the first time since the invasion of Sicily, real leaves were being granted. In batches of fifty at a time, men were being sent to Florence for five days. The leave trucks pulled out from Miramare bearing cargoes of cheerful, smartly dressed soldiers. The trucks came back five days later laden with grey-faced, wizened, weary ancients. Even the mention of the magic words *cognac* and *signoritas* could no longer bring a flicker of life into those pallid countenances.

Not all the men attempted to live two years in five days. Some saw Florence quietly and spent their money on cameos and silverware to send home to their wives and families. But these were the minority. For most of the men the Florence leave was the inevitable explosion after the years of containment. And who shall censure the infantry for how they spent those brief five days of life?

With the almost incredible elasticity that is the hallmark of the good soldier, the troops came back from the grey swamps at Santarcangelo showing a fair measure of the old pride, the old enthusiasms and the old vitality. A casual observer amongst them could not easily have guessed how much effort was required for this new regeneration. There were no superficial signs to show that the innate reservoir of strength in every man had been almost drained by this last of an interminable sequence of resuscitations.

The little world of the Regiment seemed good once more. The outside war news continued to be spectacular and morale within the unit seemed to have suffered nothing from the years. When a poll was taken to see how many of the men would serve in the Pacific after the European war was ended, more than eighty per cent volunteered – with one vital proviso – that they go with the unit, and that the Regiment remain intact.

Even the smouldering anger against the situation at home in Canada was somewhat alleviated by the report that the Defence Minister, Ralston, had resigned and had been replaced by General Andrew McNaughton. This news brought a wave of optimism – for, as usual, the truth was withheld from the troops.

"Now that our own, good old Andy is in the chair, things will be different. We'll get a break at last..." wrote one deluded soul. McNaughton had built the Canadian Army in the English years, and he was looked upon by every soldier with the affection that belongs to a good father.

None of the troops in Italy had any inkling of the depths of the betrayal that had taken place in actuality. None knew that their real champion, Col. Ralston, had been forced to resign because, after his return from the Italian visit, he had insisted on overseas conscription at once. None knew that the wily Mackenzie King had picked McNaughton, naive in politics as he was inspired in military understanding, to be the scapegoat for the Government's refusal to act.

Almost at once McNaughton announced the rough outline for the Home Leave scheme, and there was frantic enthusiasm. As it appeared in its first outline, the plan called for all long-service men to be returned to Canada by Christmas-time.

The cruel disappointment of the Triwound scheme was forgotten. Married men who had served overseas for five years were now so certain of repatriation that they refused to take their leave to Florence, for fear they might be absent when the great news came. To their wives and children in Canada and England they wrote letters hot with their high hopes, that kindled hotter hopes in the hearts of those who waited for them. These soldiers who had been forced by bitter experience to armour themselves against the thrusts of their own nation now, innocently and foolishly, took off the armour.

On November 19, they heard the truth.

The Home Leave scheme boiled down to this. Initially three men from the Hastings and Prince Edward Regiment would be picked to return to Canada, perhaps before Christmas, perhaps later. They would then have thirty days' leave at home *before being returned overseas to active service*! The whole Home Leave plan was on a point system, and it was shockingly clear that there was no more likelihood of McNaughton's promises being fulfilled, than there was that God himself would intervene.

The outrage of the soldiers was monumental. The rage of individuals was not far short of murderous. Hopes that had soared beyond the years of death and long privation, were shattered with a cruelty beyond belief. Men and officers alike shared the savage resentment of the moment and there can be no doubt that the blow was of such magnitude that it was able to do what neither pain, fear, privation, nor the enemy had yet been able to accomplish.

One of the steadiest senior N.C.O.s in the Regiment, a quiet-spoken man who had not seen his wife and children in five years, made this entry in his diary – and he spoke for all. "Shame and hellfire for Mackenzie King and his whole rotten, louse-bound crew. May they rot in hell with the Zombies that they love!"

The penultimate stab in the back had been delivered, but within the Regiment, life went on.

Numbly at first, then with the desperation of those who clutch at straws, these men who had been all but destroyed by the betrayal, rallied. Those who had no home attachments, and those who had not fallen victim to the hoax, set their own cynical example. "You've had it, boys!" they said.

The immediacy of living at the front was the salvation of many. For there was escape from thought in an utter abandonment to the essential trivialities.

Rations continued to be monotonous and of bad quality. Scrounging trips went far afield, sometimes two hundred miles behind the front where, defying the iron-bound regulations forbidding trade with civilians, men procured the little luxuries for their fellows up the line. Fresh meat was one great need, and regular expeditions went seeking unattended cows.

Each company or platoon had its specialist in the art of procurement, and in particular, in the art of keeping the vino jugs full. One of these was a man named Fuller who operated on behalf of the carrier platoon. Fuller would gather up all the loose equipment the boys had for sale, and hike off down the coast in a borrowed truck. On one November day he and three of his assistants stopped at an Italian coast hotel some fifty miles from the front. There were a number of women in the bar, all friendly. A dance developed but at the height of the entertainment the war unexpectedly returned.

A German submarine surfaced a mile off shore and with Teutonic thoroughness set about shelling the hotel and its surrounding houses into dust.

At the first explosion the Italians, including the bar-keeper, sensibly vanished. But Fuller and his crew were used to shellfire, and not used to unlimited free booze. Fuller vaulted the bar and took over as host, and to the crash of exploding shells the little group of Canadians held high wassail.

The submarine was firing its last vindictive salvo when the little truck, springs creaking with its load, pulled out into the darkness. And no one can say what the emotions of the hotel owner were when he returned at last to find no vino, but his bar piled high with sacks of pilot biscuits, old boots, ancient undershirts, khaki sweaters and well-worn blankets.

At night in almost every billet there was a party. These had become so formalized that the pattern could be intimately predicted. First there would be a feed of spaghetti cooked by some local 'mama' and served with quantities of wine. Later there would be card games, Hearts or Poker, that slowly dissolved in a vinous haze into a hilarious and drunken 'do'. In the morning there would be the inevitable thick heads and shaking hands. But in the evening there would be another party in some other platoon billet for the hardy to attend.

By day there were the inevitable parades, but even the ceremonial parades were useful now for men could forget much in the effort to appear on parade in the guise of military perfection. Even training schemes were welcomed. They occupied the mind and wearied the body so that sleep would come.

The officers played the game as well. One night there was a full-scale party and dance, and the padre was detailed to visit the rear areas and procure that crowning glory, a bevy of nurses.

"Believe me, I sweated blood over that job," he wrote. "There were three hospitals in the area, two British and one Canadian. I tried the Canadian one first, and they just laughed at me. With the whole Eighth Army to pick from? Besides, they were dated up months in advance to the lads from rear formations.

"In desperation I tried the British hospitals but at the first one it was the same story. The matron said it wasn't even any use putting a notice on the bulletin board. Completely dispirited I tried the final hospital and I must have had such a woe-begone appearance that the matron took pity on me. Anyway, she promised to mention the matter to her nurses, and if I would come back next day she would let me know.

"I went back and the matron, beaming all over told me she had good news. One of the girls would like to come to our dance.

"I picked her up the following night. A dear girl, but you know, certainly no raving beauty. The chaps were all waiting for me at the mess, thirty of them. I feared the worst, but I should have had more faith in my Regiment.

"They rushed her right off her feet. They gave her the time of her life. When it came time to take her home, the whole Mess vied gallantly with each other for the honour. When she left that night she was walking on air and carrying herself like a queen. But she gave us as much pleasure as we gave her, for she was one of our kind. She belonged to the only world that was left to us in those days."

There was a deep pathos in the heart's loneliness that is revealed by this incident – and it was shared by all ranks in the Regiment. It was the loneliness of exile.

The desire for contact with the civilian world, apart from that to be found on leaves in Italy, had long been shrinking. After the Home Leave bubble burst, the desire became almost non-existent.

During the stay at Miramare the unit was visited by a number of war correspondents and most of these 'outsiders' were viewed with a jaundiced eye. Except for a rare few the correspondents were seldom seen in times of trouble. Later, when the actions were at an end, they came forward in their jeeps and cars exuding an air of camaraderie they had not earned and that must have rung false even in their own ears. Perhaps due to censorship, and to the propaganda demands of their editors at home, very few of them wrote of events with inner truth, and fewer still seemed to know or care what the real feelings of the soldiers were. Those who cared, and tried to tell the truth, sometimes received short shrift from the military authorities. The troops observed the faking of action photographs and read the imaginative 'I was there' reports of correspondents who had spent most of their time in comfortable billets far behind the lines. They saw also that regiments from the larger cities, or with important political connections, received the lion's share of the attention, and they came to take this for granted as an example of the essential shabbiness of the civilian world. They fully understood that only bad reports could be believed, and that all good reports must be accepted with a cynical reserve.

In the last days of November the currents of rumour that invariably preceded battle began to flow again and once more the familiar tightening of the stomach muscles was felt by every man. The rumours were vague at first, then slowly they began to take on substance as reports of a grand new offensive designed to break out of the imprisoning wedge of swampland before Ravenna began to be heard.

Until that month the troops had given battle plans some credence at least. In Montgomery's day, it had been more than that – it had been certain belief in success. Later that certainty had waned and after the Gothic battles it had become heavily tinged with the same suspicion with which the men now viewed all happenings without the Regiment.

They knew that December was no time to mount a major offensive on the Adriatic coast. They suspected with something approaching certainty that any attempt to break out across the saturated swamps ahead would flounder into dismal and bloody failure. Disheartened and disgusted by the events in Canada, they approached the new battles in a state of resignation that alone could help them to fulfil their duty to the Regiment. They had only one valid reason or excuse for entering battle now, and it was not hatred of the enemy. It was because they were a part of their Regiment and because the Regiment was the one intact structure remaining in their lives, and so it must be preserved even if the cost was death.

The grand plan in brief was this. The Canadian Corps, at rest for a month, was to go forward with Fifth Armoured Division on the right aiming its thrust at Ravenna, while First Division on the left drove towards Bologna.

The weather that preceded the move forward to the assembly areas was indicative of what would follow. Once more the companies waded through a morass of half-frozen mud, remembering that a year ago to the day, they had also been on the move – to the blood bath of the Moro River and beyond.

It was at this hour that incredible news came from Canada concerning the conscript forces. The story is best told in the words of a soldier of the unit, in a letter written at the time.

"Today we heard the news that our Zombie brothers have gone on strike in British Columbia and have burned the Union Jack in protest against any suggestion that they be sent overseas. Mackenzie King has the situation well in hand. We hear that the flag-burners were fined $11.00 each and that the incident cannot be called a mutiny – just a little high feeling. This is great stuff for our morale as we go up the line. It would be funny I suppose, if it wasn't tragic. Even out her Canada has become a laughing stock and the whole world will laugh now. If this is all true and if the politicians get away with it, I don't want to be called a Canadian again."

This letter was written on December 2. A day later the sacrificial holocaust that had been grotesquely named 'Operation Chuckle' had begun.

TWENTY-ONE

Operation Chuckle

THE DIVISIONAL plan for Operation Chuckle entailed a complicated four-phase assault. The first was to begin on December 2, when Third Brigade was to cross the Montone River and, after clearing the intervening ground, seize a bridgehead over the Lamone River. Once this had been accomplished Second Brigade was to capture the town of Bagnacavallo, and cross the Senio River. In the third phase, First Brigade was to capture Lugo and exploit to the Santurno River. Finally, Third Brigade was to capture the town of Massolombardo which was considered to be the key to the enemy's control of the drowned triangle that blocked the way to Bologna and the open plains.

In retrospect it is hard to understand how the plan could have inspired any confidence even in the men who made it. In the worst of the Italian winter weather First Division was required to attack across three major rivers, several large canals and innumerable swollen drainage ditches. The intervening land was all reclaimed and, under the impact of the winter rains, had reverted to something close to its original state. All of the rivers and canals, as had been clearly demonstrated to the planning staff by air photography, presented natural barriers of formidable strength. These water-courses ran between steep earthen dykes that often stood thirty feet or more above the sodden vineyards and whose abrupt inner banks fell steeply as much as fifty feet into the angry torrents. All of the rivers and canals were in spate with currents running up to eight miles an hour. The water, fed from the high mountains, was bitterly cold.

Air photographs and agents' reports had made it obvious that the enemy intended to make a stand behind each of these obstacles, and that he had strongly fortified each line. In the northerly dykes, a complicated system of tunnels and weapon positions had been dug. The reverse slopes had been turned into thickets of barbed wire designed to trap and entangle the attackers under the muzzles of machine guns sited to the rear. It was known that the enemy was in considerable strength and that he possessed adequate resources of heavy tanks and self-propelled guns which would be waiting behind each new dyke.

The attacking forces would have no such close support. Canadian tanks could seldom hope to reach the battle areas in time to be of service and even such vital elements as anti-tank guns and other heavy weapons would be hard put to it to keep pace with the infantry. To lessen the chances of success even more, there was only a three-week supply of artillery ammunition available in Italy for Eighth Army's guns.

The First Brigade had been informed of its part in the coming operation during the last days of November, and Cameron had done everything possible to minimize the odds. Using a sand-table model he had briefed every officer and N.C.O. on the details of the ground near Lugo and before the Santurno. Tentative over-all plans that could later be fitted to the actual needs of the third phase had been prepared. When the Regiment moved up to its reserve assembly area on December 1, it had done all that could be done in advance of battle.

On December 2, after a thunderous preparatory barrage, Operation Chuckle began. Third Brigade crossed the Montone and fought forward to the town of Russi, halfway to the Lamone. But before that first day ended it was apparent that the optimistic timetable for the battle was

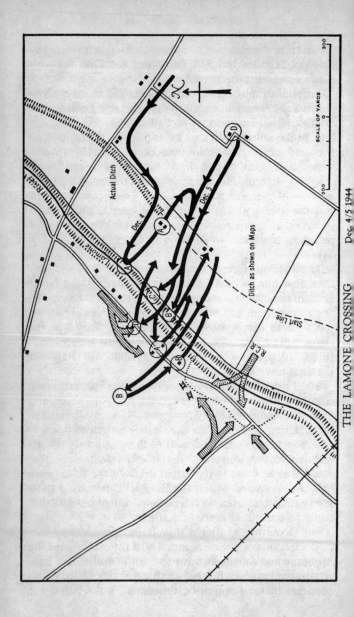

THE LAMONE CROSSING   Dec. 4/5 1944

destined to disruption. Consequently First Brigade, which had not expected to be called upon for several days, was suddenly warned to be ready to take over if Third Brigade failed to make the Lamone bridgehead. The Regiment was told that it could expect to lead any First Brigade assault which might be ordered.

By early afternoon of December 3, the Regiment was well forward of the Montone, waiting in the debris of a number of shattered Italian houses. The wreckage that lay about was not all inanimate, however. In one crumbled hut two Italian girls, both pregnant, lay dull-eyed and sick upon a pile of filthy straw. With them were two young children flaming with the fever of diphtheria. To give what help was possible, there was an ancient crone. In a corner of the floor was a pitiful little heap of rotten potatoes, the sole sustenance these people had. Soldiers glanced into that room in search of shelter from the enemy shell-fire which was already becoming intense – and turned their eyes away and went elsewhere, for there was little that men about to seek out death could do for those who had already found it.

At 1430 hours Third Brigade reported that the enemy had withdrawn across the Lamone dykes but that it was now too weak to attempt an assault across the river. Third Brigade intimated that it could go no farther.

The battalion waited. At 0100 hours on December 4, the acting Divisional Commander, Brig. Desmond Smith, again ordered Third Brigade to cross the Lamone and again that brigade replied that, in its weakened state (it had suffered more than one hundred casualties) it could not go forward. The decision hung fire until dawn had broken and then it was at last decided that First Brigade must take over, and the Regiment was warned that it must prepare to lead the assault.

The news was most distressing to Lt.-Col. Cameron. Some weeks earlier Brig. Calder, commanding First Brigade, had asked Cameron why he did not allow his second-in-command, Major Ketcheson, to command in action. Cameron had replied that, since the final responsibility in battle rested solely with him, he could not justifiably delegate full command authority to Ketcheson in the vital moments of action, although he could and did allow Ketcheson to handle the unit at less important times. The Brigadier had objected to this limited delegation of command.

"Since you won't hand over to Ketcheson voluntarily," he had said, "I shall have to order you to stay out of an action and let him take over."

"That, sir, is your prerogative," Cameron had replied. "But may I suggest that Ketcheson's first battle be an easy one – an approach to contact, for instance?"

"I will be the judge of that," Calder had said, closing the conversation.

The import of that brief discussion had remained large in Cameron's mind and it was partly because of it that he had taken such pains to prepare the plans for the Lugo action. But these plans were nullified when the Regiment moved up on December 2. And it was on that date that Calder judged the moment was ripe to place Ketcheson in command.

Cameron accepted the order only because he had no choice, but he was intensely worried. The Regiment was going into action under an inexperienced c.o. and many of the subordinate commanders were also untried. The Brigade major, a staff officer without battle experience, had been placed in command of Dog company in order to gain that experience preparatory to returning to England for a staff course. Another company was under command of an officer only recently arrived from Canada; while a third officer had only commanded his company in three previous engagements. Even in a minor action this combination of untried commanders would have been risky – Cameron feared that in the battle ahead, it might well be disastrous.

As for Stan Ketcheson, good soldier though he was, he found the situation, which so unexpectedly faced him now, was one of extraordinary difficulty. From the moment he received his orders he had no more than three hours in which to move his battalion up to the forward zone and mount his attack across the Lamone. The Regiment had been ordered to do a job that the entire Third Brigade did not feel competent to attempt. The battle would begin in full daylight and without time for reconnaissance of any sort. There would be no tank support and no means of getting anti-tank guns across the river. What was even worse, the time for firing the artillery preparation had already been fixed and the infantry would either have to conform to it, or lose its benefits. There was no time to conform.

Ketcheson recognized the literal impossibility of the operation and begged for more time. But Brigade H.Q. was under immense pressure from Division to keep the battle rolling, and no postponement could be granted.

Unwilling to commit the entire battalion in what was assuredly a futile venture, Ketcheson decided to open the action with a single company which would go forward to the south dyke and determine the strength of the enemy resistance. If possible it would then attempt a crossing.

The events which followed are related by Capt. Max Porritt who commanded Able company.

"We had barely arrived at the general assembly area when Stan Ketcheson called me to the new B.H.Q. and told me the plan. I tried to appear cheerful, knowing that Stan had his orders; but the timings were desperately short. It was 1230 before I left B.H.Q. and zero was set for 1330. I had an hour to return to my company, issue my orders, and march three miles to the start line.

"Time was slipping so fast that there was no time for reconnaissance or for formal orders. We started immediately for the river, but we had not gone half-way when we heard the artillery open up. I knew we would arrive too late to get any help from our own barrage.

"Assault boats were to have been waiting by the road, but of course they had not arrived. We marched on at top speed, but it was not until 1430 that we reached the Lamone banks. Everything was frighteningly quiet. Our guns had ceased and the enemy had not begun to reply. The platoons lined the base of the high bank, waiting my orders to attempt the crossing. But I thought I should first try to get a look over the crest.

"I crawled up the steep slope and got one quick glimpse of the river before bullets began to flick the earth about me. I was just able to roll back without being hit. My second-in-command, Capt. Christiansen, was beside me and I saw his body go rolling down the slope, his beret flying past my head. He had been shot through the skull and was dead in a few minutes.

"The enemy was alerted now and his small-arms fire dominated the dyke crest and the river gulley completely. I tried to get through on the wireless to call for artillery support, but the set went out. There was nothing for it but to take the company back a hundred yards to the shelter of some buildings. At 1600 hours a messenger reached me with the news that the attack had been postponed."

The first attempt had ended in fiasco but it had at least forced the senior commanders to take cognizance of some of the facts. The Brigadier now had time to prepare a more realistic plan. As he was completing it, Cameron again appeared at Brigade H.Q. and again asked to be allowed to return to his command. Once more he was refused and ordered to the rear, and Ketcheson was called in, along with the C.O. of the R.C.R., to hear the details for a two-battalion assault.

Under cover of a divisional artillery concentration, thickened by the fire of a medium regiment, the two battalions were to cross the river simultaneously at 0100 hours on December 5. Olafson bridging – a type of portable footbridge – was to be provided, together with assault boats.

Information as to the nature of the Lamone obstacle brought back by a hurried R.C.R. patrol was not encouraging. The patrol commander had been drowned while trying to gauge the depth of water. The survivors reported that the near-banks of the dyke rose twenty-five feet in a steep and grassy slope above the level of the farmlands, and then fell abruptly for forty feet to the surface of the water. They reported that the river was at least thirty feet broad; more than five feet deep, and flowing so swiftly that a swimming man would have little chance of survival.

It was a clear and accurate report. Yet, as the events of the next few hours would prove, someone, somewhere, must have tragically underestimated the strength of the Lamone barrier.

The Regiment possessed no air photographs of the Lamone, but it did have copies of the Italian topographical maps and as night fell, Ketcheson pored over these. He saw a lateral road running directly under cover of the north bank, with a row of houses marked along it, and he chose these buildings as the unit's first objective. After they had been taken he intended that the companies would strike inland to a depth of five hundred yards in order to establish a safe perimeter.

The Brigade plan, as Ketcheson, and the C.O. of the R.C.R. received it, had many flaws.

Chief amongst these was the planned use of the artillery. Under the conditions which governed this action, the medium guns should have been directed on rear target areas, while the twenty-five pounder gun-howitzers engaged the targets close to the infantry start line. Instead, and despite the protests of artillery officers, the 4-5 inch mediums, which fire their heavy shells on a very flat trajectory, and which require a wide safety zone, were ordered to engage the houses that lay hidden directly behind the high dyke. This inevitably meant that the path of the shells had to be low, barely clearing the dyke crests. It meant that there were bound to be hits south of the dykes, and this was particularly certain since the plans did not allow time for the medium guns to range on the targets. On the other hand the twenty-five pounders firing high angle trajectories and which had already ranged on the target area during the abortive afternoon attack, could have lobbed their shells well over the dykes with a safe margin of clearance.

The artillery-fire plan had been prepared at Brigade and there was no opportunity for the two battalion commanders to modify it. This was made doubly certain by the fact that copies of the plan were long delayed in reaching the battalions; and Ketcheson, waiting impatiently for his copy so that he could issue his orders, did not receive it until after 2100 hours.

The second flaw in the general plan was the lack of a proper appreciation of the nature of the Lamone as a physical obstacle. As a result there were no adequate provisions for assault boats and rafts which should have been available to ferry heavy support weapons into the bridgehead as soon as it was established. In point of fact, Ketcheson never even knew what assault equipment, apart from the light Olafson bridging, he was to receive, and in the end he had neither assault boats nor rafts.

The third serious flaw lay in the fact that there was no attempt to provide the Regiment with anti-tank guns. At this time a number of special two-pounder, high-velocity anti-tank guns had been received by the Division. These were light enough to be broken down and manhandled, and they were intended to replace the heavy six-pounders on difficult river crossings. Although a number of these new 'Sabot' guns had been attached to other units in the division, none was made available to the Regiment. That these defects in the Brigade plan were largely the result of relentless pressure being applied by higher formations, was poor consolation to the men concerned.

Within the Regiment's own plan there were over-sights that also stemmed from haste, and from too much pressure. In a normal battle the C.O. picks the start line for his Regiment after ground reconnaissance; and all his company commanders (and usually the platoon commanders too) have an opportunity to see that start line on the ground. In case of doubt it is clearly marked, either by guides, or by the use of white tapes.

In the Lamone battle Ketcheson had no time for proper reconnaissance, since the arrival of the fire plan was delayed until after dark, and he felt that he required the plan in order to estimate the requisite safety factor, in terms of distance, from the artillery targets. After the arrival of the fire plan there was barely time to issue the battle orders to the company commanders, and there was insufficient time for Ketcheson to give to the start line problem. Accepting the evidence of the Italian map instead, he chose a ditch which was shown as extending parallel to, and about three hundred yards to the south, of the Lamone dykes. According to the map, this was a clear and obvious land-mark, which could not be missed by the advancing companies even in total darkness.

Moving forward in the pregnant silence after midnight, the two assault companies, Baker and Charlie, stumbled over the sodden ground and the shattered vine posts, and when they came to the start-line ditch they did not see it – for on their front it existed *only* on the map. They pushed on unwittingly until the massive bulk of the Lamone dyke cast its shadow over them. It was exactly ten minutes to zero hour. From the distant south the rumble of the awakening guns came sullenly, while the black sky flickered with the beginnings of the barrage.

In the tense moments that followed, men pressed close against the bank and waited for the metallic scream of the approaching shells. On the crest of the dyke, carrying parties from Support company wrestled in darkness with the unfamiliar Olafson bridging sections. In this instant before battle, the enemy seemed unaware.

Lying on the crest, Major Cliff Broad of Baker heard the familiar wail of the heavy shells approaching and out of his subconscious mind there came an instantaneous flash of knowledge. He half rose and his voice rang out in an urgent cry of warning that was cut off abruptly as the first salvos of the medium artillery crashed into the sodden earth around him.

The distant gunners slammed the heavy shells into the breeches of their weapons and snatched at the firing lanyards, moving with a swift precision, believing that their brothers of the infantry were being well served.

In Charlie company the warning came from a sergeant who had time to cry: "Get down, for Christ's sake, boys! They're falling short!"

Both warnings came too late.

Most of the men were standing up against the dyke when the shells began to fall and for those who survived that initial blast, there was no cover and no place to hide from the appalling thing that came upon them.

Lying face down on the dyke, Broad stared with a despairing fascination at the luminous face of his watch, counting the seconds, the interminable seconds, until the barrage should end. Below him the earth shook and heaved and the red and yellow flashes of the shells illuminated a charnel scene. There seemed to be no sound, for the blasts of the thundering explosions were continuous and beyond the power of human ears to register.

A biting white smoke coiled in darkness to add its own peculiar breath of horror to the stench of burnt explosives. Phosphorus grenades hanging from men's belts had been hit by shrapnel and had exploded, spraying the living and the dead with their flesh-consuming fragments. In the inferno of those moments men ran aimlessly until they fell – their dark, contorted shapes held in momentary relief against the glare of new explosions.

Then suddenly it was done. In the silence of the aftermath the living lay immobile, stunned. And then one tardy gunner fired one final shell – the period that marked the end.

The cries of the wounded rose slowly in that final silence. In Baker company half of the men were dead or wounded, and the remainder were in a state of utter shock. In Charlie company, that had gone into battle with a strength of only two platoons, the havoc was as bad.

Men did strange things. A senior N.C.O. got down on his hands and knees and began to search earnestly for the cap that had been blown from his head. His mind was concentrated on one thing alone, the need to find the cap and salvage the cap-badge. He grunted irritably when stretcher bearers cried to him for assistance and it was not until a private soldier threatened to put him under arrest that he came back into reality.

Major Broad watched with unseeing eyes as his best friend, Sandy Moffat, came running up from the rear, desperately afraid that Broad had been killed. Broad turned on him without recognition, and with a cruel violence, and strode away.

At battalion headquarters, men waited at the radios for news that the crossing had begun. Word was slow in coming.

Half a mile to the rear Max Porritt had watched from Able company area as the barrage came down, and even he had suspected nothing.

"The barrage ended and there was silence. Suddenly I heard a scuffling and the sound of someone panting, and I saw a Support company man emerge from the ditch beside me. He seemed dazed and he was trembling violently. He babbled that everyone was dead, but I could get no sense out of him so I took him and hurried back to B.H.Q.

"He told his story then and it was grim. Then the survivors started to straggle in, some nursing wounds and all looking as if they had been through the valley of death. The artillery representative attached to us looked as if he wished the floor would open beneath his feet and let him depart from this nightmare. But even in the face of this calamity Stan Ketcheson kept magnificent control of himself.

"He got on the radio to Brigade at once and told them what had happened, then stated flatly that the Regiment could not carry on with the attack. If he threw in Able and Dog companies to make the bridgehead now he would have nothing in reserve. His face was tense as he listened to the answer from Brigade. . . . "

Brigade received the news with disbelief at first, but when the reality became certain the Brigadier contacted Division and asked for permission to postpone the assault, or at least to replace the Regiment. Permission was brusquely refused.

Ketcheson accepted the inevitable with an outward calm. At once Able and Dog companies received the order to move up. Dawn was not far away, and the men knew what could happen if they were caught at the crossing in daylight. By the time the new assault group reached the dykes the first cold and misty greyness had lightened the eastern sky. There was already sufficient light for them to avoid stumbling on the dead comrades lying in the shadows of the dyke.

Operation Chuckle proceeded in the face of a weird paradox. The enemy did not fire a shot as the two companies made their way across the half-completed Olafson bridge. There was no resistance. It was as if, for the moment, death was satiated. The quiet was frightening and strangely ominous, but there was a good reason for it.

On the left the R.C.R. had made good its initial bridgehead with two companies across the river, and the enemy – men of the 741 Regiment of the 114 Jaeger Division – had temporarily shifted their attention to the left in a counterattack against the R.C.R.

In the strange vacuum of the Regiment's bridgehead the world seemed to have reverted to a sombre hour of peace. The two companies established themselves in the row of houses by the road and prepared to move outward to their secondary objectives. Ketcheson, desperately worried about their weakness in numbers, now ordered the remnants of Baker company to cross on the left flank and plug the gap between the Regiment and the R.C.R.

Full dawn had come by this time, and a sniper peering

out of an upstairs window in Able company area saw several German vehicles coming down the road towards the huddle of farms. It was as if this had been the signal, for suddenly a spate of machine-gun and rifle fire burst over the two companies. The hour of peace was at an end.

Close-pressed on three sides by a determined infantry counterattack supported by sustained bombardment, Able and Dog tried to call for artillery assistance, only to discover that their radios shielded by the high dyke walls, had failed them. Dog company, under the command of Major Macdougal, attempted to work its way eastward along the lateral road in order to enlarge the bridgehead a little, but the enemy was too strong and the attempt failed. Able was in hand-to-hand contact on the left and both companies were suffering severe casualties. No further help could be expected, since the Regiment had no more reserves. The threatening sound of tanks moving down on the buildings made the position seem doubly untenable, and when a rumour grew and spread that the R.C.R. had abandoned its bridgehead, the survivors of Able and Dog gave way to panic.

Small groups broke away from the houses and ran for the dykes. The panic spread until it could not be contained, and a confused and spontaneous retreat began. The rumble of the approaching tanks grew louder and the distracted company officers cursed the absence of anti-tank guns whose simple presence might well have saved the battle, though they fired not a single shot. Able company rallied momentarily between the dykes, but there could now be no question of going back into the bridgehead and the company completed its retreat.

Meanwhile, what remained of Baker after the early morning slaughter, had struck off inland, unaware that it was now the sole Canadian unit that was advancing instead of retreating. It penetrated some four hundred yards from the dykes before it came under intense small-arms fire and was forced to ground in an open grain field. There was no cover here except for a single haystack, and this was soon demolished by enemy mortar bombs. The aerial of the radio was shot away, leaving Baker out of contact with the rest of the battalion.

Ordering the company to hold its position under Sandy Moffat's leadership, Broad ran back under heavy fire to the river bank. He reached the Lamone a few hundred yards west of the original crossing and here he found a distracted group of R.C.R. infantry and an artillery officer preparing to withdraw. They told him that the R.C.R. bridgehead had collapsed but they were so intent on trying to get through to R.C.R. H.Q. that Broad was unable to use their radio to contact his own regiment for orders.

Recognizing the scope of the disaster Broad sent for his company and prepared to make a final stand at the abandoned R.C.R. flank position so that at least a toe-hold might be maintained over the Lamone. The remains of his company, reduced now to less than a platoon in fighting strength, occupied the group of stone houses. Broad's signaller managed to repair his radio aerial with a length of vine wire and established a fragile contact with the Regiment.

The tanks that had broken the R.C.R. bridgehead now converged on Baker, and the houses of the defenders were simultaneously curtained off from the rest of the world by a tremendous concentration of German mortar and artillery fire. Systematically the enemy tanks began to knock down the stone walls with AP shot, while remaining safely out of range of Baker's only anti-tank weapon, the short-range PIAT.

Incredibly, Baker held out for another hour. It was still unable to get artillery support; there was no hope of its receiving anti-tank guns, and there were no infantry available to reinforce it. At 0900 hours Broad finally gave the order to withdraw. Lt. Rex Walters, commanding the remnants of a platoon, led his men into the river and they were immediately swept away and almost drowned. Only by abandoning all their equipment were they able to reach the opposite bank. Nine hours after the battle had begun for it in the holocaust of its own artillery fire, the battle ended for Baker company.

The aftermath was not long delayed.

An intercepted radio signal from the enemy commander, von Vietinghoff, reported that "the bridgehead over the Lamone which had been formed northwest of Russi, was smashed in a determined counterattack carried out with perfect co-operation from the artillery. The enemy suffered considerable casualties...."

Von Vietinghoff had not exaggerated. It was several hours before the Regiment could take stock of its physical wounds, and then it was to find that sixty-seven men had been killed, seriously wounded or left captive in enemy hands. But this was the least of the hurt. For the first time the unit had been severely beaten in the field, and for the first time its spirit had broken. The one solid thing that had remained in the world of the infantrymen had been destroyed.

For the first time, men knew that they had failed the Regiment, and in so doing knew that they had failed themselves.

Knowledge of the failure was unbearable. It knifed into them in many different ways. It is a measure of the appalling inner destructiveness of the failure that even in the first days of shock few of the men or of the officers sought to lay the blame outside themselves. It was only by slow degrees that awareness returned, and with it the knowledge that the fault lay not alone with them, but that much of it lay on those shadowy figures in authority who had forced them to destroy, with their own hands, the one true thing that remained in the chaos of their world.

It is a revealing fact that at no time was the artillery blamed. It seems to have been understood by every man that the gunners had no fault. Indeed Cameron himself later visited the artillery units concerned and carried this message to them from the Regiment. But the gunners were sick at heart at what had happened, even though they were guiltless.

In the first hours after the battle the Regiment trembled and its fabric shook with a destroying fever.

The mood of the Regiment in that moment stands out in an account left by one of the officers of Able company.

"In the heat of the shameful retreat I passed a wounded man in a slit trench on the far side of the river. He was too badly wounded to move but he cried out to me for help. I promised I would send aid as soon as I could. . . .

"We were back in the farm on the south side, holed up there, and utterly shaken. I cannot describe my feelings. But I was furious with events and I felt I would welcome an end to myself. I remember standing in the farmyard with an intense feeling of self-disgust and a supreme contempt for myself and everyone around me. Shells bursting near could not even rouse fear in me.

"At B.H.Q. Ketcheson and Cameron were staring at the maps. The Brigadier came in and asked me some leading questions – why had we not got our PIATS on to the tanks, etc. etc. I could give no satisfactory answers to anything.

"Later with an intense desire to do something that would help me not to think, I took a carrier back up to the dykes to try to find Major Macdougal and some of the other missing men. I thought I could perhaps rescue the wounded chap I had seen on the far bank as well.

"I left my revolver with Able company and putting a Red Cross brassard on my arm joined the 4th Field Ambulance Section. We climbed the dyke and found the wounded man, but we did not see another living soul.

"We had just got the wounded lad into the vehicle when someone spotted two German soldiers waving at us and pointing behind the dyke. I said I would go and see what they wanted, not really caring what happened in any event. Two of the Field Ambulance men came with me and when we got across to the far side we saw that it was lined with German soldiers wearing the *Edelweiss* on their caps and helmets. They said they had some of our wounded and would show them to us soon. I told them that I was on the medical staff of the unit but as we were talking we saw a group of our men shepherded out of a dug-out in the bank. Unfortunately they sized up my situation wrongly, and someone yelled, 'so they got you too!' "

The prisoners had not been very wrong for that officer was never allowed to re-cross the Lamone and was driven instead into Germany as a prisoner himself.

There were a good many other men who felt that nothing mattered and that only death itself would ease the pain.

That day there was an inquisition at Corps headquarters and when Major Ketcheson emerged from it and returned to the Regiment's H.Q., he stood in a doorway while enemy mortar bombs burst in the yard. It may be that in his agony of mind he would have welcomed the inevitable wound, had it been fatal. That it was not fatal was a brief concession from the hard fates of that day.

At Army headquarters, the news of the Lamone débâcle had brought deep disappointment. The great plan had failed and the offensive on Bologna had been brought to a halt. Men had need to suffer further for the failure.

Three commanding officers who had questioned orders which they believed to be impossible of execution, but who had nevertheless obeyed those orders to the limits of their abilities, were the chief victims. Both the Brigadier and the C.O. of the R.C.R. were relieved of their commands. Only the explosion of a mortar bomb forestalled a similar fate for Ketcheson. These three were singled out to bear the public ignominy for a failure which had been theirs only in its enforced enactment, and not in its design.

While higher command worked in its devious ways to justify itself, the padre went forward to his lonely tasks.

Around one great shell crater six men lay in the patterned design of flower petals spreading from the flower's heart. Beside the body of a corporal a packet of Canadian tobacco glistened in the dew and the padre remembered how, a few hours earlier, the corporal had offered him a fill from this same packet as a gesture between friends – before battle was joined.

TWENTY-TWO

The Battle Without End

THE WEATHER drew a shroud over the Lamone tragedy. For five days the rains beat down and it was impossible for battles to be fought. In its positions before the dykes, the Regiment waited in a state of coma.

Some of the officers and senior N.C.O.s partially shook off their own personal sense of defeat and began trying to repair the damage, but the days were dark and most men found it easier to crouch in the cover of demolished buildings and to let their spirits rot. Perhaps if the unit had been pulled out of the line for a few days some immediate resurgence might have taken place, but there was no such relief. The Regiment remained in this place of its shame – and the wound was kept open and palpitating by the enemy guns. Dog company perhaps fared worst, for it was close under the dykes and the enemy, fearful of a renewed attack, 'stonked' each separate building, every road and path in the company area, with thoroughness and fury.

There was no real possibility of evading the enemy fire. The marshy ground now held water within a few inches of the surface and slit-trenches filled as soon as they were dug. The only shelter from shells and weather was in the little stone farms, and the position of each of these was intimately known to the German artillery. The cold was becoming severe and ice formed every night. Wet snow and sleet beat down upon the grey morass that not long since had been the neatly patterned vineyards of a people.

There was no ebbing of the tension anywhere in the battalion area. Men drove their jeeps, or walked through the heavy mud with a constant pressure at their backs and their ears strained to the high scream of the approaching shells.

Near a crossroad behind B.H.Q. was the Regimental cemetery and even that was not a sanctuary. On more than one occasion the padre and the grave-digging detail were forced to seek shelter in the wet and open graves.

The relations between soldiers and civilians grew closer. Liberators and liberated were existing in the sympathy of shared destruction. In one platoon area an old woman rose before dawn each day to mix hot wine and the juice of a few scrofulous oranges for the patrol that would have to make its way out to the dykes and back.

On December 10, the weather moderated sufficiently to allow Operation Chuckle to continue. During the night hours and after an intense barrage, Third Brigade, augmented by the 48th Highlanders, crossed the Lamone and, with anti-tank guns in support, made good the bridgehead.

At 0800 hours on December 11, the Regiment was ordered into the bridgehead to clear the eastern perimeter as far as the village of Traversara.

Reduced to considerably less than half of its normal fighting strength, the battalion went forward over that ill-omened ground. But this time there was no real struggle. The enemy was withdrawing rapidly to the next river line and Traversara proved empty, except for a little band of Italian partisans, recently emerged from cellar hiding places.

There was no halt. New orders were issued to the Regiment and to the R.C.R. to seize a crossing over the Vecchio canal. The battalion moved out of the bridgehead on the right, the R.C.R. on the left, and by mid-afternoon, both were in contact with the enemy south of the Vecchio. Charlie company had reached the banks at a demolished road bridge and was soon involved in a hard action.

That battle had not yet been fought out when still other orders arrived. The Carleton and York Regiment was to replace the R.C.R. on the left and together with the Regiment was to drive forward to the Naviglio Canal and form a bridgehead over it on this same day.

The R.C.R. had by now made good a crossing over the Vecchio so that the C.Y.R. could pass through. But on the Regiment's front no crossing had as yet been made. The C.O. called his Orders group.

While Charlie held the enemy in action at the blown bridge, the remaining three companies led by Able were to swing far to the right and infiltrate across the swollen stream. They would then leapfrog forward to the banks of the Naviglio but, and here the C.O. made his independent decision, they would not cross nor attempt to cross, until there had been time for reconnaissance, time to plan the battle and time for support weapons to get forward. As things stood on the evening of December 11, there was still no bridge even across the Lamone and no vehicles, except for a few jeeps that had been manhandled over the dykes. By dawn the C.O. expected to have *two* river obstacles behind him, and he did not intend to add a third until the first two had been conquered by the engineers so that tanks and anti-tank guns might come up.

The attempt to sneak across the Vecchio was eminently successful. At 0300 hours on December 12, Able moved over the canal without arousing the attention of the enemy engaged with Charlie on the left. The two other assaulting companies then crossed the barrier and moved on into the chill night. By 0530 hours Able had reached its objective, a group of houses three hundred yards from the Naviglio dykes. Surprise had now been lost, and Able had been heavily 'stonked' with resultant casualties including Capt. Weese, who had just taken over as company commander after having served for two years as battalion mortar officer.

Dog company came up through a thickening fall of shells and after passing Able, pushed on towards the

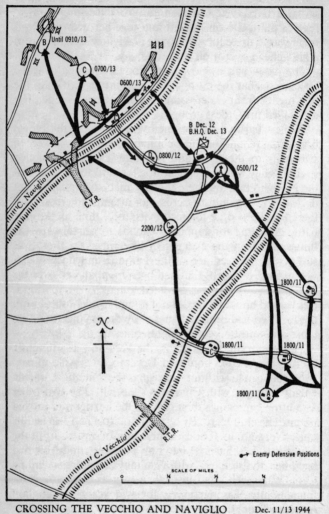

Until 0910/13

B

C 0700/13

0600/13

B Dec. 12
B.H.Q. Dec. 13

D 0800/12

0500/12

'C. Naviglio

C.Y.R.

2200/12 C

1800/11 B

N

1800/11 C

1800/11 D

1800/11 A

C. Vecchio

R.C.R.

●—● Enemy Defensive Positions

SCALE OF MILES

CROSSING THE VECCHIO AND NAVIGLIO   Dec. 11/13 1944

Naviglio dykes. The enemy still contested possession of the intervening ground and Dog also suffered casualties. These were not to be measured in the numbers of the dead, but in terms of the effect upon the company of the death of one man. He was Sgt. Van Hende and he was one of those remarkable individuals who by their very presence can inspire multitudes. Van Hende had received a Distinguished Conduct Medal only the day before and the honour had merit above most, for he was quite literally idolized by the entire company. His death brought a kind of spiritual paralysis to Dog company.

Reaching the Naviglio dykes at last, Dog attempted to send a patrol to the crest of the southern slopes but the enemy was now thoroughly aroused and an instant exchange of fire between the Bren gunners on the one side, and the MG 42 gunners on the other, soon swelled into a full-scale action. It was not limited to small arms. Having by now had much experience with attacks on their dyke positions, the Germans knew the form. Mustering all their heavy mortars and high-angle howitzers, the Naviglio defenders brought them to bear on the ground immediately behind the southern dyke. The crump of bombs and shells merged into an all but continuous roar and Dog company, unable to dig slit trenches in the half-frozen muck, was forced to retire into the inadequate shelter of two stone huts.

In the C.O.'s mind there was no possibility of an immediate attack across the Naviglio. The only anti-tank guns on the combined front were two of the light two-pounders attached to the C.Y.R. The Lamone bridges were not yet ready for traffic and the supporting tanks waited, restively, south of that barrier. There were pressing administrative problems too, for rations and ammunition had to be brought forward.

Unable to cross the Lamone the whole of 'A' and 'F' Echelons with all the unit's vehicles were crowded against the south dykes while the Regiment itself was now far ahead, with the unbridged Vecchio at the half-way mark.

Nevertheless, rations – and hot rations – went forward and the fighting companies hardly missed a meal during the two days that followed.

Long before dawn the cooks filled the insulated 'dixies' with hot food and the company quartermasters loaded the heavy containers on their jeeps. At the Lamone banks, a cable was hitched to each jeep's rear-end and it was slowly lowered down the bank to cross the swollen torrent on a light pontoon bridge. At the far bank the procedure was repeated and painfully each little truck was hauled up to the other crest.

Beyond the Lamone the jeeps scuttled forward through the smoking ruins of Traversara and up the open road, still under heavy shell and mortar fire, to the Vecchio. Here the crews portaged the heavy 'dixies', slipping and slithering down the steep slopes and across the boulder-strewn river bed. Beyond the Vecchio there was one single vehicle, a jeep belonging to Able company and driven by Cpl. Lloyd Annis. Annis' jeep had been literally carried across the Vecchio and during the whole of the battle it was the sole vehicle at the Regiment's disposal. For forty-eight hours Annis was almost continuously at the wheel, moving the wounded back or carrying the ammunition and rations forward.

Through that thunderous day the C.O. waited for news that the Lamone had been bridged – but the news never came. When dusk began to fall the Regiment could wait no longer.

The 'O' group was held at 1800 hours. The four company commanders listened intently and the strain of their uncertainties aged their faces until the outlines blurred. In the company areas men gathered their weapons with a dulled and fatalistic effort that was more mechanical than the motions of automatons. No one said the words, but each man heard them. "Here we go again." Outside in the darkness the mutter of distant guns, and the thumping crash of exploding shells became a part of the heart's beat.

News that the C.Y.R. had captured a small bridgehead

brought a brief release of tension, for the Regiment would not now have to make its own crossing, but could come up through the C.Y.R. before breaking out to the right. Relieved of the grim necessity of an initial assault there was an upsurge of hope amongst the men – a small enough revival of their spirits, but sufficient.

At 2200 hours the companies began to move.

Scrambling across the Naviglio into the small bridge-head, each company in turn swung off to seek its far objective in a night already hideous with the sounds of battle. Almost unconscious, yet directly driven, the platoons filed away into the darkness.

Before dawn all three assault companies had reached and occupied their objectives.

Baker company had the farthest to go, for its goal was a little group of farm houses called San Carlo, almost a thousand yards ahead of the Naviglio, and well off to the right. Luck and good leadership enabled the company to reach the buildings without encountering the enemy.

Charlie company, with a supporting role, headed straight out across the tangled fields and squelched its way to a point half-way between Baker and the canal. Here, in the open and with no cover save a haystack, it tried to dig itself into the saturated soil.

Able company struck out along the lateral road beneath the northern banks and was soon fighting for possession of the inevitable row of stone farm houses.

With the dawn the scraps of news that filtered back over the portable radios seemed uniformly good. Reports from Brigade indicated that the combined two-battalion bridge-head was now a thousand yards broad and, at Baker company, a thousand deep.

But to Cameron these fragments of information were meaningless until he could hear that the Lamone bridge was finished, and the Sherman tanks were moving up. Again that information did not come.

Other information began to trickle in, and the dark clouds of a grim foreboding began to gather over B.H.Q.

As dawn came full, the enemy struck back.

The messages from the signaller with Baker told that company's story. Distorted by static and by the strain of events, the signaller's voice echoed in the receiver at B.H.Q.

"Enemy C.A. with tank support coming in hard from the left...attacking from the front with MK. IV tanks... urgently need tank support...tanks closing in...."

There was a break in communications and then the voice of Major Stockdale, commanding the company. He spoke directly to Cameron. "We can't hold out," he said. "Do you wish us to remain or to withdraw?" And Cameron. "You must remain...."

Cameron's decision was of the sort that ages men and withers up their hearts. Knowing full well he was dooming Baker to destruction, he could not give the order to withdraw. There were three other companies – there was the Regiment – and the sacrifice of Baker was needed to buy time until the Shermans could come up.

At 0910 hours the radio at Baker company went off the air.

Charlie company commander, his men spread-eagled in the frigid mud of the open field, watched helplessly as the Germans closed in on the cluster of houses at San Carlo. He watched as the MK. IV tanks methodically shattered each house in turn, leaving it only a dusty rubble heap in the morning mists. He watched as a little group that had been in slit-trenches just behind the houses fled under the enemy guns towards the distant dykes. The rest of Baker company was gone.

Meanwhile Able company, holding the houses on the right and along the dyke wall had come under the attack from two S.P. guns and a strong force of infantry. The three platoons were cut off from one another and at last two of them were forced back across the dykes. No. 9 platoon, reduced to a handful of men, held its position and was overlooked by the attacking enemy.

Now it was Charlie's turn. While Baker was being attacked, the men of Charlie were unhappily aware that the enemy had seen them. But with the casual leisureliness of those who are assured of victory, the Germans left Charlie alone until Baker was destroyed. Then the full fury of the counterattack turned on Charlie. The haystack blazed into flame. The men of No. 13 platoon, off to the right and huddling in slit trenches under a heavy 'stonk', raised their heads in the heavy morning mist to find themselves staring into the muzzles of twenty German rifles and carbines. Except for two survivors, No. 13 platoon vanished and was not heard of again.

At B.H.Q., now forward almost under the walls of the dyke, the C.O. did what he could to save the situation. Dog company was ordered forward, but Dog, suffering from the effect of seven days of continuous exposure to shellfire, and from the loss of most of its officers and N.C.O.s, was in turmoil. Three times the company set out from the shelter of a building, goaded into the attempts largely by Cpl. Harry Brott, but three times enemy guns drove it back again.

There was now only the hope that the remnants of Charlie company could stave off another disaster for the Regiment. Charlie was ordered to withdraw as far as the north dyke and there to make a final effort to maintain a foothold across the river. Fighting all the way, what was left of Charlie came slowly back and took up positions in a large house already occupied by few men of the C.Y.R. and by the survivors of Baker company. The motley little group waited while the enemy tanks came down upon them in full view.

Farther left, on the C.Y.R. front, the situation was almost as desperate but here there were a few of the new twopounder anti-tank guns of the 51st Anti-tank Battery and the heroic gunners managed to hold the enemy tanks partially at bay. The whole bridgehead had now shrunk into a narrow strip hugging the north dyke; and the end seemed fore-ordained.

Max Lerner's R.A.P. had as usual been sited as close to the battle as he could manage it. The R.A.P. building was a convenient one, but at a crossroad four hundred yards behind the dyke, so that it inevitably focused upon itself a heavy enemy gun fire. The C.O. had set up his advanced H.Q. with the R.A.P. The padre has left this account of the events that took place there.

"It was just getting light on the 13th, when into the R.A.P. came the strangest assorted pair I have ever seen. At one end of a stretcher was 'Ma' Hildrieth, chicken-scrounger par excellence, who had been our muleteer at the Arielli, and who had later became a stretcher bearer. 'Ma' was tired and dirty but taking everything in his stride as usual. On the other end of the stretcher, helping to carry one of our wounded, was a German, a huge chap who must have stood over six feet tall. He was a sergeant-major, and as smart and well turned out as if he had just come off parade. We asked little 'Ma' if he'd had any trouble with his pal, and 'Ma' replied, 'Naw, he's as gentle as a lame mule!'

"About this time the big counterattack began and the really heavy shelling started. From dawn until late afternoon, the house was under constant bombardment – 'moaning minnies', 88s and everything in the book came over. Early on, a shed on the south side – from which a door led into the main room – was almost demolished by a direct hit. There were a lot of vino casks in the shed, and in between them a number of our men had bedded down and were trying to rest. The barrels were perforated, but the men miraculously escaped and ran into the main building, soaked in wine, and stumbling over each other in their hurry. The wine flowed across the floor behind them, and for the rest of the day we lived in the stink of sour vino fumes.

"As time passed the building grew more and more crowded. The remnants of Able company found shelter here, along with Dog company and the assault platoon of the Irish Regiment, which was somewhere off to the right. And then of course there was the R.A.P. and a section of the 4th Field Ambulance.

"The C.O. was directing the battle from a table in the main room where he sat smoking quietly, his ear to the radio set. In all that confusion and excitement, he was as calm and collected as if he had been at home.

"About noon I think – we had lost all track of time – Lt. Col. Joe Coke, who was then commanding the 4th Field Ambulance, joined us. He had just got nicely in the door when the most unholy 'stonk' I have ever seen came down on us. The house received a number of direct hits and for several minutes there was an uninterrupted roar of deafening explosions as shells landed in the courtyard and all around the building. Earlier we had been troubled with the problem of what to do with the big German prisoner. There was no room for him on the floor, so someone had got the idea of making him stand against the wall on a low chest of drawers.

"When that 'stonk' came down the whole milling mob of us hit the floor. There were two exceptions. Don Cameron sat just as quietly as ever by the radio, while up on the chest of drawers the big German stood at attention and never moved a muscle. As I lay on the floor, for some idiotic reason I began to think of the story in the Book of Daniel – about the graven image that Nebuchadnezzar set up, and before which 'at the sound of the sackbut, psaltery, and dulcimer' all, on pain of death, had to abase themselves.

"By this time the whole battle had begun to look like Armageddon for the Regiment. Only Charlie was left in front of us and the messages coming through from that beleaguered company were becoming increasingly desperate. 'The enemy is pressing us close.' 'We're running out of ammo.' 'What are your orders?' Cameron was standing now with his back to the fireplace and I would have defied anyone to tell what was passing through his mind as very quietly he told the signaller to reply: 'Help is coming, hold on.'

"Cameron's coolness steadied all of us, although we were sure in our minds that the promise of relief was just a pipe-dream. With enemy tanks prowling around a few hundred yards in front of us – able to cross the Naviglio at will – and remembering that behind us were two canals that, as far as we knew, had not yet been bridged and were impassable to our tanks, we couldn't see that we had a hope.

"And then suddenly we heard the rumble of tank treads on the road outside. Our common thought was, 'Well – this is it.' "

At this point the padre's story is taken up by Q.M.S. Basil Smith who had just arrived at B.H.Q. bringing with him a hot meal.

"Someone ran to the window and yelled and the rest of us crowded up and looked out too. And then we knew how the boys had felt at the siege of Lucknow when they heard the skirl of the pipes. Coming up the road was a squadron of British Columbia Dragoon tanks swinging their 17-pounder guns from side to side as if they meant business. And what was just as welcome a sight was the marching infantry of the Loyal Edmontons – the only outfit in the Army that we ever considered might be as good, or better, than ourselves. We heard later that the first of the tanks had crossed the Lamone before the bolts on the bridge were tight. They and the Eddies saved the day. And I for one will never again listen to any disparaging remarks about our armour. That squadron looked better to us than Hedy Lamarr in her birthday suit!"

The Dragoons wasted no time. Finding a ford on the bridgehead, they rumbled over the Naviglio firing as they went. One of them appeared outside the ruins of the house where Charlie company was making its final stand. It nosed around the corner of the building and was immediately hit by a German shell. The gunner leapt out of the turret, his clothes flaming, and some of the Charlie company men raced out and dragged him under cover. All the wounded tanker said was "Did we make it in time?"

They had made it in time.

The enemy had made fourteen counterattacks against

the combined bridgehead and had been stalemated only by the tenacious handful of surviving infantry and the unremitting efforts of the Canadian artillery. Now, with the appearance of the British Columbia Dragoon tanks, and the Loyal Eddies, the enemy gave up the struggle and withdrew leaving many of his own tanks to smoulder on the muddy roads.

In the early morning of December 14, the Regiment was withdrawn behind the Vecchio and for a while the battle passed beyond it.

In the eyes of the Army, and of those who listened to the bulletins of war, the action at the Naviglio had obliterated the failure at the Lamone crossing. But it was not so within the unit. The survivors were told that their feat had been given prominence on the B.B.C. news reports – and they did not care. The Army Commander sent a personal message of congratulation to them, and they listened, and did not hear it. Even the men of Charlie company to whom much of the credit for the holding of the bridge-head belonged, were unaffected. These men were beyond pride, beyond praise, beyond condemnation. They were empty of all emotions and knew nothing except a stupifying weariness. The medical officers had a term for individuals who had reached the end of their tether. They called it 'battle exhaustion' and it was a polite term that meant 'burned out'.

Waiting in the ruins of Traversara, the entity that was the Regiment lay like the last embers of a fire. Most of its substance had been consumed and there was little left save cooling ashes. Physically the exhaustion of the Regiment was just short of total. More than a hundred men had been lost at the Vecchio and the Naviglio alone. Baker company existed only as a handful of soldiers culled from the starved ranks of the remaining companies. Able, Dog and Charlie were hardly above the fighting strength of platoons. Spiritually, the wastage had been even greater.

On December 16 the Regiment returned to action.

Although the Vecchio and Naviglio had been crossed

and the C.Y.R. and Hastings bridgehead had now been extended by Second Brigade as far as the banks of the Senio, to the west the enemy still held all three of these dyked obstacles.

On December 16 First Brigade was ordered to shift to the west and launch a new assault, *a new crossing of both the Vecchio and the Naviglio*. What had been done once, was now to be done again.

There was madness in that order. The entire First Brigade was in a condition similar to that in which the Regiment now found itself. The R.C.R. in particular, had sustained heavy losses and the 48th was in hardly better condition to face a new set of river crossings. Nevertheless, the orders were issued and the 48th was told to cross the Vecchio on the night of December 16/17, while the Regiment moved up to provide close support.

The attack was made through the deepening mud on a night when the frost hardened the saturated battledress of the soldiers. The attack failed. The Regiment, huddling in its shattered farm buildings waiting for the order to go forward, heard of the failure with apathetic indifference. The apathy was hardly broken when new orders arrived for a two battalion assault on the night of December 17/18, by the R.C.R. on the right, and the Hastings on the left.

Men accepted the order without real comprehension. When H-Hour struck at 0400 on December 18, the companies that moved forward to the Vecchio dykes were hardly more than straggling little mobs of somnambulists. But their dream world was that of an all-embracing nightmare.

There is no need to dwell upon the action – if such it can be called. Cameron might have refused to commit his Regiment at all, had he not known that his refusal would simply have resulted in his removal from command. He held his duty higher and he believed, with truth, that by remaining he could still salvage something of his Regiment from the débâcle. But it was with cold and shrunken hearts that the officers gave the orders for the advance that night.

By a superhuman effort the R.C.R. secured a small bridgehead, before Dog, now reduced to eighteen men, reached the dykes. The ghost of Baker company, coming up behind, reported by radio that the R.C.R. bridgehead had already been heavily counterattacked and was disintegrating. By the time Charlie arrived, the battle was over and the brave remnant of the R.C.R. assault company had been thrust back to the south banks. Had the plan been followed to the letter, Cameron would now have given orders to his Regiment to try for a crossing. He did not give those orders, knowing that if he did, the Regiment would surely die – if not in the flesh, then in the spirit certainly.

As the enemy shell-fire rose in intensity during the bitter hours of December 18, the Regiment lay almost comatose under the explosions. It could have come no closer to oblivion, without overstepping the fatal line.

That night the three infantry units of the First Brigade received special attention. So-called 'sonic devices' were brought into the Brigade area as a cover-scheme for an attack to be staged far to the east by Second Brigade. The 'sonic devices' consisted of gramophones with high-powered amplifiers that sent the noises of tanks, vehicles and other war-like sounds roaring over to the Germans' ears. The Germans reacted by subjecting the prostrate First Brigade to a violent barrage that was repeated intermittently throughout the night.

This was the hour when the entire Brigade should have been withdrawn, carried far behind the lines out of the very sound of the guns, and given the care that belongs to the gravely wounded. But the Brigade could not be spared, for there were no fresh troops.

In Canada, the Zombies rioted.

In the morass of the Ravenna plains the battle continued. A message went back to 'B' Echelon calling for volunteers to shoulder rifles with the exhausted survivors of the rifle companies. The 'B' echelon drivers, the leather workers, sanitary men and all the rest responded to a man. They left the trucks parked and abandoned, and they came forward.

From December 21 until December 23, the Regiment continued on, too weak to drive the enemy before it and, as Cameron put it: "With only enough strength left to lean against the Hun as he withdrew."

There were few incidents of those days that emerge with any clarity from the blackness of memory. One that survives concerns an N.C.O. of the 4th Field Ambulance, Sgt. Gordon Clarke.

It was in the last days before Christmas and Baker company had moved up to the Senio banks. Having already taken one enemy occupied house, a platoon pushed forward toward a second building and an enemy sniper dropped the leading soldier. One of the company stretcher bearers ran out to the wounded man, and himself fell to the sniper's bullets. The surviving men of the platoon thrust their bodies into the half-frozen muck, and could do nothing for the two who lay ahead. Sgt. Clarke, who had no business to be this far forward, had been watching. Without hesitation he took a length of rope, tied it about his waist, and crawled into the open.

The sniper saw him well enough and all through that frigid crawl, Clarke heard the bullets smacking into the mud about him. Nevertheless, he reached the two casualties and ran his hands over their warm bodies. The stretcher bearer was dead, but the other man still lived.

While the angry sniper redoubled his efforts, Clarke tied the free end of his rope to the wounded soldier and crawled back to shelter dragging the unconscious man behind him.

It was an incident of small moment in the scope of the battle, yet it had the power to stir soldiers who thought themselves beyond reach of any emotions. Incidents like these could still fan the embers of the flame that had burned so low.

On December 23 the Regiment was at last withdrawn from the line and moved back to Cattolica for a forty-eight hour relief. The intention of the staff was that, in these two days, the Regiment should recover its strength and spirit and be fresh for action once again.

Neither the men nor the officers questioned the purpose. On this, the fifth Christmas away from Canada, the Regiment was concerned with one thing along – the fact that there was a forty-eight hour reprieve from death.

TWENTY-THREE

Resurrection

O N DECEMBER 26 the unit moved up to a reserve position near Bagnacavallo. Those last December days marked the lowest ebb to which the Regiment had ever fallen; but at the same time they marked the beginning of the turning tide and the first painful and uncertain steps towards regeneration.

The exhaustion of mind and body could be dealt with – but only if the essential faith in the Regiment itself could be renewed.

This regeneration of the spirit might have been accomplished by a deliberate fostering of the idea that the total blame for the Lamone débâcle lay outside the unit. Such an attitude would have turned the Regiment further in upon itself, uniting it in common hatred of all those who did not wear its badge. But enduring things cannot be rebuilt upon evasion, nor upon hatred.

The real measure of the unit's greatness was to be found in its willingness to accept the fact that it had failed, and that much of the blame for failure rested on itself. Men took what comfort they could from the extenuating circumstances, and they despised those on higher levels who had blundered. But the gnawing recognition that it was the individuals within the Regiment who had failed, was not to be denied.

It was from the acceptance of its own humiliation that the Regiment was ultimately reborn.

The N.C.O.s and officers set themselves to see how they had failed their men. With a kind of dedicated fanaticism they laboured to rekindle the battalion's flickering spirit. Cameron gave them their guidance, and at times it was a ruthless guidance. What could not be saved had to be cut out. Those soldiers, both other ranks and officers, who were beyond reclamation were quietly sent away for medical re-boarding. This was a drastic action, for the physical strength of the unit was now at a fraction of its operational level, and there were no indications that new reinforcements would be forthcoming. Those who left the battalion during this period did not do so under any cloud, for they were men who had long ago deserved repatriation. In the language of the day, "they had had the course". Their exhaustion was so complete that full recovery was not possible for many of them even in the environs of their own homes in Canada. Most of them had performed prodigies of endurance, and they simply had no more to give. Yet many of them left the Regiment unwillingly, and some pleaded to be allowed to stay. Theirs was a unique tragedy in a time of general tragedy.

The unit was thoroughly reorganized. Able company, devoid of all officers save one lieutenant, was broken up and its handful of survivors sent to strengthen the other three companies. From Support and H.Q. companies, drivers, mechanics, runners, administrative personnel and every man who could still handle a rifle, were gathered together into what was called 'X' company and given a combatant role. Drawing on the last of its own inner resources, the Regiment was at least able to assume the semblance of a fighting battalion once again.

The days near Bagnacavallo might easily have been given over to reaction – but this, the C.O. would not allow. He saw clearly enough that time to think, time to remember, time to descend again into the depths of the pre-Christmas days must at all costs be denied. And so a vigorous and spartan regime was introduced.

At dawn each day men were chivvied out of their billets

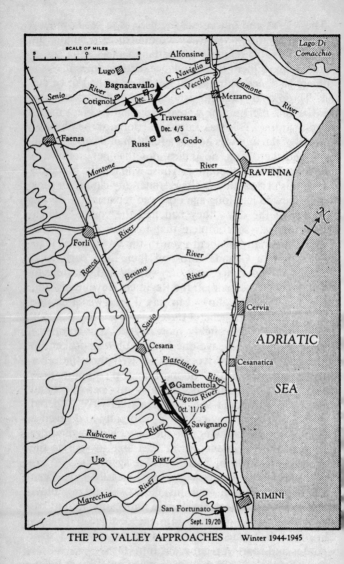

THE PO VALLEY APPROACHES   Winter 1944-1945

and set to the routine of Aldershot in 1940. Physical training and 'hardening training' became the most important elements in the day's activities. Weapon-training and the usual battle exercises were relegated to second place. Parade-ground drill with its attendant 'spit and polish' returned after an absence of almost two years. The men were worked and worked hard.

Some of them grumbled about it at first. Some of them muttered against this 'reward' for their long weeks of mud and battle. Even some of the junior officers and N.C.O.s resented the new regime. But this did not last. As day by day the old face of the unit began to reappear, its lines hardening, its contours emerging clear-cut and recognizable, the undercurrent of resistance ebbed away. Pride was returning.

Cameron, appearing completely out of character, had become a driver. But he had subtleties as well. Little things were devised to restore the pride of Regiment. A competitive PIAT shoot that had been arranged for all three units of the brigade was made into a major event. The Regiment's team practised for days under the unflagging whip of its N.C.O.s, and when the team won the competition the battalion felt almost the same satisfaction that a good victory against the Germans might have brought.

In this period when the whip was being used, it would have been logical to expect the gap between officers and men to widen. If anything, it narrowed.

One rain-swept evening a private soldier came into B.H.Q. and seeing Cameron standing by the maps, walked up and asked him for a drink. Cameron turned in some amazement but recognizing a man who had been with the Regiment for five long years, he quietly replied that there was not a drop around the place. Whereupon the soldier hauled a dirty vino bottle out of the tunic of his battledress, and with a broad smile, said, "Well then, sir, have one on me." And Cameron did.

There was the time when 'Rambler' Nobes arrived at the H.Q. and ignoring the attempts of the adjutant and the other officers to keep him out, stamped into the room where Cameron was catching an hour's rest and after shaking the C.O. awake, presented him with a chicken – a precious gift in those hungry days. These were small things, but not isolated incidents, and they were indicative of the healing of the wounds.

On January 6, for the first time in several months, a large reinforcement draft arrived. It was composed almost entirely of men from the Cape Breton Highlanders – miners, fishermen and small-town men from the harsh north of Nova Scotia. The Cape Bretoners had a hard reputation, for they were of a hard land – and at first there were doubts in the hearts of some of the officers about their potential value to the unit. The doubts resolved themselves almost at once. Although they came from a land two thousand miles away from the counties, they were the same sort of men as those who had made the Regiment. They, too, were of old stock, the sons of soldier-settlers in the days of Wolfe. They, too, were men of adversity.

On January 11 the unit returned to the line, relieving its old companion in battle, the C.Y.R., in front of the Senio dykes near Cotignola.

Winter was full upon the plains by then. Snow mingled with the freezing rains. Heavy frosts coated the muddy sloughs and the contorted skeletons of shell-torn olive trees. The war, such as it was, had been reduced to exchanges of artillery fire, patrol activity, and sniping. Shortages of ammunition on the Allied side reduced even the artillery work to the barest minimum and the Germans, also terribly exhausted by the December battles, seemed willing to remain quiescent.

Those winter days in the Senio line in miserable stagnation might have undone all the work the officers and the N.C.O.s had so far accomplished; instead the work went on and the Regiment profited by this new visit to purgatory.

Cautiously, Cameron began to restore battle confidence. Numerous patrols were organized but the objectives were

picked with exceeding care so that there would be less
danger of setbacks. Small operations of platoons or sections against enemy outposts in the Senio dykes were
planned and executed with the precision and detail that
might have gone into a Brigade battle. As a result, these
skirmishes were almost uniformly successful – and the
men who took part in them no longer knew the fear of
error and chaos when they went out into the frigid darkness with their grenades and tommyguns.

Sniping was encouraged as a major occupation and the
results were posted daily for all ranks to see. The battalion
snipers, always excellent, now began to surpass themselves, and ordinary riflemen enthusiastically joined in to
show their individual prowess. One Bren-gun team sniped
six of the enemy in a single morning and the unit's pride
in this achievement was immense.

The tendency of troops in winter lines to become slothful and apathetic was kept under close control. Contact
patrols between companies were ordered out in numbers
every night. Sentries and outpost sections were kept keyed
to a notable vigilance.

Even the remarkable activities of Brigade staff's so-
called 'deception schemes' helped restore the unit's spirit –
for these activities focused the men's antipathies where
they belonged – beyond the Regiment.

Essentially the idea of the deception schemes was that
the enemy should be kept stirred up as much as possible.
Just what useful purpose this would serve was not
explained. But a stirred-up enemy invariably retaliated,
and since the Germans had far more ammunition than
the Canadians, the results were easily predictable.

The news that Brigade had invented a new way to irritate the Germans – and a way that would be tried out on
the Regiment's front that night – would send every man
searching frantically for better shelter. The actual method
employed might be to send up a troop of tanks to do a
hurried shoot before retiring to safety, or it might be the
playing of gramophone records of 'attack noises'. What-

ever the scheme, its results were invariably the same. The Germans would call down their artillery SOS tasks, and the Canadian infantry would be thoroughly lambasted.

Although the Regiment was fast returning to its original self, its bitterness about certain happenings outside the unit remained. News from Canada remained uniformly of a nature to shame the fighting men into such reactions as a strong repugnance to wearing the C.V.S.M., Canadian Volunteer Service Medal, which was nicknamed the E.B.G.O., Every Bastard's Got One. The enemy bombarded the troops with leaflets about the repatriation plan. The propaganda was transparent, but it had its hard core of painful truth. Pictures of Canadian volunteers with flowing beards limping home to Canada on crutches in the year 1965 were not really very funny. Nor were the pictures of Zombie units, rioting in barracks while a smug Mackenzie King stood by and smirked, too well appreciated.

The attachment of the men to the Italian civilians became continually stronger, perhaps because both were often treated as sub-human impedimenta. On January 20 a Corps order was promulgated ordering all civilians to evacuate the forward areas at once. The peasant families were promptly turned out of their pitiful shacks and sent trudging to the rear. They could carry little with them, and what meagre possessions had survived the battles now had to be abandoned. The men of the unit felt a deep resentment about this, for they could see no reason why army transport could not have been used to move the people, and their belongings too.

One man, Pte. Brennan, risked the wrath of the staff by taking his truck forward to a prohibited area, where, with the help of three other soldiers, he assisted an ancient grandmother to move her most precious possession, her nuptial bed. It was a small gesture of defiance against the powers.

On February 3, after a week's rest in a rear zone, the unit moved northeast into the flat marshes beyond

Ravenna and took up the final position that it was to occupy in northern Italy. The new area, near Mezzano, had been the recent scene of a disastrous attack by the Germans who, profiting little from what had happened to the Canadians in December, launched a major counter-assault over the flooded marshes. The attackers were almost annihilated, and in early February the bodies of the dead still lay in the freezing slush.

It was an inauspicious place in which to spend the last winter month. Thaws and freezes alternated almost daily and the roads vanished in quagmires that were often four feet deep. No vehicle movement was possible over most of the area and the Regiment had to use boats on its supply route. The foot soldiers slogged knee deep in muck. The country was so flat that no-man's land had been extended to almost a mile in depth. Patrols splashed miserably about during the nights, disturbing little groups of half-wild pigs that were fattening on decomposing German corpses.

While there had been no large actions during January and February there had been the usual sad attrition of static warfare. Men had died from sniper fire and from shelling. Sickness had taken its toll as well, and the Regiment, which had never regained its full strength, was again much weakened physically. Reinforcements arrived in pathetic trickles; men from every branch of the service drafted into the infantry to fill the gaps. They were good men for the most part, all volunteers of course, but their years in the Service Corps, the Anti-aircraft Artillery and the Ordnance had not fitted them for infantry warfare. They were the flesh of an army that was being forced to practise self-cannibalism in order to keep the fighting units in existence. They were further sacrifices to the politicians at home.

Within the battalion they posed a special problem in integration and it became necessary to carry out programs of basic infantry training while in the field, a final and definitive indication of the depths of the home betrayal.

On February 15 the unit took a heavy blow. Lt. Col. Cameron was promoted to full Colonel and ordered to leave at once for England. There was only one consolation and this was that, by February 15, the Regiment's spirit was again almost what it had been before the December shambles. Cameron had managed a hard task with skill. He had commanded the unit through some of its best days, and through its darkest hours, and he had not failed the Regiment which had adopted him, and of which he had become a living part. His personality, with those of Kennedy, Graham, Tweedsmuir, Sutcliffe and Salmon, was deeply woven into the fabric of the unit.

Not long after Cameron left – to be replaced by Major Alan Ross, a one-time Black Watch officer who had long since become a Plough Jockey – the unit was withdrawn from the line to Cesanatica on the Adriatic coast.

February was ending, and with it the long winter. Spring suns again shone hotly on the hardening sea of mud and the mists of black memories were dissipating. The news from the world battlefields was uniformly bright and for the first time men could glimpse the end of war.

Cesanatica was alive with rumour.

The one that said the unit was being shipped home to Canada was greeted with cynical derision. But other rumours were less fantastic. One thing seemed sure; the unit had fought its last battle in Italy. Whether the future was to take it to the Pacific, or to Northern Europe – Italy would soon be left behind.

In point of fact, First Corps was about to depart for Germany and Holland, there to join First Canadian Army for the last campaign of the war. The move was shrouded in the deepest secrecy, and only the Italian civilians really knew the truth about it. They were not slow to impart their information to the troops and when the convoys began to move out of Cesanatica, rolling south along the coastal road, most of the men knew the ultimate destination.

But first there was to be an interlude; one of the happiest interludes in the memories of the Regiment. It brought with it ten days of spring in a little town of the Adriatic coastal mountains. The place was called Ripratransone and it clung to a soaring ridge overlooking the glaring blue of the sea. Its people were gentle, friendly men and women who had been spared the worst of war, but who yet understood the mood of men of many battles.

Alan Ross could now give the men what they had so well earned; and discipline and routine were relaxed sufficiently so that, for these brief days, they could find some semblance of the almost forgotten freedoms they had known so long ago.

There were endless spaghetti dinner parties in Italian homes; endless escapades when the vino flowed a mite too freely. There were expeditions into the lovely mounded hills and into the green valleys and there was a plethora of eggs, fresh meat, chickens, and those other simple things that meant so much to the fighting man. There were even women – those improbable beings whose very existence had seemed mythical for so long.

Ripratransone was noon-day festival after the long night. Men breathed deeply and without fear and there was a contentment over them that they had not known before.

On March 2 the people of Ripratransone stood on the steep, cobbled streets and watched the Canadian vehicles grind slowly down the switchback road towards the line of the coast highway. Men in khaki looked back from the open trucks and waved their hands in what was for many a sad farewell.

For four days the convoy wound its way across the spine of Italy and then down at last into the Arno Valley, through Florence to a sandy pine forest not far from Pisa, and a place called Harrod's Camp. It was a transit camp – and the Army once again. The usual foul food, the usual niggling regulations and restrictions. No one was allowed to leave the confines of the camp – even to see the famous tower that leaned, beckoningly, on the flat horizon.

The men grinned to themselves and went about the soldiers' ways of circumventing the blind dictum of authority.

On March 10 the companies mounted the gangplanks of American landing ships in Leghorn harbour. The exiles stared at the well-fed faces of the friendly Yanks as if they were denizens of another world. They gaped with amazement at white bread and butter, at canned wieners and frozen chicken, at ice cream and at cigars. They accepted the lavish generosity of their hosts with the pleasure of children at a birthday party and they gorged on these unaccustomed and almost forgotten things. They did not notice at first when the engines turned and the moorings were cast off, but then, one by one, they became aware of the trembling of the hull.

Those who had been below climbed quickly to the narrow decks and joined their fellows. And they stood, silent and no longer jubilant, staring across the widening waters at the blue haze of the Italian mountains, and at a land whose memories would haunt them always down the corridors of time.

TWENTY-FOUR

The End in View

IT IS NOT until long after peace has come that soldiers' memories of war really begin to live. While war still lasts, the new events bury the old with terrifying swiftness and too deeply for a waning strength and will to resurrect until time's intervention brings a desire for the exhumation.

It was so with the Regiment as the landing ships butted their ways across the Tyrrhenian Sea. Italy, that land of death, vanished from view and with an almost equal abruptness it passed out of the conscious minds of the men aboard.

In the hours of that gentle crossing the Regiment seemed young again; fired with the exultation of escape, and with the rising excitement of an unknown future. Ahead, the coast of France rose from a mirrored sea. Beyond that coast there was, of course, another war, but a war that could not help but be relief and betterment after the atrocious months in northern Italy. Meanwhile there was a changing world that raised men's hopes, that cleansed them of much bitterness, that gave them solace in forgetfulness.

The ships landed at Marseilles and the troops disembarked and boarded the waiting trucks with some of the excitement of a village baseball team about to drive across a county to a game against some well-known rival. There was the same exuberance; a little foolish, and a little sad.

In the relief of their escape the troops could find no fault with France as the convoys began to roll inland up the valley of the Rhône. The women were all fair, the men all fine. The wine exquisite and the country lovelier than God contrived. War had not lived here; it had only brushed its fingers on the land and left no darker traces than occasional clusters of burned-out German transport caught by Allied fighter aircraft on the roads.

The convoys rolled into the north. The long days were not long enough for men to stare out over a verdant countryside that each one made familiar in his own mind, because of his desire that it be familiar. The miles unravelled and there was the knowledge that England, the second home and the beloved one for many, was drawing nearer. There was more than the reduction of space – there was the shrinkage of time as well. The end of war itself was coming close – closer with each mile the convoy travelled.

Aix, Valence, Lyon, the Côte d'Or, Sens, Montereau, Cambrai. And then the cemeteries of the first world war; neat, ancient, mossed and weathered into time beyond the present, and incapable of stirring more than idle curiosity in the troops who saw them from the passing trucks. *That* war was ended. *This* one was ending fast, and death no longer held the pride of place.

On March 20 the convoys entered Belgium and dispersed near the little village of Westmalle. Most of the Regiment found itself quartered in an improbable domain – a Trappist monastery and one, moreover, that was noted throughout Belgium for the fine quality of the beer it brewed. It was a strange resting place for the men from the Ravenna marshes. Untouched by the war, its atmosphere was heavy with medieval sanctity. Beyond it, in the evenings on pass to Brussels, there was the contrast of an uninhibited outburst after two years of repression. The men were not slow to learn the way of things in Brussels which, at that time, was the capital of Europe – rich to bursting with the affairs of the black markets brought into being by the Allied troops.

Now at last there was repayment in part, and long belated, for those who had served the unit through so many years. Leave parties to Blighty just across the Channel were begun. Groups of fifty to a hundred men – with those who had landed at Pachino having first priority – took ferry to England. The ferry was, incredibly, the *Canterbury Belle* which had carried the Regiment from Brest to England in the days of France's collapse in 1940. The survivors of the 'Cook's Tour' days had made a long detour to repeat that passage. Now they found England changed and many of them felt like wanderers returning from a far Odyssey. Everywhere the Americans were in command of the amenities and some of the men found themselves sharing the bewilderment and resentment of those English troops who also were returning home for the first time in many years. Those who went to England had a bleak foretaste of the truth – that there is no return to the land of a soldier's memory for that land does not exist. At leave's end they came back sobered and quiet, to the only place that would not change – the Regiment.

Twelve of the oldest serving soldiers left for Canada in late March and they, too, setting out in the grip of the narcosis of anticipation, were rudely shaken by reality as their homesick letters to the unit soon revealed.

For the balance of the Regiment the stay in Belgium was one of nearly unadulterated pleasure. Training went on but the troops did not take it very seriously, for with the constantly optimistic battle news they knew that war was almost at an end. Many believed they would not again see battle. And in any case *they* were the veterans. Their fellow Canadians wearing the shoulder patches of the Second, Third and Fourth Divisions were treated with some condescension. The names of Carpiquet, Falaise and the Scheldte meant as little to the men of the Regiment as the names of Cassino, Ortona and Ravenna meant to those Canadians who had fought their war in Northern Europe. But the soldiers of First Division knew that they had been in action almost a year longer than their fellows. They had nothing to learn.

There was also a disdain for First Canadian Army, as it was represented by its staff. During the final months in Italy even First Corps H.Q. had lost some of its stolid unimaginativeness and had come to share the general easy spirit of Eighth Army. As for First Division, it had long since learned to relax the rules when they were obviously designed to do no more than irritate the fighting troops.

But in Belgium, the Regiment soon found that First Canadian Army was deeply concerned with the trivial non-essentials, with the petty regulations and restrictions made by men who themselves possessed too little certainty, and too little imagination. First Corps, arriving from Eighth Army, was instantly suspect and a flood of jealous regulations descended on it. It became a serious dereliction for a man to refuse to put up his 'Spam' medal. (The Canadian Volunteer Service Medal.) Personal idiosyncrasies in dress and behaviour were considered major crimes. New dress orders attempted to ensure that every soldier be the mirror image of his fellows. Worst of all, the fighting men who had for five years worn the tight, buttoned-up collar of the standard battle dress – and worn it with pride if not with comfort – were now issued with black ties and collared shirts. The tie and open neck were the hallmarks of the conscript soldiers in Canada – of the favoured ones. The tie itself was known as the Zombie tie, and the resentment of the volunteers who were now ordered to wear this symbol of shame was most outspoken. Nevertheless, there was a reason for the order.

During these last months of the war a few thousand Zombies had actually been sent overseas in an effort to still the growing clamour of a nation's conscience. Not more than eight thousand in all ever joined combat units, and probably not more than a third of these saw any action. Nevertheless, they were in Europe, and it was imperative – so thought the Canadian Army – that no distinction in appearance exist between the unwilling newcomers, and the men who had fought the war.

There were a good many other things that changed. At Westmalle, the Regiment was issued with 'Plumber's Nightmares', otherwise and officially known as Sten guns. Much of the unit's fighting equipment, worn and shiny after two years of battle, was replaced. But the biggest change, and the one that really hurt, was the fact that Eighth Army's famous Crusader Cross had disappeared to be replaced by the meaningless geometric pattern of the First Canadian Army flash.

On April 2 the Belgian interlude came to an end. On the following day the Regiment was ordered into the line, forsaking the joys of Brussels for the desolation of the Reichswald Forest inside Germany.

There was no hesitation. If anything the troops accepted with pleasure this opportunity to display their talents before the eyes of the rest of the Canadian Army.

There were, however, some thoughtful glances from the older soldiers as the convoy moved forward into an area that had known real battle. Here were the familiar signs again – the shattered farms, the diversions around great craters or blown bridges, and the blatant rawness of recent crosses in muddy ground. But there was also the stimulus of an entirely different type of country. This land bore no resemblance to Italy. It was a tamed land and it had nothing of the natural menace of the Italian mountains, or the Sicilian deserts. The houses – those that remained – bore little relationship to the squat stone hovels of the Adriatic plains. Here there were tress and forests and regulated fields and an order that even war had not completely disrupted.

In the evening the unit reached the Reichswald and went into camp to await the morrow. It took an indigestible piece of news to bed with it.

Alan Ross, still a major and acting C.O. only, was not to be allowed to carry on in command. The Brigadier had decided to replace him with an unknown from the 48th

Highlanders. This news did not greatly affect the new reinforcements, but the older soldiers, the N.C.O.s and officers, were properly irate. Ross had served the Regiment for a long time. He had displayed outstanding leadership in battle and, since Cameron's departure, had handled the battalion with skill and good effect. The fact that he was to be passed over in favour of an outsider made no sense. It was inevitable that the new appointment should appear to be a deliberate slight on a first-rate officer and on the Regiment itself.

Fortunately no irreparable damage was done, for the unit had learned to take rebuffs of this nature in its stride. Lt.-Col. Rennison, coming into what might have been an unpleasant situation, showed considerable understanding of the unit's feelings and the new effectiveness of the Regiment was unimpaired when, on April 12, it moved forward into action.

The battle situation in the west had reached its apogee by the first week in April, and everyone, including the enemy commanders, was perfectly well aware of what the final outcome must be. The great double-encirclement of the Ruhr was complete and the heart of the German Army had been cut off from its limbs. Holland, defended by the 25th Army Group under von Blaskowitz, had also been cut off from Germany. Second British Army was moving east well into the Reich and the Russians were moving west at a frightening pace. The war had now become a process of liquidating the enemy armies piecemeal. First Canadian Corps joined in the final phase. Its task was to drive west from Zutphen, across the Ijssel River, and cut Holland and the 25th Army Group in two.

At 1000 hours on April 12, the Regiment tasted action in Northern Europe for the first time. Loaded aboard Water Buffalos (a species of amphibious tank), the troops were ferried swiftly across the Ijssel River close to Zutphen. There was no enemy opposition, but this did not detract from the excitement of the hour. The very prelude to the battle, even before it had been joined, was enough to surprise the men from Italy.

There were the Buffalos; ponderous, armoured carriers that took water obstacles in their stride. Men marvelled at the safe and effortless crossing of the river.

And overhead; not just a single flight of war-weary Kittyhawks against the German Army, but an endless stream of aircraft – a ceaseless, returning, flowing stream.

And the armour; not just a single squadron of worn old Shermans, but an entire reptilian army of fighting tanks, armoured troop carriers, self-propelled guns, flamethrowing tanks, bridging tanks, mine-clearing tanks, bulldozer tanks and many other strange and novel types.

And the guns; there was no ammunition shortage here. The fire of division and corps artillery was thickened into a steel mattress of destruction by the guns of the army and the army group; by batteries of rocket projectors; by regiments of heavy anti-aircraft artillery no longer needed against the defunct Luftwaffe, and now throwing their airburst shells over the flat farm lands to reach down, viciously, into the slit-trenches of the enemy.

Moving up as Brigade reserve, the Regiment felt once more, and for the last time, the intoxication with the powers of destruction – an intoxication that was unmatched, except in the memories of those surviving few who could remember Pachino and the Sicilian beaches. The elation of destruction did not last long for, as darkness came, there came with it the awaited orders. "Before first light the unit will pass through the 48th and strike inland for Apeldoorn."

Before the light had come, a Charlie company platoon patrol moved out from the scarred village of Hoven, into the new battlefield, with a crossroad some miles to the west as its objective. With the coming of dawn there was a return to the reality of dying.

The platoon met the enemy just short of the crossroad and there was a bitter clash. Disorganized in their administrative areas, the remnants of a hundred regiments of infantry. ss, Jaeger, Luftwaffe troops and many others were fighting now with a fierceness one step removed from maniac fury. Knowing the war was lost, they fought against the knowledge and against the promised retribution. They fought with a purposeful savagery – or, and the numbers were about equally divided, they dropped their weapons and walked out to meet and hasten the inevitable end. There was no way of knowing what they would do. Machine gunners who could have massacred a Canadian platoon fired no shots but walked into captivity from behind their silent guns. Then there were those individuals who, by-passed by the advance and swallowed by the victors in a foreign and hostile land, snatched up a rifle and sniped at the backs of passing soldiers until they themselves found death.

The crossroad was taken in an hour and the balance of Charlie company, with a squadron of tanks from the First Hussars, drove on against spasmodic resistance.

The pace of the advance seemed impossibly fast. There was no halting even to mop up by-passed enemy strongpoints that might turn their guns on the backs of the advancing tanks and infantry.

By noon Charlie had advanced several miles and was fighting hard for a thick pine woods not far from Teuge. Off to the left somewhere, the R.C.R. was driving westward on a parallel course.

In the late afternoon Able and Dog companies went forward through Charlie and carried the assault to the near banks of the great canal which runs just east of Apeldoorn. The two companies rode on the backs of tanks, shooting up pockets of resistance as they met them, and passing on to find the next before the first was silenced. Prisoners were streaming in – more than two hundred and fifty passed back through the battalion that day – but the Regiment had suffered, too, and thirty men were dead or wounded before nightfall.

The mounting tempo of the battle was maintained all through the night. Long before first light on April 14 Dog and Baker were assaulting the buildings along the canal bank that guarded the as yet intact bridge to Apeldoorn. Grenades blew hollowly in shattered rooms and the rattle of Stens and Schmeissers vied with each other in the dawn. A platoon of Baker company ran forward to the bridge and at the moment when they had only fifty yards to go, the bridge vanished behind a lurid orange flare, a boiling column of white smoke, and the shattering reverberation of the demolition.

Now, and now only, did the tempo ease. It had been a good second day, with one hundred and eleven German prisoners, another forty Germans dead, and only five casualties within the Regiment. Nothing more could be done until a bridge was built, or until some way to cross the river had been found.

At nightfall came news of a further respite, with the orders that the R.C.R. and 48th were to fight up to the canal upon the flanks and make the crossing.

Bemused by the swiftness and confusion of the battle from the Ijssel, the Regiment dug in and waited while overhead the never ending whine of Allied shells was drowned by the almost ceaseless roar of aircraft engines. This was a strange war even to men who had lived at war for nearly two years now.

On the night of April 16/17, the R.C.R. and 48th reached the canal and crossed into Apeldoorn securing the eastern half of the city before dawn. The Regiment climbed on its tanks and moved across the river, past the advance positions of the 48th and into a city waiting for liberation, and half crazed with its own emotion. The enemy had gone and the only shots were those fired into the air from the C.O.'s pistol as he sought to clear a path through the civilian throngs. The Regiment's first objective, the Palace of Queen Wilhelmina, was reached only after a prolonged struggle to escape the civilians. Here B.H.Q. was established on the palace lawns. The pandemonium in the streets was rising, but for the moment the 'liberators' were partially forgotten. The Dutch were intent on satisfying their desire for revenge on their own compatriots. Women who had been seen with German soldiers were seized and shorn; collaborators, and there were many of them in Holland, were hunted down by the orange-brassarded men of the Dutch Underground.

There was but little time for the troops to gaze at this fantasy of liberation, for there was still war beyond the next row of trees. By 1000 hours the tanks and their encrusted infantry were driving out of the city into the pine woods, the tank guns swinging ready to blast each suspect bush, or house, or shadow by the road. Then the shadows took on substance and at another crossroad the enemy struck back at point-blank range with heavy mortars and with 88s. Able company and the men who had once worn the Cape Breton badge went in and cleared the crossing. Dog at once led off again towards the village of Nieuwmilligen.

The battle was beyond easy hearing of Apeldoorn by now, but things of interest were still passing in that place. An officer from the Regiment, passing to the rear to bring up new supplies, was startled to find himself observing a strange tableau. By the Palace gates an entire platoon of the 48th Highlanders, in full fighting order and with fixed bayonets, was preparing to attack the grandiose old structure. The officer could not believe his eyes. He stopped his jeep, got out, and walked towards the war-like group and their commander – an officer whom he knew.

"Hey, Jim," he called, "what have we here? A palace revolution nipped smartly in the bud?"

The other spun on his heel, recognized his interrogator and grinned wryly. "Hell," he said, "you damn Plough Jockeys *would* arrive just now. All right, you'll find out anyway. See these reporters?" And he swept his arm toward a bevy of war correspondents and photographers. "Seems they're writing a yarn about how we stormed the Palace – and they need illustrations to go with it . . . and, well hell . . . you know how these things are . . ."

While the 48th platoon was making its bayonet charge

against the empty palace, Dog company and its tanks had driven forward to the edge of a dense pine forest near Nieuwmilligen and had encountered the enemy in strength, determined to halt the Canadian advance which was now threatening to cut Holland in half and to strike down upon the major German bastion guarding the cities of Utrecht and Amsterdam.

The confusion automatically attendant on an advance as rapid as the Regiment's had now become almost impenetrable. Rennison, moving up to join the lead company, became enveloped in the smoke and confusion of a flame thrower attack while a frantic R.S.M. sure that he had mislaid his C.O., searched for him high and low.

Each man was at war now, almost independently of his fellows and against an enemy as vicious as he was dangerous. The troops in the Nieuwmilligen woods were almost all SS and many of them were Dutch SS. Each Nazi SS trooper knew well what his fate would be when Germany was gone, but for the renegade Dutchmen who had joined the SS, that fate would be even more terrible. And so they fought this, their last battle, with the particular savagery that only civilized men who have abandoned civilization can achieve.

One incident displays the character of that day's battle. Slightly to the rear of the advance companies, a regimental stretcher bearer was administering morphine to a mortally wounded comrade when, from a range of only a dozen yards, two Dutch SS men exposed their hidden position in a ditch and fired at the stretcher bearer and his charge. Miraculously the Red Cross man was not hit. But he had had enough of a noncombatant's role and, snatching his dying comrade's tommygun, he cut the Dutchmen down.

All afternoon the battle in the pines went on. 'Crocodiles' – tanks mounting flame-guns – methodically sprayed their sticky agony into the underbrush while the coils of smoke rose to obscure the world. From the flanks the ear-shattering crack of 88s mingled with the dull thunder of Canadian artillery shells. The feathered pines shredded into white and splintered skeletons.

Charlie and Able companies, relieving the exhausted men of Dog, pushed grimly forward, close-in behind the tanks, their vulnerable friends.

Dusk was coming now and the nostalgic scent of burning pines rose to a still sky, veiling the stench of charred flesh and the harsh, throat's agony of cordite fumes. The smoke was lifting and the battle dying as the two lead companies reached the far side of the forests.

Occasional artillery salvos rumbled loosely overhead. From the west, retreating German mortars stopped long enough to fire a few hasty bombs. But the woods were growing still.

Not far behind the lead troops Cpl. Fenton, of the three-inch mortar platoon, found the frayed ends of a broken telephone wire leading from his mortars to the forward Observation Post. In a few moments he had spliced the raw ends together, and then suddenly his hands relaxed and let the thin cable fall to the sandy soil. His body slumped, falling forward on the wire that was already carrying the words of living men.

He had come from the counties. He had joined his Regiment in 1939 and had fought with it and lived for it ever since that day. He was one of the last of the 'originals' and only a week earlier he had refused his repatriation ticket-of-leave to Canada for the transcendent reason that he could not leave his Regiment until the end.

On April 17, 1945, as the evening light dimmed over the forests of Nieuwmilligen, Cpl. Fenton took his ticket – not one of leave – but one of transfer to that other, that swollen regiment of shadows that had grown through the red years even as the living regiment had dwindled in death.

As he had been amongst the first to come, now he was the last to go – the last to take his warrior's transfer to the unseen ranks of the White Battalion.

For the Regiment, the war was done.

The Years Ahead

THE WAR WAS DONE.

On April 23 the Regiment went out of action, and in the early days of May, word came that the enemy in Northwest Europe had surrendered.

In Canada, in the United States, there was a tumultuous jubilation. In those places farthest from the battlefields the night was riven with hysteria. It was not so in the places where the war had been.

In the countries that had been brutalized there was an attempt at celebration, but oddly attenuated and somehow empty. Civilians stood about in streets, or gathered in cafes and bars, drunk with the knowledge of deliverance but devoid of strength to shout and throw their caps into a sounding sky. They needed time to recognize the change.

In the tented camps, in the billet houses, the troops who had fought the war heard the news and they went out to the nearest bars and drank themselves into the only sure surcease that had been theirs through so many years. They slapped each other's backs and cried, "*Tedesci's* done. The war is over, chum!" but the words conveyed little to their inner minds.

Peace does not come overnight to men who have spent years in uniform and who have lived with war. The shadow comes first – but months are needed until it gains full flesh.

It was so within the Regiment. The slow progress to peace demanded many months for some; for others it demanded a life-time yet to be lived out.

The physical entry into peace was slow enough. Four full months elapsed before a troop train pulled into Belleville station, and the Regiment came home. Those four months were the aftermath.

On May 6 the Regiment, then resting near the town of Elspeet, was ordered to proceed across the German lines to Amersfoort and carry out the 'relief' of the large German garrison in that Dutch town.

An advance party moved at once to a canal before Amersfoort, a canal defended by the German Army. The patrol reached the near bank and there the leader held a heated discussion with a German officer, while field-grey and khaki kept their weapons at the ready. In the end the German brusquely ordered the Canadians to turn back. He had heard no official word of peace and, barring that, there could be only war.

The next day the advance party fared better. General Blaskowitz's 25th Army Group had apparently passed the word that the war was ending, and the patrol crossed into the German lines. In jeeps and carriers the handful of Canadians drove through the bulk of a German ss division, still armed and, by the look of its men, uncertain about accepting peace at all. Those who took part in that strange journey were haunted for weeks afterwards by the cold horror of wondering when the steel would strike them in the back.

No shot was fired, and on the following day the c.o. arrived in Amersfoort and, over drinks and cigars, conferred with the German General in command of the area. It was a friendly but military meeting as the Hastings and Prince Edward Regiment formally 'relieved' the enemy garrison.

Then, on May 8, the unit was ordered to move across Holland, through Amsterdam to the coastal city of Ijmuiden where some twenty thousand Germans had concentrated. Along with the R.C.R., the Regiment was ordered to surround, disarm and formally make prisoners of this vast assemblage of the enemy.

Enough time had elapsed since the cessation of battle for the Dutch to grasp the meaning of the end, and their delayed reactions took effect coincidental with the unit's journey. In towns and villages across the flooded land the convoy found itself engulfed and almost washed over the dykes by a wave of humanity. The Dutch are a staid race, but when they broke loose, they simply flung off all restraint and went berserk. Flowers crushed wetly underneath the tires. Women, fat or bony, young or aged, clambered aboard the vehicles until some trucks disappeared from view entirely. Civilian men along the routes gazed with a queer and vacuous expression, their mouths foolishly agape and their hands in violent motion as if to compensate for throats too hoarse to cry aloud.

This was only the preamble to the frenzy that had seized on Amsterdam. That the regimental convoy got through the city at all was a miracle. It was not surprising that a good number of men disappeared en route; and there was enough truth to make a good case of their later contentions that they had been literally kidnapped by the Dutch.

For the first time the phrase 'liberation' meant something more than legalized looting and it was a heady experience for the troops to find themselves idolized by an entire nation. The men who had come to the unit earlier and who had remained through Sicily and Italy took the outburst with a certain cynicism, knowing that in a day or so the tide would slow and that in a month, it would have turned. The younger men, the newcomers who had swelled the ranks in the final weeks of the war, saw themselves as shining knights in khaki armour, and for them there would be particular disillusionment as peace grew strong.

At Santpoort, near Ijmuiden, the unit took up position as a guard force surrounding a huge German fortress.

There were conferences with German generals and even an actual relief of German guards by a regimental contingent. Old soldiers in the unit watched uneasily.

It was a period of fantasy. Men walking into Santpoort, unarmed and bound for an evening's entertainment, stood aside to let armed German platoons under German officers go goose-stepping by. Men were sent off on detached duty to act as guards for German food convoys – and they were not guarding the Dutch from the Germans – they were guarding their erstwhile enemies from the Dutch.

Slowly the picture changed. Regiment by regiment the Germans in the area marched into Santpoort, surrendered their arms, were searched for loot and were caged inside a vast prisoner compound. In the warehouses taken over by the unit the stacks of MG 42s, *Faustpatronen*, artillery weapons, grenades and ammunition grew mountainous. In one day the R.C.R. and the Regiment together sorted and disarmed ten thousand of the enemy and on that day the atmosphere of unreality reached its peak and began to harden into the realization that the war was truly done. For a few more weeks the excitement of events sustained the men, but with the final departure of the last contingent of the enemy on the long road home to Germany, excitement waned and the presence of a strange doldrum began to grow apparent.

There remained nothing further for the Regiment to do – save only wait for dissolution.

And now the thing that the years of battle, even the bitterness of defeat in the field, had not been able to accomplish, began to happen of its own accord. The Regiment was disintegrating and passing from existence. The walls of the home that had sheltered so many men in death and despair, in victory and exultation, were crumbling as the storm which had created the reason for them, passed beyond sight and hearing.

Piecemeal, the walls collapsed.

In early June those men and officers who had volunteered for service in the Far East left the unit taking with them the hard core of the old soldiers. Drafts for direct repatriation to Canada removed most of the remaining men who had been with the unit for so many years. Those who stayed included exchange drafts which had been torn from their own regiments and posted to the Hastings and Prince Edward simply because their homes happened to be in Military District No. 3 in Canada.

On June 13 the unit moved eastward to the town of Soest, but by then it had become no more than a façade, thin-walled, and functioning largely as a glorified holding unit into which men from a dozen units were placed to wait the return home. In the last days of June even the Regiment's weapons were removed, to be shipped east for other hands to use against the Japanese.

It was a time of sadness for those who had known the home in the days of its strength. Men who had prayed for peace found themselves fighting against recognition of what peace had brought them. Already, with the peace less than three months old, nostalgia had come and with it the beginning of a wave of memories.

On September 1, the Regiment left Holland and after a brief pause in England, sailed for home. On October 4, at 0900 hours, the troop train halted in Belleville station.

On hand to greet it were those who had come home during the war years, wounded beyond further battles; there were the low-category men of the Second Battalion who had hungered for five years to join their regiment, and who had been denied; there were the civic deputations with their speeches, and the promises of reward, promises that would fade as all promises do in the end; there were women and children who stood quietly and watched and did not see the ones they sought, for these were dead.

They gathered, all of them, to see an empty scabbard, for the sword had vanished. And when the shouting and the tumult of the bands was at an end, the darkness closed in over the two counties; and the beloved creation, which had lived and breathed with the blood and breath of four thousand men through five long years, was gone.

Glossary

'A' Echelon	The administrative group in immediate support of the rifle companies
AP	Armour-piercing
A.W.L.	Absent without leave
B.H.Q.	Battalion headquarters
Besa	Machine gun used in Canadian and British tanks
Bren	The Canadian infantry light machine gun
'B' Echelon	The rear administrative group of the regiment
C.O.	Commanding Officer
C.S.M.	Company sergeant-major
Compo Rations	Composite British rations boxed in unit quantities sufficient for one platoon for one day
C.A.	Counter-attack
C.Y.R.	The Carleton and York Regiment
D.R.	Dispatch Rider
Flashes	Shoulder patches identifying the regiment and its division; or a corps or army
Fiumare	A seasonal Italian river
Faustpatrone	A shoulder-fired rocket projectile used by the Germans against tanks and roughly equivalent to the U.S. Bazooka
F.O.O.	Forward Observation Officer, of the artillery
'F' Echelon	That section of the regimental transport concerned with actual fighting
Hour (system)	The army system of indicating times; numbering the hours from one to twenty-four in each twenty-four-hour period
H-Hour	Equivalent to Zero hour
HMT	His Majesty's Transport
I.O.	Intelligence Officer
L.M.G.	Light machine gun

367

ME 109	German fighter plane
MG 42	The standard German infantry machine gun
M.O.	Medical Officer
MK. IV TANK	The standard German medium tank
MK. V	German Panther tank
N.C.O.	Non-commissioned officer
Nebelwerfer	General term for large calibre rocket projectors used by the Germans
NAAFI	Navy, Army and Airforce Institute; an organization operating service canteens.
'O' OR ORDERS GROUP	Conference called by the commander to issue battle orders to his subordinates
P.O.W.	Prisoner of war
P.P.C.L.I.	Princess Patricia Canadian Light Infantry
PIAT	Projector, Infantry, Anti-tank: a shoulder operated weapon, firing a short-range, hollow-charge bomb
Q.M.	Quatermaster
R.C.R.	The Royal Canadian Regiment
R.S.M.	Regimental Sergeant-major
R.A.P.	Regimental Aid Post; the unit medical officer's establishment
SL	Start line – for an attack
S.L.I.	Saskatchewan Light Infantry
STONK	A sudden concentration of shell-fire on a limited target
SOS TASKS	Emergency firing of previously ranged artillery tasks, on the demand of the infantry
S.P.	Self-propelled; usually referring to guns of heavy calibre mounted on a tank chassis
SCHMEISSER	The German standard machine-pistol: equivalent to the tommygun
SS	The elite Nazi party units of the German Army
Torrente	An Italian river, usually seasonal
Tedesci	The Eighth Army name for Germans, adopted from the Italian epithet
TAC. (H.Q)	Tactical headquarters; an advanced operation centre for the unit commander
T.O.	Transport officer
VEREY (FLARE)	The Verey pistol fired a signal or illuminating flare
WREN	A corruption of WRNS – Women's Royal Naval Service
Wehrmacht	The German Army
W.N.S.R.	The West Nova Scotia Regiment
ZOMBIE	The derisive name applied to conscripts called up in Canada but excused from overseas service
21-CM. GUN	German heavy artillery

20-MM. CANNON	Light automatic cannon, usually intended for anti-aircraft use
39ERS	Volunteers who enlisted with the Canadian Army in 1939
48TH	The 48th Highlanders of Canada
88-MM. GUN	The standard anti-tank gun of the German Army; often used as a multi-purpose gun against troops, aircraft, or tanks. A very high velocity weapon.
81-MM. MORTAR	Standard German infantry mortar; equivalent to the British 3-inch mortar

Index